Love *on*
Lavender Island

A LAVENDER ISLAND NOVEL

Love *on* Lavender Island

A LAVENDER ISLAND NOVEL

Lauren Christopher

 Montlake
Romance

Text copyright © 2016 Laurie Sanchez

Published by Montlake Romance, Seattle
www.apub.com

Amazon, the Amazon logo, and Montlake Romance are trademarks of Amazon.com, Inc., or its affiliates.

ISBN-13: 9781503935358
ISBN-10: 1503935353

Cover design by Eileen Carey

Printed in the United States of America

To my family and friends . . .
You were all there for me when I needed you most.
I can't thank you enough.

CHAPTER 1

Paige Grant knew she wasn't as wide as this window. But right now—with her butt on one side and her torso on the other—she was forced to recalculate.

She wriggled her hips one more time, stretching for the dusty wood floor she could *almost* touch with her fingertips, and then . . .

No. She pulled back. That's the last thing she needed: to get stuck and die out here on top of Lavender Island's highest mountain. Alone. Squeezed into a window. Undiscovered for days. Fingertips reaching along the floor for something that looked remarkably, embarrassingly, like a piece of cheese.

She pushed her hips back across the sill and bobbed her foot to find the toehold she'd just had on a rickety old bucket. She bounced her foot several times, almost panicking, but finally landed on it with a whomp. Relieved, she slowly squirmed over the sill.

Dang. Nothing like a tight window and a stuck butt to shatter a girl's confidence.

She plopped back into the grass and brushed her hands together. She'd have to come up with plan B. Or C, really. Or maybe she was on

D now. She'd already tried the front door, of course. She'd tried the back door to the kitchen. This was the living-room window—the lowest. Maybe she could try the kitchen window?

She stepped through the mud that had accumulated from recent May rains, her wellies making squishing noises as she rounded the tiny ranch house. Weeds and stalks of hardy annuals shot up through the ground to hug the weathered adobe walls, with clusters of green dappling the rest of the muddy, neglected yard.

She walked around to the dining-room window and wiped a circle of dirt from the panes to peer inside. All the furniture was gone— Gram's couches, her Victorian chairs, her dining-room hutch, the blue delft porcelain pitcher she always had in the center of the dining table. All that remained was a dusty kitchen table and a few ladder-back chairs, one of which looked broken. The place had really been left to ruin. Paige had known that—her mother had told her—but seeing it in person made her shoulders slump.

She glanced to the north and instinctively ducked behind a tree. She had every right to be here, of course, but she still didn't want anyone from the Mason family to see her. She took another look at the rented golf cart she'd driven up here—the only transportation allowed on the island—and found it to be adequately tucked behind some bushes. The Masons probably couldn't see it from their adjoining property.

She didn't have to worry about George Mason seeing her, of course. Paige had read about his recent death from a heart attack in the *Lavender Island Gazette*. And Grandpa Mason—at least that's what the town called him—was long gone. One of the young sons, Noel, had flown off the island a year ago in one of the family's famous red Cessnas and had never come back. But that still left Adam. The son Paige least wanted to see. His Cessna was tied right in front of the airport hangar on the far end of the property. Still here.

What did he look like now? She could still recall, in vivid detail, Adam's looks of disdain throughout her awkward teen years. He was five years older and wouldn't give her the time of day, despite her many attempts to put herself into his line of vision. She could remember every dismissive brush-off, every slight from him since the time she was ten. Of course, she hadn't seen him since she was thirteen—the year her unrequited love was at its worst. The year he finally noticed her. And the year he laughed at her. She'd made a fool of herself and probably deserved it, but she still could never forgive him.

So out of sight, out of mind with Adam Mason was just the way she liked it.

Not that he'd been entirely out of mind, since she did ask about him from time to time. She'd heard he'd never married and didn't even have a girlfriend. She'd heard he hardly ever came to town, and some islanders hadn't seen him in years. All she could picture was some bent-over, flannel-garbed, wispy-haired, missing-toothed recluse, probably rotting away, becoming thin and wiry with age and isolation. Who lived on a mountaintop, on an island, away from people his whole life? A weird hermit, that's who.

But despite her efforts to avoid him right now, she would eventually have to deal with him. She knew that. She just wanted to be better prepared.

Now that both his father and her grandmother were deceased, people were starting to come around and offer money for their side-by-side properties. Or, rather, *his* enormous property and Gram's teeny-tiny corner that made up the final rectangle, like a small, uneven bite taken out of a sandwich. Despite the offers, Paige and her family had something else in mind. She just didn't know how Adam was going to respond. Or . . . well, she could guess. And she was dreading it. But she needed to ask. Eventually. For now, she ducked farther behind the trees in case he had eyes and ears out on his property.

The kitchen window was higher than she remembered, and she had to go back and retrieve her bucket, position it carefully against a rock, then stand on top to peek inside.

Yes. This could work. Paige quickly got to work jimmying open one side. She freed it and got ready to hoist herself up on the sill, but then she stalled.

And came to her senses.

This was ridiculous. She wasn't going to do this anymore. She'd go back down the mountain, verify which key was which, and behave like a normal human being. She was too old to be hoisting herself through windows—women approaching thirty didn't do this, right?

A movement past her shoulder sent her slamming against the wall with a squeak-scream as a small, furry thing flew past her ear and landed on the sill. When she finally willed her eyes to open, she realized it was a kitten. An adorable little kitten, actually, that looked as if it would fit in a teacup. It glanced over at her from the sill, then playfully jumped inside. Paige peered in as it looked back at her from the dusty floor of the kitchen.

"Wait! No! Here, kitty . . ." She held her hand out, trying to coax the kitten back to her, but the little thing simply lifted its chin and looked the other way.

"Come here, sweetie." Paige glanced back at her golf cart. Did she have some food she could lure a kitten with? She couldn't just shut the window now and leave. She ran to the cart and shuffled through her backpack until she found some grapes and cheese. Did cats like cheese?

She returned to the window with the snacks. The kitten wasn't immediately visible. Paige jumped up, leaned through the sill, and waved the cheese around.

"Here, kitty . . ."

Her voice came out strained as her belly pressed against the frame. She wriggled farther toward the sink counter, which she could *aaaaalmost* reach. *Damn.* She pushed herself forward on her hips another inch and stretched toward the inside. *Aaaaalmost.*

A few old tchotchkes—a cat soap dispenser and an old dishdrainer plug—skittered to the hardwood floor as she waved the cheese and threw her weight forward. She wouldn't mind just toppling in at this point. She could break her fall. But her hips kept her from budging.

Damn. Was she just eating too many paninis these days?

Another wriggle.

Another curse word.

Another wriggle.

A new curse word.

She took a deep breath and thought about backing out. But no. She was too far in now. And she had to find the tiny calico. She could do this. She tried another hard squirm.

Nothing.

Her heart rate picked up a little, and she let it get to panic rhythm as she wondered who would come looking for her if she really got stuck. Her sisters didn't even know she was here. Her mom knew she'd come here, of course, to start their plan, but wouldn't think to send out a search team if Paige didn't respond for a week.

Paige forced herself to be calm. She tried her old trick of summoning favorite femme fatales from her most beloved movies: Katharine Hepburn. Lauren Bacall. Those were always the movies she checked out late at night at the Hollywood Film Library after her part-time shift was over. She couldn't get enough of her favorite leading ladies. She wished she could be more like them—strong, tough, knowing what they wanted and taking it. Unfortunately, that level of bravado and sophistication was becoming more and more elusive to her. The actress who most paralleled her life these days seemed more along the lines of Lucille Ball.

After another three minutes of panicking and wondering what Lucy would do, a snap of twigs outside had her jerking forward. Then the voice she figured she most *didn't* want to hear came low over her shoulder, a man's deep tenor.

"You going in or out?" he growled, from what could only be eye level with her behind.

Somehow, without looking, Paige knew exactly who it would be. It was the bent-over, flannel-garbed, wispy-haired, missing-toothed recluse.

Staring right at her bottom.

Just her luck.

Adam Mason took his sunglasses off, pushed his hat back on his head, and peered carefully at the mighty-fine female bottom wriggling its way through Helen Grant's old kitchen window.

This would definitely fall under the category of one of his more interesting patrols, but he wasn't here to enjoy the scenery, as nice as it was today.

"You need help?" he called.

He didn't imagine this was a serious break-in—the golf cart badly hidden behind the bushes pretty much gave that away. It was probably some photographer who wanted scenic shots of an abandoned building against the pine trees. That had certainly happened before. But you never knew. Squatters had happened before, too.

"I'm, uh . . . stuck," said the intruder. "Who's that?"

"Adam Mason," he barked.

The body stopped moving.

"Adam *Mason*?" The voice seemed to have grown smaller. She almost sounded like she recognized his name. But he ignored that and focused on how he was going to get to the bottom of this. A rusty smile escaped at his own joke.

"Yes," he said when he finally got the smile out of his voice. "Now back out of there."

"I, um . . . don't think I can." Another wriggle.

He tried to look away. Sort of. Normally his patrol wasn't this amusing. Or curvaceous. But he always took full responsibility for keeping Helen's old property safe, so he'd have to focus here.

He cleared his throat and tried to keep his eyes on the ground. "Would you like to go the other way?"

"Yes. Can you grab my feet and hoist me through?"

He caught hold of the muddy rain boots and gave the intruder—and her shapely, jean-clad legs—a gentle shove. She toppled to the floor, all arms and legs and softly uttered curse words. While she was still picking herself up and dusting herself off, he fished out the key to the kitchen door and pushed his way in with the handle shake and shoulder shove the back door always required.

Inside, the intruder had scrambled to her feet and was facing him with a stance and expression that didn't seem warranted—as if *he* were the one intruding. Her mouth dropped open, and she stared for what seemed like an eternity. Then, suddenly, in a flurry of movement, her hands flew to her hips, her brown eyes flashed, and her honey-colored hair swirled about her shoulders. Despite the mud and dust covering her, she was too well dressed to be one of the vagrants he'd had in here before. Plus, of course, the golf cart. But she didn't have a camera around her neck, either. And now she was throwing him a glare that had just enough familiarity at the edges to force him to rack his brain. It was a look that made him want to protect his balls for some reason. Had this woman kicked him there once? It was a distinct possibility.

"Who are you?" he finally asked.

"Adam, it's *Paige*." She looked disgusted with him and turned toward the kitchen.

His hand shot out to keep her from moving. It was just instinct. But she looked shocked, and her disbelieving eyes met his.

"It's *Paige*," she repeated.

His mind backflipped into his past as the flash of her eyes struck a memory. But he couldn't quite place her. He squinted and took her in again.

"Paige *Grant*," she said with rising irritation.

He blinked. *Paige Grant? Damn.*

He'd forgotten one of the Grant girls was named Paige. Was she the youngest one? There were two young ones he remembered who seemed like twins. He'd wondered when one of the Grant women would get here—assumed it would be the mother, Ginger. Now that his father had passed and offers were starting to come in for the fifty-acre mountaintop property, he figured the Grants would be getting offers, too, to complete the last five-acre corner. He'd always wondered whatever happened to his almost-stepmother, Ginger. Though most of the time he chose not to remember her at all—she hadn't exactly been his favorite person.

The only Grant he ever saw anymore was the oldest daughter, Olivia, sometimes in town on Lavender Island. He remembered her always being pleasant, though quiet and almost too shy to talk to.

This must be the surly little sister who had always shot him glares through her goth eyeliner. She'd been about thirteen, as he recalled.

Although, honestly, she looked nothing like he remembered her.

"You don't have a key?" he asked, trying to reach for some logic to put all these pieces together. Why the hell was she crawling through the window, making him come investigate when he had a million other things to do?

Her shoulders seemed to relax, and—if he wasn't mistaken—a slight smile formed at the corners of her mouth.

"I like a challenge," she said.

Adam sighed.

Just his luck.

Adam Mason—or this attractive person who claimed to be him—was not at all what Paige had expected. He wasn't flannel-garbed. He wasn't missing-toothed. And he certainly wasn't thin or bent over. Instead, his muscular body loomed in the doorway, much taller than she remembered, his shoulders wide and his hands hanging low on his hips. The wispy, wheatlike hair she recalled from their teen years was now trimmed and pushed thickly away from his face, giving him a mature air while still making him seem windblown somehow—as if he'd just flown in from the sky. His eyes had aged beautifully, too—not a lost-boy cloudy blue anymore, but a deep, storied blue, the color of the sky before a storm. And dark eyebrows made them look more intense. Even wise.

The only thing that was the same from her memory was the scowl.

"You're *here*," she said absurdly, not quite able to reconcile everything at once, not quite able to admit how unjustly handsome he was.

"Yes." He shifted his weight in his cowboy-sheriff stance. "I was going to say the same thing."

His voice was deep and smooth, kept in a low tenor that seemed to strive for tolerance. He glanced over her shoulder, as if he wasn't sure she was alone, and then waited patiently for her to say something. Finally, as if he'd tired of that, he readjusted his stance. "What are you doing here, and why are you breaking in?" he asked.

Paige scrambled to get her thoughts in order. She had planned to approach him and launch into a carefully rehearsed speech: They wanted him to wait to sell, for three more months. And, further, they wanted him to loan them certain areas of his land to put on a huge wedding for the old-time movie star Dorothy Silver. It was a crazy request. Paige suspected he wouldn't go for it. He wouldn't have the best memories of either Paige or her mom. And a hermit like him wouldn't want the hoopla of a huge Hollywood wedding happening up here on his tiny mountain. But her mother had insisted she at least ask. This could be a big boon for their wedding-planning business.

But Paige hadn't intended to meet him, and make the request, like this—muddy boots, butt in a window, twigs in her hair, with him barely remembering her. And damn, why did he have to look so good?

He seemed to tire of waiting for an answer and turned to take in the surroundings: the tchotchkes on the floor, the neglected wall paneling. He glanced toward the window and pulled the curtain back with an index finger. "I assume you're here to talk about the offers we're getting?"

She willed her heart to beat normally. "Yes."

She didn't know what was wrong with her—it felt like raw, animal fear. She didn't know if it was from his being nothing like she expected or from her being launched right back into her thirteen-year-old self: stomach jumping, hands shaking, words turning to cotton on her tongue. He smelled like wild grass and whittled wood. And took up so much space in this kitchen. And looked amazing in that hat and those jeans. She took another deep breath and had a strange, nagging thought that if she could get out of this room, she'd regain some of her sanity. Maybe being on Mason-Grant land again was part of the problem.

"I'd like to talk to you but would like to talk somewhere else," she said, willing her voice to stay steady.

He turned and gazed at her. "What's there to talk about? I've almost made my own deal, but you're free to do as you please."

"Yes." She swallowed. "I'd just like to talk to you about a few things."

Adam crossed his heavy forearms and fixed his attention on her. "What things?"

Her heartbeat continued to escalate, but she told herself to breathe deeply. She wasn't going to let this guy intimidate her. Their families had had long, messy involvements with each other—the Masons and the Grants were like two wild vines, weaving in and around each other's thorns over the generations, sometimes strangling the other vine and sometimes caressing it. The Masons had continued to be nice and polite to Helen, but there was certainly no love lost on other generations, especially her mother, Ginger—Adam definitely had reasons for hating her. And many of the Masons were probably already suspicious of Paige—the next generation of complication.

She would just have to be firm. And convincing. Greta Garbo . . . Joan Crawford . . .

She squared her shoulders. "Maybe we could meet this evening in your family's lobby?"

His family resort would be the impersonal, removed space she could use. Plus, it would give her enough time to clean up and look somewhat like a professional, like her mother had begged her to do. At least she could dust the dirt off her face and run a comb through her hair. She pushed her hair back now and tried to face him with an expression of confidence. She knew she must look like a crazy person.

Adam hadn't moved an inch—his legs were spread in a gesture of obstinacy, his jaw set. The only movement that gave away the fact that he was still breathing was his jaw muscle.

"I don't think there's much to talk about," he murmured. The hardening of his eyes clued her in that memories were starting to come back to him.

"Let's meet anyway. For old times' sake." She tried to keep her voice light.

Adam, however, didn't look amused. Instead, his face hardened even more, if that were possible, and he glanced out the window.

"My staff doesn't know all the details," he said in a deep monotone. "I'd rather not meet in my lobby."

His lobby? *Damn.* It really hit her for the first time that Adam was the new patriarch of this place—all this land, the ranch, the airport, the orchard, the pond, the resort. She'd been told that, of course. But it was a different story viewing it firsthand—seeing how much property this was, how much work this was, and how pulled together he was at only thirty-four. She'd been selling him short, thinking he was up here wasting away. He was up here hanging on to an empire.

She tried to meet his eyes, but too many emotions were making it hard—shame that she'd misjudged him, embarrassment that he might remember too much from that summer, anger that he didn't remember her at all, and a frustrating chemistry that was making her blood race in a way that apparently her body hadn't been able to shake for sixteen years.

He shifted his stance. "If you insist on talking, let's meet at the Castle this afternoon," he said. "Do you know where that is?"

"Of course I know where it is. I've only spent a million summers on the island." She looked away. Facing Adam Mason again also caused a regression to her snappish, nervous thirteen-year-old self, too.

But everyone who lived here knew where the Castle was. It sat at the very top of Castle Road, the steepest of the five main roads leading out of Carmelita and into the unpopulated interior of Lavender Island. It was where island visitors went to catch romantic panoramas, and where locals went if they didn't want to be seen.

She took a deep breath and tried to pull herself together. When she glanced back up, he was studying her carefully. She squinted at him. "You *do* remember me, don't you?"

He waited too many beats to answer, but he finally gave a slight nod.

She didn't believe him. He didn't remember her specifically. He remembered her family—probably Olivia, definitely Ginger—but he didn't remember her. Story of her life. He hadn't paid any attention to her then, and he was probably looking right through her now. But that was fine. She needed to make this deal. And memories and feelings would just get in the way. It was like her mom always said: *Don't play the fool, in business or in love.*

Paige's mom—along with Dorothy Silver and probably Gram in heaven—was counting on her. She needed to keep her wits about her.

Paige motioned with her hand toward the door. "Thanks for letting me into Gram's place, then. I'll meet you at the Castle. What time?" As soon as she saw how badly her fingers were shaking, she snatched her hand back and put it on her hip.

"How about two?"

Paige nodded. That would give her a chance to clean up a little. And run that comb through her hair. And get her feelings in check. And remember what decade her hormones belonged in.

A movement to her left caught her eye. "There you are!" She leaned down to get the kitten to come toward her, but it stalled in the living-room doorway. "She jumped in here and I didn't want to close the window on her."

"That's Click." Adam bent down and scooped the kitten up in one swift move.

Paige tried to ignore how easily the cat went to him. And how sweet his enormous hand looked cradling it. He'd been half terrifying her here—looking huge and scary and much too controlled. But seeing him holding that kitten reminded her of the boy he'd once been, the one she'd crushed on, the one with the vulnerability softening his edges. She cleared her throat when the man met her eyes.

He stared at her, waiting another five uncomfortable beats—three of which seemed to be him contemplating whether she really was who she said she was—then maybe another two where his brain seemed to be registering a few more memories. Finally, he strode toward the door.

"See you, Calamity June," he said, with his usual note of dismissal.

Paige's back stiffened.

He did remember.

CHAPTER 2

Paige chose a table in the Castle dining room that had beautiful views of the sunlight-dappled patio and fire pit.

Since she'd never lived a life of intrigue, she'd never stepped foot in here. Who in a million years would have dreamed that the first time she'd visit, she'd be sneakily meeting none other than Adam Mason? Insanity.

She adjusted the table lamp, straightened the tablecloth, smoothed her cotton maxi dress—which had felt great to slip into after a morning of sweeping and scrubbing—and stole a quick look at the mahogany-paneled bar. He wasn't here yet. Just how she liked it. She always tried to be early. It was one of the many business strategies her mother had taught her—to have the advantage of getting settled before the client walked in.

Ginger had been imparting all this business advice with the hope that Paige would follow in her footsteps. Paige didn't have the heart to tell her she wasn't interested. And now, with her mother ill, it was even harder to come clean.

Her mom had always bemoaned the fact that Paige scrambled around, working clusters of part-time jobs. She currently worked part-time at the Hollywood Film Library, part-time finding roles in commercials, and nights at the corner yoga studio. Her mom would tsk and shake her head, saying Paige should give that up and become the businesswoman she was meant to be—maybe take over Ginger's event-planning business that catered to celebrities.

Paige really didn't want to. She used the acting thing and the Hollywood Film Library as her decoys—everyone knew she loved movies and had been appearing in commercials since she was fifteen. But what she really loved was the yoga studio. She didn't look like a typical yoga teacher. She wasn't long and lean, or even particularly graceful. She didn't go barefoot all the time, wasn't a vegetarian, and didn't have a perfect behind. But teaching yoga part-time made her feel whole and fulfilled. The problem was she couldn't figure out how to transform it into a career that her mom thought justified her college degree, so Paige simply kept quiet. For the time being, she'd help her mother. With the cancer diagnosis, Ginger needed Paige right now.

Paige pored over the menu and ordered a bottle of red. Her mom was definitely right about this arriving-early thing. Paige was able to calmly read the menu and have a drink to tamp down her Adam jitters. She pictured him again and let out an involuntary sigh. She truly hadn't expected him to be so . . . *normal.* Better than normal, really. She thought about the fact that he'd never married. And the rumors that he never left the mountain. Now she wondered about that. What had gone on all those years up here? Had he just lived a solitary life, with his brother and George and a few old ranch hands, and that was it? Working like a plow horse every day and doing nothing else? Sure, he was some kind of land baron now, with all that property he'd inherited, but had the cost for that been a hermit's life?

The waiter brought her bottle, and she waited as he poured. She didn't recognize him. The staff and chefs for the Castle were said to live off the island, coming here for four days at a time and staying in the hotel itself until they were ferried back to their homes in Los Angeles. It was all part of keeping the island's secrets.

She sipped the wine, nodded to the waiter, then waited until he walked away so she could gulp down half the glass. As soon as she felt the first buzz of relaxation, she was able to sit back and take in the beauty of the place without her nerves going into overdrive. The dining room was nearly vacant, but her favorite view was outside: those interior island peaks were gorgeous and mysterious.

After a few minutes, and a little more Zen buzz, she decided she was missing the best views, and some good sun, and asked the waiter if she could move outside.

After she was reseated among the pine trees that surrounded the flagstone patio, enjoying the scenery and the way the sun danced through the oak leaves across the patio, Adam walked in.

Paige straightened her back and twirled the wineglass between her fingers, trying to look as unruffled as possible. He was just so ridiculously good-looking—so unfair for a guy she'd hoped would amount to nothing. He'd thrown on a dinner jacket over his blue jeans—to meet the restaurant's dress code, she supposed—and the effect was disarmingly sexy. He took his hat off as he made his way past the tables, the sun backlighting him, and his amble seemed to gain strength—as if he absorbed it from the trees, the stones, the smoky scent of the fireplace on the patio. He nodded to the waiter who stood by the bar. He was clearly at home here. Her disadvantage.

"Glad you found a seat," he said, glancing at the surrounding empty tables.

She attempted a smile, but her lips got stuck on her teeth, and she quickly took another gulp of wine. "This was a good choice to hide from your staff. Come here often?"

"Why do you ask?"

"Just wondering what kind of a secret life you're living these days."

He glanced up from underneath his eyebrows as he slid smoothly into the chair across from her but didn't bother to address that accusation.

She needed to knock this off. Her nervousness with him was making her say crazy things. She tried to relax her shoulders and sink into her chair like Bette Davis might, but worried she wasn't pulling off the look exactly. She probably looked drunk.

"I guess I owe you an apology," he said.

She did a double take—not quite ready to hear those words—as her heart rate escalated. "An apology?"

"For not remembering you."

She straightened in her chair. That wasn't the apology she'd been hoping for. Not that she'd lain in bed awake at night thinking about apologies from Adam Mason, of course. For something like sixteen years. But whatever. He was at least being polite.

"At first." He cocked his head. "Then I did."

Up this close, at this tiny patio table, a citron candle flickering under his chin, Adam exuded a strange mixture of strength and relaxation. Every element of his body had a solidity about it, as if his muscles were rocks from the earth. His jeans, his shirt, his jacket, his windblown hair—they all had the same natural air, as though he were one with this place. As if he came from its soil. Which, she supposed, in some ways he did. The strength was the part that made her nervous.

"Do you remember a lot from back then?" Her voice came out in a too-high octave.

His frown became suspicious. "What are you asking?"

"Nothing. It was a strange summer."

He gave her another of those looks from behind now-furrowed eyebrows, this one with something that might be irritation.

"What's done is done," he said. "Is there something you wanted to talk about?"

Paige focused on the candle. No, there wasn't. She didn't want to get to know him again and stare into those blue eyes while she heard his story—everything that had happened since that summer. She didn't want emotions to enter the scene. And she didn't want *him* to remember, exactly. She tried to repeat another of her mother's favorite rules to herself about never letting hearts get in the way of business, but she quickly gave it up for another gulp of wine.

"Not really," she said. "I'm just here to do business with you."

He nodded. "Great. Let's talk business, then."

The waiter came over to pour another glass, but Adam ordered a scotch instead. She studied him as he tossed his jacket over the back of an adjoining chair and rolled his sleeves up. Dang, he had beautiful forearms.

"So why don't you start?" he asked.

"I'm sure you're getting lots of offers to sell your property."

"I am."

"We are, too."

"I imagine."

"We heard you were close to making a deal with Dave MacGregor. He offered to buy from us, also."

"He's offering the fairest price so far—beyond fair, really. I'd advise you to take it."

"Well, that's the thing. We want to keep the land for a little while longer. For an event. An important event."

Adam kept his gaze steady. The brief glimpses of friendliness and professionalism he'd shown a minute ago had already slipped away. Now he was wearing his old scowl—the one all the Masons tended to wear when dealing with the Grants.

"You're welcome to do whatever you want with your land," he said.

"The event is the wedding of Dorothy Silver to Richard Crawford—their second marriage to each other, actually. She wanted to re-create the wedding they had on Nowhere Ranch in the 1950s. Remember, the one from the movie—"

"*Last Road to Nowhere*," he filled in for her. "Yeah, I got it. But what does this have to do with me?"

Of course. He was probably all too familiar with the movie that had made his family's ranch and airport famous and brought in visitors from around the world. She was losing him. He sat back with a barely lassoed impatience.

"My mom runs a wedding-planning business now, and this wedding could put her over the top. We want to do this for Dorothy. She made friends with my grandmother when she was here filming, and she's a regular at the Hollywood Film Library, and—"

"I'm familiar with Dorothy Silver," Adam said edgily. "But what does this have to do with me?"

"We're hoping you'll supply the ranch."

He frowned again. "What's wrong with your property?"

"Dorothy wants all of Nowhere Ranch, where they did a lot of the filming."

"You could use your building and the yard around. Should be plenty of room. The views are the same—you can see the ocean from anywhere."

"She wants the whole thing, like the old movie set. She already brought us blueprints. She wants the horse stables and the airport and the resort and everything. And especially the orchard."

"The *orchard*? Why the orchard?"

"She found it romantic."

Adam barely suppressed an eye-roll. "MacGregor might be interested in loaning it to you once he becomes the new owner."

"He's not. We brought that up when he offered to buy our piece."

Adam shook his head. "Sorry. I can't wait. I want out of here, and I need to take this deal."

"But if you—"

"Look, I'd like to help you out, Miss Grant, but—"

"Oh, I'm sure you want to help." She couldn't help the snap that came out in her voice.

She slumped in her chair. This was pointless. Adam was exactly how she remembered him—so in his own little world, so unconcerned with anyone else that he couldn't even let her get her explanation out of her mouth. When she was a thirteen-year-old gawking girl, his introversion seemed mysterious and movie-star-like. But as she got older, and was able to look back on it, she recognized it as selfish and uncaring. Especially after what happened that summer.

The waiter brought Adam's scotch, and he quickly downed about half of it before giving her another of his scowls. "Honestly," he said, "your grandmother meant a lot to me."

The comment felt like a reprimand. She looked away.

"But I've had this deal under way for some time now," he went on in his measured voice, "and I need to leave."

"Why do you need to leave?"

The frown he gave her made it clear it was none of her business. And, in business, that was true. But she wanted to know for personal reasons. Maybe he would find it funny that she'd had such a crush on him. Maybe she could tell him she'd followed him around that whole summer. But—given the way her heart was still palpitating now, and the fact that it had been a terrible summer for him with long-lasting consequences—she decided she'd better not start confessing. He probably wouldn't find it funny at all.

"Don't answer that," she said, her hand fluttering to the table. "What I mean to say is that Dorothy Silver wants to buy the entire property when we're done. And she'll double MacGregor's price."

That shut him up. He leaned back in the chair and studied her carefully. The irritation was off his face, and he peered at her with interest now. "Double?"

Paige nodded.

"You could get that in writing?"

She nodded again.

"Why doesn't she buy it now?"

"She wants to make sure we can fix it up to look like it did back then."

"Sounds like a lot of work."

"That's why she's paying double."

A blue scrub jay landed on the flagstone bench surrounding the patio and loudly squawked its dismay. Paige had forgotten how angry those scrub jays always seemed to be. Adam stared at it and took a few gulps of scotch, then turned his glass in his hand. "I'll think about it," he said.

"I don't know what there is to think about. She's willing to pay *double*—that's good money."

"Like I said, I'll have to think about it." His tone shut her down.

Normally she'd be able to hang in there, applying the new business acumen she was learning from her mom, but he was unnerving her. And his roped forearms weren't helping.

She closed her eyes and told herself to get a grip.

"I was sorry to hear about your father," she said.

Adam stiffened, then drew one hand off the tiny table. Extra air swirled between them.

"That makes two of you, then—you and the casino." He took another long gulp and scowled toward the bar. The comment, and the pause, felt like a tiny, tentative thread of connection. She wanted to seize the thread—it was the one commonality she shared with this man—but he turned a frown toward her, and the moment felt lost. "So where are you staying?"

She wanted to linger over the topic of George for a moment—or maybe the brief vulnerability she saw in Adam's eyes, or maybe that loose thread of connection—but she zeroed in on his question instead. Mostly because she didn't have a very good answer.

"I'd planned to stay in Gram's house, but I didn't realize what bad shape it was in," she admitted.

"Yeah, that's not a good idea. Don't you have a sister by the harbor? Can you stay there?"

"You remember my sister?"

"Vaguely."

"How do you know my sister lives by the harbor?"

He gave her another of his you're-testing-my-patience looks. "It's not a good idea to stay in the house," he said firmly. "There are probably raccoons living in all the closets by now. I took care of it up until a few years ago, but Helen had me turn off the electricity and close it up. I can get everything back on for you, but it'll take a couple of days."

Paige had noticed the lack of electricity. At least there was still running water, but she could tell it hadn't been run in some time.

Her mind lingered over Adam's last comment. "*You* took care of the house all those years?"

"I just watched over it."

"You did that for my gram?" She could hardly keep the note of incredulousness out of her voice.

Adam glanced up but chose not to answer. He seemed tired of her already.

"So when is this wedding?" he asked instead.

She straightened in her chair. *Is he considering this?* She casually took a sip of wine and hoped her voice didn't squeak as she answered. "August 7—just like the movie."

He nodded. "And what do you hope to have done by then?"

She tried not to look too enthusiastic as she scooted her chair back to reach into her tote. "I brought the blueprints."

Despite trying to look cool, she managed to get her chair legs caught on the wood floor, which sent her shoulder rocking into the table. Her wine sloshed as her hand flew out to steady her glass; then she pushed her hair out of her eyes.

"Don't get excited," he drawled. "I'm not saying yes. I just want to know what your thoughts are."

"Here, let me show you." She spread the top landscaping blueprint in front of him.

He lifted his glass out of the way and looked as though he was sorry he'd asked. "Can you sum it up?"

She resisted rolling her eyes. He sure hadn't gotten any friendlier.

She threw her hand in the air as if she were painting a scene. "Wildflowers. Gazebo. Horses grazing—"

"Wait. Wildflowers?"

"Yes, wildflowers. In the meadow between our houses."

"It'll be August."

"I'm sure we can find something."

"We're in a drought. What do you think is going to grow in that meadow in August? It's going to be brown and filled with weeds."

"I'll take care of the wildflowers, then."

"And what gazebo are you talking about?"

"Remember in the movie? There was that beautiful white gazebo, where they shared their vows."

"That didn't exist, you know. It was a dummy set."

"We could build a real one."

"Who's 'we'?"

She cleared her throat. "Well, *I* could build a real one . . ."

"And whose horses are you planning on using?"

"Don't you still have horses?"

"I sold them."

"I just saw them when I was driving down here."

"They're with me for three more weeks. Then a new owner is taking them."

"Do you think you could talk the new owners into—"

"Listen." Adam rolled the blueprints back up and pushed them across the table at her. "This sounds like a lot of trouble. I have a million things to do, and enough of my own problems, and I truly can't help you with this. If you want to fix up your own property, I'll help you with whatever you need, in honor of Helen, like turning back on the electricity or finding island contractors for you, but I can't spend time or money working on extraneous things like planting wildflowers in a drought or building a gazebo in the middle of a bison ranch. I'm trying to sell my place and move on. I'm sure you understand." Adam stood and reached for his wallet.

She stared at him, panic setting in. He couldn't go now. She wasn't done. Her mother would be disappointed in her. Dorothy Silver might fire them. And Dorothy would definitely not get Paige the part of playing her in the new movie. Paige had barely been able to breathe when Dorothy had first suggested it—her first serious role. If she could make enough money on that, she might be able to open a yoga studio.

"Maybe I could help you with something in return?" she sputtered. His blue eyes and sexy scent, coupled with the strangely distant intimacy of their shared history, were throwing her off her game. She finally had to look away.

"What are you going to help me with?" He frowned and gathered his jacket off the back of the chair.

She scrambled to think of something, shoving the blueprints back into her tote. "I'm sure I could help you with something. What sort of help do you need?"

"If you have any ranching skills, I could use those. Or flying skills. I have a half-manned, barely operating airport right now. The ranch is flailing. The airport is on its last leg. I'm trying to pay off my father's debts, and it's all I can do to keep my head above water. So if you have any help to offer with any of those things . . ." She watched him check his pockets for his keys.

His admission warmed her heart a little. Both the words and the dropped voice sounded like intimacies shared with a good friend, someone you'd known from the past, the same someone who knew your father had a gambling problem and who you could trust not to judge. But she knew better than to read too much into it—years of misjudging men's words had done a number on her. She immediately dismissed the maybe-intimate words and focused on how to solve this. How could she help him?

"My skills lean more toward event planning," she admitted quietly. "Or acting." She was still a bit shy about mentioning yoga. "And maybe a little baking, cooking, or babysitting."

He froze and glanced over at her, but then—as if she'd imagined it—he went back into motion, shrugging into his jacket.

"Wait," she said.

He turned back toward her.

She desperately searched his face for the smallest hint at what had caused that pause.

"Did you need some baking?"

He tugged his sleeves down at the wrist. "Why would I need someone to bake for me?"

"Cook?"

Adam continued straightening his cuffs. "I have a cook."

"Babysit?"

He went back to patting his pockets, looking for his car keys. But she thought she saw it: the slightest hesitation.

"Do I look like I have a baby? I don't need anything from you, Miss Grant. Thank you."

"Well, I hope you'll think over my proposal and idea." She got the blueprints back into her tote, still eyeing him to find any cracks. "Dorothy Silver's price is unprecedented, and it will be more than worth your time. Think it over. I'm happy to bring the blueprints back. Until then, I'll try to stay out of your way. Here's my card." She handed him her event-planning card. It was the first one she'd used from the box of five hundred she'd ordered online for ten bucks. She'd ordered some, too, that read, "Yoga Instructor," but they still sat in their cellophane. "When do you think you'll have an answer for me?"

"Thursday. By the way, the food's good here," he said, shoving the card into his jeans pocket without even looking at it. "Have anything you want, and tell them to put it on my tab. In honor of Helen." He took the last swig of his scotch.

Paige toasted back with her wineglass. "In honor of Gram."

She brought the wine to her lips and watched him go. He tilted his hat back and ambled out the door, and she stared over the rim of her glass and wondered at the bewildering pounding of her heart.

She wondered if it was due to the fact that she might have lost this round; the fact that she thought she saw a win for the next round; or the fact that she couldn't stop staring at him, thinking, for some reason, that she'd been brought to this moment—this exact, final moment—since the very first day she'd laid eyes on him down by the Lavender Island harbor, sixteen years ago.

She sincerely hoped it was one of the first two.

CHAPTER 3

Paige slipped back out of her maxi dress in the powder room off the kitchen—glad that no one was around to see her get twisted in it and almost crash through the wall—and tugged on an old pair of yoga pants and a T-shirt. Then she got to work on Gram's house.

She spent half an hour sweeping the rest of the kitchen floor with the old broom she found behind the double Dutch door, sending too much dust swirling into the air, only to have it settle slowly in the rays of late-afternoon light that were coming through the windows in a beautiful way.

As she swept, she thought about Adam's reluctance to cooperate, his impatience, the suspicious looks he kept giving her . . .

She sighed.

That man always made her feel more than she wanted to.

She thought back to that night, many, many years ago, when they'd all sat around a bonfire on the beach as teenagers, and he'd leaned in toward Samantha Sweet, whispering something into her ear.

She and Adam had known each other for a few years at the time. Or, more accurately, she'd known *him*. He'd seemed unaware of her existence. But as their parents dropped each other off and picked each other up during their summer romance, Paige's thirteen-year-old self had conjured a relationship between her and Adam as she stared surreptitiously at his teenage swagger through the living-room window of Gram's ranch house.

Gram had two houses on Lavender Island—the little cottage down in the island's only town, Carmelita, plus the huge ranch house up on the fifth peak of the island. Paige, Natalie, and Olivia had preferred the cottage in Carmelita, where they'd visited their grandmother every summer since Natalie was born, along with a bevy of other tourists who got off the ferries and fell upon the tiny harbor town for the glorious summer months.

Lavender Island was twenty miles long and eight miles across at its widest, but the tourists and almost the entire population spent most of their time in the three square miles of Carmelita. As grade-schoolers, Paige and her sisters loved running up to Main Street in their bathing suits and flip-flops, visiting the candy shop, ice-cream shop, and toy shop that lay between E and F Streets. As preteens, they loved snorkeling in Heart's Cove and swimming at the public beach near the harbor. But that particular summer, the summer Paige turned thirteen, they were dragged up one of the back roads, way up one of Lavender Island's remote, interior hills, and forced to stay in Gram's ranch house. Without Gram. With their mom instead. All because their mother had fallen in love for the millionth time.

Paige sulked for the first few days—how were they going to get down the mountain to see Gram or go to the candy store or go snorkeling? But once Paige lifted her sulking head and glanced out the window—and laid eyes on eighteen-year-old Adam Mason riding a horse across the property—her protests died on her tongue. She didn't know what all her swirling feelings were about, exactly. All she knew was that Olivia had a boyfriend at school, and Paige was pretty sure this boy on the horse should be *her* first boyfriend.

Twice she'd walked across the meadow to dinner at his house, along with her mom and sisters, but he hadn't taken note of her. He might have had a second-long linger at Olivia, who was closer to his age, but mostly he kept his head down, his mop of blond, wispy hair covering his eyes as he wolfed down his food, then whisked away from the dinner table as quickly as possible. He had a younger brother named Noel, who was Paige's age, but Noel reminded Paige of a little elf and was thoroughly annoying—constantly playing tricks on Paige and her sisters. She tried to ignore Noel as best she could. She only had eyes for the brooding, scowling, mysterious older brother who wouldn't look her way.

Paige's school friend Cathy took the ferry over to visit a week later, and the two girls would sit on the ranch rails and watch Adam ride his horses in the distance. Cathy verified that he was a fine specimen to watch. In rapid order, they begged Paige's mom to let them go to the weeklong beach camp down in Heart's Cove, where they'd learned that Adam was a counselor and the horse-riding instructor. Paige's mom was completely distracted with George and said yes immediately.

During the first few days of camp, Paige and Cathy memorized Adam's every move, his every voice inflection, his every head snap to get his sun-bleached bangs out of his eyes, and his every uttered word. She and Cathy would go back to their shared beach tent and titter together in the darkness, writing everything down in their diaries with colorful gel pens and Lisa Frank stickers and giggling over whether he'd even looked their way or not. (Usually not.)

But that night, the night of the bonfire, she stared at him with a new feeling. As she watched him with Samantha Sweet, another counselor his age, she had her first real pangs of jealousy and longing. She felt them painfully, all the way into her belly, but couldn't make enough sense of the emotions to express them to Cathy. Instead, she was compelled to sneak away while Cathy was learning to play the ukulele—to spy on Adam and Samantha still sitting alone by the bonfire. As Paige peered around a tree at them, Adam nuzzled Samantha's neck and sent her giggling up into the woods. He grabbed a lantern and followed the pretty camp counselor while she crooked a finger at him. And Paige grabbed another lantern and followed.

They ran, laughing, up the hill. Paige had a hard time keeping up, her lantern shorting out every ten feet or so, emitting frightening electric sparks for a second. But she managed to track them to the old boathouse that sat high on the hill. She peeked around a pine tree as Adam set his lantern down and put both hands against the wood on either side of Samantha, smiling at her in a playful way. He said something to her, low, out of Paige's earshot, but the way Samantha melted against the building made Paige die with curiosity. She wanted that for herself. She didn't even know what, exactly, she wanted, but she knew she wanted Adam to look at her in just that way: that admiring, adoring, fascinated way. She wanted to make him smile like that. She wanted to make him follow her like that. She wanted to make him stare, wide-eyed, and lean in, and nuzzle, and kiss, and laugh—just like that.

Once the kissing began in earnest, Paige studied Samantha's movements carefully. Samantha grabbed at Adam—at his shirt, at his belt buckle—and started tugging him inside the boathouse. He took one quick look around and followed her in. Within minutes the lantern went off, and Paige saw a soft glow coming from the high boathouse windows, bouncing shadows off the walls. The glow looked romantic and intimate, like candlelight. Just like in the movies.

Paige sighed. Blinking against the darkness and suddenly coming to her senses about how long she'd been gone and how obsessive she was becoming about Adam Mason, she turned to find her way back down the hill. A twig snapped behind her. She sucked in her breath. *What was that?* A second snapping sound followed and sent her tearing out of her spot, fleeing down the mountain, lantern abandoned, tripping through the wild grasses and over gnarled tree limbs and tangled vines she hadn't even noticed on her way up.

At the base of the hill, as soon as she saw the campers' lights, she sighed a relieved breath and joined the rest of the group in another campfire song by the cabin, her voice shaky and uncertain, her memory not able to let go of Adam's sly smile or the scary twig snap or what Adam and Samantha might be doing in that cabin.

But within twenty minutes, life changed.

Because within twenty minutes, the hillside was ablaze.

Chaos erupted. People ran everywhere, counselors shouted, someone called the fire department, sirens roared. Paige stood like a statue in the center of it all, feeling the heat coming down the hill, watching orange-and-black shadows play across panicked faces. As fire trucks screeched up the roads and heavily equipped men poured out of the cabs and into the woods, Paige raced to the nearest firefighter. "There are two kids up there!" she shouted.

The fireman couldn't hear her as the cacophony of the night continued around them. He shuffled her toward one of the counselors, down by where the orange firelight was reflecting in the navy ocean, and kept his sights on the hillside amid shouts and still-arriving sirens.

"Wait!" she shouted again in desperation. She raced around until she found Adam's boss and grabbed his arm. "Adam is up there!"

A shadow of disbelief, shock, then anger passed across his face before he turned and began waving his arms, yelling the information to others.

Paige was escorted farther down the harbor with the other kids, away from the blazing hill, and their parents were called.

Paige found Cathy crying against a set of harbor chains and threw her arms around her. Soon Ginger and George came screeching up in their golf cart. "Where's Adam?" George barked. He had always scared her. She pointed tentatively up the hill, and George's characteristically angry face suddenly had a moment of worry and shock before contorting into rage again. Ginger clutched Paige and Cathy to her side and pulled them away from the crowd, checked with their counselor, and took the girls home. Up at the ranch, it was a long night of worry and staring out windows for Ginger, while Cathy and Paige finally fell asleep around two.

In the morning, Ginger told them the ending: Adam had been found, with a girl, Samantha Sweet. Both teens had been questioned.

The girl's parents had been called from the mainland. The reason for the fire was still unclear.

Paige had torn a paper napkin into shreds, listening.

Natalie—Paige's younger sister by a year—came bounding into the kitchen, breaking the tension and worry by demanding some cereal. She asked if she could follow Cathy and Paige to the harbor.

"I don't know if we're going today." Paige tried to tamp down her sadness. She couldn't believe Adam had been questioned by the police. At least he was safe from the fire. Although, clearly, he had another firestorm to deal with.

"We should go," Cathy said. "It'll keep our minds off of everything."

She wanted Cathy to have a good time. Paige didn't particularly appreciate that Natalie always wanted to tag along with her friends, but she acquiesced to let Natalie come. The three of them spent that day in the harbor. And Paige had never stopped thinking about Adam.

Paige snapped herself back into the present and stared at the table where she and Cathy and her mom had sat that morning long ago. She took a deep breath and continued sweeping, wondering if she should do a quick mop to make it even cleaner. But then she glanced again at the falling light and remembered Adam's comment about the raccoons. *Egads.* She'd have to investigate that before it got dark.

She tiptoed up the staircase with the broom. The ranch house was small by ranch standards, but it was still a sprawling two-story spread—larger than anything Paige had ever lived in while in LA. Moving slowly along the dusty wood hallway, she glanced inside each bedroom and felt completely overwhelmed. Nine years was a long time to leave a house vacant. The only way to tackle this would be to focus on one room at a time. And for now, first things first.

She flung each closet door open, broom in front of her, stifling a scream, and let another shiver run through her. As the light fell, her uneasiness grew. Some of the closets felt stuck, and others were so filled with clutter—decaying boxes, old suitcases, stacks of paperback novels—that she couldn't open them all the way. She poked the broom inside each one to see if she detected any movement. The idea that critters could be living in there, or might crawl back at night, had shivers racking her shoulders.

Maybe she should stay with Olivia or Natalie down in Carmelita.

She glanced out the window—it was probably only seven thirty. She could make it down the mountain in an hour and drop in on either of her sisters—Olivia; her husband, Jon; Paige's niece, Lily; and brand-new nephew, Aaron, who now lived in Gram's old cottage on C Street. Or she could show up at the door of Natalie and Elliott, who'd moved in together in Dr. Johnson's old place, much to Paige's surprise. As much as all three girls had loved Lavender Island as kids, Natalie and Paige had agreed, early into their teen years, that it wasn't a fun place for anyone over the age of fifteen and under the age of eighty. But Natalie had come to visit last spring and had fallen in love with a visiting scientist. The idea that her younger sister had fallen in love before she had, and had fallen in love enough to stay on this old-people island forever, had left Paige a little shocked.

Paige shrugged off the idea of calling either of her sisters, though. She hadn't wanted them to know she was here. Not yet anyway. She'd tell them once she got things ironed out with Adam Mason.

She made timid sweeps with her broom at the last closet just as the light began falling into a dusky purple. A mouse ricocheted out, and Paige screamed. She coughed at the swirl of dust that flew out behind the mouse and broom. But no big critters, at least. Despite Adam's warning, they didn't seem to have made homes here. Maybe she could stay, after all. There *was* running water, and she'd brought a lantern. She could set up her sleeping bag downstairs. It would be like camping, only with a roof over her head. Not that she'd been camping since she was thirteen.

She headed outside to retrieve the lantern, sleeping bag, her yoga mat, and bottled water out of the golf cart before night fell completely, bouncing them against her hip on the way back in. As she approached the back steps—damn, they were rotting out, too—the same tiny kitten wove its way through her legs.

"Hey, pretty girl." Paige set her lantern down to pet her, trying to remember her name. Did Adam say Click? "What are you doing back here?"

She lifted Click and glanced over her shoulder—hoping she'd get the same visitor who followed last time. But . . . *no*. She couldn't wish that. She couldn't go there again. She just needed to make this deal with Adam, and then mind her own business and stop thinking about him. He'd already made her childhood angsty—she didn't need him to mess with her adult years, too.

She went inside, set up the sleeping bag, and laid out a grapes-and-cheese dinner for her and Click, who snuggled into the crook of her arm. Paige pulled out a book, petting Click as she read. She'd put in a few nights of this, wait until Adam got the electricity back on, then finish cleaning up and hope that Adam would come around on the ranch-sale idea by Thursday. Her mind kept drifting to ideas for Dorothy Silver, but she kept dragging it back and tried to concentrate on her book. No sense in worrying about the Silver wedding on a large scale—or the moneymaking acting role Dorothy might give her—until Adam made a decision. She wasn't even into the second chapter when a sharp scratching noise against plaster echoed through the house.

Click skidded across the floor and sought refuge behind the pantry.

"What was that?" Paige whispered.

She tiptoed across the floor toward the banister with her lantern. Was the noise coming from upstairs? Her mind raced with possibilities—the raccoons, first and foremost—but each sound was different and unidentifiable. Now it was a rustling.

She scrambled back for her cell phone, which she'd turned off to save the battery, and gripped it tightly as she crept around the corner of the living room. As the stairs came more and more into view, her lantern light splashing shadows across the rails, she looked upward and froze—just as another shadowy outline of a body at the top did the same.

CHAPTER 4

He was tall, huddled in the dark, a sweatshirt hood covering his head and most of his face, still as a statue, just as she was.

A scream erupted from Paige's throat as she dropped the lantern and flew down the hall. She ran back through the kitchen, scooped up Click, and dashed out the back door into the cool night air.

Her screams turned to shrieks as she sped into the yard. She sucked in deep breaths as she whirled to see if the figure was following her. *No one.* Click clawed her way out of Paige's arms, and Paige wrapped her hands tighter around her waist as she realized her other hand was empty. She'd dropped her phone?

Panicked, Paige glanced around the grass, then gave up on the phone and sidled toward her golf cart, keeping her eyes on the house. Through the moonlit darkness, she saw the figure slip out the side door of the house about seventy feet away. He pulled his hood up around his head and began hobbling down the path toward the dark woods, half running, half stumbling toward the shrubbery.

The sound of horse hooves came up behind her, and she spun again in the darkness, heart in her throat, only to see Adam ride up.

"What's the matter?" he yelled as he leaped from his horse.

"Th-th-there was someone inside. He's there." She pointed. "Or he *was* there. He went toward the woods."

Adam steadied her, but his attention was already on the path. "Which way?"

She shakily pointed.

He swung back onto his horse. *What the hell is he doing?*

Terrified, she took a step after him, but he raced off at a gallop. She turned and inched toward the golf cart again. There was no way she was going back, even for her phone. She couldn't believe she'd dropped it. Some brave femme fatale she'd turned out to be.

She sidestepped faster, glancing between the house to detect any more movement and then at the woods to look for Adam's return. Where could that intruder possibly have been hiding? Had he been upstairs the whole time? She'd never checked the bathrooms—could he have been hiding in a tub or shower stall? Her shoulders rolled into a violent shiver.

Crickets trilled around her, making the night seem deceptively peaceful as she took the last few steps. Click crept out of the bushes and cautiously returned to Paige. When they were almost inside the cart, Adam and his horse exploded out of the trees on the other side of the house. Click sprang away again.

"I couldn't find him," Adam said as he thundered up beside her.

He dismounted, breathing heavily. His dark-denim shirt, rolled up at the forearms, blended into the night as he straightened his hat and moved into his customary hands-hanging-on-his-hips Western pose.

"I thought you were going to stay with your sister?" He sounded angrier at her than at the intruder.

"I never said that."

"I told you this place isn't safe."

"You said there were raccoons inside, not hooded men."

He gave her another aggravated look. "There are sometimes vagrants," he admitted. "Or sometimes hikers looking to get out of the rain. I try to patrol up here at least once a day. Tonight I saw the lantern flickering up here and thought I'd come investigate. Then I heard your screams."

He met her eyes for the first time. And, slowly, his face softened.

She blinked back for several seconds—soaking in his furrowed brows, his worried eyes, his protective stance. It was the first time Paige had ever seen him direct any kind of positive emotion toward her. But these were not emotions that she could rightfully take from him. They didn't belong to her. Never had. She'd always wanted attention and concern from Adam Mason, but they had never been hers.

"You really shouldn't stay here until we can get the electricity back on." His voice dropped into an even-more-protective softness.

She cleared her throat and tried to pull herself back into the present. She ignored the sexy voice, disregarded how it would sound in bed or how those arms would feel wrapped around her. Twenty-nine-year-old women were too old for crushes, weren't they? It was easier if she looked away.

"I'll find somewhere else to stay," she murmured.

"What about your sister?"

"It's a long story, but I can't really go there right now."

He looked through the darkness back at his own place and seemed to hesitate for a second, but finally he took a deep breath. "You can stay at the resort." He motioned with his shoulder.

Back to where a lot of it had happened. Back to that summer. Back to when they were kids, and their parents were in love, and he thought her mother had had him thrown in jail, and they'd split their parents up, and all hell had broken loose.

But she didn't know if she wanted to go back to those places.

And the hesitancy in his voice sounded like he wasn't so sure, either.

She gazed at Gram's place, picturing the figure at the top of the stairs, and another shiver went through her. A cold gust followed, and she wrapped her arms around her middle. Finally, she turned toward Adam.

"Are you sure?" she asked.

"You can stay in one of the resort rooms."

She couldn't shake the image of the hooded man. The idea of another intruder moving into her personal space tied her stomach in knots. Her fear of that was much worse than the fact that her hormones, around Adam Mason, had suddenly seemed to forget they were no longer thirteen.

"You have rooms open?" she asked.

"Plenty. As I said, the place has been floundering. We're closing it, but we have one more dude group soon, so the rooms are still made up. They're coming Thursday. You can have the room until then."

Another type of panic shot through Paige. "*Closing* it? Why are you closing the resort?" Her mind jumped from one difficult truth to another. This was not going to help with the Dorothy Silver situation at all—the wedding guests and huge wedding party would need a place to stay. But she'd have to revisit this problem later. Adam was turning away. And she had too much to worry about. Starting with tonight. She needed a safe place to sleep. Needed to stop noticing Adam's muscles. Needed to stop imagining what those strong, tanned hands would look like tracing along her body. Needed to stop shivering . . .

"I have to get my phone," she said quietly. She wanted to appear to be a strong, fearless woman to this man—pulled together, longing for nothing, no one to laugh at—but that was simply not going to happen. He made her feel weak in a million ways.

Turning to watch her from under the brim of his hat, he waited patiently for her to make a move. "Do you want me to go in? Just tell me where to look."

For a second she pretended he was smitten. She pretended he thought her a beautiful, sophisticated damsel in distress. But then her shoulders felt as though they had bricks piled on top of them, and she didn't feel much like a sophisticated damsel. Her loose yoga pants and wild hair didn't help. She was no good at this. This capturing-the-attention-of-sexy-men thing. Besides, she just wanted to sleep. Maybe the adrenaline from running out of the house from an intruder had simply whisked the last cells of hope and energy out of her body.

"I don't know where I dropped it," she admitted. "I can go in."

He frowned, and studied her as if he wasn't too certain, but he led the way, holding his hand up until he looked around to make sure the place was clear.

In silence, they traveled along the already-dusty-again floor, refocused the lantern beams so they had a little light, then collected the sleeping bag and the strewn grapes and cheese.

"Is this all you ate?" he asked, frowning at the cheese.

It felt like more judgment about her ridiculous life, and she didn't have the strength for it right now, so she ignored him and threw it into her backpack. When she spotted her phone, she tossed it in, too, then pulled the pack onto her shoulder. "All right, let's go." She couldn't get out of there fast enough.

She led the way out the door and back into the misty night air, where they piled her items into the golf cart to the sounds of chirping crickets. Click peered at them from behind one of the wheels.

"Here, sweetie." Paige bent and found a long twig, dragging it in front of Click until she leaped close enough to grab. "What's a dude group, by the way?"

Adam threw her sleeping bag into the cart. "Dude-ranch visitors. I've got a bunch of corporate sorts coming to experience a few nights on the range and corral some bison. In fact, one of them is MacGregor."

That was exactly the kind of experience Paige figured Dorothy's guests would want—maybe not the bison part, but the eating-around-the-campfire-and-riding-horses part. Could she pay him to do one more dude ranch? Would the ranch belong to MacGregor by then?

But now was not the time to get into this—Adam was looking longingly toward his house, as if he just wanted to get this night over with, and she was tired herself. She needed her pj's. And a comfortable bed. And to stop noticing how good he looked with the moonlight in his hair. Or how intimate it felt looking at him in the dark. Or wondering whether he made love to women with the lights off . . .

"Lead the way," she squeaked.

Adam swung onto his horse and led them down the dirt path that curved onto the main road. She bumped along behind him in the golf cart, pushing it to its whopping twenty miles per hour, feeling as if she were driving a clown car. These rental carts were slower than the ones the islanders owned. She floored it and tried to peer through the darkness at the old, familiar landscape. When she'd gone to the Castle earlier, she'd taken a different road down the hill, but now she was heading straight through his property for the first time in eons.

The meadow was still there—a circular piece between their properties that stretched for about an acre and sometimes had wildflowers in bloom. It was the land that most connected them. Gram used to say that the flowers bloomed when the families were getting along, but even as a young girl, Paige had doubted that. Right now, the flowers were closed to the night sky, but during the day, Paige had seen pretty yellow, white, and lavender wildflowers in bloom.

To the right, just before the woods started, was a quiet pond and, in front of that, was the apple orchard Dorothy wanted featured as part of her wedding ceremony. It was small but beautiful, with trees in straight rows and neatly kept patches of bright-green grass between each row. It had been George's pride and joy, and he'd always yelled at the kids to stay away. He'd babied his apple trees all year, especially into the summer months, and every fall the Masons held their annual Apple Fest that the entire island looked forward to. Paige's family was always gone by then—back on the mainland after their summer visit—but Gram talked about the Mason Apple Fest all the time. It hadn't been thrown for years, according to Olivia—ever since George had had his first heart attack. Now the apple orchard was too dark for her to see, but Paige knew she'd have to talk Adam into making that part of the wedding experience. It was a key scene from the movie.

Beyond the apple orchard, in a large clearing, was Mason Field, the only airstrip on the island. In front of the lone hangar were three small planes—one possibly Adam's. The other two might belong to his brother or an island resident, since the Masons had always provided tie-downs for anyone flying in.

On the other side of the property—several acres away—were the stables and corral, along with a few storage sheds and a large pasture where the Masons handled the island's bison. Most of the year the bison were free to roam the island's interior, grazing on the grass, kept in control by the island's conservancy group, but when it was time for immunizations, the bison were rounded up and brought to the sorting pens at the Mason ranch.

Paige glanced around at all of this in the dark. As soon as the sprawling house came into view, a flutter of butterflies went through her stomach. Her mind immediately conjured the lovely, earthy smell of summer sage outside their kitchen window; she could hear the collar of the Masons' little puppy Denny; she could see her mother's bright-coral summer lipstick as she looked across the table at George, right where the morning sun came streaming through the kitchen window. The Grant girls often had breakfast at the Masons' that summer, even after the fire—or the first fire anyway—the five of them cavorting over there in the mornings across the meadow, Ginger with her three daughters, and Cathy, all in dresses. Sometimes Adam would be there, but only as a quick shadow, hustling out of the house, buttoning up a shirt, mumbling that he was going to see Samantha. After the fire, Samantha's parents had tried to take her off the island in the middle of her summerlong counseling duties, but she'd managed to convince them to let her stay and finish out all the camp weeks. It had only given Paige more misery, as she would watch Adam tear off to meet her anytime he could.

After Paige parked her cart in the empty lot, she followed Adam through the huge oak double doors of the resort and tried to look away from his strong legs and snug jeans as he leaned over the lobby desk and shouted for someone named Mendelson. She sighed deeply and looked for a way to divert her attention.

The lobby, while eerily empty, was beautiful—not at all what she remembered. The update boasted a vintage aviator theme that highlighted Mason Field. There were enormous old propellers on the two-story-high walls, historical photos hanging throughout, and leather-bound logbooks lining the mantel of a massive flagstone fireplace that erupted through the center of the lobby. Sixteen rooms lined the wing off one side: eight on the first floor and eight on the second. The other side of the lobby had a door that led to the family kitchen, and behind that was the family home.

The renovated resort felt old and new, and small and enormous, at the same time—small enough to feel cozy, but enormous in its high ceilings and oversized stones. But the dimmed lighting and silence also made it feel like a place marching toward death.

"What's up?" A young blonde girl—with the edges of her hair in bright blue—came around the corner in a Grateful Dead T-shirt and took her place at the check-in desk. Paige wasn't even sure where she'd come from. A back office? The family home?

"Amanda, where's Mendelson?" Adam asked.

"Not in yet."

Adam frowned and made a frustrated sound. It made Paige feel better that, for once, neither she nor her family was responsible for a Mason scowl.

Amanda looked Paige up and down as she licked some kind of potato-chip dust off her fingers.

"Can you get Ms. Grant here set up in a room, then?" Adam asked in his deep voice, avoiding Amanda's eyes.

Amanda glanced between Adam and Paige a few times—as if trying to assess the situation—but finally pulled out a keyboard from under the check-in computer.

"Which room do you want her in?" she asked.

"Eight-A."

She nodded as if that meant something to her. Paige wondered if that was the farthest room in the wing, as far away from Adam as possible.

"Are you hungry?" he asked, turning toward Paige abruptly. "That cheese and those grapes couldn't be your dinner."

His voice sounded more irritated than truly concerned. That indifference was what Paige needed to remember. *Her* hormones might be going into overdrive at the sight of him, but he'd been treating her like a veritable stranger the whole day. A pain-in-the-ass stranger, in fact. She'd do well to follow his lead.

"I'll be all right," she said. "I'm mostly tired."

He gave a curt nod, then strode through the door that led to his own residence.

"It's on us," he told Amanda over his shoulder.

Amanda frowned at his retreating back as if confused, then focused her eyes back on the screen.

"Nonsmoking okay?" she asked.

"Yes."

"One queen okay?"

"Yes."

Amanda went into efficiency mode, printing a confirmation, getting a key, folding it into a map.

The girl leaned across the counter and pointed with her pen. "We're here. Your room is straight down that way." Her voice fell into the rhythm of boredom that was the hallmark of teenagers everywhere. "Jacuzzi is open until . . . well, it's closed now, but it's normally open until ten. There's a light continental breakfast from—oh wait, tomorrow might be the last day for that. It's eight to eleven, but we probably won't have it after tomorrow. If you'd like riding lessons or maps to get down to the harbor, come see me in the morning. I assume you just flew in?"

Paige glanced up. She didn't really feel like telling her the whole story. Not only that, but her mind kept dragging over how young this girl looked to be working in a hotel this late. Was she thirteen? Fifteen? Sixteen? The heavy eye makeup and dyed blue tips were throwing Paige off. "Something like that," she said.

The girl's scrutiny swept across Paige's clothes, yoga mat, and backpack, then seemed to drag over Paige's ring finger. She clicked her pen several times. "Is there anything else I can help you with?"

Paige hesitated. She sort of wanted to ask some questions—like why were they closing the resort, and who normally worked this desk, and whose kitten was Click, and how old was this girl, and where did she live—but the weights on her shoulders reminded her that a good night's sleep was in order first. "No," she said.

The girl's bored nod, Adam's quick dismissal, the hauntingly quiet resort, and the looming flagstone fireplace all made Paige feel insignificant as she dragged herself toward the room she'd been assigned.

She put a few of her things away in the drawers, then flopped onto the bed and closed her eyes. It had been a long, outrageous day. She should fall asleep now and get ready to wake up early and get back to work on Gram's place.

This was going to be a strange week.

And Adam was definitely looking like he remembered things.

And Paige didn't know how he was going to feel about that when he put all the pieces together.

At half past midnight, weary and exhausted from his toes to his scalp, Adam pushed back from his desk. His eyes lit on the remains of the cold enchiladas, still sitting in the tinfoil container from Rosa's Cantina. He picked it up and scraped at the bottom with a plastic fork, wondering if Paige had eaten hers. At least he'd ordered something for her. Damned if he was going to be responsible for her collapsing from hunger as well as possibly getting attacked by an intruder in the house he was supposed to be watching.

He couldn't believe he'd let Helen's house get invaded again, and this time with an innocent occupant inside. He was off his game. He'd always yelled at his father and brother and ranch hands for even one moment's slip into irresponsibility—you had to be constantly alert on a ranch this big—but now here he was, doing the same thing. He needed to concentrate.

Of course, it was harder these days with everything going on. Deaths. Wills. Memories. Ghosts from the past . . .

The late-night silence of the office crept up around his ears—an office that had grown eerier and lonelier as time marched on. The depression that wanted to settle around his shoulders was something he instinctively kept staving off—every time the sense of loss entered his head, he shoved it out of the way. He knew he'd need to address it at some point, but for now he'd put one foot in front of the other, sell this damned place, leave this damned island, and then let reality catch up with him.

He tossed the foil container into the trash and let a new level of irritation rise that he'd thought of Paige Grant again. He'd gone almost the entire evening staying focused on other concerns. But for the last half hour, his mind kept drifting to her. He wondered if it would be weird if he went to check on her.

It would.

And he shouldn't.

She was none of his business.

But she'd rattled him. That was the bottom line.

She felt like a strange, long-lost, hazy, shifting piece of an unfinished puzzle. And the worst part was that she wasn't the only piece. Between her and Amanda, his world was shifting on its axis.

Not that his world was engaging to begin with, but at least he used to know where he stood. He knew his land, his animals, his ranch hands, his family history. He was like those massive old trees out in the perimeter of his ranch—bent, scarred, gnarled, and sometimes leaning, but still standing, anchored by powerful roots the size of branches.

But Paige was definitely an anomaly and felt like another lightning strike. He'd never had a very good memory for sentimental details, and he dismissed plenty of elements from his brain at the end of each day so he could concentrate on the ranch. So when he'd first seen Paige, he'd had trouble even conjuring the right era to place her in. But then, slowly, he began to remember: She was Ginger's daughter. She'd been one of the young campers. She'd been there the night of the first fire. She'd been there when he got home from jail after the second one, too, sitting at his father's dining table. Or maybe that was the next day. He wasn't sure. But she'd been there that summer, with her goth eyeliner, staring at him as if she wanted him to combust. He remembered the townspeople had talked about her that summer and said she'd "saved" him from the first fire, although he'd never believed that, caught up as he was in everything that was going on with Samantha. He remembered that he and Paige had talked one night, late, in the hangar. She might have been crying. He recalled that everyone called her Calamity June. And that she'd hated him for some reason.

The rest was cloudy, like most of his teenage years. That whole summer had been a shit-storm anyway. It ended after the second fire, down by the stables, when Ginger and George had sat at his dining table and announced they were turning him in. They'd sent for Samantha's parents. Her parents had taken her away. He'd been thrown in the Carmelita jail, where they held him on a jaywalking warrant, of all things, so they could buy some time, then ferried him over to the mainland, where he spent another week in the county jail. When they released him on lack of evidence, he came home on a late-night ferry to a scowling father, a suspicious town, no girlfriend, and what felt like a life filled with distrust.

Normally he wouldn't care that he couldn't remember the details of that summer. He liked life that way. Forgetting could be good.

But, for some reason, with Paige Grant here now, he felt as if he was going to remember.

Whether he wanted to or not.

And the fact that he couldn't quite drag his eyes from the sexy woman who'd once been the thirteen-year-old girl who was nearly his stepsister was disturbing in ways he didn't want to examine right now.

Back in his bedroom, Adam peeled off his shirt to get into bed, but he suddenly thought of a better way to relieve some of his ache and fatigue.

Within minutes, he was in a towel at the back of the resort, his bare feet thudding across the redwood deck to the Jacuzzi. With the dude group coming in a couple of days, he wouldn't have the place to himself anymore. Might as well take advantage of it now. He snapped the lights back on, but only half—he didn't want to wake his only resort guest— then he reset the timer behind an elderberry bush and tossed his towel on the deck. In seconds, he lowered himself into the bubbling cauldron.

Gaaaaaaaaaaaaawd, that felt good.

His head fell back against the lip of the tub, and his arms floated weightlessly to the surface. His mind was finally able to relax. No more thinking of the past. No more thinking of the present or any of his responsibilities. No more thinking of this night. No more thinking of Paige Grant.

About fifteen minutes into a very nice reverie regarding a pinup girl and a bathtub, a twig snapped. He jerked to attention and scouted the bushes, assuming he'd see a raccoon or opossum. But a human form took shape behind the shadows of the cypress trees.

"Who's there?" he barked, pushing to a sitting position, the water gently sloshing.

Silence followed, then a rustling of bushes. As Adam watched, a very shapely shape stepped out from the shadows.

He groaned inwardly.

"I couldn't sleep," said a familiar voice.

CHAPTER 5

Paige shoved branches aside, picked her way through the bushes in her slippers, and stumbled onto the planked wooden deck, where Adam came fully into view. She stalled right on the edge—still not certain this was a good idea. She plucked a few twigs from her hair, then gripped the elbows of her velvet hoodie and waited to get a sense of Adam's mood.

She'd seen him enter the hot tub from her window—she'd heard the lights clank on, then peered through the thick panes to see his waist slip into the bubbling water. The angle of her room and the dim lighting allowed her a long, guilty ogle. She'd gaped at his flexing arms as he slowly lowered his body; then she'd stared at his strong chest as he took deep breaths and dropped his head back to settle in.

She'd enjoyed her view for five glorious minutes before pulling on her hoodie and scrounging up the nerve to pad across her patio and down the back path to the deck. She would just thank him for sending the dinner.

Yeah, that was it.

As she hesitated at the edge of the deck, Adam squinted at her through the darkness, the blue lights from the water dancing along his face and sending luminescent shadows across his jaw. His arms came up level with the ground, shoulders glistening under the moonlight, as he stretched his biceps along the back of the tub. Then, in a gesture that was either irritated or defeated, he let his head fall back to the edge of the tub and closed his eyes again.

"Did my staff see you walk out here?" he grumbled.

Ah, his mood. Sulky.

"I . . . I don't know," she said. "Who is your staff? That girl?"

"Mendelson is there now. Did he see you?"

"I came the back way. Anyway, I'm not sure why he'd care."

"He's supposed to be watching you."

"*Watching* me?"

Adam shook his head. "Never mind. Come out from those bushes. There are raccoons back there."

Paige leaped forward, then crossed her arms against a shudder. She'd never been meant for a wooded life, with creatures and insects. That was another reason she never came to the island's interior anymore. She smoothed her velvet hoodie and stepped across the deck.

"Why is your staff supposed to be watching me?" she asked.

He gave a long, put-upon sigh and shifted slightly against the lip of the tub. "Would you believe I was worried?" he mumbled, his eyes still closed.

"No."

A beat passed, and then he smiled.

"What's so funny?" she asked.

"So *distrustful*, Paige."

Her heartbeat picked up. She wasn't sure if it was because of that intimate whisper in his midnight voice, or the fact she'd never heard him say her first name like that, or the idea that he'd finally paid enough attention to her to form an opinion—and a shockingly accurate one at that—but it all seemed dangerously sexy. She told herself she should leave. Or at least look away. But first she allowed herself another clandestine ogle of his glistening chest.

"Why are you out here?" he asked with his eyes still closed.

She cleared her throat. "I, um . . . wanted to thank you. For the dinner." She tried to remember her earlier feeling of gratitude and replace it with her current irritation that he was assigning his staff watch duty over her.

"No problem. Figured you had to be hungrier than you were letting on. And I felt a little responsible for the situation you were in."

A cacophony of crickets chirped rhythmically behind her. She padded around the side of the chaise and sat on its edge, smoothing the velvet of her pant leg. She should go now. But she didn't want to. Adam's presence gave her a zing that she hadn't experienced in a long time, and it was a nice jolt. She hadn't had that giddy rush of attraction for eons—that adolescent feeling of energy that tended to be lost once real jobs and bills and boyfriends who cheated on you entered the picture. She didn't know if she was experiencing it with him because he was the one who made her feel that way when she *was* an adolescent, or if it was because of something about him specifically that she'd experience no matter when in life she met him. But he definitely gave off that chemistry. It was addicting.

They sat in silence, listening to the crickets' trills. She searched for something to say. Normally she was good at small talk, but it felt weird with Adam—they were like strangers, but not really. They knew too much about each other's families and pasts to be real strangers, so instead they were caught in an uncomfortable middle ground: arm's-length intimacy, unfamiliar familiarity.

"Nice night," she finally said. *Lame.*

He glanced up, peeked out of one eye as if surprised she was still there, then laid his head back down without comment. He was probably tired of her already.

She kicked off her slippers and wriggled her toes against the rough planks, then tried to find something innocent to look at while she thought up more of her scintillating conversation.

Her eyes flitted over the rows of chaise lounges, a cluster of pots holding half-dying geraniums, a deck table with a newspaper still folded on top of it. She wondered who took care of all this. Did Adam do everything now? Her gaze kept being pulled, though, like a magnet, to his biceps, illuminated in the blue lights from the hot tub. Rivulets of water ran down his hairline, dampening the hair around his face and at the base of his neck. His eyes remained closed. His throat moved a few times in a visible swallow.

"You're different than I remembered," he said, surprising her out of the darkness.

His jaw formed a shadowed triangle underneath his chin, the late-night blond stubble creating a gentle outline. His lips were full and beautiful. They were closed now, as if he'd never spoken, and Paige was suddenly unsure he'd even spoken at all. But as it slowly dawned on her what he'd said, she felt her stomach tingle. "Different how?"

His lengthy pause made her wonder whether she should continue this conversation. This could be dangerous territory. He could piss her off. He could turn her on. He could laugh at her. He could charm her pants off. She had no idea which way this could go. She stared at the remaining live geraniums in the pot, at their ruffled leaves, at their bright-red petals.

"What exactly did you remember?" she asked as her pulse raced. She was in uncharted area now, without a compass.

The water sloshed as Adam shifted. He still hadn't opened his eyes. "I remembered you wearing a ton of black makeup and looking like you were going to pull out a grim-reaper scythe." The lights from the spa danced along his chest, his jaw, like an aurora borealis, throwing flashes across his skin. He was grinning now.

"That was my goth stage," she said. "Black eyeliner was crucial."

His grin grew wider. "How long did that stage last?"

"Too long, as far as Ginger was concerned."

The low rumble of the spa bubbles and the crickets' rhythmic chirps grew louder over the next minute as Ginger's name threw a pall on their rising friendliness. *Way to ruin the mood, Paige.* She did appreciate that Adam let the Ginger comment lie, though. He probably had plenty more to say about her mother. It was part of their weird connection again—the one that kept them from being complete strangers, although that would be easier. The things they had connection over were things neither of them wanted to talk about.

Although, now, with him in a slightly relaxed mood, it might be a good time to clear the air.

"I'm, um, sorry for all that Ginger did. Back then," she blurted.

The spa bubbles shifted as Adam repositioned for comfort. His face lost its friendly grin and went into neutral.

Paige cleared her throat and went on. "I hope our pasts—and your past with Ginger—won't affect any decisions you make about selling this place, or possibly working with us on the Dorothy Silver wedding."

He kept his head back and his eyes closed as he answered her through barely moving lips. "Business is business, Paige. I never let personal issues interfere."

She nodded. *Good philosophy.* Ginger, ironically, would be proud of him for that line.

"Well, it couldn't have been easy for you," she said quietly. "I'm sorry for any pain my family may have caused you."

"No need. It's not your apology to make."

A shot of guilt went through her. This was the hard part. Although Ginger was the one who had actually broken Adam and Samantha up—had Samantha sent away, had Adam thrown in jail—Paige had had a hand in it. But, to Adam, Paige had been invisible. And apparently even now her part in everything was invisible. It was best she just leave things that way. At least for as long as they were negotiating.

Like he said, business was business.

"So did you and your goth friends hang around the Industrial Tech building and smoke cigarettes?" he asked.

A smile escaped her lips. Maybe he wanted to move on, too. "Art building. But I didn't smoke. I drove a fast car instead."

"Ah. A girl with a fast car is a dangerous thing. This rebelliousness lasted awhile, then."

"It did." Paige stood and took a few steps toward the tub. "I loved that car. It was a bright-yellow 1970 vintage Mach 1."

Adam gave a low whistle. "That's a serious muscle car. Where'd you get that?"

"I inherited it from my aunt. It always pissed my mom off that Aunt Susan gave it to me."

"Tell me you left the black hood stripe."

"Of course."

"Loud?"

"Very."

He smiled. "Ginger must have loved that. You must've been a handful. I didn't have a fast car—I had a plane. But I was definitely one of the kids at the Industrial Tech building with the cigarettes."

Paige giggled. "I'm sure George loved the smoking."

"Yeah. When I was fifteen, he made me smoke a whole pack at the kitchen table one morning while he watched me. That kicked my habit."

"He probably did you a favor."

Adam made an odd sound in his throat but said nothing to that.

Paige allowed herself another long look at him. She wanted to know more about his boyhood—what drove him to be so isolated, why he'd always been so angry. But that boyhood scowl from her memory made a lot of sense when she thought about the fact he'd grown up with George. She'd never thought of that at the time. George had always scared her, too. She didn't really blame Adam for being an introvert, or avoiding her and her family in whatever way he'd known how. It was probably a chance to escape, much in the same way her black eyeliner and Mach 1 were—a chance to feel some sense of control over a life that seemed as if it was happening against your will.

"You took me by surprise when I saw you," Adam said suddenly. "You didn't match my memory." He readjusted his arms against the edge of the tub.

"Because I didn't have my scythe?"

He chuckled. "Something like that."

The crickets resumed their chorus as Paige wriggled her toes again. She wasn't sure how much she wanted to tell him, or how much she wanted him to remember—she definitely didn't want him to put the pieces together that she'd been the one to tell on him to her mom. But he was letting her in a little, and she didn't know how to resist. He was like a drug.

"You weren't how I remembered, either," she found her voice saying. She almost wanted to slam her hand over her mouth.

Adam gave a low laugh and finally looked right at her. He looked as if he was going to say something to that, but the water suddenly sloshed as he lowered his arms. He shifted forward, pressing his palms along the bench, and cleared his throat. "Listen, Paige, the timer on these bubbles is going to go off in about ten seconds, and once they stop, you're going to get a view you very well may not want, so I suggest you give me a second to get out and grab a towel."

Paige could hardly take her eyes off the new position he was in—his glistening shoulders, the way his muscles flexed in such a testosterone-driven way. She felt like her thirteen-year-old hormones were shooting off fireworks again. But then she forced her adult brain to put together what he was saying: He was *naked* in there? She wondered how inappropriate it would sound to say she'd actually love the view. It had been a while. But instead she slowly turned her back.

She heard the water slosh again and his bare foot slap the deck as he hoisted himself out of the tub.

She tried to make small talk to keep her mind from picturing what he must look like. "Do you always come out here and enjoy your hot tub naked?"

His towel shook out. She heard it ruffle as he dried himself. The jets suddenly died with a hiss, and the deck went silent. He didn't seem as though he was going to answer that.

"What do your guests say?" she pressed, trying to keep the nervousness out of her voice.

His footsteps slapped heavily against the wood, coming toward her around the side of the tub. "Sometimes 'thank you,'" he said over her shoulder.

A loud clank rang into the night, and suddenly the entire deck was draped in darkness. Paige stifled a scream.

Adam mumbled a few curse words under his breath. "I'm here," he said calmly. His touch on her elbow caused her to jump. "Sorry. I forgot the timer was set for only twenty minutes. Take four steps this way." He tugged at her elbow, but the blackness was so disconcerting, she froze. She took one awkward step, but she couldn't get a sense of her footing.

"Paige, it's okay. The hot tub is right behind you, and if you move to the right, you'll fall. I'm right here. Trust me. Move this way."

His hand was wet and warm. She could have sworn the hot tub was the other way, but she'd twisted a bit when she'd heard the clank, so maybe she was turned around. Fear could do that. She could smell the chlorine on him, could sense heat emanating from his skin. She felt drips on her shoulder and wondered if he was standing so close that they were coming from his chin or his hair. She wanted to trust him. His palm pressed firmly into the back of her elbow, soaking her velvet jacket. The heat traversed the fabric with ease. She remembered the arms, the wrists, the strong hands she'd just been ogling, and thought about them touching her now in this darkness.

"One more step," came his voice.

She begrudgingly gave him one more; she couldn't help but do it with resistance. Stepping into unknown blackness had always scared her. She had a hard time trusting any people at all, let alone men. Let alone *this* man, who could've easily hated her and her mom for sixteen years.

After her last faltering step, she felt his hand move away. His towel ruffled again. As her eyes continued to adjust and her breathing returned to normal, his outline started to materialize, and she could see that he was about six feet away, his back now to her, drying off his shoulders, his chest, his abdomen, not a care in the world. As his towel slipped, though, she turned away quickly.

"You okay?" he asked. Ruffle, ruffle.

"Mmm-hmm."

"Are you sure?" he asked. Ruffle, ruffle. She wondered what he was drying off now.

"Yep." She glanced away and tried to focus on a cypress tree until it came into full view. The moon had disappeared behind a night fog.

He chuckled from behind her. "Are you always this nervous around water? Or is it the darkness?"

"It's . . . uh . . . well, yes, I get a little nervous around both." *And naked men I've been fantasizing about since I was thirteen.*

"Accidents or something?"

"You could say that."

"Is that why the townspeople always called you Calamity June?"

She managed a haughty lift to her chin. "I haven't been called that in years. And I'd prefer you didn't, either."

She suddenly noticed a pain shooting through her toe. She bent forward to take a look and thought she saw drops of blood, although it was hard to see in the dark. *Damn.* How was she going to shake the nickname Calamity June if things like this kept happening to her?

"I think I might . . . uh . . . have a splinter or something."

He came up from behind her, his towel now secured around his waist, his hair standing damply on end.

"It *is* June 1 now," he said, bending to look at it. "You're bleeding. Here, follow me. I'll get you something for that."

Paige followed him through the dark, trying to ignore the June 1 comment, focusing instead on the crickets chirping around them.

Instead of heading through the glass lobby door, Adam walked toward the back steps of his own place. *I'm going into his house again?* Paige took a few deep breaths for calm.

An old border collie came trotting out the door and nuzzled up against Adam's leg to greet him. Paige stared at the dog and recognized his coloring. "Is that *Denny?*"

Adam glanced back at her. "Yeah. You remember Denny?"

"He was a puppy when we used to come over."

"That's right. He's an old man now—sixteen—but still the most loyal dog ever. You have a good memory, Paige."

Danged right I do. She hobbled behind him, trying to keep her eyes trained away from the body she remembered all too well, and from the towel outline of his apple-shaped bottom, but she failed, and bumped right into the stair rail. He turned and gave her a look that had a mixture of disbelief and pity, then opened the door for her and Denny.

The Mason kitchen was exactly as she remembered: too much wood paneling, cast-iron cabinet handles, a huge butcher-block table for eight to the right. It was, in fact, the same table where she'd sat with her mom, late one night, telling George what had happened with Adam and Samantha. It had been the night George had sent Adam away.

Paige stared at the door Adam had disappeared behind, remembering it led to the bedrooms. As she waited for him to bring back a Band-Aid or a pair of tweezers or whatever he'd disappeared for, rubbing her arm where she'd bumped into the rail and staring at her toe that was still bleeding, she heard a noise in the hallway and glanced up.

Around the corner came Amanda in a pair of low-cut pajama bottoms and a tiny T-shirt that left a band of smooth, flat stomach showing. She shuffled across the room in a pair of UGG boots that were crumpled down at the sides.

"Hey," she said, heading toward the fridge.

Adam strolled out of the hallway, now in jeans and a T-shirt, holding a box of Band-Aids. Paige turned to stare at him, then Amanda, trying to put the pieces together.

"Amanda, you remember Ms. Paige Grant from earlier tonight?" Adam said, walking through the room to hand Paige the box. "Paige, meet Amanda, my daughter."

The box and all thirty-six Band-Aids skittered across the floor.

CHAPTER 6

Paige shoved the last of the Band-Aids back in the box, then tried to focus on her toe, which was propped up now, at Adam's insistence, on a chair.

Adam came over with a basin of warm water, tweezers, and tape. He made small talk about fixing the wooden planks around the Jacuzzi, which she tried to focus on, but all she could think of was the fact that he had a teenage daughter.

A *teenage*.

Daughter.

It didn't take much calculating, or a DNA test, to figure out that the daughter was his and Samantha's. Once Paige looked at her more closely, right before Amanda grabbed a Coke out of the fridge and escaped to a back room, she could see the resemblance clearly. Samantha had always had a glamorous look about her—long hair that fell in soft curls around her face like Veronica Lake's, which was what Paige had assumed Adam, and all men, liked back then. Amanda didn't have that glamour about her—the dyed-blue tips looked more rebellious than glamourous—but she had the same almond-shaped blue eyes Samantha had and the same delicate nose. Her lips were full and pouty like Samantha's, although Amanda's held no smile.

But where is Samantha?

When she finally got up the nerve to ask, Adam glanced up from his position near her foot. "Dead," he answered, low, finally getting the splinter out. He cleaned up the remaining drops of blood on the floor and tossed the rag aside.

"I'm so sorry," Paige sputtered. "Did you . . . did you two marry?"

"No." He washed his hands at the kitchen sink.

He didn't seem ready to give more information than that, but he was sort of trapped here now, with Paige sitting on his kitchen table, so she thought she'd try to drag a little more out of him. "Did you co-parent, then?"

"No." He dried his hands on a towel behind him.

Paige figured he was only going to give answers one sentence at a time. Adam didn't exactly seem like the kind of guy who would tell his life story. She tried again. "Did you get to see Amanda often?"

"I didn't even know I had a daughter until six months ago." He closed a cabinet that had the first-aid kit inside and looked around, as if searching for keys. "Here, why don't you go out this way?" He indicated the door to the lobby.

Six months ago? Paige tried to make sure her mouth hadn't dropped open as she slid off the table to put weight back on her foot. She followed his momentum toward the lobby, hobbling along while her mind still whirled.

"Six months ago?" she whispered up at him as she passed him in the doorway.

He reached forward to open the next door for her. She could smell the clean, chlorine-mixed-with-sandalwood-soap scent that wafted off his T-shirt as he herded her into the voluminous lobby.

"That must have been a shock," she pressed.

"Mmm." He guided her past the lobby front desk, where he waved to a thin, balding man that must be Mendelson, then ushered Paige along the flagstone flooring, past the stone fireplace, and toward her room.

"Where were they living all these years?" she asked.

"I should introduce you to Mendelson. I'll introduce you to the staff tomorrow. They can help you around here until I get your place secured. We'll have it ready before the dude group comes."

Paige let him derail her for a second. "How many staffers are there?"

"Fifteen or sixteen."

"What do they all do?"

"Eight ranch hands, sometimes ten in busy seasons. A maid for the resort. A cook. Someone mans the front desk twenty-four hours. Kelly works in the daytime, a woman named Joanne works early evening, and a guy named Little fills in on days off. Mendelson works overnight. Joanne also handles the wedding planning, and Mendelson coordinates the dude-ranch visits. Little does my handiwork."

Paige nodded at the litany of information she barely heard and gave a courteous pause before pressing more about what she truly wanted to know. "So where were Samantha and Amanda living?"

He gave a defeated sigh. "Alabama."

"What did Amanda say when she arrived here?"

"Listen, Paige." They arrived at 8A, and he turned to face her. "I'm tired. You must be tired. Let's do this another time. In the morning I'll send Antonio over to the house to look at the points of entry the intruders might be finding. And Pedro from town is going to take a look at the electric lines. Seems a line went down from our last storm, and they did a quick fix because they thought the property was going to be donated or abandoned. But now they need to look into it deeper. They'll get it done, though. I told Pedro you needed the electric back on in a hurry. In the meantime, why don't you stay around here for a day?"

"Here?"

Adam glanced around. "Yes. Here."

"I can't stay around *here*."

His scowl reappeared, with a bit of hurt lacing the edges of the irritation. "It's not so bad."

"I mean, I have to get to work. I need to get into Gram's house tomorrow."

He shook his head. "I need one day."

"I can't spare a day."

The frustration was back on his face. "I need a day."

She shook her head.

"Paige. *One* day. Let me get it secured."

She wanted to argue. But he looked tired, and she was tired, and he'd helped her quite a few times already today, and she didn't want to put him through any more paces. Guilt had been rising into her throat as she'd realized that she and her mom had split up not just a teenage couple but an entire family—Adam, Samantha, *and* Amanda. And it had had terrible, long-lasting effects.

Paige thought of Amanda again, how sullen she looked, how scared she must be, and how she'd just lost her mother. She'd just learned of a father she might not have even known she had. She'd probably been dropped off here on this island mountaintop, away from life as she knew it, all against her will.

And Adam, meanwhile, was probably trying to figure out how to deal with all of this.

Without anything more to say—except, maybe, a heartfelt *I'm sorry* that she couldn't yet get out of her closing throat—Paige nodded and headed into her room.

Paige's head was a fuzzy haze of robin's-egg blue and seashell pink when she came out of her restless sleep. As she moved to stretch, a strip of sunlight streamed through her window like a spotlight, catching her in the eye. The previous day's events started to come back to her in flashes: the sweeping, the cleaning, meeting Adam at the Castle, the Dorothy Silver deal going south but having some hope. And then, slowly, the night's events: the intruder, Adam on his horse, the hot tub, the lights going out, the splinter, Adam's *daughter* . . .

God.

She moaned against everything—the long, emotional day, the disappointment at not being able to close a business deal, the guilt she ultimately felt at breaking up a family, the dull ache in her legs and arms from all the sweeping . . .

She rolled over and squinted against the sun.

What time was it?

She snatched her phone from the nightstand. Eight. She should be cleaning by now.

But Adam had requested she not go over there today.

She stared at the ceiling and went through a mental checklist of the house, thinking of all the things that would need to be fixed or touched up. There was a water leak in one part of the ceiling that she realized might be coming from an upstairs sink. There was a broken closet door upstairs, a chipped mirror in one of the bathrooms, a busted toilet handle in another, a loose balustrade toward the top of the stairs, some scratches in the wood floor in one of the bedrooms, and the whole house could use a fresh coat of paint. She needed to get the interior and exterior in decent enough condition that Dorothy could come by to give them the go-ahead on the wedding. Then she'd have to jump through hoops to make the whole thing look just like the movie for the actual wedding. It was a lot to take on. But overall, it was doable.

If she could get started, that was.

She swung herself out of bed, unrolled her yoga mat, and spent an hour doing her favorite asana practice, ending with a long corpse pose to help stretch her muscles.

Then she settled at the room's side table and came up with a game plan. She opened her laptop and created an Excel sheet of the projects she'd need to tackle, typed steps to get each done, and listed target dates. She spread out the landscaping blueprints on one table to study them again, then propped some photos up from the movie along one wall. She stepped back to gaze at the pictures. The place did look magical back then. The gazebo was a bit too big—much larger than a normal one—almost the size of a town-square bandstand—but it looked pretty in the middle of the meadow with its bright-white paint and flowers at its base. She remembered Adam saying it had been a movie prop, so it had never actually existed, but it was a key element of Dorothy's wedding dreams. Paige would have to build her one. She just hoped Adam would let her build it in the meadow between their properties. If not, she wasn't sure where she would put it.

First things first, though. Today she'd head into town to get started on some supplies to make the house more habitable.

And hope she didn't see her sisters.

And try to forget about how guilty she felt now about Adam and Amanda.

Once she got ready, she drove her golf cart down the mountain and into town, hoping she could avoid Adam. Her emotions were all over the place, and she wasn't sure how she felt about facing him again. The chemistry she'd always felt with him was mixing dangerously with the memories, the fantasies she'd had, the anger and frustration that he'd ignored her, the lack of forgiveness she'd carried for the last several years, and now her guilt. Everything was swirling together in a complicated storm of lust, adoration, resentment, attraction, dismissal, and obsession. It was too many feelings to have for one person, complicated with too much passing time. And now she was asking him to do a very big favor for her family.

She turned her golf cart at the base of the mountain on N Street and puttered her way around the edge of Carmelita. Joe's Mercantile was on one side; Karen's Sundries was on another. There was a bookstore called Book, Line, and Sinker that she'd always loved, right next to the toy shop Once Upon a Toy. There was a little hardware store on Main Street that would probably become her best friend over the next few months. She knew the clerk there—an elderly gentleman named Mr. Clark—who always had the prettiest flowers out front, including the gerbera daisies her sister Natalie favored. Elliott routinely bought them for her each month. Natalie had told Elliott last March that she loved him so much she would be ready to take the leap when the daisies went all the way around the house. They were at three-quarters now.

And Paige was jealous.

This realization over the last couple of months surprised her. Mostly because long-term relationships were not her thing. She made the worst choices of men imaginable, and seemed to pick cheaters or other men she couldn't trust—one after another. She was ready to give up and assume she'd never get married. She didn't want children anyway. She could be one of those women she admired in the movies—like Katharine Hepburn, maybe, flitting from man to man, adventure to adventure, but never marrying. The other advantage to that lifestyle was that she wouldn't have to subject anyone else to her Calamity June life. Paige felt as if drama followed her everywhere—car crashes, bee-sting allergies, birds falling from the sky and landing on her head. She'd nearly been hit by lightning once. And even though it had been sort of exciting as a teenager, and even in her early twenties, and everyone said they loved hanging around her because she was like a walking *I Love Lucy* episode, it was starting to become tiresome. And worrisome. And she was starting to think she had a curse.

Paige spotted the entrance to the island's only market and pulled into the gravel parking lot behind the large wooden wagon filled with fresh flowers. Lavender Island was a floral color-fest, especially at this time of year. The climate was Mediterranean, and there was always an explosion of colorful flowers to highlight the Spanish-style architecture—sea lavender (after which the island was named), regular lavender, geraniums, poppies, blooming ice plant, jasmine, roses, Queen Anne's lace, baby's breath, bougainvillea. The island was always gorgeous and alive. The changing color was what Paige loved most about Lavender Island. Everything that stayed stagnant she distrusted.

Paige grabbed a bouquet of irises she'd put on Gram's dining table in the old blue delft pitcher she'd found in a cupboard, then wandered through the aisles, basket on her arm. She ducked her head when the store owner, Mr. Fieldstone, looked her way. He probably wouldn't remember her, but she kept her sunglasses handy just in case.

Soon she heard two women giggling by the paperback section.

"Here's one of my favorites," one woman said. "Have you read this one, Marie? It's not erotica, either, but I love it. The hero is a whale watcher, and he manages to do a little sightseeing of his own, if you know what I mean."

Giggles.

It sounded like Doris and Marie, two of the islanders who lived at the Casas del Sur senior-citizen apartments in the harbor. They'd both known Paige's grandmother and were also friends of Natalie, who now worked at Casas del Sur full-time. They would surely say something to Nat if they saw Paige there.

"Oooh, and this one's good. This is about a rancher," the Doris voice said.

Paige flattened herself against a display of paper towels and began sidling into the next aisle.

"Oh, speaking of ranchers," the Marie voice said, "did you see Adam Mason down here the other day?"

Paige froze. A paper-towel roll almost toppled to the floor, and she quickly caught it and shoved it back in place.

"I did!" the Doris voice said. "I think he was looking at curling irons."

"Curling irons?"

"I couldn't figure out why, either. I can never figure him out. He's such a quiet man. I was going to offer to help, but I'm never certain if he welcomes chitchat or not."

"Probably not. You'd overwhelm him with your version of chitchat."
Both women giggled.

"Anyway, I wondered because I hadn't seen him around since
George's funeral, and when I thought I saw him down here, I was
relieved to see him out and about," the Marie voice said. "He's always
been so standoffish. But I wonder if he needs help up there."

"Help with what?" Doris asked.

"Help with anything. He's all by himself. And I heard he's moving. I'd
hate to think he's leaving just because he's overwhelmed by that resort. He
has a whole town here who would help him. Do you think he knows that?"

"I heard he's got a young girl up there," a man's voice piped in.

Paige peered around the corner. *Ugh.* Kilner Kileen. He was always
a troublemaker. He was a worse gossip than anyone else in this town.

"A young girl? You mean a girlfriend?" Doris questioned. "That
would be good for Adam."

"No. *Real* young," Kilner added. "Like yay high. Like jailbait."

Paige resisted the urge to stomp around the corner and shove Kilner to
the ground. She wanted to explain that the young girl was Adam's *daughter*.
She hated rumors. Especially slimy, sexual ones started by creeps like Kilner.
It was one of the things that made this island deplorable. She couldn't imagine how Natalie and Elliott and Olivia and Jon could live here all the time.

"I'm just sayin' he's maybe got some funny business goin' on up
there," Kilner added.

Paige bit her lip. It was hard not to whirl around and shake some
sense into that idiot. But this was not her information to share. She had
no idea what Adam wanted the townspeople to know. And besides, she
tried to remind herself that she, too, had believed much the same about
Adam's hermit ways not too many hours ago.

"Hmmm." Doris didn't sound convinced.

A silence fell in which Paige imagined the two women to be looking
at more paperbacks, or maybe trying to move away from Kilner.

Paige inched slowly around the paper towels and slid her sunglasses on as she heard the front doorbell. She really didn't want anyone to see her here. Who knew the place filled up at ten a.m.? She spun away from the door and stared intently at whatever was on the shelf nearest her. *Great.* K-Y Jelly. Trojans on the next shelf. She kept sliding until she was in front of the tampons, at least.

Kilner paid for his purchases, trying to get some agreement about his conclusions regarding Adam, but Mr. Fieldstone didn't seem interested in feeding that fire. Kilner eventually shuffled out the door. The bell on the door handle seemed to cheerfully celebrate his exit.

"Well, that doesn't sound right," the Doris voice said, lower now, presumably just to Marie. "Adam seems like a nice young man. Although there was that curling-iron thing . . ."

A silence went on for about a minute; then Paige heard someone sigh. "I had always hoped they'd revive that apple festival," the Doris voice added. "I guess they never will."

"Remember those *pies* Ellen used to make?"

The women's voices moved toward the front counter.

"Oh yes. And remember the dunking for apples and all the fun games? So much fun."

As they moved farther away, Paige inched toward the back. She'd find her WD-40, her granola for tomorrow, a few pieces of fresh fruit, and get out of there with her flowers. Mr. Fieldstone looked rather distracted, and wasn't making small talk with anyone, so she'd move quickly.

And stop thinking about Adam.

And Amanda.

And rumors.

She didn't need to take all this so personally. These were not her battles to fight. Adam and Amanda were not her family to defend, and Nowhere Ranch was not her business.

She needed to keep her heart safe and out of the way, and just get business done here.

CHAPTER 7

Adam took careful note of the morning's crosswinds and shifted his frame in the Cessna, adding a few extra knots of airspeed as he glanced at the ocean whitecaps and made his way back to his airport.

It had been a rough night. He hadn't slept well, and he'd been up since daybreak to fly this charter. Now that his client was safely landed in LA, Adam could enjoy the flight back and take a few deep breaths.

And try to get his mind off everything.

It wasn't easy. As if fixing the place, finding a fast buyer, and getting Amanda back to Alabama in time for the start of art school weren't enough to worry about, he now had Paige Grant in his line of vision. And he didn't know why she was rattling him.

At the beginning of their hot-tub conversation, all he'd been able to see was the young girl who'd caused so much trouble for him that one summer. And the one who, like him, had been blamed for those fires. Those were the rumors anyway. Half the town thought she'd done it, and half thought *he* had—Calamity June or Adam. His dad had gone with Adam. And had him thrown in jail, after Ginger threatened to report him if he didn't. It was the beginning of the end between him and his dad, their trust forever severed since that day.

So he didn't have great memories of that time. Or of Ginger. Or of Paige. But the more he'd talked with Paige last night, and the more she'd sauntered around the side of the tub, coming closer and closer, the more he'd started to see her as a different person.

She'd grown up. Obviously. He'd struggled to reconcile her sexiness in the velvet pantsuit—the way her curves made the color change and made him want to reach out and touch—with the young girl in the goth makeup. It had been easier to keep his eyes closed so his body didn't betray him underwater. He needed to separate the two images of her. This new Paige was here to do business. This new Paige seemed smart and shrewd. Although she'd started out her negotiations with silly, romantic notions about wildflowers and gazebos and elaborate weddings, he could see now that she meant business and planned to get things done. And—especially interesting—this new Paige was someone he could relate to. Her stories about being a rebellious teen in Ginger's world had made him smile. And reminded him of himself. And, frankly, of Amanda. He wondered if he and Paige Grant had met at a different time—and under different circumstances—they'd have been friends.

Although if she'd looked that good in velvet, maybe not.

He dipped his wing slightly. Out the window his island came into view, and he felt the usual peace that brought him. Though now the familiarity was tinged with an ache in the back of his throat. He hated to lose his mother's family's airport. He'd always felt as though he was his mother's keeper—responsible for her and her memory—ever since he'd lost her. His dad had not cared about her family's airport, so Adam had taken it on. His brother, Noel, had moved to Phoenix a year ago, and there was no way Adam was going to lasso him back to the island. Noel had made his escape, and Adam was happy for him.

And now, with Amanda here, he wasn't going to tie her down, too. She wanted to leave. He understood that. Amanda had been embarking on her own dreams right before her mother died—she'd told him she'd been accepted into a prestigious art school she'd always wanted to go to in Alabama. And Adam wanted to give her a chance there. After losing her mother, he couldn't let her dreams slip away, too. He'd be letting go of his mother's legacy—and might never forgive himself for that—but he couldn't screw up his new daughter's life. Guilt and failure were warring with guilt and failure.

And guilt and failure were winning.

He dropped his wing deeper into the wind and searched for his visual cues. The recent May rains had left the Southern California island interior beautifully green, and he enjoyed the view as he tracked a herd of bison moving together through the center. There were three herds of free-roaming bison here on the island, initially brought here in 1952 for Dorothy Silver's movie and never removed. His family had been contracted to help with herd control for many years, helping to ship bison off the island to the Dakotas, where they were allowed to roam free. But his dad had started drinking during those years, and eventually the Lavender Island Conservancy took over, implementing a new birth-control shot to manage the population in a simpler but equally humane way.

A few years ago, however, they'd come back and asked if Adam could take it over. He'd proven to be a great bison wrangler in his early twenties, and the company didn't have anyone to match him. Adam contracted with them, much to his father's dismay—George had always thought he'd gotten screwed over by the Conservancy. Adam had rebuilt the sorting pens and working chutes on his dad's property, then took on one herd, then two, then all three, and eventually made it into his own business. His dad kept running the resort. Noel ran the airport. Then, last year, when his father died, everything fell apart. Adam struggled to keep three businesses afloat by himself. But it was too much now.

His family's tiny airport slowly came into view, and he pushed his shirtsleeves up and tightened his seat belt. He dropped his other wing just enough and added a little uphill rudder, eventually crabbing toward the gravel runway.

The island airport was tricky for most pilots because it looked deceptively flat, although in reality it was a slight hill and needed to be approached as if you were coming out of a ditch. But he'd been flying this since he was fourteen and could do it with his eyes closed. After one glance at the family's tattered wind sock, and four or five more dips of his wing, he let his wheels descend and finally crunch on the ground.

The impact rose through his soles in that warm, familiar sense of landing home. The steering mechanism vibrated under his hands. Leaning back, he pulled the sixteen hundred pounds of steel to a bouncing, wheel-popping, teasing-the-air, exhilarating stop.

Dust swirled. Silence welled. He closed his eyes while sounds of regular life—birds chirping, the sound of Denny barking across the gravel—all dragged him gradually back, as they always did.

Slowly, he crawled out of the plane.

"Glad to see me, Den?" he asked, scratching his old border collie behind the ears. "You might be the only one today." Adam shifted his backpack onto his shoulder and tucked his sunglasses into his shirtfront, then strode across the dirt expanse, past the cactus garden, across the meadow, and up his wooden steps.

At the faded back door, he ran through his usual routine: he stamped the dust off, let Denny in, grabbed yesterday's mail off the kitchen counter, checked on Amanda, saw she was still sleeping, then flipped through envelopes as he continued his trajectory through the wooden house and into the resort lobby.

"Hey, Kell," he said to his receptionist, pretending to gaze at an invoice that had just arrived.

"Hi, Adam. Thanks for coming back so fast."

He glanced up to see her balancing on top of a swivel stool to reach a shelf above the mailboxes, giving him a clear view under her skirt. He quickly looked away, as he always did with Kelly. Although she flirted with him relentlessly, she was much too young for him. Plus, he was in no position to be thinking about women these days anyway.

"You, uh—" He ran his hand along the back of his neck and kept his eyes down. "You need a hand with something?"

"I need this container with some of our old receipts." Her voice strained as she reached for a willow-colored box on the top shelf.

"Let me get it."

He waited until she got down, then crawled up onto the stool and retrieved the box she was reaching for.

"So you brought in a new guest last night?" she asked from below.

At the mention of Paige, the nervous feeling that had started in his gut began gnawing upward, pressing against his lungs.

"Yes," he said.

"I thought you weren't bringing in any more guests? Isn't this dude group going to be the last?"

"This was an exception."

Kelly didn't respond to that but instead reached for the leather-bound hotel registry on the opposite end of the desk and dragged it, like a boulder, toward her. The monstrosity had belonged to Adam's father. Although Adam had finally convinced him to put everything on the computer, the thick registry still remained, filled out in Kelly's loopy scroll.

"Amanda didn't register the new guest in here," Kelly said, running her hot-pink, gnawed-off fingernail down the ledger. She wasn't getting along very well with Amanda and seemed to like pointing out her faults.

"It doesn't matter anymore, Kell," he said softly.

He didn't mean to meet her eyes. But when he did, he saw tears start to well there, and he had to look away.

"Why don't you take a break?" he asked gruffly, moving some things along the counter so he didn't have to look at her. "I have some bookkeeping to do."

"I'm fine. Take your bookkeeping to the back," she said. "I'll stay here."

He headed for the cramped office he'd built between the lobby and the kitchen. It was about the size of a closet—really just part of the hallway—but it served their needs and kept a buffer between the house and work. And now between him and Kelly. And tears. And the inevitability of their futures.

Adam plopped down at his father's oak rolltop desk and pressed his fingers against the bridge of his nose, closing his eyes against the last will and testament that sprawled before him. He'd read it at least seventy times, looking for loopholes that might let his father's employees have something to keep.

He rubbed his forehead again and thought about the worst part of the whole thing—*was he becoming just like his father?*

George Mason's cynicism, his distrust, his paranoia, his anger—Adam was starting to see it in himself. The older he got, the more cynical he got. And the more cynical he got, the angrier he got. He didn't want to be this way. But dealing with his father's debts and probate was aging him and making him similarly angry and bitter. And now with Amanda . . . he just couldn't become that kind of father. George had been volatile, verbally abusive, always blaming. Adam knew George's heavy drinking played a big part in that—as well as George's years of blatant irresponsibility and gambling and womanizing—but he always worried there was some gene being passed down, too.

He pressed down the horrible awareness and scanned the will again. George had stipulated that Adam could keep the furnishings in the main house, the animals, and all the items in the garage, along with the box marked "Private" in the hangar. And, of course, the planes. Everything else would go into probate.

Adam's chest tightened. At least he hadn't lost the planes. If he and Noel did, indeed, have to unload the land, those Cessnas would be the only thing left. One was his and the other Noel's, and they shared a

Grumman S-2T they kept prepared with fire retardant that had been used for the island for years. He was surprised that his father had given them over so freely. Flying was a source of constant discord in their family.

Adam's mother, Ellen, had been an airwoman in the military. And, although his father had initially fallen in love with her for her streak of adventure—so the story went—George later saw it as something to resent. George had resented her wildness. He'd resented her fierce independence. And he'd resented the fact that he'd had to stay on this land to keep it in her family. Of course, he'd made the best of it. He'd created an inn-like resort around the airstrip and made a living through the income it brought. But when the boys were born with their mother's renegade spirit—that same spirit that longed to be free and propelled them into the sky as soon as they could reach the dials—George seemed to resent them all, both before and after her death. Maybe he'd been worried they'd all be free before he was.

Adam swiveled his desk chair and reached for his cell phone.

His buddy Bob picked it up on the first ring.

"One of the Grants is here," Adam said.

Bob had been his father's accountant for forty years and had always been a father figure to Adam. Even when George was alive, Bob was the one who'd taught Adam to hold doors open for women, helped him get decent car insurance, and knocked him hard once on the back of the head when he saw Adam grab a girl's ass on the boat dock and told him never, ever to do that in public again. As an old friend of George, Bob also knew George's indiscretions, his problems, his failings as a father. And he seemed to want to make them up to Adam.

"Is it Ginger?" Bob asked.

"No. One of the daughters."

"Is that so? Huh. Is she at the resort?"

"Yeah. I gave her a place to stay."

"What's her plan?" Bob asked.

Adam relaxed in his chair. "She wants to put on some crazy wedding for Dorothy Silver, and then sell to her."

"Dorothy *Silver*?"

"Yeah, do you remember her?"

"Who wouldn't?"

Adam smiled. Bob always had a thing for old screen legends. He still had pinups in his den of Marilyn Monroe and Rita Hayworth, much to the amusement of his wife, Gert. "Well, the daughter, she, uh . . . she wants to use some of the land over the next couple of months and then wants me to sell to Silver, too, at the end of the summer. She says Silver is willing to pay double."

The silence that followed confused Adam. He'd expected Bob's normal bark of laughter, but none came.

"Bob?"

"Yeah, I'm thinking. Or maybe remembering. What did you tell her?"

"I put her off until Thursday, when MacGregor will show up."

The lack of response made Adam more uneasy. Bob had been the family's financial adviser for years, and Adam trusted him completely. The problems they had right now stemmed from Adam's father ignoring Bob's advice.

"So do you think it's something I should consider?" Adam asked.

"I could call around and see how serious she is. But with no formal offer, no, it's not something we should consider. I know you're in a hurry. MacGregor is paying cash and ready to go—and probate always takes longer, so the cash will move things along. Let me think on it. Oh, hey, Gert wants to talk to you."

He heard the muffle of a phone being passed.

"Adam, dear?"

"Hey, Gert."

"Did you find the flatiron like I told you?"

"Uh . . . wait, flatiron? I thought you said curling iron."

"No, I said *flat*iron. Girls of Amanda's generation use flatirons, dear."

Adam sighed. Amanda's birthday was in just a couple of weeks, and Gert had been pushing him to buy her something. Amanda had been crushed about having to leave Alabama so quickly and had left many of her personal items behind. Gert had suggested a few things Amanda had lamented leaving, including a "flatiron." He'd first pictured something you'd flatten clothes with, but Mr. Fieldstone had pointed him in the direction of hair products. And then he'd forgotten the term. He'd stared at curling irons the whole time, at their different "barrel sizes," which confused him. Adam had ended up leaving in a huff, perplexed.

"I'll go back," he told Gert. He couldn't let this defeat him. Certainly he could handle one teenage girl's birthday present?

"Okay, write it down, dear: *flat*iron."

"Got it."

"Do you want me to get it for you? My hip's been giving out, but maybe Bob could take me down the hill and we could—"

"No, no, that's okay. You rest, Gert. I'll get it. I promise."

"And a card."

"A card?"

"A birthday card. Get something nice, and write something meaningful inside. It might be hard for you two to communicate right now, but take this opportunity to write something nice to her."

Adam nodded. Gert was probably right. He and Amanda had gotten off to a rocky start, but he just needed to try harder.

"All right, dear," she said. "You take care."

"You, too, Gert."

"Maybe you can come over one of these nights soon for some red velvet cake. It looks like you're losing weight. I'll pack you a few dinners, too. Bring Amanda."

"Thanks."

Adam hung up and pinched the bridge of his nose to keep a head-ache from coming on. He was going to miss Bob and Gert. He'd always said he wanted to leave this island the entire time he was growing up, but now that it was becoming a reality, damn . . . he would miss some of these people.

He glanced out the tiny office window and did a double take at Paige Grant walking by. He wasn't used to seeing guests—especially between dude groups—walk along the back way, along the planks that ran in front of the pine forest. Seeing her made his pulse race. *Damn.* That almost felt like good, old-fashioned attraction. He'd nearly forgot-ten what that felt like.

Back in his more randy, carefree days, he'd felt plenty of attraction. He'd enjoyed a string of females every summer, as far back as he could remember, because when you lived in a resort town, there were new girls every season.

As he got older, though, the "summer girls" became part of normal life, normal expectation, and Adam realized he had no taste for the local girls anymore. The local girls were around forever, while the summer girls were deliciously temporary. No strings, no messy breakups, no expectations of forever. Adam had had enough worry and responsibil-ity in his life. He certainly didn't need girls tipping the scales. So the summer girls grew up and became summer women. And Adam grew up relishing them. It had worked his whole life.

But ever since his dad's first heart attack six years ago, he'd only had time for the most basic of actions and reactions: get up, take care of the ranch, haul feed, fix fences, take care of the hotel patrons, take care of the horses, rinse, and repeat. Impressing new women, or thinking about things beyond his fence line, never seemed to enter the picture.

But now, as he stared out the window at Paige, he remembered how she'd gotten his blood pumping the day before. How she'd made him smile. How he'd felt strangely protective of her when she'd encountered that intruder. How he'd felt bad when the lights clanked out at the hot tub and she'd been scared. How he'd felt that twinge of nervous empathy crawl through his arms when he'd removed that splinter in her foot . . .

He watched her walk along the back porch to her room—her arms loaded with two big bags—and suddenly wanted to talk to her again.

But some kind of sense kicked in, and he told himself to ignore her. His life was a shit-storm. He had no right thinking about, or looking at, a woman right now. Especially a woman to whom he could offer nothing. And especially a woman who wanted something from him, business-wise, that he couldn't provide.

He rustled some papers, moved some things around on his desk, tried to concentrate on the month's payroll. But as he glanced up at Paige through the window again, his blood started thrumming, his heart started working, and he took a deep breath.

Ignoring her was going to be like ignoring lightning.

CHAPTER 8

The next morning, Paige sprang out of bed, practiced ninety minutes of pranayama breathing exercises, went into her favorite hatha-yoga moves, then popped open her laptop. She was eager to get going on her renovation.

She was also nervous about seeing Adam again. But since he'd seemed busy with his own work this morning—she'd watched him head out to the stables when she glanced out the window while unrolling her yoga mat this morning—she decided to just stay focused on her own work and keep her head in the game.

First, she needed to chat with her mother. The fact that her mom wasn't calling yet was good. It meant she trusted that Paige was doing fine. Which had bought Paige another twenty-four hours without having to get on the phone and mention Adam's name. Ginger Grant was amazing at reading her daughters, especially when it came to men, and Paige was afraid of what her voice would reveal when she gave her mom a rundown.

Not only that, but she didn't want her mom to read into her possible failure to get Adam to agree to the Dorothy Silver sale. Even if he didn't agree, she thought she might be able to at least get use of the meadow for the gazebo, but she didn't want to get her mom involved in the tug-of-war. She'd handle it on her own.

She piled her hardware supplies and groceries into her golf cart, then puttered across the property. As soon as she got everything set up, she grabbed her phone and sat at Gram's dining table.

"Mom? How are you? I haven't heard from you for a few days."

"Oh, darling. I'm sorry. I spent last night in the hospital."

"What?"

"Now, dear, it's nothing. Mrs. Terrimore from next door took me. It was fine. They monitored my heart rate and did an EKG and made sure everything was—"

"An EKG?"

"Paige, please. It's fine. I'm fine. Now, how are you? How is everything going there with the esteemed young Mr. Mason?"

Paige winced at her mom's judgment. Ever since they'd come up with this plan, she'd been calling Adam that, when she wasn't directly warning and reminding Paige about his jail terms.

"It's . . . fine. Wait—was this the same type of test they took last time?"

"It was different. So what's he like?" Paige could practically hear her mom's long fingernails impatiently drumming the kitchen table.

"Different how?"

"Paige, please. I'm fine. I'm the mom and you're the daughter. You are not supposed to worry about me. I have lots of friends here taking care of me, and I promise to tell you if anything serious comes up. Now tell me about him."

Paige made a mental note to have a talk with her mother's doctors as soon as she returned. Obviously she'd never get the real story from her mom. The doctors had taken an EKG once before, when the chemo treatments had first begun, but it worried her that they were taking another.

"What's he like?" Ginger pressed again.

Paige tried to turn her attention back to defending the boy her mother never knew she'd crushed on so hard. If Ginger had known, she'd have used it in their constant arguments regarding all the bad decisions Paige had made.

"He's . . . not like I remembered." It was the only thing she could think to say. She knew that too many adjectives would give her away.

"Paige." Her mother's voice held the timbre of warning. Paige could picture her, her silky auburn bob shimmering. It was a wig she began to wear after the first couple courses of chemo, but it almost exactly resembled her real hair from before. She habitually reached up when she was nervous, pushing a few strands back with the tips of her narrow, French-manicured fingers. "I hear something in your voice."

Paige pressed her lips together. She knew her mom would read things into this. "Mom, it's fine. Tell me more about why you went to the hospital. Was it your legs? Were they checking for blood clots?"

"First tell me about Adam."

Paige was trapped. She tried to think of vague descriptions. "He's . . . uh . . . *tall.* Polite. Smart. He has a loyal staff up here, and—"

"Oh, Paige, for goodness' sake. You're attracted to him, aren't you?"

"Mom."

"I know you. 'Tall' means attractive, 'polite' means charming, and 'smart' means savvy. I'm just worried about you. You can't make good business decisions if you're swept away by the man."

"Mom."

"This is just like that summer."

"It's not like that summer."

"Then it's just like later, with Terry Connor—remember him? Remember how you got swept away, and I ended up having to fire him as the wedding photographer?"

"This is not like Terry Connor."

"And Brandon Nichols? Remember the DJ that you got wrapped up with, and he ended up as a no-show on the Brewster wedding?"

"Mom, I was *eighteen*."

"Paige, you wouldn't keep things from me, would you?"

A wave of nausea swept through Paige. Her mother always used that line—it had been her trump card. It was how she got Paige to tell her about the first boy she'd kissed, the time she'd been only thirteen but tested all the wine in the fridge, the time she'd snuck out her mom's car overnight to meet some friends at the beach. That line was like a truth serum.

"Paige?"

"It's fine. Everything is fine." Paige sank back into the chair and waited for God to strike her down.

"Because I'm counting on you. And so is Dorothy. Do you need me to come up there?"

"No."

"I think you need me."

Paige gripped the phone and closed her eyes. "I will be *furious* if you come up here. You just had an EKG. You need to rest. Everything is fine. Adam is fine. He's polite and smart—and by that I mean *polite* and *smart*—and he seems to be a hard worker. He's not in any kind of trouble with the police, like you were worried about. That's it. Now stop. He needed to discuss some things with his lawyer, but I'm in discussions with him now about the gazebo and the orchard, and it's going to be fine. I'm cleaning up Gram's place and researching local vendors. But this place is in serious disrepair, Mom. Also, most of the wedding vendors are in LA, so that's a huge hassle, getting everything across on a ferry, and the staff we'll need to take care of it will be enormous. But I'm working on it and—"

"Paige, don't tell me you can't do it."

"No, I'm not saying that. I'm just saying—"

"We need to pull this off."

"I'm not saying—"

"Don't lose this deal, honey."

"I'm not going to lose it. I'm just saying—"

"Just get Adam to lend us at least some of the land. Especially the orchard, plus the area for the gazebo. We'll take care of the details later."

"Of course."

"*Great.* Great. You're doing great, baby. Is he anything like his father?"

Paige stalled over the sudden shift. "What?"

"If he's anything like his father—"

"Mom, stop talking about Adam. Let's move on. I wanted to ask you about the size of the gazebo and—"

Her mom continued as if she hadn't heard her. "He'll be shifty, wily. Is he good-looking? George was so good-looking—with that blond hair and those blue eyes . . . he looked like Robert Redford. And Adam is probably charming. He got into all that trouble, remember? With that girl? What was her name?"

"I have to go now." Paige couldn't bear to tell her mom about Samantha, or Amanda. Her mom would have no sympathy. Ginger had always thought of Adam as a troublemaker at best and a deviant at worst. And, when business was her mom's primary objective, she had that uncanny way of turning off her heart. "Are you sure you're fine?"

Her mother seemed almost disappointed to be snatched from her memories of George, but she cleared her throat and said yes.

"Are you doing the yoga moves I taught you?"

"Yes, actually, they're quite good, Paigey. They do make me feel better."

Paige smiled. She'd been working on a set of yoga moves specifically for her mom's chemotherapy-induced body aches and was now expanding the repertoire for chronic conditions like arthritis and fibromyalgia. She'd been receiving great feedback so far from Ginger and some of her friends.

"Do you want me to call Mrs. Terrimore to check on you?" Paige asked.

"For God's sake, Paige, I'm not ninety. I'm fine. I have a cell phone."

"But you don't pick it up."

"I listen to the messages," she said indignantly.

"Have Natalie or Olivia called you?"

"Olivia called last night."

"Do they know you were in the hospital?"

"Paige, please. We're driving each other batty. Maybe we'd better hang up. I'll call you again tomorrow night. Be good. And stay smart around Adam Mason."

"I will."

"You're a smart girl."

"I know."

"Don't let him take advantage of you."

"Take *advantage* of me?"

"Just be smart."

"I will."

Paige hung up and looked out the window. The rising sun cast an orange glow through the pine branches lining the back of the property, dappling the green ground with what looked like gold dust.

Leaning against the countertop, she sighed.

This was going to be a delicate dance.

As she continued to stare out the window, gazing at the patterns in the grass left by the leaves, a figure in a cowboy hat caught her eye. She sucked in her breath and slid away from the window.

Could that be Adam?

And why was she *hiding*?

Dang. She leaned forward and peeked out the window again.

A few more cowboys joined the first. All over her yard. Young, old, with great bodies. *What in the world?* It looked like a Chippendales show out there.

She saw her favorite cowboy leading the pack. Adam said something to one of the older guys, then tugged on his brim, wiped his palms on the thighs of his jeans, and stepped up to her porch.

"Howdy," Paige said when she answered the door. She meant it to be sort of funny—she felt as if she were suddenly in a Wild West film.

"I brought some helpers," he said.

She glanced over his shoulder. A couple of the young ones were inspecting a broken fence, and another was peering into the cellar. "I see."

"This is Antonio, my super." Adam pointed to the older guy, who was climbing the porch steps.

"Hello, ma'am."

Being called "ma'am" for the first time made Paige's brain stall. For some reason, she thought of her agent, Dirk—was he right? Was she going to be washed up in Hollywood before she ever began? But a second later, there was something oddly satisfying about it. It felt sophisticated. She briefly wondered at what age Lauren Bacall and Rita Hayworth were first called "ma'am."

"Call me Paige," she said in her best Rita Hayworth voice.

"Paige." Antonio tipped his hat toward her.

"Antonio's crew will replace the cellar door," Adam said. "They'll also patch up some holes on the roof and put a new screen over the chimney for raccoons. My wranglers there will fix your fence. That's Luke, Gabe, Gordon, and Joe."

Paige studied the four. All were muscular and young and cute. When Paige and Natalie were still early twentysomethings, they'd always joked that Lavender Island had a terrible shortage of that age category—which was part of the reason they'd never wanted to come here. Little did they know the hot twentysomethings were up on the hill, working on this ranch with their muscles bulging out of their cowboy shirts.

"Thank you for the help," Paige said. "But I don't know if I can afford all this."

"The labor's on me," Adam said. "And the materials for the fence and roof are items I had left over. These safety issues are things I meant to do for Helen anyway."

"Thanks, Adam." Although he'd intimidated her before—and had been causing a flurry of emotions pretty much every time she looked at him—she now sought his gaze and bravely held it to convey her appreciation. She didn't even need to call on Ava Gardner or Lana Turner for courage. She simply let her heart fill with sincere gratitude and met his stare. "Truly," she added in her own voice.

For the first time, she saw him falter. All this time, she'd seen him as a rock from the earth—confident, dismissive, not caring a lick whether she existed or breathed. But in that one moment, when she said "truly" and held his gaze for maybe a second too long, she saw his expression flicker with uncertainty or confusion. He almost looked flustered.

He cleared his throat and pivoted on the porch. "I, uh . . . I have a generator for you. It'll get you by for a few days until we can get the electricity problem fixed."

"A few *days?*"

"You can sleep at the resort—I have your room reserved through Thursday—but the generator will allow you to at least charge your phone and a few power tools. Pedro and I will arrange to get the electricity fixed by Thursday."

"Thursday?" Paige felt her shoulders fall. This would make things harder. But it wasn't the end of the world. She could work around this and still stay on her deadline. "Okay, the generator will be great."

She made herself busy (and tried not to stare out the window) while Adam and his biceps hauled and situated the generator. As he stepped away, he adjusted a few balustrades around the porch that were coming loose, then inspected the bottom step that was starting to fall apart. Her eyes traced his every move as he wandered out to the fence line to get the wranglers started on the fencing project.

Paige put her water glass down and went to adjust the curtains in the dining room so she could get a better view. From atop a dining chair, she tugged and tugged, trying to get the one side over without snagging. At one particularly forceful tug, though, she lost her balance and fell into the window screen. As if in slow motion, she found herself tumbling—along with the entire screen—outside the frame and straight into the grass.

"Ooof!" Her belly and elbows broke most of her fall. She could hear the men shouting and running toward her. She slowly rolled over and stared into the sun.

"*Ma'am?* Ma'am? Are you okay?" It was two of the younger guys, staring down into her face.

"I'll be fine once you all stop calling me 'ma'am.'" It was one thing when you could adopt a Rita Hayworth stance, but another altogether when you were spread-eagle in the grass.

Adam's face joined the others to stare down at her, too—but his held a note of amusement. He extended his hand to help her. "Enjoying the view?"

She let him lift her, brushed off her elbows and her pride, and tried to stand tall.

"I'm fine." It was all she could do to keep from batting him away. She had embarrassing falls and stumbles constantly—she was quite used to awkward adventures—but she didn't usually do them with an all-male audience who treated her like a senior citizen.

"I'm fine—I'm fine," she said as Gordon reached for her elbow. She hustled out of their view as quickly as she could. But halfway around the corner, her gait turned into a limp.

She dragged herself up the porch steps and tried the door. *But . . . damn.* Had she locked herself out?

Her forehead dropped to the wooden doorway.

"Need help?" she heard over her shoulder.

Adam. She didn't lift her head. Now he'd seen her with her butt in a window, a splinter in her foot, falling out a window, spread-eagle in the grass, and locked out of her own house. She might as well have a sign over her head: **Paige Grant: Awkward since 1987**.

"I think I'm all right."

"You look like you're locked out."

She sighed. She might as well face the fact that she was never going to be able to hide her gracelessness from him. She was never going to look like Faye Dunaway or Anne Bancroft to Adam Mason.

"I think I left the side door open."

She heard his heavy boots come up the steps and a set of keys clink. Then his arm was reaching around her. In seconds he had the key in.

"I'll give you these extra keys now," he said over her shoulder. "I only had them when Helen needed me to check on things. Unless, of course . . ."

The door fell open, and Paige stepped inside. "Unless what?" She glanced back.

"Unless you have these situations often." He was definitely trying not to smile.

She limped into the kitchen. It was hopeless. He'd never taken her seriously back then, and he wouldn't take her seriously now. She wanted to talk to him about letting her use the meadow regardless of the sale, but now didn't seem to be the time. Right after she'd been sprawled in the grass and all.

She poked at a few keys on her laptop.

"Are you going to be okay?" He pushed the keys toward her across the dining table.

"I'm fine," she snapped.

"Your hip, I mean, are you sure you—"

"I'm *fine.*"

He lifted his hands in a surrender position and backed toward the doorway. "Just making sure."

"No need."

He frowned at the fruit cups sitting on the counter. "Is that all you're eating?"

She really couldn't handle any more of his observations regarding her sad life. "Don't you have to be going now?"

He blinked back at her. "Sure."

She followed him to the door and watched him head down the steps.

"Thank you for the generator," she mumbled.

He lifted a hand and kept walking.

Paige watched him saunter away with his languid, sexy stride and wondered how she'd ever turn this ship around.

First step: stop acting like a goofball.

Second step: let him see her being capable.

She knew she *was*—capable, that was. In her normal life, away from the island, she felt efficient in many things. But for some reason, whenever she was here on Lavender Island, she launched back into old behaviors. And coming face-to-face with the boy who'd laughed at her attempts to be cool in her developmental years didn't help. Not that he appeared to remember. But it was still hard. She simply didn't seem to know how to be competent in front of him.

But a lot more was riding on this now than pride—she had business reasons to impress him. Not to mention her mom counting on her. And Dorothy Silver. And getting that part. And then, of course, her dream of the yoga studio.

She was just going to have to pull herself together once and for all.

She'd be a different person around Adam Mason.

Starting right now.

CHAPTER 9

For the next couple of days, Paige woke every morning, yanked open her hotel-room drapes, did her pranayama practice and asanas in the best patch of sun she could find, then drove across the meadow to do more work on Gram's house.

By day three, she'd managed to get all the downstairs windows clean. The floors were mopped, the cabinets were wiped, and at least seven repairs had been started. Paige had even started searching for gazebos online. She found an enormous one—it was perfect—and sought out a private shipping company to bring it over when it was time. Now she just had to talk Adam into lending her the land to build it on.

By the end of the third day, Paige stood back, hands on her hips, to admire her work. She could almost see now how beautiful this place would be again, once it had its full face-lift and was filled with cozy furniture. Click seemed to approve, as well, as the kitten leaped up onto one of the newly cleaned sills to check out the views.

Paige was exhausted, though. And she knew she should probably talk to Adam, but she didn't know if she had the energy to look like the new pulled-together woman she needed to project. She also wanted to return the empty propane tank for the generator, but she didn't want to show up looking this spent. Maybe she'd just slip it onto his porch, hope not to see him, and go back to the room to shower and relax. Then she'd get her act together and talk to him.

She dragged her things onto the flatbed part of the golf cart and headed back across the meadow. The sky was turning a dusky blue, the dandelions blowing gently in the evening air. She'd come to love these bookend times of day—the hour the sun rose over the meadow, then the hour the sun decided to set, making its hesitant decision to disappear. She loved the feeling that the sky was holding on to something wonderful—only to give in, and then slip into sunsets that became even more vibrant and beautiful.

Her wheels bumped around the edge of the resort. It had been nice having a few days off from Adam—and the tiring work of trying to be someone more sophisticated, or at least tamping down her hormones. After making such a fool of herself, then being plagued with memories of his flexing biceps as he hauled that generator around, not to mention his seriousness and intensity that she knew must be amazing in bed, she'd had a terrible time getting him off her mind. It was exhausting.

At his back porch, Paige hopped out of the cart and pulled the propane tank onto the top step, pushing her hair out of her eyes and wiping away the line of perspiration trickling its way down her cleavage. As she turned to make her quick escape, she caught a glimpse of him walking through the field.

Damn.

His sleeves were rolled up, his shirt disheveled, giving credence to the long, hard day they'd apparently both had. The falling amber light caught the lines along his face, giving his eyes an otherworldly air as he kept them focused on her. He took the porch steps two at a time.

In the twilight, his eyes had softened to the exact color of the sky behind him. All this time, Paige had thought they were the color of a coming storm, but, in fact, they could also look like twilight, if you looked at them the right way. And if you liked him. And if you saw him with that June night sky right over his shoulder.

He leaned into the opposite porch rail, waiting for her to say something.

"Thank you again for the generator," she said. "It's been a great help."

"I see you're returning the tank—do you need a fill-up?"

"I can handle it from here—I'll get my own tank in town."

"It's no problem. I'm going to town tomorrow."

"I'll do it myself."

He studied her for a long moment. "Suit yourself."

She watched him wander toward a bench and admired the languid way he moved. He took a seat to take off his boots. On one side of the bench was a wicker basket filled with firewood, and on the other, a basket brimming with pinecones. Paige had never thought of the Mason residence as particularly homey before, but with Adam manning the helm now, there was kind of a warm look to the place. Denny came out of the dog door and sat beside Adam to complete the setting.

"There's a gathering tonight at Rosa's Cantina," Adam said, interrupting her fantasies of living in an L.L.Bean ad with him. "Antonio and Tanya the bartender are getting engaged. You're welcome to come."

"Oh wow. Antonio the super?" Paige was instantly happy for him.

"Yes. Big night. The food will be good. You can come and help yourself. I'm sure no one will mind."

His eyes were so intense. His forearms were so sexy. "No thanks," Paige blurted.

As soon as the words left her mouth, she questioned their wisdom. She *was* starving. And it might be fun to socialize.

She'd figured out that Rosa's Cantina was part of an almost secret town up here. Or not a town, exactly, but a street. A dirt road, really. But it had Rosa's restaurant, the bar, a gas station, a tiny market behind the gas station with a few basics like milk and eggs, and about two dozen small homes—the residents of which all seemed to keep the

Mason ranch running, along with the resort and the airport. As a kid, she'd never noticed the dirt road back there, being about a hundred acres away. And as an adult, when she would visit, she never came anywhere near this mountain. She wouldn't mind checking it out now.

Yet with Adam looking this good, and her known weakness for him, and her new plan to act like a sophisticate, she wondered if seeing him in a party atmosphere might be dangerous. Throw in a couple of drinks and another few gazes into those intense eyes, and she might end up in his lap.

"What are you going to do for dinner, then?" he asked.

"I'll find something. I'm just exhausted."

"You don't seem to eat much." He set both boots at the end of the bench. "Why is that?"

She shrugged. She didn't feel like defending her choices to him. "Women don't eat as much as men."

"Says who?"

"Says Dirk." She practically threw her hand over her mouth. How had that slipped out?

He lifted his head. "Who's Dirk?"

"He's nobody."

"Well, he must be somebody if you're listening to his advice."

She sighed. "My agent."

His frown created lines between his eyes. "What do you have an agent for?"

"I'm an actress."

She could have sworn a slant of doubt moved across his face, but he seemed to dismiss the comment and went back to tending his boots.

"Well, it has been a long day," he said, "and I can understand that you're exhausted, but you need to eat. If you don't want to go to Rosa's tonight, I could order you something and have it sent to your room again."

"You don't have to do that."

"Did you like the enchiladas?" he asked, ignoring her protest, looking as if he just wanted to get down to business.

"A salad would be good."

"You've got to eat more than salad. You're working hard out there."

She felt herself blush. Working hard, she had the impression, was something Adam admired. "I did like the enchiladas a lot," she mumbled.

"I know just the thing." He pulled a cleaner pair of boots from under the bench, and his thigh muscles tightened underneath his jeans as he tugged them on. "Are we done here, then?"

The switch from the kind gesture to the brusque dismissal confused and annoyed her, so she simply nodded.

He stood and moved toward the screen door. "You can come through here. It's getting dark."

"I'll go around. I'm a mess."

Adam watched her hand sweep across her body, but his gaze lingered somewhere around her hips, then seemed to stall at her breasts before he finally made it to her face. Once he met her eyes, he held them.

"Dirk's an idiot," he said quietly.

Her heart pounded. Having Adam's gaze drag up her body like a fingertip was more thrilling and unexpected than she could handle right now. She turned on her heel and scurried back to her cart, fumbling with the ignition key while he and Denny stared after her.

Finally, the thing lurched forward, and she tried to gun it across the grass back to her room.

She'd have to weather this one.

A storm might be brewing, for sure.

Adam let Denny into the house and shrugged out of his jacket. He was wiped. Between pounding fence posts up by the corral, shoveling sawdust, checking on bison, cleaning horses, pumping fuel for Brunner's plane, fixing a broken stair post in the barn, and helping Paige with Helen's property, he was sore from the cords of his neck to the ligaments of his arches. He wasn't in the mood to go to Antonio and Tanya's party tonight.

But damn, talking to Paige had perked up all kinds of body parts.

She looked worn-out but still incredibly sexy—her honey hair escaping along the nape of her neck, her blouse open at the collar just enough to reveal a sheen of sweat across her chest. It was enough to nearly undo him right now.

As soon as he'd invited her to the gathering, he'd questioned his sanity. Having her there and spending time with her after he'd had a few drinks probably wasn't a good idea. His thoughts were getting not only more and more lascivious but strangely protective, too. He wasn't sure what he'd do or say. His instincts ran from wanting to make sure she ate to wanting to pummel that idiot Dirk for making her feel she shouldn't. He wanted to take care of her. He wanted to take her exhaustion away. He wanted to unlock doors for her and save her from intruders and be some kind of hero to her . . .

He pulled out his phone and started scrolling for Rosa's number.

"Amanda?" he called into the other room.

Amanda came shuffling around the corner in her fluffy boots and slithered into a dining chair, staring up at him. She was so obedient. But he sort of wished she'd argue. Or not come. Or be belligerent. Or at least *talk*.

He put his phone away. "How was your day?" he tried. It was always his sorry start.

"Fine." It was always her dismissive end.

He had no idea if this ghostlike wordlessness had always been part of her personality or if it had started when her mother died, but either way it seemed sad. He wanted to fix it. He felt it was his job. And yet he didn't know how. And he didn't know how to ask. Talking things out was not one of his fortes in general, and talking things out with a fifteen-year-old girl was way out of his wheelhouse.

"Did you do anything fun today?" he asked.

"No."

He scratched Denny behind the ears and studied Amanda. With the setting June sun coming in through the window, hitting her face like that, he was suddenly struck by how much she looked like his mom. He turned to get his bearings, putting a few coffee mugs into the sink.

"I wanted to ask you about dinner," he said. "I'm going to Antonio and Tanya's engagement party tonight, but it's adults only, so I can order you something ahead of time. Or I can make you something. Mama Mendez can't make it tonight."

Antonio's mom, Teresa Mendez, was their full-time cook in the evenings, but her mother had fallen sick in Mexico, and she'd left for a month to take care of her.

"I'm not hungry," Amanda said.

Adam blew out an exasperated breath. Was this a girl thing? It was one of the nine hundred or so things about women that he'd never understand.

"You must be hungry," he said. "It's eight thirty and you probably haven't eaten all day."

"I'll make something later. There's sandwich stuff."

"What sandwich stuff?"

"I'll find something."

"Let me order you something."

"Okay. I'll do the enchiladas, I guess. Can I be excused?"

He sighed. He had no reason to say no. He could beg her to stay, beg her to talk, beg her to eat a snack, or eat with him, but she'd only do it with that sullen look of hers, staring at him through that thick makeup while moving food around on her plate. He shrugged. "Suit yourself."

He heard the chair legs scrape and then the shuffle of her slippers as she headed back to her room. Where she'd stayed for hours. Days. Weeks. But then suddenly she stopped and turned toward him.

"Can I go down to the harbor?" She tilted her head and threw her hand on her hip.

He wiped his brow with the back of his hand. *Damn.* She really did look like his mom. And she hardly ever asked for anything. Now that she had, it was something he couldn't give her. At least not right now. His heart felt heavy in his chest.

"It's kind of late now, and I have to go to the party. How about tomorrow? I can take you then."

"I can find my way."

"You don't drive."

"I'll take a cart."

"The hill's too dangerous in a cart. Especially at night."

"Paige does it."

He blinked back his surprise. He hadn't expected to hear Paige's name spoken by Amanda, and it felt like worlds colliding. Without thinking, he glanced toward the porch, where he'd last seen his little role model.

"Well, Paige is a grown woman, and she can do what she wants," he said. "You're fifteen. And you can't. I'll take you tomorrow."

"I'm almost sixteen!" Amanda gave him a good, old-fashioned eye-roll and huffed through a dramatic pivot. Then she stomped away, back to her room, where she slammed the door.

Adam stared after her, blowing out his breath, and then turned toward Denny, who was staring up at him, cocking his head to the side.

"How the hell did we get into this mess, Den?"

Denny gave him a good bark that had just as much male confusion wrapped in it.

Adam pulled his phone back out of his pocket, made his call to Rosa's, and ordered two enchilada meals, then stared out his kitchen window at the hangar.

Now there was another wall of frustration. He had some cleaning out to do.

The hangar was old, filled with dusty boxes stacked high on one wall and along shelves at the top of another. The domed ceiling ran about fifty yards back, and was once used to house some of the fire planes after World War II. But these days, only his and Noel's Cessnas and the one fire plane stayed on the property permanently, and none used the hangar. He kept them tied outside, for easy accessibility. And they had several ties they rented out to others who wanted to fly in privately. The hangar, therefore, had grown to be an enormous storage shed since the 1950s. There must be 170 boxes in there.

He trudged across the meadow. He had about a half hour until the takeout would be ready, so he'd get started on this now, then come home and get ready for the party.

He wandered inside across the hangar's dusty floors and started looking up at the boxes piled along the sides. He was specifically looking for the box marked "Private" that his father's will said would be there.

He wasn't really interested in finding it. It was just on his list of things to do. It didn't intrigue him in the least that his father had a private box. And if it so much as dared to have some pathetic letter of apology for being a terrible father, or for not "being there" for his sons and all that bullshit, Adam was going to have to hurl it against the wall and blow the place up.

But he looked anyway. His eyes roamed over the cardboard: "Logs 1950," "Logs 1960s," "Winter," "Movies," and one box marked with a big fat pen with the scrawl, "OIL."

He saw nothing that said "Private."

He gave it a half hour, scouring one entire side, but then gave up. He'd have to start hauling these boxes into a moving van at some point and find storage for them once the place sold until he could go through this crap.

But his half hour was up. And no luck. He'd head over to Rosa's.

And he'd start thinking about something much more pleasant, like Paige Grant.

He wondered if it would be weird if he delivered her meal in person.

◆　◆　◆

Paige unloaded her belongings into the corner of the room and crashed on the freshly made bed. She stretched her arms over her head and rubbed a new knot out of her left shoulder as she allowed herself to play back her porch encounter with Adam.

About fifty times.

The way he'd looked at her was something she'd never experienced. At least from him.

Part of her wondered if she could use that to her advantage: if he liked her, maybe he would be more likely to cooperate about the wedding.

But as soon as she had that thought, Paige batted it away. *Damn.* Maybe she was becoming more like her mother every day. That would be Ginger's plan. And while Ginger would highly approve of heavy flattery and flirting to get a deal done, Paige was not that kind of person. Ginger thought of it as guerilla-warfare tactics—all was fair in love and business—but Paige could never quite get on board with those methods. Of course, that was probably why her mom was a successful businesswoman while Paige was barely able to pay her bills.

She rolled off the bed and limped her way into the bathroom, where she started a hot shower, then peeled off her clothes. She thought she might have heard a knock on her door, but she ignored it and crawled into the steamy shower, letting the droplets wash away the dirt, the dust, the day.

When she got out, she saw a rectangular piece of paper slipped under her door that almost looked like a bill, but when she opened the door, she saw instead a napkin and a tinfoil meal sitting in her hallway. The napkin read, "For you. From Adam."

She walked the meal back to the table in her room, laid it down, and stared at the napkin for an unreasonably long time.

And tried to ignore the fact that her heart was not hardening. In fact, it was pounding crazier than ever.

CHAPTER 10

Adam slid his chair toward the table and fingered the pale-green napkin that lay on the pink-and-lace tablecloth at Rosa's. He and Bob had decided to come to the party early so they could grab a real meal and have time to talk. The rose that had been tucked inside the napkin fell out, and Adam hastily shoved it back as he glanced across the table at Bob.

"This is very romantic," he said drily.

Bob smiled, creating lines like parentheses around his eyes. His bushy white eyebrows—which matched the snowy tones of his hair—bent in the middle as he studied the table and flickering candle. "Want to eat in the bar?" he asked.

Adam shoved himself to his feet before Bob even got the entire question out. They flagged Tooey, the headwaiter, to let him know he had an extra table available.

Rosa's bar was even darker than the dining room, with shadows cast across the wooden floor. Silver nut bowls lined a mahogany counter that ran the length of the east wall, and a full-length mirror lent a Wild West look. Two pool tables took up one side, and a jukebox stood on the other. Rosa had put up white streamers across the front of the bar with paper bells hanging from them.

Adam studied the scotch selections as he dragged the bar stool up. "How're the horses, Joseph?" he asked the bartender.

While Adam helped himself to the bowl of nuts, Joseph filled him in on the new pony, born two months ago, and asked if he could bring it to Nowhere Ranch's corral in a month to train with Kelly. Adam started to say yes before remembering he might not even be there in a month. He ordered a Glenfiddich neat and changed the subject.

After they studied the menu, Bob leaned on his elbow.

"So Ginger wasn't the one to arrive, huh?" he asked.

"No, it's one of her daughters." Adam took a long swig of scotch.

Bob took a sip of his own drink and winced at the burn. "Which one? I think I've met them all."

"I had, too. But I barely remembered her. This is Paige. The youngest?"

"No, Natalie is the youngest. I remember Paige, though."

Adam nodded.

Bob's eyebrows rose, and a smile spread across his face. "She's probably a hard-ass now, right?"

"Well . . . I wouldn't use that term exactly." Adam recalled his reluctant appreciation of Paige's ass in the window the first day he saw her and realized he'd call it something other than "hard." Maybe "round," "tantalizing," with that perfect curve at her back . . .

He cleared his throat. "She was at the fire," he said instead.

"Ah, that's right," Bob said. "She's the one who saved you, right?"

"I wouldn't put it that way."

"Seems everyone else did."

Adam shrugged and took a sip of his scotch. He couldn't think about that now. He could hardly admit to himself that Paige was the same girl at the fire, the same girl who'd sat at his dad's dining table, the same girl who might have been his stepsister if things had gone differently, and the same woman now who was rattling him in ways he didn't understand.

"How's Amanda anyway?" asked Bob.

"Better. I think."

Bob nodded. "So what did you need my help with?"

Their dinners came, and they both leaned back. As soon as the waiter was gone, Bob lunged into his steak, and Adam filled in more details about Paige's plan to sell to Dorothy Silver.

"It's an interesting idea," Bob said, "but frankly I don't know if you can wait that long."

Adam stared at his plate for a long time. He didn't know why he was even bringing this up. They'd had a plan; he'd already put the wheels in motion. He knew he needed to hurry and leave for Amanda—everything should keep moving forward. But, for some reason, Paige's presence, and Paige's idea, kept causing the record to skip.

"Though, I have to say . . . ," Bob said, his voice drifting off toward some unspoken idea.

Adam glanced up. "What?"

"Something doesn't feel right with MacGregor."

Adam nodded. "I've been feeling the same way."

"But MacGregor's offering cash. If you're in a hurry, it's the easiest thing to do."

"I'm in a hurry."

Bob nodded. "When's he coming anyway?"

"Tomorrow."

Bob paid attention to his meal for a couple of minutes, giving Adam the amount of time he needed to make friends with this new reality.

"I'm sorry your dad put you in this position," Bob said. He always seemed to apologize for George, as if he could've talked him into other financial arrangements—like putting Adam and Noel on titles as partners, or otherwise saving parts of the property from probate—but Adam knew what a mule his father had been.

"It's not your fault, Bob."

"We'll make it work," Bob said, his voice drifting off.

Adam nodded yet again.

"But now"—Bob's eyes twinkled as he looked up from his dinner—"I want to hear more about Paige, and why you get that look on your face every time you say her name."

"What look?"

"*That* one," Bob said, pointing with his fork.

Adam looked away and pushed some potatoes around his plate. But as he glanced up, he caught a glimpse in the mirror of something that made his gut tighten. "Looks like maybe you can see for yourself," he said.

Bob looked at him with confusion, and Adam nodded toward the mirror. "She just walked in."

Paige stood in indecision in the doorway, her earrings brushing her cheek, staring at Adam at the bar with an elderly gentleman.

Maybe this was a terrible idea.

She clutched her laptop closer to her chest. Maybe she should eat in the dining room. She could actually get some work done, which was the lame excuse she'd given herself for coming here in the first place.

In full makeup.

In her favorite outfit.

Wearing her lucky pair of earrings.

As she took a step back, however, Adam turned in the bar stool and looked right at her. He didn't exactly motion her over. In fact, he didn't move at all. He simply stared.

Since he'd caught her eye, though, she told herself she shouldn't be impolite.

"I thought you weren't coming," he said when she arrived at his shoulder. "I left something at your door."

"Yes, thank you. I, uh . . . I decided maybe I'd get out a little. Get some work done." She lifted her laptop satchel for proof.

"Ah." Adam nodded.

Paige turned to the older gentleman, who was studying her with interest.

"Ms. Grant, this is Bob Hastings. Bob, Paige Grant." Adam turned to flag down the bartender with something that looked like sheer desperation.

"Nice to meet you," Bob said enthusiastically, holding out his hand. "I'm Adam's accountant. How's your mother?"

Paige blinked back surprise. "You know my mom?"

"I've known the Masons and the Grants for a long time. Lived here on Lavender Island since the seventies. I met you when you were a little girl."

"Oh. Well, nice to meet you again." She shook his hand.

"Why don't you join us?" he asked.

Adam suddenly coughed, chaotically, then slammed his chest with his fist.

"Thank you, but that's okay," Paige said. "I need to get some work done. Thanks for the invitation, though."

Before Bob could argue—he looked the type to always put forth an effort of gallantry—and before Adam could start choking again, Paige retreated to a quiet back corner. She felt silly moving so far away, since the room was practically empty, but she needed to get out of earshot. She didn't want to appear to be spying on what looked like a possible business meeting. And who knew—maybe it was even about the Dorothy Silver sale. Of course, her mother would probably approve of spying. But even though Paige wanted to do her mother proud, she still couldn't bring herself to take on Grant-women guerrilla tactics. Becoming her mother's daughter would have to come in steps.

She chose a table against the window and stole one more look at the bar. Adam was still watching her. An unrecognizable thrill shot through her, and it had nothing to do with furthering her position in a business deal.

Biting her lip, she chided herself. She couldn't get herself worked up like she had sixteen years ago. This guy was exciting her on every level, but he'd already broken her heart once. And there was no way she was going to let it happen again.

As her mom said, she was just going to have to be smart.

"Are you determining the angle of the creases in her slacks or how many buttons she has undone to her bra?"

Adam looked with embarrassment at Bob, who was smirking at him relentlessly.

"My life is falling apart," Adam said, turning back toward his scotch. "How could I look at her with anything but dismissal?"

"Well, I've got a fifty that says you're looking at her with something other than dismissal."

Adam stabbed at his dinner. "Listen, regardless of how beautiful a coral snake is, you stay away."

"Those are the poisonous ones?"

"'Red touching yellow kills a fellow'?" He waited for some recognition to alight on Bob's face, but when none came, he shook his head. "Bob, you're not much of a mountain man."

Bob's eyes crinkled at the edges, and he let out a warm chuckle. "Sometimes ignorance is bliss. Sometimes you just want to enjoy beauty for beauty's sake and not worry about what's poisonous or not. Aren't those snakes generally reclusive unless you bother them?" Bob looked at him for a long time, chewing his steak.

"Are you giving me hell, old man?"

Bob laughed into his potatoes. "I'm just saying I've known you a long time, Adam, and I've seen you through many a girlfriend, but that woman looks more your type than anyone I've quite possibly ever seen."

Adam pushed his plate away and stole a look at her over his shoulder. "Too bad she's a beautiful coral snake."

Bob took another sip of his scotch and suddenly moved off the bar stool, getting out his wallet.

Adam looked at him with alarm. "Where are you going? We haven't even talked yet."

"Listen, son," Bob said. He threw several bills onto the bar. "Let me pay for your dinner, and let me buy that lady a bottle of wine, and I want you to walk over there and apologize for whatever you did or said that's making her sit way over there. Then I want you to sit with her and have a couple of drinks and ask her to dance at least once and celebrate with Tanya and Antonio tonight. You've looked like something the cat's dragged in for the last three years, and seeing that look on your face right now makes me happy. So make me happy tonight."

"I've got to get back, Bob. There's so much to do. I've got books to keep, and—"

Bob chuckled into his wallet. "You must be losing your touch, son, if you can't stay up late enough for a few drinks and some dancing and still get your bookkeeping done."

"Amanda doesn't like to be alone in the house late at night."

"I'll swing by and bring Amanda some pie. I'm sure she'll be fine. Denny's with her, right?"

"Yeah." Adam glanced over his shoulder. Maybe Bob was right. He'd aged about twenty years in the last five. And Paige was looking incredible. And it had been a long time since he'd sat across a table over a flickering candle to have a few drinks with an interesting woman.

Paige was funny and smart and intriguing, and he hadn't been around a woman in years who'd captivated him quite like she did.

"Send her a chardonnay." Bob clapped Adam on the shoulder and left.

Paige looked up from her screen and noted that Friendly Bob was heading for the door. She wondered if something had gone wrong between the two men. She forced her eyes back to her laptop but stopped absorbing a single word.

"This is from the gentleman at the bar." A waiter suddenly set a bottle of white wine on the table. "Would you like me to pour?"

Paige nodded and waited until the waiter was gone, focusing on breathing, then glanced at Adam. That, apparently, was all the welcome he required. He slid off the bar stool and began a reluctant gait toward her.

"Mind if I join you?" he asked stiffly.

She didn't know. He looked too good tonight. She'd forgotten to factor in that part. The ever-present hat was now off his head, dangling at his side. His hair was pushed off his face, making his eyes more prominent and blue. The work shirt had given way to a crisp white button-up, which he wore under a tweed jacket, and his dark jeans curved around his thick thighs before falling over black boots.

Her voice couldn't seem to form the words *no* or *yes*, so she simply made a spasmodic jerk toward the extra seat and closed her laptop.

"I was getting some work done," she said. "Is that what you were doing with Bob?"

He gave her a wan smile as he slid into the chair. "Are we back to talking about business already? I was going to say you look nice tonight."

She straightened her shoulders and stared at her wine. She *did* think she looked nice. The silky top in a gorgeous mustard color made her feel grown-up and sophisticated for once.

"Thank you. So were you talking to Bob about my proposition?"

He took a swig of his scotch. "I was, in fact."

"And?"

"I'm sorry, Paige. Unless MacGregor doesn't show up at all tomorrow, I don't think I'm going to be able to take Dorothy's deal. But tomorrow is Thursday. So I'll give you my final word then."

Paige's shoulders slumped. This was not what she wanted to hear. But she held out a tiny sliver of hope that MacGregor might not show up. And if he did, maybe she could at least borrow part of the meadow for the time being—just to get the gazebo erected—and they could make sure it was a temporary structure. The orchard she could work on later.

"But I didn't come over here to talk to you about land," Adam said, glancing around the room.

The bar was starting to fill up, and Adam seemed to nod at almost everyone.

"What did you come to talk about?" she squeaked. Moving this to a social rendezvous could be dangerous for her.

"Bob wanted me to cover three things."

"What three things?"

"One is to have a couple of drinks with you."

She nodded toward the bottle. "I think we can handle that. Thank you for the wine." She had to make sure she didn't drink much. She pushed the extra wineglass toward him. "Do you want a glass? Or three?"

"I'm good." He lifted his scotch. "And the wine's actually from Bob."

An odd disappointment fell through her stomach. She gazed at the flickering candle in a leaf-shaped bronze holder and wished she hadn't just felt that. She wasn't supposed to let herself get hopeful about gallantry from Adam Mason.

He stared at her for a few beats, then laughed with embarrassment and shook his head. "But I should've taken the credit," he said softly.

Her fingers nervously stroked her wineglass stem. "So what are the other two things?" she managed to ask.

"The second is apologize," he said.

Apologize? A new panic seized her. Was he remembering more from the past? Did Bob know more about that summer than he let on?

When Adam didn't continue, she had to prompt him through dry lips. "Apologize for what?"

"For whatever I did or said that made you sit over here instead of joining us."

She relaxed back into her seat a little, but her heart continued to thump as she wondered how much she could admit: *Feeling guilty for contributing to the breakup of a family? Feeling guilty for having a mother who sent you away? Being the one to tell on you? Lusting after you anyway? Reverting to a hormonal teenager every time I'm near you?* The list was long and pitiful.

He patiently waited for an answer, staring right into her eyes, but just then a man's voice bellowed across the room.

"A-*dam*!"

A man Paige recognized as Antonio from earlier came barreling across the wood floor, followed by a crowd of three men and four women.

"Paige, right?" Antonio said, leaning over to shake her hand. "This is Tanya." He pointed behind him. "And Joe, Little, Tony, Jen, Sherryl, and Kelly." Paige glanced up to see Kelly, whom she recognized from the front desk. Kelly gave her a quick wave before plopping into a chair nearby.

For the next half hour, the friends and ranch hands danced to never-ending songs on the jukebox. A country band took over around ten, and bottles clinked in several toasts to Antonio and Tanya. Every time the new couple kissed, everyone took a drink—until they started making out on the dance floor, and everyone finished their glasses and ordered another round. Paige didn't mean to take so many sips of wine, but the kissing went on and on. The group laughed at story after story, explaining details to Paige when necessary so she'd get the jokes, especially when they were about Adam, and next thing she knew she was relaxing and having a great time.

Adam laughed along but kept glancing across the table at her nervously. She enjoyed watching his dimples make brief appearances.

When the music got louder and faster, and the malty scent of spilled beer hung heavier in the air, Little leaned over and asked Paige if she knew how to dance.

"I do all right."

"Thought so." He smiled and held out his hand.

Little was anything but, but the man could bust a move. He was all over the floor, his body jiggling in impressive hip-hop moves that made him look like some kind of gelatin dessert. Paige did her best to keep up with him, and, after the second number, when she glanced back at the table, she noticed Adam staring at her. He took a sip of scotch and looked away.

At the end of the night, once they'd toasted Antonio and Tanya about a million times, once they'd all danced with one another, and once their tables were littered with beer bottles, Paige finally pushed herself to her feet and announced that she had to go home.

"I'll take you," Joe said. "I'm heading out myself."

"I'll take you," Adam said, pushing his chair back. He glanced briefly at Joe.

Paige turned toward Adam, coming up to his chest. "Are you sober?" she whispered. She wasn't sure. His hair was mussed, his grin a little cocky. He had a recklessness about him that didn't seem his normal self.

"Not entirely, but neither is he," he said, low. "We'll walk."

She nodded. She didn't know if this was a fun Adam to be with, or a very, very dangerous one. Because he looked too sexy. And too easy. And she wasn't entirely sober, either. And she knew liquor made her Calamity June side come out and made her confess all kinds of things . . .

She watched him grab his hat, set it on his head, and nod toward the door.

And then had the frightening but thrilling thought that this night could go either way.

CHAPTER 11

The night air carried the warm, earthy scent of California sage as Adam tried to slow his pace to let Paige keep up. Crickets chirped along the dusty roadside, filling the silence that grew between them. His boots and her heels crunched together in perfect rhythm. But then he heard her panting.

"Can we slow down?" she asked.

Damn. He hadn't realized he was walking too fast for her. He slowed immediately and glanced at her shoes. They made her legs look great—he couldn't help but notice that—and they made her move in the sexiest way. But they couldn't be easy to walk in, especially along a dirt road. He wished he could pick her up and carry her.

"So . . . ," she said on a deep breath, "what was the third thing?"

He frowned. "Third thing?"

"The third thing Bob wanted you to do. He wanted you to have a few drinks with me, apologize, and what was the third thing?"

"Dance with you."

She looked up at him quickly. When she seemed to collect herself, she shrugged. "But you didn't."

He wanted to read her tone as disappointment, but he wasn't sure. "No, I didn't."

Their shoes crunched along the gravel. Adam had to admit *he* was disappointed. It would have been nice to have held her for a moment, even if he didn't know how to dance. He'd thought about asking her five or six times. But honestly, he didn't trust himself. With the way she'd made his blood race all night, he thought his second scotch might have had his hands roaming a little too far.

"Your friends are nice," she said suddenly. "I didn't know you had an entire community up here. Do you go out with them often?"

"Not as much as I used to. But they're good people. We grew up together here."

"Little sure can dance."

"Yeah, I noticed you were dancing with him a lot."

He'd had strange flare-ups of jealousy all night. Every time Little or Joe or Tony would look her way, he wanted to jump in and intervene. It was misplaced, he knew, but there it was.

"That's because someone who was *supposed* to be dancing with me, on Bob's orders, wasn't asking."

He glanced down at her. "I can't tell if that's disappointment on your face or relief."

"Depends."

"On what?"

"On how well you dance."

He chuckled. He was glad Bob had forced him to stay and relax with her—he hadn't smiled as much in five years as he had in the last three hours.

"Actually, it's probably for the best," she said.

"Why is that?"

"I probably had too much to drink. And when I get tipsy, I'm always afraid of what I'm going to do or say."

"This sounds interesting." He smiled down at her.

"*Blathering* is what it is."

An enormous dirt clod seemed to come out of nowhere, and she stumbled over it and grasped his forearm. He caught her and helped her right herself.

"Sorry," she said.

She hung heavily against him, and it felt so good—the warmth of her body, the feel of her hand, the silkiness of her skin and clothes. It had been a long while since he'd walked a woman home. Or even dated anyone seriously, where you noticed things like how good they smelled, or how nice they felt leaning on you. And he was shocked to have those feelings about none other than Paige Grant—the girl with the goth eyeliner who'd maybe saved him from a fire and whose mother had completely altered his young life. But now he was looking at a sexy, grown woman who had the same spitfire energy, and he was enchanted.

She leaned over and carefully slipped off each shoe. "Anyway, what I'd really love is if you'd start answering my questions."

He smiled at that and tried not to stare too much down her top. "Have I been skipping your questions?"

"You most certainly have." She shook one pointy toe at him. "You're skipping the most important ones, actually."

"What have I skipped?"

"Samantha. Remember? I asked you after you took the splinter out. I wanted to know what happened there."

She turned and started charging up the hill.

"Are you going to be okay without your shoes on? There's a lot of glass on the ground here. And snakes. And scorpions."

"I feel like I'll fall if I keep them on."

"Might be better than the glass and snakes and scorpions. You can lean on me."

She looked around the ground, as if the scorpions would be right there for proof, then shivered and slipped her shoes back on. She didn't lean on him—just forged forward—but he wished she would.

"So you're skipping your question again," she said.

"What was it?"

"Samantha."

Their feet made soft crunching sounds along the dirt road for another minute before he answered. He hadn't thought about it much himself. It was what it was: a situation he hadn't seen coming, but now he must take responsibility. That was most of his life. Thinking about it, or talking about it, didn't seem necessary. He just kept getting out of bed, putting one foot in front of the other, and doing what must be done.

"There's not much to tell," he said. "I got a call from a lawyer in Alabama about six months ago who told me Samantha Sweet had died, and that I had a daughter named Amanda. And about two days later, Amanda showed up on my doorstep with three suitcases."

They let the crickets fill the silence while they rounded the next corner.

"How did Samantha die?" Paige asked.

"Cancer."

"She was so young."

Adam nodded.

"So those are the *events* of what happened," she said, "but I'm wondering how you and Amanda felt about it, and why Samantha didn't say anything about a baby all those years before."

"I don't have the answers there. Maybe she just didn't want to be with me."

The fact that Samantha had chosen to have and raise a baby by herself rather than name him as the father was something he'd been wondering about for the last six months. He must have really let her down. He'd let everyone down that summer, he knew, sometimes for events he hadn't even been responsible for, like the fires, but Samantha's silence when she found out she was pregnant hurt the most.

It didn't matter how he felt, though. As far as he was concerned, he just had to fix everything.

"So, since she had cancer, Samantha probably knew she was dying?"

"I imagine so."

"And then she told someone you were the father, so someone would take care of Amanda?"

"I suppose."

"So she *chose* you, in the end?"

He hadn't thought about it that way. But he imagined that's what had happened. Her parents had died in a car crash years ago, he'd learned, but she still had some distant relatives in Alabama she could have sent Amanda to. So Paige was right: Samantha had, in the end, decided Adam might be a good father for their daughter, after all. A bolt of confidence rose from somewhere deep, and he watched their shoes cover the dusty ground for the next minute.

"That looks like quite a view." She pointed.

Through a thicket of pine trees, they could see a hint of twinkle lights far below. She was right—it was called Top of the World, and it had been a popular make-out spot when he'd been a teenager.

She was halfway up the next rock before he knew it.

"Be careful," he called. He hated how old he sounded. He wished he still had a spirit like hers.

She nimbly scaled the smooth stepping-stone rocks, then suddenly paused. Her shoes seemed to be getting in the way again, and she bent and peeled each one off, her focus still on the top of the rock. He couldn't take his eyes off her. Until, that was, she tossed the shoes at him. Adam caught each one.

"Come up here with me," she said.

"How much exactly did you have to drink?"

"C'mon."

He hesitated. Climbing the Top of the World at midnight with a beautiful girl was something he'd done as a teenager, but it seemed inappropriate right now, while he had so much responsibility and so many things on his mind. But somehow, everything about Paige seemed lively and a little inappropriate. And she made him smile. And she made him forget for a few minutes that he had the weight of the world on his shoulders.

He dropped the shoes and hauled himself up within seconds, following her onto the next ledge, where she'd crept around the corner and now sat with her legs curled beneath her to take in the view.

Below them, toward the east, Nowhere Ranch unfolded—his resort, orchards, airport, and stables, laid out like a patchwork quilt, deep blue-green velvet in the moonlit darkness. To the south, the island's harbor and Carmelita rolled out, its city lights sparkling by the sea. A few boat lights could be seen in the ocean, as well as the reflection in the night water, but then the black ripples fell off, deep and still, as if they were at the end of the earth. Way out along the horizon, across twenty-six miles of sea, the lights of LA shimmered as if it were light-years away.

"I haven't done this in a long time," he said, settling beside her.

The smile she sent his way felt like his night's reward.

"You used to come here?" she asked.

"All the time."

"What's it called?"

"Top of the World."

"That's right!" She let out a breath of relief. "I couldn't remember. I vaguely recall it, but I don't think Ginger would let us come out this far. What did you do up here?"

"Make out." He threw her a grin.

Her laughter bubbled into the night. "I'll bet. How many girls did you bring up here?"

"Ah. A gentleman never brings more than one girl at a time."

She laughed.

He'd forgotten how good it felt to laugh with a woman—someone who could make you forget the things you wanted to forget and remember the things you wanted to remember. Someone who could remind you how beautiful city lights were from a mountaintop. Someone who could make your heart hammer a little, and confuse you about whether it was due to an uphill climb or to the fact that she looked stunning in the moonlight.

"Did you ever bring Samantha up here?" she asked, twisting her body toward him.

"Probably."

"I was always jealous of her."

He lifted his eyebrows.

"I'd see you whisk away with her, like from the campfire or something, and I'd always get jealous. I always wondered what you were doing."

"Well, you were probably a little young to be wondering what we were doing."

She laughed. "Maybe. You know, she might need to hear you talk about her mom."

"What?"

"Does she have any idea how you felt about Samantha?"

"Are we talking about Amanda now?"

"Yeah, sorry. That's another thing I do when I've had too much to drink—I change the subject a lot."

"I'll try to keep up."

"Try harder, buddy. So does Amanda have any idea how you felt about Samantha?"

"No, I wouldn't imagine . . . I barely remember myself."

"You don't remember how you felt about her?"

"Not really."

She looked thoughtful about that for a second, then gazed back over the view. "Well, make something up. Kids need to know they're wanted and loved, and if Amanda knows you didn't even know she existed, she probably assumes you don't want or love her. But if she learns that you sincerely cared about her mom, she might feel there could be some feeling that will trickle down to her. It's the same thing as—*ahh! Crap!* What was that?"

She leaped up and started batting her hands across her hair.

He jumped up with her. "What's wrong?"

"Was that a—*crap!*" She ducked again, then grabbed his arm and tugged him in the other direction. "Are there *bats* out here?"

"Oh. Yeah. I think there's a cave up there on that next—"

But she'd yanked him toward her and was leaping off the rock slab as the bats swooped in their direction.

"Paige, wait! Be careful."

She whisked herself down two more ledges in incredibly impressive moves, then pulled him into a tight crevice so they could hide until the bats passed by. She pressed her back against a rock and glanced around the ledge above their heads. "Are they still coming out?"

He poked his head around the formation. Sure enough, in the distance, about seventy of them continued their trajectory to the south. "I think the coast is clear."

"Bats seek me out."

"What?"

"I'm attractive to them."

He stepped back into the crevice with her and smiled. "Well, I can see you being attractive to a variety of species, but *bats?*"

"Birds, too. Hummingbirds especially. And some insects."

He lifted his eyebrow.

"They find me and dive-bomb my hair. It happens all the time. I think I'm cursed."

"Cursed?"

"Bad things follow me around. Calamities, if you will. Birds fall out of the sky and land on my head, bats dive-bomb me, I fall out of screens, I get myself stuck in window sills and laundry chutes—that kind of thing."

"Wait. There's a laundry-chute story?"

"I'm serious. It's a curse."

"Maybe it's a blessing."

She rolled her eyes. "How is being dive-bombed by bats and falling out of screens a blessing?"

"Maybe it gives you a life filled with fun and adventure, and maybe people like being around you."

She looked up at him in the sweetest way, her eyes filled with thanks and vulnerability. She stared out at the empty night for a minute and then gave him another once-over. Inexplicably her hand reached for his shirt, and she pulled him toward her, stumbling just a little. She leaned in, slightly, and tilted her chin toward him.

Did she want him to kiss her? He wanted to. He'd wanted to have his hands on her all night. He moved his arms toward her shoulders but then stopped himself.

She smiled up at him. "You want to kiss me, don't you?"

He grinned and glanced away. "I do, yes."

"Why aren't you?"

He sighed. "Because you've told me twice now you've had too much to drink, and it's an asshole move when a guy already knows that."

She stepped closer toward him and then stumbled on a crack in the rock and fell into his arms. *Damn, she has soft skin.* This time he didn't take his hands away.

"That's very noble of you. But it's probably smart on both our parts to leave now." Her delicious-looking bottom lip pouted, and her voice was tinged with a strange awareness that sounded too lucid for the state she claimed to be in. "Are the bats gone?"

He leaned out. "They are."

She nudged him toward the opening of the crevice. "Let's get back."

His chest fell from disappointment, but he knew it had been the right thing to do. He made sure she got down safely, then jumped down beside her as she tugged on her shoes.

"We can sing songs on the way back," she said, pulling on the left one.

"Why would we sing songs?"

"Because that way neither of us will think about how stupid we were back there."

He wasn't sure exactly what she meant by that—whether it was stupid of her to almost be kissed or stupid of him to have missed his chance—but he nodded and followed her back to the dirt road, shoving his hands into his pockets.

And when she launched into a wailing chorus of "Goodnight, Irene" as soon as they started down the road, he burst out laughing.

Damn. This girl was cute.

CHAPTER 12

The dude group arrived at eight the next morning. Through sleepy eyes and a mild hangover, Paige watched them assemble in the meadow. She hoped MacGregor wouldn't show. But she'd told Adam she'd be well out of the way by the time anyone arrived, so she scrambled out of bed to make sure she had her things packed and rushed outside to pile everything into the golf cart. She'd have to practice her asanas later.

She also wanted to clear out before she had to face Adam again.

Her eyebrows throbbed. But the worst part was remembering how much she'd flirted with him, and how much she'd revealed, and how she'd stumbled into him several times. And then . . . oh God . . . having the bats dive-bomb them, and then *almost kissing him* in the crevice. And then . . . did she *sing* all the way home?

She groaned.

This was not being smart. This was not proving to him how capable she was.

This was being foolish.

This was being weak.

This was being a disaster.

As she scurried to find Click and make her getaway, the dudes hauled large duffel bags toward their rooms, dressed in full Western gear—shiny boots, bright flannel shirts, and spotless ten-gallon hats. There were eight of them, of varying ages from thirty to sixty. Adam brought up the rear, in his more faded, natural colors, deep in conversation with an older gentleman who Paige thought might be MacGregor. Her shoulders fell.

She and her mom had never met MacGregor in person, but she was pretty sure—based on how much attention Adam was giving him—that was him. He'd shown up. Which didn't bode well for her.

She tore her eyes away from the man who was ruining her plans and . . . well . . . from the *other* man who was ruining her plans. Neither had seemed to spot her. This would be a good chance to make her escape.

"Mornin', miss," said one of the freshly minted cowboys leading the pack.

Paige smiled and quickly resumed her packing. She just wanted to get out of there.

"Good morning from me, too," said another.

Paige turned and gave another brief nod. She had the sense a bunch of locusts were descending.

"Can we help you with anything?" another youngish one said. Without waiting for an answer, he strode over, dropped his duffel bag, and reached for her sleeping bag.

"I'm fine, thank you." She took the bag back.

"Are you going to be part of our riding group?"

"No. I'm just—"

"Rooms are straight ahead." Adam had come out of nowhere and lifted the duffel bag of the urban cowboy and shoved it a little roughly at his chest. He pointed in the right direction.

The cowboy took off with his adopted new amble.

"Mornin', Paige," Adam mumbled, still watching the cowboy's retreat.

Her pulse kicked into a silly rhythm at his looming nearness again, his handsome face frowning into the morning sky, his hair brushed back under his hat. She glanced at the chest and arms she'd practically thrown herself into last night and then had to turn away slightly so he wouldn't see her blush. Should she say something about the almost-kiss? Should she apologize? Should she—

"And who's this?" came an older man's voice behind them.

She and Adam both tore their gazes away from each other to turn toward the voice.

"Mr. MacGregor, this is Paige Grant," he said. "Paige, Dave MacGregor. You two might know each other—Dave, Paige and her mom, Ginger, are the owners of Helen Grant's property across the way."

Adam sounded so pulled together. She reached up and smoothed her hair down.

"Ah, yes, the Grants." MacGregor reached for her hand. "Well, aren't you pretty?"

Paige shook back. She didn't know what being pretty had to do with anything, so she ignored that.

Adam turned and suddenly seemed to glare at MacGregor, or maybe just into the sun. He directed the man toward the rooms. "That way."

MacGregor stared at Paige for another few seconds, then nodded to them both and loped away.

Adam stayed planted, hands on his hips, watching MacGregor leave. "How're you doing? I wasn't sure how your head would feel."

"I'm good," Paige lied.

She was a little hungover, but she didn't want to focus on how irresponsible that had probably been. Besides, the pain medication she took was doing its job. Damage controlled. Her greater worry was what Adam might think of her flirting last night.

"I'm, um, sorry about last night," she blurted. "Especially if I said or did anything inappropriate."

He finally looked at her. His mouth quirked up at the side. "Inappropriate?"

"The, um . . . flirting. Or trying to get you to kiss me." She scrunched her face up. It sounded so ridiculous. Like some college coed, not an almost-thirty-year-old businesswoman. "I hope we can forget that ever happened and go back to business." She flapped her hand around.

As Adam stared off toward the horizon, the sun lit the side of his face. "If that's what you want," he said.

"Yes." She breathed the word more than said it. "Yes. Please. Let's just forget that even happened. I see MacGregor showed up, after all."

He glanced once more at Paige with a polite nod. "He has."

"I hope we can still come to an agreement for the wedding? Maybe we can still work something out? I was thinking maybe the orchard—"

"Paige."

She looked up at him. His amusement had slid off his face, replaced now by his familiar scowl.

"Let me meet with him first."

She nodded.

"The electricity should be back on at your place. Pedro said it would be ready today."

Paige nodded again and watched Adam amble away. She threw her sleeping bag into the back of the cart and took off for her new home.

She needed to keep this situation under control.

Adam had a busy day with the dudes. The first day was usually allowing them to get settled, giving them a tour of the property, and introducing them to the horses. They were at the stables now, getting their first lessons from Joseph, who did the horse-trail tours when he wasn't bartending at Rosa's.

It was great to have something to do. It kept his mind off Paige. He'd had a lot of fun with her last night—it was the first night in a long time he'd just relaxed and enjoyed himself, and he'd thought they were even making a connection—but her abrupt 180 this morning reminded him that she was just doing business here. Much like Ginger.

Ginger had started a relationship with his father that summer and had eventually gotten him to fall in love with her. But his father had failed to separate business from pleasure and had started signing over land to her by leading with his heart. Or other body parts. Adam still wasn't sure. Regardless, Ginger had acquired all the land south of their house and one hundred feet of meadow before George even knew what hit him.

Adam had to be smart. And not make the same mistakes.

He liked Paige a lot, especially the way she was last night—so gorgeous and open. But there was no way he was going to be an idiot about this. She was here to do business. And he knew now that she saw last night as a mistake. Thank God he hadn't actually kissed her.

He plodded into the kitchen after finishing up in the stables and found Amanda taking up two dining chairs, sitting in one and leaning over the other with a nail-polish brush poised over her toes.

"Hey, you wanted to go down to the harbor today, right?" he asked.

"No."

"Yes, you did. That's what you said yesterday. I can take you now."

"I don't want to go anymore."

He set his bridle down on the counter and frowned at her. "Why not? What happened?"

"It was a onetime thing."

He leafed through the mail. "I'm sorry. What was the onetime thing?"

"Nothing."

He frowned. It was so damned hard to talk to her. She seemed to look at him with nothing but disdain, if she looked at him at all. But then his thoughts drifted to what Paige had said last night: maybe Amanda just wanted to know how he felt about her mom. He took a long look at her.

"Your mom used to paint her nails like that when she was about your age," he said.

Amanda's head snapped up. She stared at him for about ten seconds, which was ten seconds longer than usual. "She did?"

Encouraged, he went on. "Yeah, she had long fingernails, also, and I remember she used to have a different color on every day. Or at least it seemed that way to me."

It was a weird thing to remember about Samantha, but there it was. He hadn't thought about her in years, and this was a strange place to start, but that was definitely a memory. Pink, black, blue, silver, white—she had different colors all the time. He remembered staring at her toes when they'd sit in beach chairs and wriggle their feet in the sand. She had toe rings, too. But since he'd found Samantha's toe rings rather sexy, he decided not to mention that part to Amanda.

"Did you like my mom's fingernails?" Amanda put the lid on her polish and turned more toward him.

He shrugged. "Well, I was an eighteen-year-old boy, so I liked everything about your mom."

Amanda smiled.

He did a double take and couldn't help but stare as she toyed with the bottle of polish. She'd never smiled at anything he'd said before. And here she was, smiling for a good two seconds.

"What else did you like about her?" Amanda asked.

Damn. His blood started racing with something that felt like joy. Amanda was talking to him. In a sweet, smile-in-her-voice way. Paige was right. She was probably craving information about her mom, and maybe just needed to know that he'd cared for her. Why hadn't he thought of this?

He wandered toward the fridge and pulled out some leftover apple fritters, remembering that Amanda had gobbled one up when Gert brought them over the other night. He popped two of them into the microwave.

"I liked a lot of things about her," he said to buy himself some time. He had to think. What could he remember about Samantha? "She was beautiful, of course," he said, hitting the buttons.

"What did she look like then?" Amanda asked.

"Kind of like you, really. She had long hair like yours. She had blue eyes like yours. She always wore sandals, like you do. Except when we were on the horses. Then she had these brown boots with flowers all over them." He chuckled. He hadn't thought about that in years, either, but there it was. The other kids had made fun of her flowery cowboy boots, but he'd thought they were pretty. Growing up with just his dad and brother and a bunch of burly ranch hands, he'd found everything that was feminine about girls fascinating.

The microwave pinged. He found a towel to grab the hot plate with and walked the fritters over to the kitchen table.

Amanda was fidgeting with her polish bottle. "How did you two meet?"

He set the plate between them and pulled up a chair. He had to rack his brain for that one. He didn't dare make something up: What if Samantha had already told her the story, and Amanda was testing him?

He slid the plate over to buy some time. "Have one."

"I'll have half," she said, breaking one in two.

He couldn't believe she was finally eating something with him.

"So how did you meet?" she asked again around a big bite of pastry.

He strained for some memory. A vague image came to him, of Samantha sitting across from him at a campfire. "We were both counselors here on the island one summer. I had been doing the camp for a couple of years, but one summer she came from the mainland and joined the staff. I remember seeing her across the campfire and feeling like a lightning bolt hit me."

Amanda smiled at that.

Paige was absolutely right. Amanda just needed to know that he had cared for her mom and, by extension, that he now cared for her. He reached back for any memory he could conjure. Unfortunately, most of what came up was randy eighteen-year-old boy stuff. But he tried to think of something G-rated he could share.

"She was good on horseback," he suddenly remembered.

"Really?" Amanda crinkled her nose. "I can't imagine my mom riding a horse."

"Yeah, we rode almost every day."

"Seriously?"

Adam nodded. "I was the riding instructor, so I think she used to pretend she needed lessons so I'd take her out every day."

Amanda laughed.

"She liked this horse we had named Bartlett." He couldn't help but smile at that. He'd loved Bartlett, too. "He was a beautiful brown-and-white Appaloosa. She was great with him. She liked the trails that went along Heart's Cove."

"Really?" Amanda picked at her fritter.

"Want me to take you out there sometime? You could ride the same trails she loved."

"I don't know how to ride."

"I'll teach you. I'm a pretty good instructor." He winked at her.

She looked away, but she didn't say no.

She finished her half of the fritter and started playing with the nail-polish bottle again. "Did my mom have other friends here?"

"She had lots of friends."

"Anyone who's still here?"

"I'll think about it. I have to remember who was here back then."

She nodded, then scooted abruptly from the table.

"Where are you going?"

"I'm going to clean my room."

Adam knew she simply said that anytime she wanted to *escape* to her room, but he let it go.

He'd thought things were going so well. But now he ate the rest of his fritter in silence.

Paige drove back up the road in the golf cart, the wheels straining on the hill, and put her hand on her packages so they didn't fly out. She'd decided she couldn't go another day without a few more hardware supplies, or else too many of her projects would fall behind schedule. But she still hadn't wanted her sisters to know she was on the island. She'd grabbed a wide-brimmed baseball hat, shoved on a pair of large Jackie-O sunglasses, and hoped for the best.

Mr. Clark at the hardware store hadn't even given her a second glance, and, because of her success, she'd decided to make a quick stop at the market to get a few more groceries and snacks.

Now she jiggled Gram's kitchen door with one hand while balancing her bags with the other.

Suddenly she sensed a figure over her shoulder.

She whirled into one of her self-defense moves.

"Whoa!" Adam moved out of her elbow's range as her bag went flying.

Her granola bars skittered across the dirt, her orange and apple rolled off the edge into the grass, and the fresh flowers she'd bought from Clark's fell in a heap.

Adam put his hands up in apology. "Sorry. Didn't mean to scare you." He lunged off the porch to pick up the runaway fruit.

"I didn't expect anyone here." She bent for the granola bars and then lifted and shook out the poor flowers. "I guess . . . I guess I'm still a little jittery about intruders."

He took two of the bags, dropping the collected fruit into one. "It *is* quiet at this time of day," he said. "I usually like it."

He looked as good as he had that morning—still in faded blue jeans, but now with a fresh gray T-shirt that outlined his muscles. His hat sat familiarly low on his forehead, and the look he gave her out from under the brim didn't seem as scowling. It looked *curious*, maybe. Confused. Probably at the weird woman he didn't really know how to deal with. She was trying to do business with him, but also flirting with him. Now he knew she was cursed. He knew she was prone to stumbling. And talking too much when tipsy. He knew she'd had a crush on him when they were younger, and that she acted just as silly and giddy now if the moonlight hit him in a certain way. He knew she couldn't fit through a window and that she attracted bats and insects. And that she might kiss him at any given moment.

"That's not all you're eating, is it?" he asked, scowling at the granola bars.

She turned to work her key and jiggle the door. "Is there something you want, Adam?"

The door gave way, and she lunged inside, unloading her bags onto the dining table. Once her arms were empty, she turned to find him hesitating in the doorway. "You can come in."

He entered as if the house were haunted and added the other two bags to the mix, staring at them as if searching for something to say. He probably didn't know how on earth to deal with her at this point. She should put him out of his misery.

"Is this about MacGregor?" she asked.

"No. That's not why I'm here. I did talk to him today, but he's remaining tight-lipped about his plans. He said he wants to experience the dude ranch first. So I don't have an answer for you yet."

"Is this about that almost-kiss last night?" she blurted. *There.* That should get rid of him.

He rubbed the side of his nose and avoided her eyes. "That's no problem, Paige. I knew you had too much to drink."

She began organizing the few food items. "It won't happen again. I mean, the blathering and the trying to get you to kiss me and everything—that won't happen again. The having too much to drink might, if we're being honest."

"Not a problem."

"Well, I have been a problem, right?"

She watched him squirm. This was always where her conquests usually ended. Adam would never be interested in her because she was the comedienne. The Lucille Ball. Guys found her fun to hang out with, but she wasn't the elegant, classy woman men fell in love with and wanted to get into bed with and wanted to see again. Why couldn't she *ever* be the classy, sexy Lauren Bacall?

"You weren't a problem," he said. "You were fun."

She started slamming her groceries onto the cupboard shelves. "Even this past week—the house, the electricity, the shattered window, the bats."

"You're not a problem, Paige. Fixing the house up can only help me sell, too. And I came to say thanks and ask you a favor, in fact."

Her hand stalled halfway to the cupboard with a jar of peanut butter. *A favor?* She half wanted to know what it was and half wanted to drag out the suspense for a few more minutes so she could enjoy this new Adam—this one who was perhaps a little embarrassed and damned cute. She turned toward him.

"First, I need to thank you," he said.

"*Thank* me?"

"For what you said about Amanda last night. You were right. She needed to hear me talk about Samantha."

"You talked with her about Samantha?"

A flash of pride shot through her that he'd listened to what she'd said last night, and that he'd acted on it, and—most important—that it had worked. Paige was glad that Amanda probably got to hear a little affirmation and love. But then, as he nodded, a crushing sense of jealousy pervaded her. And, of course, embarrassment came right on the heels of that. She was happy for Amanda and didn't want to deny the girl any happiness, but her old childish jealousies about what Adam loved about Samantha were shoving to the forefront again.

Paige unloaded her cans of green beans.

Adam, meanwhile, tapped his finger on the edge of the table in a distracted, erratic rhythm. "So the favor. I, uh . . ." He shrugged.

She folded her paper bags and stared at him, waiting. Whatever it was, it might work to her advantage. If she could help him with a second thing and prove she wasn't a complete fool, he might more seriously consider helping her with the whole Dorothy Silver situation. Even if MacGregor was planning on buying the property, maybe she could still borrow the meadow for a short time. If they timed it right, she could have the whole gazebo deconstructed again by the time he moved in. She just had to figure out how to ask Adam about it.

"Do you know what a flatiron is?" he suddenly asked.

The question startled her for a second, but then she remembered the conversation she'd overheard in town the other day. She smiled as she folded the last bag. "Yes, I do."

"Is there any chance you could help me find one for Amanda?"

She looked at him sideways.

"It's for her birthday. I'm thinking you understand her, and I don't know what I'm looking for. I know you just got back from town, but I'll drive. And I've got faster wheels. I'll even throw in dinner."

She tucked the bags into the pantry. It *would* be nice to spend more time with him. She could maybe have a second chance at a first impression. Or was it her fourth chance at a second impression? Or her third chance at a third impression? Either way, she was trying to impress him in a business sense now, not trying to get him to notice her body. Right?

But she shouldn't go back into town. She'd barely gotten through town those first two times without being spotted.

"I'd like to help," she said. "But honestly, I'm trying to keep from being seen. I don't want my sisters to know I'm here yet."

"Ah. That's right. The long story. Maybe you can explain all that to me." He wandered into the kitchen and looked around a little. "I can help you keep a low profile. And we don't have to eat dinner there—we can bring something back."

"What about the dude group?"

"I have three more hours while they're out on a practice ride. We can have dinner—just us. I'll make something at my place."

Paige was surprised that he wanted to spend so much time with her after her revelations last night. Maybe he didn't think she was crazy.

"You cook?" she asked.

He gave her a crooked grin. "I didn't say I'd *cook* something at my place. I said *make*. I'm thinking sandwiches."

"Sandwiches are part of your repertoire?"

"It's a pretty limited repertoire. It's that or eggs or salsa."

She smiled. She felt as if she'd received a second chance. "Sandwiches sound fine. You're on."

CHAPTER 13

They rumbled back to town in Adam's Ford F-150. Paige had to admit it felt good to be in a car with some power again, versus those wimpy golf carts. And sitting so close to Adam's flexing forearms didn't hurt, either.

"I thought cars weren't allowed on the island," she said.

"In town."

"But we're going to town."

He threw her a sly smile. "We'll park on the outskirts."

"Are you *always* a rebel?"

He looked truly surprised by that. "There may or may not be a rebel in this car, but it certainly isn't me."

"Aren't you the one who smoked the cigarettes behind the Industrial Tech building and flew the fast plane?"

"Those were my young and stupid days. And planes are supposed to fly fast. I've never been called rebellious in my life."

She turned to gawk at him.

He glanced over at her. "What?"

"Are you forgetting who you're talking to here? Remember, I knew you when you were a teenager."

He stared out the window for a minute, then laughed. "You probably remember more than I do. Maybe you're right. Okay, I haven't been called rebellious since I was twenty. How's that?"

She sat back in her seat. "I'll buy that. Do you miss it?"

He kept his eyes on the road for another two turns, then shook his head. "I've had a lot of people to take care of. My brother, Noel, got to be the rebellious one. Or the irresponsible one, I guess. And everyone loves him. So maybe I'm a little jealous of that, but I don't miss being rebellious."

"You wear the cloak of responsibility well anyway," she said. "Thank you for taking care of me last night. You were very honorable."

She thought she saw him lift his eyebrows at that, but he didn't answer.

But she felt as if she could move on now.

"I'm glad you talked with Amanda," she said.

His smile came back. "She gave me about ten minutes of her time. But that was ten minutes more than usual. And only because I talked about Samantha."

Paige took a deep breath. She couldn't decide if she wanted to know what good things he'd said about Samantha or not. But maybe she could be the better, more mature Paige. She dove in. "What did you tell her about her mom?"

"For some reason, I remembered that Samantha always painted her toenails and fingernails wild colors. Amanda was painting hers, and it triggered the memory. And then I remembered that Samantha liked horseback riding. And I told Amanda that her mom was pretty and looked like her."

Paige nodded. That wasn't so hard. "That sounds perfect. How did she react?"

"Like I said, she only gave me ten minutes. But she smiled once. And she looked right at me. And she shared half a dessert with me. I call that a huge success. I can't thank you enough."

They pulled into a dirt parking lot at the base of the mountain and readied to walk the block over from there. The lot was huge—designed to hold tourist buses and other large vehicles that were used on the back canyon roads and throughout the hilly interior. Paige glanced around as they crossed the street into the main part of town, hoping not to see Olivia's or Natalie's golf carts.

"She asked if Samantha had any other friends on the island," Adam said as they shuffled along Main Street. "Would you consider yourself a friend?"

Paige blinked back her surprise. A *friend*? Not at all. Samantha was the source of every one of Paige's first bouts of jealousy.

"I didn't really know her," she said to get out of it. "She was a lot older than me. You older kids hung out pretty separately."

Adam nodded. "That's true. Do you remember anything about her, though? Maybe you could say a few things to Amanda?"

"I could try."

Damn. Insult to injury. But Paige would do it for Amanda. She felt so sorry for her.

Paige yanked her sunglasses out of her bag and shoved them onto her face, ducking once more to make sure she didn't see anyone she knew.

Adam slid a grin down at her. "I hardly recognize you."

"Yeah, this isn't working. It probably wasn't a good idea to chance this twice in one day."

"Wanna wear my hat?"

"I didn't think that thing ever left your head in the out of doors."

"Special circumstances." He plopped it onto her head, and it fell slightly over her eyes. She pushed it back a little, but—between it and the sunglasses—it did a decent job of hiding her face. Plus, her sisters would never in a million years think to look for her under a cowboy hat. Or walking alongside Adam Mason.

"So what's this long story that's causing you to hide from your sisters?" he asked as they arrived at the market.

"Maybe I'll tell you at dinner."

Adam opened the front door for her, the bell jangling their arrival. Mr. Fieldstone looked up from the counter. He seemed to be reading one of the romance novels Doris had been recommending the other day, and he marked his halfway spot with a Lavender Island postcard.

"Hey, Adam," he said.

Adam nodded. "Mr. Fieldstone."

"Come back for that curling iron? Oh, hey, is that the little lady who wanted it? I've been hearing you might have a new girlfriend up there."

Paige dashed behind the first aisle.

"Uh, no. That's . . ." Adam glanced up at her and pointed lamely while he let the thought trail off.

Paige made a shushing pantomime and motioned frantically with her hand to follow her.

He ducked behind the aisle with her, barely suppressing a grin. "Is this your idea of not calling attention to yourself?" he whispered.

She tugged his arm toward the hair supplies, and they landed in front of the display together, investigating the flatirons. Paige was surprised there were so many.

"Let's go with this one," he said.

"Why that one?"

"It's the most expensive. It must be the best."

"Wait. It depends on her hair. Let me read the boxes."

Paige studied each model, then found the one that would suit Amanda's hair texture best and shoved it at him. He asked about the magnifying mirrors, brushes, and hair bands next, so she picked out an array of items that seemed like things the teenager would want or need, then tucked them into his waiting arms and sent him to the counter.

"Wait. Gert says I need a card."

They made their way to the other end of the store, Adam grabbing a few more things on the way, like luncheon meats and a loaf of bread. Watching his arms get more and more loaded, Paige found a basket to hold everything; then she let Adam read the cards while she selected wrapping paper.

"Do you like this?" she asked, holding out a tie-dye pattern that looked like Amanda.

He nodded absently as he kept reading.

She thought it was sweet that he took the birthday cards so seriously. After reading four or five more, he shook his head. "None of these seems right."

"What's wrong?"

"I don't even know her. These are sentiments a dad would have if he knew the slightest thing about his daughter."

Paige reached out to put a hand on his forearm. Once she realized how intimate it seemed, though, she quickly jerked it away.

But not before he had traced all her movements.

He cleared his throat. "Anyway, Gert said I should write something. I'd find something plain, but I want something that doesn't have flowers on it. That doesn't seem like Amanda."

"You're right. She did have a Grateful Dead T-shirt on the other day—does she like music?"

He seemed to think that over. "She does have her earbuds in all the time."

"You said she was painting her nails?"

"Yes."

"How about this one, then?" Paige selected a card that had a picture of bluish-silver nail polish bottles and a pair of headphones on the front, with a simple "Happy 16th" on the inside.

"Perfect." Adam nodded and turned toward the counter.

As they rounded the side, though, Paige spotted Olivia coming through the door with eight-year-old Lily.

"Oh no!" She flattened herself against the chip display.

Adam slid back with her. "Sister?"

She nodded.

He peered through the stems of some balloon bouquets. "Niece?"

Another nod. She was too afraid to speak and have her voice carry. Lily would probably notice her before Olivia did—they'd spent so many weekends playing together when Paige visited, so many evenings rubbing each other's backs and singing songs. Lily had called her cell just yesterday expressing disappointment that Paige wasn't visiting this weekend.

Adam leaned down toward her ear. "Slide out around the back of the aisles." He slipped his car keys into her hand. "I'll meet you at the car."

His deep, whispered voice, combined with his warm breath dancing along the edge of her ear, sent a soft shiver down her arms. His hand spanning the small of her back solidified the thrill. But she felt the shove. She scurried down the aisle, toward the back, and crossed carefully past the paper plates, the canned-soup display, and an impressive sculpture made with Gatorade bottles. She tugged the cowboy-hat brim lower over her eyes and readjusted her sunglasses.

At the main aisle, she took a few more peeks around the corner and then made a dash for the glass door. Just as she barreled through—the bell bouncing chaotically against the glass—she thought she heard Lily say her name.

She moved faster down the sidewalk until she could cut across the alley behind Once Upon a Toy. She knew a shortcut back there. Once in the alleyway leading to the parking lot, she broke into a jog across the pavement as her cell phone began ringing out the chorus of "Dancing Queen."

Damn. Olivia's ringtone.

◆ ◆ ◆

Adam found his little masquerader crouched in the front seat, ten-gallon hat pulled low over her eyes as she peeked over the dashboard.

"Good work, Bonnie." He couldn't quite contain his grin as he tossed the bags in the back.

"Not bad yourself, Clyde."

Adam gunned the truck out of the parking lot, dust flying behind them.

"Though you were a little slow to the getaway car," she said. "What took you so long?"

"Mr. Fieldstone decided he needed to interrogate me on my new girlfriend."

"Ah. Yes, apparently you and your other new girlfriend are the talk of the town."

"What are you talking about?"

"When I was down here a couple of days ago, a few of the locals were discussing you in the market. Doris and Marie, I think, and Kilner."

"Oh God, Kilner."

"I know. He's the worst gossip ever."

"What were they saying?"

"Well, Kilner had apparently glimpsed Amanda and was speculating on who she was."

Adam looked over at her with a wince of disgust. "Do I want to know?"

"No, you don't."

"He's such an idiot."

"Agreed. I would have defended you and explained that she was your daughter, but I didn't know what you wanted them to know."

"And you're trying to keep a low profile."

"I would have defended you anyway."

He glanced at her again and lifted an eyebrow.

"Seriously. I don't like gossips," she said.

"Well, that wasn't the girlfriend Mr. Fieldstone was talking about tonight. He meant you."

They bounced over some uneven terrain, and Paige's heartbeat escalated—she wasn't sure if it was the bumping tires, or the fact she was sitting so close to his thigh and forearm, or the fact that he'd just mentioned her and "girlfriend" in the same sentence, but she was enjoying herself.

"I'm sure you had a wonderful time explaining that," she said. "You didn't give *me* away, did you?"

"Nah. I said very loudly that you were my mistress."

Paige's pulse accelerated even more.

"Did you seriously say *mistress*?"

"Yeah." He laughed.

"Who uses the word *mistress* these days? That doesn't even make sense."

"That's your main objection? My word choice?"

"You're going to set off a whole new slew of rumors, you know. No wonder everyone talks about you—you're probably feeding them all kinds of stories."

"No one needs to feed them stories, Paige."

They stared out separate windows for a second, possibly thinking about the rumors that had spread about each of them so long ago.

"But that *is* kind of funny," Paige admitted. "Mistress."

Adam met her smile. "Your sister and your niece were both staring out the window after you left, though. I don't think my ploy worked, and you might have been noticed."

"I know. Olivia called my cell. She left a message that Lily thought she saw me. But then she had a good guffaw over the cowboy hat and seemed to dismiss the whole preposterous notion."

Adam frowned. "What's wrong with cowboy hats?"

She laughed. "Nothing, Mr. Mason." She plucked his hat off her head and set it back on his own.

"Don't call me that."

"Why not?"

"Reminds me of my dad." He readjusted the hat lower toward his eyes and then glanced over and soothed his harsh tone with another playful grin that sort of melted her for a second. "So if we go back and I make you dinner, will you tell me the long story?" he asked.

"Your making me dinner was payback for my coming down here with you. We're already even."

"Ah. Of course. You drive a hard bargain, Bonnie."

"I've been told, Clyde."

"Name your stakes, then."

She thought that over. "I'll tell you the long story if you tell me the whole story with Samantha."

"You already know it."

"I was tipsy, remember?"

"There's not much to tell."

"I'm sure there's something to tell."

He shrugged. "You'll be disappointed, but if you insist."

"I insist. So have you ever seen the one with Faye Dunaway and Warren Beatty?"

"*Bonnie and Clyde*? Sure."

"You have?" She sat up straighter. "Do you like old movies?"

"Remember Bob? He's a big fan. He makes me watch them."

"Really? Do you have a favorite?"

"I'll have to think about that."

"What's Bob's favorite?"

Adam laughed. "Anything with a beautiful woman in it."

"Did he see *Bonnie and Clyde*, then?"

"I'm sure he did."

"I always loved Faye Dunaway."

"You look like her, actually."

Paige leaned back in her seat and inhaled the deep, masculine sandalwood scent of him that pervaded the cab, then marveled that he'd told her she looked like a young Faye Dunaway.

"I always thought she looked so sophisticated," she said, almost as much to herself as to him.

"You're very pretty, Paige."

Her heart might explode. She stared out the window and waited for something terrible to happen. But when nothing did, she tempted the curse and kept talking.

"Thank you. But I really mean sophisticated. I always wanted to look sophisticated, classy, and get those meaty, serious roles, you know?"

"Oh yeah, the acting. What kind of acting do you do, exactly?"

"Mostly commercial work. My mom got me into it when I was fifteen."

"Wow, that's a long time."

Paige shrugged. "It was a slow build. I'd just do one commercial a year when I was a teenager, but it saved me a nice college fund. Since then, I've ramped it up a little because it pays the bills."

"What commercials have you been in?"

"Um. Recently? Well, last year I played a soccer player for a tampon commercial, and an older sister who gets bonked on the head in a Toyota commercial, and for the last three years I've played a recurring role as a piece of broccoli."

Adam slid a glance her way. "Broccoli?"

"There's money in dental commercials." She tried to inject her voice with as much dignity as she could muster. "Anyway, Dirk's trying to get me a real role."

"Oh, that's right. Dirk—the idiot who thinks you need to lose weight."

Paige let a grateful smile slip. "Thanks, Adam."

"You're welcome, Paige."

Adam shoved the door open in his pine-paneled kitchen and motioned for Paige to take a seat. He dropped half the bags on the kitchen counter, then took Amanda's gifts and wrapping paper to the back bedrooms.

"She's not here," he said when he came back out, rolling up his sleeves.

"Where does she go?"

"Sometimes she takes a walk by the pond, or sometimes to the stables."

Paige watched him scrub his hands and forearms with some kind of industrial soap.

"Do you want me to help you wrap everything?"

"No, I'll do it late at night when she's asleep."

As he rummaged in the fridge, all she could see was his behind, which filled out his Levi's quite nicely, she couldn't help but notice. *Damn.* Sixteen years later and she was still gawking at him as if she were thirteen. Would she *ever* stop finding him attractive? She tried to distract herself with a stack of paper napkins on the table.

"So tell me the long story." He brought his head out of the fridge and threw a bunch of cheese selections on the table.

"You don't really want to hear it."

"Sure I do."

Paige began making paper fringe. "Well, my sisters and mom and I don't see eye to eye about what to do with Gram's house."

He came back with two knives, two plates, some mustard, and the three loaves of bread he'd just bought at the store. "That's not a very long story. So you and your mom want to sell, and your sisters don't?"

"It's not that simple. My mom and I want to revitalize it for Dorothy first."

"So what's your connection to Dorothy Silver?"

"My mom and I are fangirls of the old movie stars. Dorothy Silver is someone I've always idolized—I, of course, watched *Last Road to*

Nowhere a million times, with Gram's house in it and all. And I knew Gram had been friends with Dorothy back when the filming was going on up here. So anyway, I work at the Hollywood Film Library in Beverly Hills, and—"

"Wait. I thought you were in commercials?"

"Well, you know, between roles. I work there most of the time. I'm the receptionist. And lots of movie stars come in and want to rent space to watch old movies for research. So one day, Dorothy Silver walked in. I about died. I introduced myself to her and told her I was Helen Grant's granddaughter and visited Nowhere Ranch all the time, and she invited me to lunch. So I went, and when I told her about my mom, she told me about her upcoming wedding to Richard Crawford and asked *my mom* to do her wedding." Paige shook her head. She still couldn't believe it. "My mom's wedding business could use this lift. Mom's been ill for the last year, and our business has taken a hit."

Adam stalled opening the mustard jar. "I didn't know that."

"Cancer."

Adam put everything down. "I'm sorry, Paige."

"I know Ginger's not your favorite person, so I didn't want to say anything."

"No, she's not. But I'm not an asshole. I don't like to hear that about anyone."

"Thank you. She's strong. Her prognosis is good, and she'll fight with everything she's got. But chemo has taken its toll, and she's been too weak to handle a lot of business. She didn't want to give up this Dorothy Silver opportunity, so she asked me to help. And then—do you want to hear the most amazing part?"

"I haven't heard it yet?"

"Dorothy wants me to play her in a movie about her!" Paige could hardly keep the squeal out of her voice. "The casting starts the day after the wedding, so she said she'd fly me to LA immediately and tell the director I had her highest endorsement."

"Sounds like a dream come true for you."

She sighed. "It is." She didn't mention that the real dream was simply getting the money for the yoga studio. Adam would surely find that silly.

He kept his eyes on her as he unscrewed the condiment jars. "And your sisters?"

"My sisters think we're being stupid. They want Mom to rest and get well. They don't think I'll get the part anyway. They think Dorothy will back down on everything. They want to donate the property to the island historical society, or sell to MacGregor. But . . . I don't know about MacGregor."

"What do you mean?"

"Something didn't seem right about him when he was making his phone calls to us over these past months."

Adam looked up at her. "What specifically didn't seem right?"

"I can't explain it. It's just a feeling."

He frowned. "You're not saying that to get me not to sell to him, are you?"

"Of course not. You can't do business on feelings."

He nodded. "Agreed."

Paige continued shredding the napkin while Adam pushed the condiments across the table toward her.

"So you're here, basically doing all the work yourself, with Ginger sick and your sisters not on board?" he asked.

"Well, I'm supposed to be assessing the situation. And . . ."

She pretended to survey the luncheon meats.

"And what?" he asked.

She shrugged. "And talking you into helping us."

He pushed the bread choices in her direction. "Paige, I'm sorry for the situation you're in, but I can't make financial decisions based on that."

"I understand. I'll take that one." She pointed to the rye.

"I have to hurry and sell, or this place is going to lose even more money. And Amanda—she wants out of here. She was accepted into a prestigious art school in Alabama, and I'd like to get her back there before school starts."

"Amanda's an artist?"

"I've never actually seen her art, but I did see the letter of acceptance."

"I could see her wanting to escape the island. I didn't like it as a teenager, either."

"I'm with you. When I was a teenager, I wanted out of here in the worst way."

"It seems a little stifling."

"Agreed."

"Too much gossip, too many rumors, hard to escape a reputation."

"You're preaching to the choir."

"I don't know how my sisters can stand it. They say it's nice if you're in love, though."

He slid a plate across the table to her. "Is that right? Maybe that's been my problem."

Paige smiled and studied the sandwich he'd just made her, thinking of how simple and comforting it looked, like something from her childhood. He'd even cut the sandwich in half. She poked at her crust and tried to get up the nerve to ask the question she'd been wanting to ask: "So you've never been in love, then?"

Adam's mustard knife halted. "That's a pretty big question."

"Is that your way of saying you don't have an answer?"

"No, it's my way of saying that question might cost you."

A little prickle of awareness ran down Paige's arms. "Cost me what?"

He opened a bag of potato chips. "A revealing answer about yourself."

"Like what?"

"Tell me about the last boyfriend in LA. Or the current one."

Paige froze. She thought maybe he'd ask about her family, not her love life. Could she continue talking to him this way and keep things professional? If he flirted with her, could she resist flirting back?

But she knew he would go only so far with these questions. He was as aware of their precarious situation as she was—she needed land from him, and involving any kind of feelings would be stupid for either of them. As long as they both stayed distant, and kept things light, they could make this friendly. She'd just have to be sure not to flirt back. Too much.

"It was, um . . ." She thought briefly about making something up. Her love life was rather embarrassing, pathetic as it was. But then she changed her mind. She hated liars.

She picked up her sandwich. "The last man I dated was Todd."

He made a motion with his fingers to give him more.

"He was an investment banker. I met him at a party. He had a dog named Duncan."

"I don't care about his damned dog, Paige."

"You don't?" She smiled playfully.

He chuckled and studied a potato chip. "No."

"What *do* you care about?" she asked between bites.

"Why and when you broke up."

The potato chips suddenly demanded her attention. She couldn't maintain eye contact with him now. This was definitely flirting.

"Well," she finally said, "the 'why' involved a heart-shaped, voice-recorded frame."

Adam sat back in his chair in a languid pose and propped his ankle on his knee. "You'll have to give me more than that."

"He used to go on these business trips, just for a day or two, and one day I was over there while he was packing, and he had this little red heart-shaped frame he was putting in his suitcase. So he showed it to me, and it had a picture of *me* in it."

The fact had stunned her at the time. They'd been dating for only four weeks. The idea that he had a framed heart photo of her for his suitcase, like some married businessman, freaked her out.

"So he wanted to record my voice on the frame, too," she said. "He wanted me to say, 'I love you.' Right into the frame!"

She waited for Adam to mirror the shock she always felt when she told this story, but—like everyone else—he looked at her as if he couldn't see the problem.

"And you . . . weren't there yet?" he asked, trying to follow along.

"Not at all."

"How long had you been together?"

"A few weeks."

He nodded thoughtfully. "Sex yet?"

She raised her eyebrows. "I don't think that's any business of yours."

"Just trying to put the pieces together," he said, shrugging innocently.

Her cheeks were suddenly getting hot, and she made a big show of moving things around her plate.

"And when was this?" he asked.

"Four months ago." She pushed the plate away. "All right, my turn. So have you ever been in love? Were you in love with Samantha?"

"I'm still working on Ted here."

"Todd."

"Todd, right. So you broke up with him because he wanted you to say you loved him after a few weeks, and it's a personal policy that you don't make those kinds of decisions after just a few weeks."

"Right."

"And that's why you broke up?"

"Well, no."

He moved a few chips around and waited for the rest of the story. She almost didn't tell him. It was so pathetic. "I broke up with him because I found another heart-shaped frame."

"And?"

"It had someone else in it."

"Where did you find it?"

"In his bedroom drawer."

"You were looking in his bedroom drawer?"

"I have trust issues."

Adam nodded.

"Don't nod like you understand this," she said. "He was a jerk. He was lying to me, and sleeping with someone else, and he couldn't be trusted. Men can't be trusted. I'd been through this before, and that's why I was looking in his bedroom drawer. I felt vindicated that I was right."

Adam stared at his plate of chips.

"And we're done with Todd," she said too loudly. "He's not very interesting. It's my turn now."

Adam looked ready to argue, but the back door swung open from the lobby, and Mendelson popped his head in. "Hey, chief. The riders are back."

"I'll be right there." Adam scooted his chair back and gathered his jacket and keys. "Sorry, Paige. You can stay as long as you like. Have more sandwiches. I have to start a campfire."

Paige watched him walk out and instantly regretted getting so worked up. She never knew when to shut up. Adam made her so nervous. Had she just admitted that she could turn into a psychotic drawer-searching lover? And that she had trust issues?

If he'd had even an inkling of an idea about letting her kiss him (just once) or maybe taking her up on that dance (just once), she was sure those thoughts were gone now. She probably looked like a lunatic. A real femme fatale. But not the gorgeous, sexy Lana Turner kind. More like the wild-haired, raging Glenn Close kind.

She ate the rest of her sandwich in silence and then cleaned up the table.

Adam was probably done with her now.

Which, really, was the best thing.

Her mom might even be proud of her.

Adam jogged out to the riders and swore at himself for being such an idiot. Was he just asking about Paige's *boyfriends*? What the hell was wrong with him?

He had a business to sell, a prospective owner to impress, a dude ranch to run for a weekend, a staff to take care of before he closed up, and a daughter to move off the island and enroll in school in a couple of months.

Trying to learn more about Paige was getting him nowhere.

He could be friendly with her—she'd helped him out with Amanda, and he liked helping her with Helen's place, and he liked smiling at the things she did and said—but everything had to stop there. He had to stop watching her lips. He had to stop asking about her boyfriends. He had to stop caring whether men gave her heart-shaped frames, or how long she waited to have sex with them, or how long ago they may have broken up. Those details were not his business. And no matter to him in any way whatsoever. And he didn't even know if he could trust her—she might be striking up a friendship to get him to hand over land. Just like Ginger.

They could have a tentative friendship over the next few weeks, but that was it. He was leaving. And she was too dangerous to have meaningless sex with: she wanted something from him, and he couldn't let himself forget that.

Although she didn't seem the type to be manipulative. Despite her skillful mother, her goth-eyeliner past, and her love for adrenaline and adventure, she had a vulnerability underlying that bravado that was impossible to miss. And he didn't want to hurt her. She'd obviously been hurt by jackasses in her past, like Ted or Todd, and maybe even this Dirk guy. And he didn't need to be part of a new parade of jerks. Lord knows he could be. And maybe it was because he'd taken care of Helen and her dogs and her house all those years, but he felt oddly protective of her granddaughter. Not that Paige was like a house or dogs or property, but something about her made him want to protect her. And that meant from guys like him.

His attempts to get closer had to stop now.

The cowboys were gathered outside, with Joseph and Mendelson starting the campfire and getting the grill fired up. They usually did a cookout on the first night—it gave the guests a chance to get to know one another, and gave the wranglers a chance to assess who would be able to do what on the rides, especially the overnights. Of course, this dude group was a little different from most—MacGregor was just trying it out with his guys to assess if he wanted to take it over. He wanted the property either way, but he wasn't sure about the dude-ranch business. Adam didn't blame him. It was a lot of work. But he'd show him a good time anyway. And they had the bison to bring in.

"Hey, gentlemen," Adam said, touching the brim of his hat.

The other guys greeted him and asked him to join their campfire. He didn't usually—he typically acted as working wrangler—but in this case he was also a salesman. Joseph nodded his approval—he had the grill under control.

Adam sat down and shot the breeze with them, hearing about their first ride, knocking around some numbers with MacGregor, swapping stories with one of the others about rounding up cattle, which Adam explained was very similar to rounding up bison—only the bison were bigger and meaner. They would be doing that, too, later in the week.

"So how long have you known Paige Grant?" MacGregor asked, leaning toward him.

Hearing her name in such an unexpected way had Adam swiveling his head. "What?"

"Paige Grant. How long have you known her?"

"I, uh . . . I've known her family a long time. Why?"

"I want her property. If we expanded this"—MacGregor swept his arm toward Helen's place—"we could have a whole mess hall set up over there, with the view."

"I don't think the Grants are interested," Adam said.

"Oh, I know they aren't. That's why I asked how long you knew her. I saw her here this morning and wondered if you knew her better than I thought you did. And, more important, if you could use your influence to get her on board." MacGregor winked and followed that with a slimy smirk.

"Like I said, I don't think she's interested."

"If she's not interested, then I might not be, either."

Adam hid his sudden urge to bloody that smirk right off MacGregor's face. He adjusted his hat to get his anger under control.

Then he glanced in the direction of Helen's house, at the meadow where Paige wanted to start preparing for the Silver wedding, and realized things were about to get a lot more complicated.

CHAPTER 14

Paige traipsed through the meadow back to Gram's house to resume her most recent project.

But this time her thoughts kept stalling on Adam, and stayed there, swirling in confusion. She wanted to stay distant from him because it was easier to get business done, yet she loved making connections with him on a personal level. She wanted him to take her seriously, yet she loved how he smiled when she said something funny. She wanted to stay away from him so he didn't hurt her or break her heart again, yet she loved being near him and getting to know the adult Adam.

She was a mess.

It was maybe a little dangerous how much she actually *liked* him. She wasn't going to protect her heart this way. Even at the height of her past adoration, she'd always been aware of his arrogance, his stand-offishness, and his swagger—just the kind of confidence teenage girls swooned over, but women could quickly fall out of love with. Now she saw that that old standoffishness ran deep. It was less a confidence and more of a wall he put up, perhaps to protect himself, perhaps borne of losing his mother and growing up with George instead, and then developed by having so much responsibility put on his shoulders at a young age.

Learning these things about him, though, was not helping. It was not protecting her heart. It was not getting business done. It was not helping her mother, or helping Dorothy, or landing her a high-paying part, or furthering her dreams of a yoga studio.

She unlocked the door and threw her purse on the table. Click had been hiding around the side of the house, but she now made her way in right behind Paige.

"Hey, Click." She scooped up the kitten and carried her into the kitchen.

She hadn't even tried the electricity earlier that day, but now that it was dark, she welcomed the new fix.

She flipped on the switch.

Nothing.

Flipped it again.

Zero.

Click squirmed out of her arms, then landed with a tiny thump and began winding around Paige's legs, mewing.

Paige tiptoed through the darkened kitchen toward the circuit breaker, wondering what calamity she could have brought down on her shoulders now. A drip . . . drip . . . drip sounded in front of her. Coming from up high?

As the pieces started to come together for her, she frantically grabbed for Click. Just as her fingertips curled around the kitten's belly, a loud crack sounded, then a whoosh. Pieces of wood crashed to the floor. Insulation and dust swirled at her feet.

Paige screamed and flew out of the kitchen.

Click rocketed out of her arms—through the air—toward the open door.

And, next thing she knew, Gram's upstairs bedroom fell through the floor.

◆　◆　◆

Paige and Adam stood outside the house in the cool night air, staring up at it, Adam with his hands on his hips. An emergency vehicle's yellow lights flashed across his face.

"You're going to need a place to stay," he said.

Paige sighed and ran her hand down Click's back in the crook of her arm. She would. It would take a few days to get some industrial fans out here, clean up the leak, fix the plumbing, repair the floor, and make the house habitable again. This was going to set her project back two weeks at least.

"You can stay at my place," he said, his eyes still on the house.

"But the dudes are there now," she said. "You gave up my room. It's okay. I'll find a place in town."

"I have an extra room in the house."

Oh no, no, no, no. Paige's mind whirled through calculations of who would be hardest and easiest to avoid—Adam or her sisters. And Adam came out on the "hardest" end.

"I can't impose on you for that," she said. *But mostly I don't know if I can sleep, with you in a bedroom nearby . . .*

"Think of it as a favor," he said. "I have to leave on a pack trip with the group tomorrow, and I wasn't sure about leaving Amanda alone for three nights. She doesn't like to be in that big house alone, out in the middle of nowhere. It might be nice if someone stayed to keep her company."

"I don't know."

"C'mon. It works out for everyone." He tried to give her an encouraging smile, but doubt flashed in his eyes, and he looked away.

Paige followed suit.

This felt a little dangerous.

Like playing with another kind of fire.

Paige sat on the edge of the bed in Adam's guest room, staring through the window on the north side at the moon hovering over the pond.

She was truly cursed. This newest calamity was going to set her back too far, in both time and money. Her sisters were right about her, and her mother was right to worry. How on earth was she going to get all this fixed up and still plan a wedding for three hundred?

A knock sounded at the door, and she jumped.

"Paige, it's Adam."

"Come in," she said, even though she really couldn't take any more of him today—or of embarrassing herself in his presence. She didn't want him to see her in her SpongeBob SquarePants pajamas. Or with her hair all disheveled, or feeling as if she wanted to cry. But this was his house, so she'd be polite and then say she needed to turn in.

His footsteps sounded behind her. She reached up to smooth down her hair and realized there was still plaster in it.

"Are you okay?" His deep voice dropped to a low decibel—soft, tentative, as though he thought she might break apart. And, for some reason, that was all it took: the little piece of plaster in her hair, her deep-set frustration, her growing fear, and topped with his full-of-concern voice. Her nose prickled and tears threatened.

"I'm fine," she choked out.

He walked around the side of the bed and stared at her for a minute, as if she were a wild animal he wasn't sure what to do with. "Can I sit down?"

Afraid her voice would betray her if she spoke, she nodded. Her fingertips brushed the first errant tear from her cheek.

The bed creaked under his weight. A silence stretched between them. He leaned forward, elbows on his knees, and clasped his hands in front of him.

"Listen, Paige, I know you've been through a lot with that damned house, but I want you to know that I'll help with whatever you need when I get back. I already called Pedro to get his ass back out here ASAP, and I have two of the best plaster guys I know coming out tomorrow to lend you a hand. Okay? When I get back, we'll get it fixed up."

She sniffled and wiped at her face again. "Thank you for arranging that. You didn't have to. It's not your responsibility."

"I know. But I see you trying, and I admire how you keep picking yourself up and going, even when things aren't going your way. I want to help."

"I told you—I'm cursed."

"You're not cursed, Paige."

"When I'm here on the island, I'm cursed."

"The bats and the birds and all that?"

"Well, electric problems, too. Car accidents. Fires. Floods. You don't want to get messed up with me." She tried to give her voice some levity, but it wasn't coming out right. Instead, tears sprang forward again. And as soon as she thought about the truth of what she'd said, the tears burst out in an ugly cry, and she turned away.

"Oh, hey."

She sensed he was going to reach out to her but then seemed to change his mind. She probably looked like a terror.

"Hey, don't cry. We'll get it fixed up. I promise. I'll fix it for you."

The sweetness of that, combined with how pathetic she felt, made her want to cry even more, but she tried to pull herself together.

"What else do you need help with?"

She glanced over at him. What she needed was the meadow. But could she say that now? Would that make her too much like her mother? Or would she just be being honest?

"I did find the perfect gazebo for the ceremony," she said hesitantly.

He nodded slowly. "And?"

"I wondered if I could order it and start putting it up in the meadow?"

A thin veil of suspicion dropped over his features as he nodded and stared at the ground. "You do know that some of the meadow is in your family's name, right? My dad signed it over to your mom."

"I did know that, but I wasn't sure how much."

"About a hundred feet from your side door."

Paige nodded. From what she could tell in the movie, the gazebo sat more like two hundred feet away, right in the center of the meadow.

"If you overshot your mark less than fifty feet, I think I could overlook that," Adam said. "And I could probably talk MacGregor into it."

"Really, Adam?" Paige breathed out a sigh of relief. It wouldn't be exactly like the movie, but Paige could alert Dorothy to it and suggest enough angles to take pictures that no one would be able to tell.

He nodded but still wouldn't meet her eyes. "So no worries tonight, okay?" He rose.

She gave a chaotic nod.

"Stay as long as you like. Make yourself at home. I'll see you when I get back?"

She was relieved he was leaving. Her nose started to drip, and she didn't want him to see her looking any worse than she already did. She gave a quick nod to whatever he said and let him escape out the door.

As soon as he was gone, she flung herself onto her pillow and let herself sob, half with relief that this setback might not be as disastrous as she'd thought, and half with worry that she was more like her mom than she wanted to believe.

The next morning, Paige straightened her pajamas and shuffled into the kitchen to find the coffeepot. Her eyes were puffy, her throat was sore, and she felt spent from crying into the night. But she was at least relieved not to have to face Adam in this ugly state—she'd heard the entire group and their horses leave at four thirty.

A rustling sounded behind her. She whirled to see Amanda.

"So are you Adam's new girlfriend now?" Amanda continued into the kitchen and reached for a coffee cup. "You're making enough for both of us, right?"

"I, um . . ." Paige hit the "Off" button and quickly added enough for a second cup. "Sure. Your dad allows you to drink coffee?"

"I don't think he notices. I just drink the second cup he leaves in there."

"Okay. Well. Then." Paige wasn't sure how to handle this. She wanted to take her part of the bargain seriously about staying with Amanda, but Adam hadn't gone over any rules to follow. A cup of coffee wouldn't hurt a sixteen-year-old, right? Paige was pretty sure she was drinking coffee at that age. Probably doing exactly what Amanda was doing—sneaking the last cups out of a parent's machine.

Amanda fetched the extras—the creamer from the fridge and then a box of sugar from a cupboard. She seemed to know what she was doing. And thank goodness for the sugar. Amanda readied everything along the counter and then stood next to Paige, watching the coffee finish up.

"So are you?" Amanda asked.

"Am I what?"

"His new girlfriend?"

"Oh. No. Definitely not. I'm just a family friend. My gram used to own the house across the meadow. I used to spend summers here on the island. When I was about your age, in fact."

"Really?"

Paige gave a halfhearted, not-yet-induced-by-caffeine nod. She tried to duck her head to hide her puffy eyes. She might have to find some cucumber slices or tea bags or something.

Their coffee signaled its preparedness, and Paige poured the two cups. Amanda loaded hers with creamer and sugar and then passed each of the add-ons to Paige, who followed with nearly the same ratio.

"So has Adam told you about my mom?" Amanda's voice dropped, the maturing teenager gone now and replaced with a young girl filled with uncertainty.

"Yes." Paige sipped her coffee. "I knew your mom, in fact."

"You did?"

Here she went. She could do this. "Yes, she was a counselor at the camp down by the harbor, and I was one of the campers."

Amanda twisted toward her, mug in her hands. She looked very old and very young at the same time, cocking her head and staring at Paige.

"Actually, I guess I was younger than you," Paige went on. "I was thirteen. Your mom was about seventeen, and she led a lot of the girls' groups I was in. She was very pretty."

A tiny smile moved its way across Amanda's face.

"You look just like her," Paige added. "She was a good counselor. We all liked her. She had a great voice, and I remember she taught us some fun campfire songs. She also taught us how to French-braid hair."

Amanda's smile was full now. "What else?"

"Let's see . . . I remember her mostly with your dad. He was nuts about her. He stared at her all the time when we were sitting around the campfire, making lovebird eyes."

Amanda laughed a little—a combination of a little girl's giggle and a teenager's quest for subtlety and reserve. "Do you remember anything else?"

Paige's mind went straight to the fire. And to Samantha's parents—Amanda's grandparents, now that she thought about it—coming to the island to drag her away. And to Samantha and Adam's fight to stay. And to their constant escapes to the boathouse. And to all the drama that ensued.

But she couldn't tell Amanda those memories, so she took another sip to buy time and finally remembered something else. "She taught me how to make friendship bracelets."

Amanda laughed and stared into her coffee. "So you're not Adam's girlfriend, then?"

Paige blinked at the abrupt shift in subject. She didn't have a lot of experience talking to teenagers these days, and she wondered if she'd have to keep on her toes for these conversations. She also noted that Amanda never called him her dad. "No, I'm not his girlfriend."

"Then he's not the one who made you cry last night?"

Paige's cup halted midair.

"Tea bags will help that swelling go down." Amanda brushed sugar granules off the countertop. "I read that in *Seventeen* magazine."

"Thank you. I was thinking cucumbers."

"Tea bags are better."

Paige smiled.

"So I'm glad it wasn't Adam. Because I'd have to get mad at him. And maybe hide his Tabasco. Guys shouldn't make girls cry."

"Thank you, Amanda. That's sweet of you. I was just, um, sad and frustrated because of the house falling apart."

"Oh yeah. That sounded bad last night. I saw the emergency trucks."

"I'll bounce back." Paige lifted her chin.

She could do this. She always did.

And what kind words from Amanda.

"Hey, can you take me down to the harbor today?" Amanda asked.

Paige tried to keep up with the new change in topic and backpedaled with her brain. *Damn.* She should have asked Adam if there were any rules for Amanda. Was she being played right now?

"Does your dad let you go down there?"

"Yeah, he just won't let me drive."

"Well, that's smart."

"He said you were a grown woman, though, and you could do whatever you wanted, including drive the golf cart down the hill too fast even though you're not supposed to."

Paige lifted an eyebrow. "He said that?"

Amanda nodded.

A warm, tingly feeling slid through her veins that she was being discussed by Adam when she wasn't there. Although he was obviously extolling her more rebellious virtues. But still.

"Well, I think I can take you to the harbor today if you want. What time do you need to be there?"

"Three o'clock."

Paige nodded. "Okay. I have some work to do at Gram's most of the day, but I'll come back to get you this afternoon."

"Great." Amanda smiled and bounced off to her room.

Paige hoped this wasn't a terrible decision. She didn't know how to talk to teenagers, or fulfill requests, or avoid being played. She especially didn't want to make a bad decision in her brief stint of watching Amanda that would make life harder for Adam when he returned. And, truth be told, she wanted to impress him: he'd asked for a favor, and she wanted to come through. Especially after he was doing her such a huge favor with the meadow.

That's all this was.

He was doing her a favor, and she was doing him one.

As friends.

With Adam Mason.

Who would have ever thought?

CHAPTER 15

For the next few days, Paige and Amanda developed their routine. They'd start every morning with their shared coffee; Paige would do her hatha yoga on the front porch; Paige would head over to Gram's to oversee the damage repair and do what she could without getting in the way; they'd meet again to drive down to the harbor at three; Paige would pick her up at five; and then Paige would deliver Amanda for dinner at Bob and Gert's. Paige thought she was doing a pretty good job of her end of the bargain.

"Would you like to stay, too, dear?" Gert would ask each evening as she popped her head out the door and her gold-colored chignon shimmered.

Paige shook her head each time. Gert seemed like a lovely woman, but Paige didn't want to get too invested with Adam's friends and family, or too attached to the people here. "No, thank you—work to do," she'd say. Then she'd roll her cart back down the steep mountainside driveway.

The place Amanda had wanted to go at the harbor every day, it turned out, was the Friends of the Sea Lion rescue center, where Paige's hopefully-soon-to-be-brother-in-law Elliott worked.

Afraid Elliott or someone would recognize her, she shoved her sunglasses on tighter as she accelerated by, pulled down the borrowed cowboy hat, then parked a little up the road, waving to Amanda and ducking away.

During one of their morning coffee klatches, Amanda admitted she was going to the sea-lion center because of Garrett.

"Garrett Stone?" Paige had met Garrett several times during her stints helping at the center during their heavy-intake days.

Amanda nodded and blushed.

"He's cute, Amanda! And very sweet. How did you meet him?"

"His brothers work here on the ranch, and he came to visit them a few times."

"Who are his brothers?"

"Gabe and Gordon."

"Ah, of course." Now that Paige thought about it, the brothers all did look alike. It made sense now.

Amanda smiled, her spoon making tinkling noises against her mug. "But don't tell Adam."

"Why not?"

"He looks at Garrett funny when he's up here talking to me."

"I'm sure he's just being a protective dad."

"Well, I don't know what that means, but don't say anything, okay?"

Paige didn't really know what that meant, either. She'd never had her dad in her life—he'd left when she was a preschooler—so she didn't know what it would be like to have a father who wanted to protect you and had only your best interests at heart. At first she was sad that Amanda hadn't known that, either, but then it occurred to her: Amanda was getting a second chance. A wave of happiness swept over her for both the teenager and her dad.

"I think you'd be okay to tell him, but I won't say anything until you're ready," Paige said.

Amanda's shoulders relaxed on a sigh.

Paige just hoped again she was doing the right thing. She didn't want to ruin anyone's second chances.

On the day Adam was due to return, Paige puttered back over the hill from dropping Amanda off at Bob and Gert's and then pulled her cart around the back of Adam's ranch.

She would go in and pack, then quickly escape before Adam came home.

Gram's kitchen had been well repaired. The flooding was cleared up, the walls were being dried, and the new beams were going in. She probably could have gone home the night before, but she'd told Adam she'd stay the whole time with Amanda. Also, she sensed that Amanda liked company in such a sprawling house.

But, quite frankly, Paige didn't want to be around when Adam got back.

She'd missed him. Just remembering how sweet he'd been the night before he left, the way his voice rumbled in her belly, the secure presence of his forearms so close to her SpongeBob pajamas, the heat from his body, and the way he smelled—that whittled-wood-and-sandalwood smell that infused his house—made her long for him even more.

She wasn't thinking of him as a business partner.

Or as a friend doing favors.

She was a mess.

And being too near him would be flat-out dangerous.

The back door opened just as she finished throwing the last of her things into her backpack. Adam's heavy footsteps fell across the hall's wooden floor. Her pulse started to race.

"Amanda?" he called. "Paige?"

Her heart lifted to hear her name on his lips. Maybe because he remembered she might be there. But this was her falling for him again. She packed faster.

"I'm here."

She threw the last of her things into her bag and snatched up the cowboy hat she'd been borrowing to go incognito to town. As she swung toward the hall to rehang it, Adam materialized in her doorway.

He leaned in the doorjamb, a tired frown chiseled on his face. Blond stubble dotted his jaw—clearly a few days of riding behind him—and his eyes had a sleepy alertness that might seem paradoxical on anyone else but looked just right for a wrangler. He wore his riding clothes, with a thin sheen of dust on the thighs of his jeans. He looked tired and rugged and strong and sexy, and she wanted to climb him like a mountain right now.

"Where's Amanda?" he asked, breaking the spell.

"She's, uh . . ." Her voice came out in an embarrassing squeak. She cleared her throat and tried again. "At, um, Bob and Gert's. For dinner."

She whirled away and grabbed at a few items of clothing she'd left on a chair. Mostly she didn't want him to see her blush. Her wayward thoughts were suddenly getting more and more wayward.

"When will she be home?" he asked from behind her.

"She's been getting home about nine." She found a bra she'd flung onto the floor and a pair of underwear, and she wrestled with her backpack zipper to shove them in. "I think they watch a movie with her after dinner."

She told herself to simply ignore his rugged look and all that brawny sexiness. Maybe she could bolt for the door without looking up at him.

"So, um . . . thanks for letting me stay." She made a move, but he still stood in the doorway.

"Paige."

Ah, that deep voice. She was a goner. She knew she shouldn't, but she looked up at him.

"I'd like it if you would stay," he said.

Once again, he'd rendered her speechless. He'd probably been the only man able to do that ever in her life—back when she was thirteen, and now that she was almost thirty. She tried to make sure she didn't have a foolish, gaga look on her face. She wasn't drooling, was she?

He seemed to misread her silence as a refusal.

"I know I look like crap," he said. "And I probably smell worse. But if you could cool your heels for five minutes while I take a shower, I'll make a better entrance and say thank you properly, and maybe you'll stay for a quick dinner."

Paige didn't even know what the hell "thanking her properly" meant, but it sounded amazing.

"Um . . . okay." She was so damned easy.

She tried to ignore the dimples that appeared on his face as he nodded once and ambled back toward his room.

She might be in trouble.

Adam scrubbed the dust and dirt off his body, then stood in the shower for a minute, letting the water sluice over his head and contemplating where he might want to go with this.

Or where he *should* go.

That made more sense.

Where he *wanted* to go was easy—he wanted Paige. Desperately. Under him, on top of him, didn't matter. He wanted her in any way he could have her.

Walking up to the house, seeing Denny run toward him, knowing Amanda might be inside, and knowing Paige would be there, too, had given him the strangest sensation he'd ever experienced. As if he could imagine all of them greeting him like that, forever. But as soon as he had the thought, he dismissed it, focusing on petting Denny outside instead. Because Amanda and Denny were a given. But Paige was a strange addition to the equation. Because *forever* and *women*—even beautiful, vivacious women whom he'd been thinking about for days on the trail—were not words Adam thought of in the same sentence.

But he had to admit, he'd been thinking about her for a bizarre amount of time. Partly because MacGregor kept bringing her up, asking when Adam might start to put some pressure on her to sell, suggesting that he might do so by hinting at a promise of a relationship. "Women don't go for simple sex like we do," MacGregor had said, as a disgusting trail of spittle and barbecue sauce ran down the side of his face. "But if you promise them a future—a house, a baby, a dog—they'll roll over for anything you want. Try that, maybe."

Adam had clenched his fists, resisting the urge to pummel the smirk off MacGregor's face. He'd told himself he just had to listen to this crap for a few more days. Once they were in escrow, he could hate MacGregor all he wanted. And then all he'd have to worry about was keeping Paige off MacGregor's radar: Who knew what slimy tactics he'd pull with her, or if he'd pressure her to sell to him?

Over the few days, and at every mention of her name by MacGregor, Adam had ground his teeth.

She was too sweet. And vulnerable. And tough. All at the same time. She was fighting tooth and nail to fix that place. But what he admired even more was that she kept lifting herself up when things were going wrong. She came off as funny and confident most of the time, but seeing that vulnerable side of her brought out every fixer instinct he'd had. He wanted to fix her house, fix her sisters, fix any asshole boyfriends she'd had in her past, fix MacGregor's smirk, and make life easier for her.

Then came the lascivious thoughts. Which he'd planned to avoid. It wasn't lost on him that he'd agreed to lend her land as soon as he'd seen her cry. That made him more like his father than he cared to admit—blurring the line between business and beauty, responding to a woman who could make you feel things and do things that you might not do if you were in your right mind. The only difference was that George

Mason was further mired by having sex with his women, including Ginger. And Adam wasn't there yet. And he didn't intend to go there. It would just complicate everything.

So to walk in and see Paige looking fresh and strong and happy to see him, filling him with hope and that strange warmth he hadn't recognized, had simply sent him into a spiral of confusion.

Then finding out that Amanda was gone, which gave him a few hours alone with Paige, had suddenly put his libido into overdrive. And seeing Paige's bras and panties on the floor hadn't helped. Thank God she moved that lace out of his line of vision while he tried to cast his eyes away. Her cartoon pajamas the other night were cute, but that lace would be his undoing. He had to stop imagining what she wore to bed, although he'd come up with an entire wardrobe over the last four days. Which, in his mind, he'd stripped off every night.

Damn.

He was going to have to control himself.

He was not a slimeball like MacGregor, with barbecue sauce and spittle drooling out of his mouth. He was not a pushover like his father, able to be manipulated because he couldn't control himself.

Plus, he *liked* Paige.

And he should protect her, as Helen would expect.

And she'd been through a lot. She needed someone to help her and be on her side.

So he was going to be a gentleman. He would make her dinner, thank her like a human being, and then help her stay or go—whatever she felt more comfortable with, given the state of Helen's house.

He turned the shower off and told himself to behave.

And stop thinking about what she wore to bed.

And how he'd take it off her.

God help him.

◆ ◆ ◆

Paige wished she had something nice for Adam to come home to—maybe some kind of food he liked—but she hadn't planned to be here when he returned. While he was showering, she scoured the fridge for leftovers, then spotted the strata Amanda had made the other morning. She pulled it out of the fridge, heated it up, threw together some lettuce and spinach leaves in a salad, and set everything on the table.

"What's this?" he asked emerging from the bedroom hallway in clean jeans and bare feet, buttoning up his shirt.

"Dinner."

"You cooked dinner for me?"

He looked so stunned and—if she wasn't mistaken—touched that she almost wanted to lie and say yes. But she couldn't.

"Um . . . no. I didn't cook it. Amanda did. She pulls together whatever you have in the house. This was bread, ham, and eggs—I guess from your limited repertoire of sandwiches and eggs. But either way, it's here for you. You look exhausted."

"Amanda made this?"

"Yeah. Did you know she could make a strata?"

"Not at all." Still looking baffled, he made his way to the table, then rubbed his hand over his jaw. "So all this time, she's known how to cook, but she's been suffering through my attempts?"

"Maybe she didn't want to hurt your feelings." Paige smiled. "Here, have a seat." She joined him at the table. "Did MacGregor have a good time?"

"I think he did."

"Did he make any decisions?"

"Unfortunately, he still won't commit to a sale. I think he's playing games with me. Can you be patient for a while longer?"

Paige shrugged. "I'm not going anywhere."

He motioned with his fork to an empty plate. "You're going to join me and eat, too, right?"

"I wasn't going to stay. I'll just grab something later at—"

"Paige, really. Share this with me."

She sighed. Sitting here with Adam, acting as if they were actually dating, or at least friends, might be painful or thrilling—she wasn't sure which. She didn't want to get hurt by pining after him again. She didn't want to get close, or fall head over heels in a crush and have him not return any sentiment whatsoever. But she was older now. Maybe she could handle it. She let him cut her a slice.

"So what did you and Amanda talk about?" he asked.

"I got a chance to talk to her about her mom—any good things I remembered. And—oh! Was it okay that I took her down to the harbor every day? She wanted to go. And was it okay I let her drink coffee?"

He smiled. "Coffee was okay. I think she's been sneaking mine. Where was she going in the harbor? She'd asked me about that, too."

"To the Friends of the Sea Lion center. I think she was volunteering."

"Really?"

Paige wanted to tell him about Garrett, but she didn't want to break Amanda's confidence. Amanda had so few people here she knew or could trust that Paige didn't want to ruin that. Instead, she stabbed at her salad so her face wouldn't give anything away.

"Thank you again for the use of the meadow," she said. "I ordered the gazebo. It should be here in a day or so."

Adam looked away and nodded silently.

"I hope you think I did a good job here in return," she added nervously. "Amanda was great."

Adam cut another piece of strata with his fork. "It was nice having you here when I came home."

He kept his eyes on his plate.

Paige's fork halted in midair. She'd always dreamed of hearing words like that from Adam Mason. Said low, just like that. In this dim lighting, just like that. Eating dinner with him, just like that. And actually hearing them was as wonderful as she'd ever imagined. A warmth curled down like smoke into her stomach. But she didn't quite know what to do with the information. And she was now doubting she'd even heard him correctly. She put her fork down and wondered how she might get him to repeat that.

"So what movies do you think Bob and Gert had Amanda watching?" he asked. "Did she tell you?"

"Yes!" Paige felt a rush of relief at the change of topic. "They started her on the classics—*Casablanca, North by Northwest, The Maltese Falcon,* and *Roman Holiday.*"

Adam smiled. "That sounds like Bob's lineup. He's a big Humphrey Bogart and Gregory Peck fan. Did she like them?"

"She did. She said she loved Audrey Hepburn, especially, and that Bob had promised to rent *Breakfast at Tiffany's* next."

"Ah. Holly Golightly."

"I told her she needed to see *Last Road to Nowhere,* too, since this very house is in the movie. She seemed pretty impressed."

"Impressed?"

Paige nodded.

"We'll have to do that, then. I think I have it here somewhere."

"You do? I haven't seen it in ages."

He motioned toward another room. "It's probably a VHS. We'd have to dig up my dad's old VHS player."

"We could do that!"

He glanced up, and she realized she wasn't quite sure she was included in "we." But then he looked over his shoulder toward the other room. "Do you want to look?"

"Sure."

He scooted his chair out and wiped his mouth, then led her to the next room. If the kitchen seemed to serve as a bit of a community room for the resort workers, this room, behind it, through a closed door, looked as though it might have been intended as a private living room for the family. However, white sheets were thrown over the furniture, and there were no lamps or light fixtures—the room was entirely cast in darkness, as if family living was no longer practiced here.

Adam lifted a few sheets to look in some bookcases and cabinets, then walked back toward her.

"What is that room?"

"The living room. We closed it up when my mom died."

"It's looked like that since you were *ten*?"

He shrugged. "I got used to it. It's always been that way."

"It might freak Amanda out a little."

He frowned at the room as if he were seeing it for the first time and nodded. "I never thought about that. I should fix it. Anyway, I guess we moved the VHS tapes. Maybe they're in my room."

She followed him down the hallway, past the guest room where she'd stayed, past the room where Amanda stayed, and into a huge room that looked as if it had been added on in the back. She glanced around, then stepped inside while he barreled toward a large walk-in closet in the back. The room was simple and clean and natural, just like him. Tan walls mimicked the color of summer California hills, while a denim comforter echoed the color of the sky. The bed held a cluster of plain white pillows. The furniture was a little mismatched, but neat and clean, and there were several prints hanging on the walls: images of airplanes and aerial views. An enormous old propeller hung from the wall nearest the light switch, the red paint rusted and chipped as if it was a historical piece. There were no personal photos anywhere—no family photos, no pictures of a day at the county fair, no nieces or nephews, no pictures of Adam with his dad or brother. A swift, unbearable ache hit Paige, suddenly and brutally, when she remembered again that Adam had grown up without a mother. Maybe, for him, life and childhood had simply been something to get through, not something to remember with photographs.

"Not here, either," he said, emerging from the closet. "There's one more place, but I'll have to check later."

She wanted to see this movie with him. The idea of curling up with him on a couch seemed wonderfully appealing. It felt like something that might solidify their friendship. "Where might it be? I'll help look."

"I'm thinking we might have moved that old stuff out to the hangar, but you don't want to go out there. It's become an old storage shack with a bunch of shi . . . llings in it."

"Shillings?"

He smiled. "I'm trying to stop cussing. Around Amanda. And now you. Growing up here with my dad and brother and a bunch of ranch hands, I've developed quite a mouth, but I'm trying to be more civilized. Anyway, the hangar's got a bunch of *stuff* in it. But I'll look later myself, maybe this weekend. I'm looking for something else out there anyway. In fact, I might have seen the box of movies."

"I can help." As soon as she said it, she nearly regretted it. She knew that hangar. She'd been there with him before. It had been the place that had sealed her heartbreak. He obviously didn't remember, and she didn't need him to.

But maybe it looked different now. "I don't have anything to do tonight," she said tentatively. "Let's look."

"Are you sure?"

He didn't look so certain himself, though probably for different reasons.

"Absolutely." And she led the way with a confidence she wasn't sure she felt.

CHAPTER 16

Adam lifted the lantern, undid the lock, pulled the main slider back from the hangar entrance, and stared inside. The smell of sawdust and sagebrush wafted out.

"I thought I saw a box that said 'Movies' when I was here earlier," he told Paige over his shoulder.

"What were you looking for earlier?" She took a few steps into the hangar behind him.

"My inheritance." He put the lantern down so he could search the stacks of boxes with both hands. "Apparently it all fits in a little box marked 'Private.'"

He didn't even try to edit the spite out of his voice. He didn't want anyone's pity, least of all Paige's, but spite was something that could flow free.

"George left you a box?"

"Apparently."

"Do you know what's in it?"

"I don't care."

"How could you not care? It sounds like an adventure movie."

He glanced at her to see if she was kidding, but she didn't appear to be. For the second time, he wished he had her spirit. He'd love to be as optimistic and happy as she always seemed. He thought he might have been that way once, back when his mom was alive. When he and Noel used to play and not have any worries. When his mom was always there for him, waiting in the kitchen, making apple pies for him or whittling her little flutes. He glanced at Paige and wondered if that might be some of her draw to him—that constant joy and hope. As it was, it felt like it might be. He liked being near her. His soul felt lighter.

And he hoped he was giving her something, too. Her relief at being able to build that damned gazebo in his meadow was a great reward. He loved being able to bring that look to her face. And he wasn't being manipulated, as his father had been. They were just two friends helping each other out because they had empathy and respect for each other. That's all this was.

He wandered farther into the dark hangar, hanging his hands on his hips and staring up at the boxes in the area he'd been before. He wanted to find this movie for her, too.

The boxes were marked "Spring 1980," "Summer 1980," and "Fall." Those might be ranch records. Or airport records. It was hard to tell. He knew the one that said "Movies" had been over—

"I found it." He steadied one of the lower sets of boxes and climbed up to reach the one with the movies, finally dropping it down to the hangar floor. It landed in a rattle of VHS plastic and a swirl of dust that came up into the lantern beam. When he jumped down behind it, Paige was no longer at the entrance.

"Paige?"

"I'm here."

He looked over toward the workbench that took up about eight feet of wall on the other side. She was standing in front of it, looking up at the rows of flight logbooks that lined the wall above the bench.

"This place is like a museum," she said.

He followed behind her with the movie box in his arms and plopped it onto the table. "Sure is. We have flight records here dating back to the 1940s."

"That's amazing."

He opened the box flaps and started looking through the VHS tapes, flipping them one by one: *Top Gun, Sixteen Candles, The Breakfast Club* . . . but *Last Road to Nowhere* was nowhere.

"Sorry," he said. "I thought it would be here. Wrong era."

"Bring the box in anyway. Amanda might like some of those eighties movies, too." She turned to look again at the books. "You and I had an argument here once."

His hands, already closing up the box, stilled. "What?"

"That summer. I yelled at you. I might have hit you in the balls."

"*Might* have?"

"Okay, I did."

He let go of the box and turned toward her. She was still staring at the books, her hand on her throat. The lantern light was coming in from the back and, as she stepped forward, it shone straight through her dress. He thought about mentioning it to her but, bastard that he was, decided not to. He cleared his throat and tried to look away.

Concentrate, man.

"You hit me in the balls?" he asked.

That sounded familiar. He stretched for the memory. He could almost reach it. They'd been standing near here, in fact. She'd been young, her face puffed from crying, her brows knit in anger. "What did I do?"

"Well, not enough to deserve that. I was just a newly hormonal teen."

He pushed the box back and turned more toward her. "Tell me. I'm trying to mend my asshole ways."

"Along with the cussing?"

"That's right. Not doing very well. I'm trying to mend my . . . *jackal* ways? How's that?"

"You could've gone with jerky."

He chuckled. "Thanks, Paige."

She turned her face away, then let a silence linger as she stared at the logbooks. "I wasn't going to admit to any of this."

He stepped closer. Something was starting to feel dangerous about this conversation, but he couldn't stop himself. "Is it something *I'm* apologizing for or you?"

"You . . . or me. Both, maybe."

This just got more interesting.

The light made her look almost ethereal, illuminating a halo around her hair and shoulders. She looked angelic. But the devil in him couldn't help but note her shapely thighs and the outline of a beautiful behind that the light also provided.

He rubbed the back of his neck to force his eyes downward.

"I'm sorry for my part, whatever it was," he said.

"You were just ignoring me. I should be the one to apologize."

She turned and put her arms behind her, up on the workbench, which raised her breasts into an illuminated silhouette of the most beautiful form. He cleared his throat and rubbed his neck harder.

"I followed you out here," she said.

He stopped and looked at her.

"You and Samantha," she added. "I had been playing in the orchard, and I saw you guys run in here, so I followed you. You had been making out with her over there." She nodded her head to the other side of the hangar. "Her clothes were coming off. So were yours. And I bumped into this table, and a paint can went crashing to the floor, and you both turned and stared at me. Do you remember any of this?"

He shook his head.

"So she grabbed her clothes and went running out, and you came over here, zipping up your jeans, and lit into me. You called me a sneak and a pervert, and asked what I was doing over here. And I didn't know what a pervert was, exactly, but I called you one back and swung the paint can and lobbed you in the balls."

He didn't remember any of this. But he kind of liked the image of a little spitball Paige, swinging a paint can at his junk. A small grin escaped.

"Sounds like I got what I deserved."

He could sort of picture the scene now. He didn't remember being here with Samantha, but he could vaguely remember Paige. What he remembered were her puffy eyes.

"You were crying," he said, as the memory came into clearer focus. "I remember that. Were you crying because of what I said?"

"The paint can I swung at you came back at me and opened, and red paint spilled down my front. And then you laughed at me. And you tried to call Samantha back in here to see it, but she was gone. So you had the laughs to yourself. You called me a clown."

He frowned. "Damn, Paige. I'm sorry. I was a stupid kid."

"I'm sorry, too. I shouldn't have been spying. Maybe I just wanted you to notice me." She leaned her body against the bench. "I wanted your attention. I had such a crush on you."

She laughed again, but the words hit him hard in the chest. She'd mentioned that before, during their walk from Rosa's. But he'd thought it was the wine talking.

"You had a crush on me? Way back then? My idiot self?"

She smiled. "I wanted you to look at me like you looked at Samantha. But you always ignored me—probably because I was a clown to you."

"No, probably because you were thirteen."

She smiled. "Well, that's true, too."

"Trust me, Paige, if I'd met you a few years later, I'm sure I would have been thinking differently."

"Differently how?"

"Differently like I am now."

He hadn't meant to admit that. He hadn't meant to tell her that his brain had been locked on her ever since she'd arrived—either trying to remember her, trying to figure her out, trying to protect her, or trying not to admit to himself that he was flat-out attracted to her. But he didn't have the luxury of that. Somehow attraction to Paige seemed as if it came with a whole maze of other thrills, which sounded fun. But irresponsible. And—especially with Amanda here now—Adam simply couldn't be irresponsible. That ship had sailed long ago.

But she definitely looked as if she didn't mind he'd admitted that.

She took a step toward him. He took a step back. She moved into the light again, and he couldn't help but look at her hourglass body.

"What are you thinking about now?" she asked.

He tried to swallow. What could he admit to? That he was horny? That he was lonely? That he'd been fantasizing about her for days on the trail? That he could picture taking her right now against this worktable? He didn't know what she could handle hearing. He cleared his throat.

"Well," he finally tried, "I don't think you want to know all my thoughts. But I can tell you that you look amazing in front of that lantern. And that your clothes have been see-through ever since you walked into the beams. And that I've chosen not to alert you but have enjoyed looking at you instead." His voice had fallen into a huskiness that he didn't recognize.

She took another step toward him. He didn't take a step back this time.

She put her hand against his chest and stepped closer still, and for a brief, insane moment he thought he might warn her. This would be a risky thing they were embarking on here, both of them trying to sell land to separate people, wanting the other one to help seal their own sale, and both still reeling from their parents' mistakes—in their own and each other's lives. But then she leaned up and kissed him.

Her lips were everything he thought they'd be—yielding and sweet, with the promise of warmth and suppleness everywhere on her body. Paige was everything soft and silky and curved that he craved. Before he knew what he was doing, he slipped his hand behind her head and pulled her toward him, giving extra attention to that pouty bottom lip that had been driving him nuts for the last week. He wanted to devour her—her lips, her body, her softness, her comfort. He'd kissed plenty of women in his lifetime, but Paige felt different— she felt forbidden, wild, like something he'd been meant to find long ago but had lost his way.

They banged up against the table, and he pulled them a little farther down the wall—farther into the shadows—and slipped his hand around her bottom, the other thing he'd wanted to touch since he'd seen her stuck in that window. It was as soft and fit in his hand as well as he'd imagined. He loved where it met her thigh: he could feel the sweet half-moon there, outside her skirt. He had to touch inside . . .

He pushed her back, hiding them both from the light, and scrambled for the bottom of the skirt with both hands. Her hand grasped his, and he felt a wave of embarrassment for how adolescent he was behaving—that feeling of overzealousness, as if he'd never seen a naked woman before. But this particular woman felt, in a strange way, like something that, perhaps, he *had* never experienced before.

He pulled back again to make sure she was okay with this.

His answer was gazing up at him—her eyes had become half-lidded, her arms came up around his neck, and she looked at his lips with a teasing smile.

And that was pretty much all the invitation he needed.

He dove back down to taste more of Paige Grant.

Responsibility be damned.

◆　◆　◆

Paige closed her eyes and waited for the thrill of Adam's hands, which overcame her, warm and firm, fingers spread, slipping under her blouse, down toward her skirt, over her bottom, dragging back up to her rib cage, grazing the undersides of her breasts, then back down to her behind again. He kissed her bottom lip, running his tongue along it, pulling it gently between his teeth until her blood pulsed, and sending a thrilling sensation to every fleshy part of her before settling, languidly, between her legs.

She tilted the bottom half of her body toward him, yearning for pressure, wanting his hands to touch her under her skirt. But his hands, instead, did a controlled exploration up her back, past her rib cage, his thumbs stroking her breasts, causing her to jerk in anticipation. She brought her heels back to the ground. She tried to stay calm. This, after all, was what she had longed for. She wanted to enjoy every second.

She pressed herself against him. "Don't you want to take my blouse off?" she whispered.

Adam smiled against her mouth. "I've wanted to take every one of your blouses off." He kissed the hollow behind her ear. "But I can't be sure the wranglers aren't coming here. How do you feel about getting caught?" He kissed her neck, sucking hard, and the sensation brought her off her heels again.

She gasped for breath. The idea of getting caught was at the top of her turn-ons, actually, but she was embarrassed to mention it. She'd waited too long for this—sixteen years, to be exact—to screw things up.

"I'll be discreet." He pushed her back into the darkness, his hands memorizing every curve of her body, first outside, then inside her clothes. He slipped his tongue into the nook behind her ear, and she sucked in her breath while his fingers moved along her inner thigh, under the skirt. The closeness of his fingertips was causing her to ache and throb, and she moved her thighs toward his hand.

"God, I've wanted you," he whispered into her neck.

Her heart soared. This was what she'd always wanted—Adam crazed for her, Adam touching her, Adam desiring her body. She knew she was supposed to keep business separate from her feelings toward him, but right now she couldn't separate anything. She held his hair as he kissed her neck, and arched her back to give him better access. His fingers moved her panties to one side, and she gasped and arched farther, just as a sharp beam of light came crashing into the hangar. Vaguely, Paige could hear the crunch of tires on gravel.

"Adam? Paige?"

A door slammed.

Adam lifted.

Paige scrambled upward from the table and pushed her skirt back down. This wasn't the kind of discovery fantasy she'd had in mind.

But dang, that whole kiss had been a fantasy.

"We're here, Amanda," she called in a shaky voice.

CHAPTER 17

Paige heard Adam bite off a few swear words and break his fall against a cluster of old paint cans, then quickly work his jeans back in place. He ran his hands through his hair, whispering a steady stream of curses under his breath.

"How're you doing?" Paige walked out into the light so Amanda might focus on her. "How was dinner?"

Amanda was trying to see around her shoulder into the darkness, frowning, but Paige kept walking toward her, shading her hand over her eyes to block the headlight beam. "We were looking for some old movies for you," she said to distract her.

"For *me*?" Amanda looked around again.

Paige waved hello toward the car, and the headlights snapped off.

"Yes, did you say you didn't get a chance to see *Last Road to Nowhere*? That's what we were looking for. We, um . . . didn't find it." She ran her hand down her hair to make sure it wasn't all over the place, just as Adam emerged with the box in his arms. He looked disheveled and sexy and slightly dazed.

"We were only able to find these eighties movies." He cleared his throat. "Not sure if that's your thing?"

Amanda frowned at them both, looking around the hangar with suspicion. But then her face softened as she saw Adam holding the box.

"You were finding those for me?"

"We were," Adam said.

"Can I see them?"

"Box is heavy. I'll carry them into the house for you."

As he continued his trajectory past her, the car turned off and Bob stepped out.

"Sorry, Adam. Amanda didn't know where you were. We saw your dinner dishes half-eaten, and she got worried."

Adam threw Bob a glare as he continued marching across the meadow, box on his shoulder, but Bob just swallowed a smile, gave Paige a wave of apology, and crawled back into the car.

"Let's go see what movies Adam found," Paige said, grabbing the lantern off the floor and putting her arm around Amanda. "You might like some of these."

Once back at the house, Paige watched Adam and Amanda go through the VHS tapes and pick out those she'd like to see. Amanda kept calling the tapes "vintage," which made Adam laugh.

"Your grandfather probably had some old record albums out there, too," he said, inspecting each of the tapes.

"Really? Vinyls?" Amanda's eyes grew wide. "Can we go find them?"

"Sure, we can look. His taste might have leaned more toward country, but I think he might have had some jazz and rock, too."

"Let's go look!"

Adam smiled. "How about during the day? It's dark out there right now. Paige and I had a hard time."

He glanced at Paige but then quickly cut his eyes away.

Paige could hardly look at him, either. *What had that been?* That was lunatic lust that had been released there in the hangar. Adam kept glancing at her, then rubbing his hand over the back of his neck as if he wasn't sure what had just happened himself.

But as far as Paige was concerned, that was *hot*. And he was hot. And she wanted a repeat. Or at least a finish.

Adam had been everything she'd always fantasized he'd be—aggressive, passionate, unstoppable. She watched his hands move the dishes off the table and thought about how he'd moved them over her body, how they'd cradled her breasts, how they'd cupped her behind, how they'd explored as if he couldn't get enough of her.

He glanced up at her again, seemingly asking what she was thinking, but Amanda said something, and he turned away.

He and Amanda eventually found the old VHS player under one of the sheets in the darkened living room, tucked a few more sheets into the upholstered crevices so they could sit on a couch and face the old television, then Adam brought a few lamps into the room and tested them.

"Better?" he asked.

Amanda nodded enthusiastically.

He came back into the kitchen to clear away the dishes, and she followed behind him while he complimented her on her cooking.

"I used to cook all the time at home," she said.

"Why didn't you tell me?" Adam turned on the sink. "You're welcome to experiment with whatever food you want here. Just tell me what you need from the store."

"I bake, too."

"No kidding?"

Paige left them to continue their conversation and went to gather her bags. She wanted to leave them like this. Adam looked so happy, and Amanda's face had softened into pleasant surprise when she'd realized that Adam was interested in something she could do.

Paige wanted more of Adam herself—*definitely*—and more of his hands, and more of that mouth, and more of those kisses. But she also wanted Amanda to have what she needed from him.

"I should go," Paige announced from the kitchen door when she had everything assembled.

Both Amanda and Adam looked up with identical expressions.

"No!" Amanda said. "We want you to watch the movie with us."

Paige glanced at Adam, who nodded, although he still seemed unable to completely meet her eyes.

"Just one movie," Amanda said.

"One?" Paige laughed. "How many are you planning on watching?"

"Maybe three. But stay for the first one. Your pick."

Adam lifted his eyebrows and gave her a slight grin.

She stared back at these two people she was coming to care for—with their identical begging eyes and hopeful smiles—and dropped her bags. She knew her heart was approaching a danger zone. She knew she might get hurt. She knew she was becoming too attached. But she'd be careful.

Very careful.

"Okay, just one," she said.

The next morning, Paige rubbed a crick in her neck and opened her eyes as she struggled to figure out where she was. When she blinked a few more times, she was able to peer through the dim lighting at draped white sheets, pine wall paneling, and a blackened television. Her head was on a pillow propped on a rolled couch arm. She got up on her elbow and looked around. Adam's living room.

But where was Adam?

And where was Amanda?

And what time was it?

She pushed off the blanket that had been laid over her and padded out to the kitchen area, where daylight fully assaulted her eyes. By the way the sun was coming through the window, it looked as though it could be nine or ten a.m. Amanda's coffee accoutrements were stacked along the kitchen counter.

Against the back of the coffeemaker was a note on an index card:

Made enough for the three of us. Had to lead a ride today. Enjoy. —A

There was one cup left. Still warm. Paige poured, added the creamer and sugar just the way she liked it, and leaned against the counter, wondering where Amanda was. As the taste swam through her senses, she sighed at the richness of Adam's coffee and glanced again at his note.

She wanted, of course, to think about business. She needed to call her mom. She needed to do her asanas. She needed to get at least four more things checked off her remodel list today and recruit a few strong men to help her haul the heavy two-by-fours and gazebo roof up the hill. She expected the pieces on the noon ferry.

But, instead, her eyes kept drifting to the note. She was intrigued, for one, that this was Adam's handwriting—this scratchy, up-and-down, almost-out-of-control writing. She thought about how out of control he'd been last night in the hangar and realized how much she'd loved that—*she* did that to him. Paige Grant. She'd made Adam Mason lose his mind. It had been what she'd wanted as soon as the first teenage hormones had flooded her body, and now it was playing out as the most amazing adult fantasy.

She took a sip of coffee and pondered her decision not to talk about that summer with him. Maybe they should. To clear the air. She didn't believe he'd started those fires. But she should tell him her part in talking to her mom and George about seeing him at both scenes, and how that might have been the conversation that truly got him sent away. She'd been telling the truth that night she'd sat with George and Ginger at the

Mason dining table—Adam *had* been there—but her point had simply been that the fires could have been started by many others besides her, so she shouldn't be singled out and blamed. She hadn't done it. Certainly, Adam would now understand those were the knee-jerk reactions of a teenage girl, and she truly hadn't meant to get him in so much trouble? Besides—did he still think *she* started those fires way back when? How could he kiss her like that if he believed that about her?

Yes, she should probably talk to him.

But, then again, they weren't starting a relationship here, and she didn't want him to think she thought they were.

Adam was not a long-term kind of guy, and he was ready to bolt off this island with Amanda as soon as he could. He didn't want any messy involvement with Paige. She got that. She'd just enjoy his hands on her and their temporary friendship while they did business together. She didn't have much hope of Adam selling to Dorothy Silver anymore—MacGregor almost seemed like a done deal. But with Adam's help, maybe she could make the wedding work, after all. She'd continue with her plans. And she'd protect her heart.

That was a good plan.

She blew on her coffee and congratulated herself.

And tried not to worry that she got a strange, warm feeling in her stomach every time she glanced at the note and caught sight of that recklessly scrolled *A.*

Adam headed out with the dude group for their first bison run. They'd corralled them to this side of the island during the four-day trek, but now they needed to get them onto the ranch and into the pasture. Normally, Adam did it with a bevy of ranch hands, but when they could, they timed it with a dude group. Their guests got a kick out of the bison roundups.

But he was having a hard time keeping his mind on work today.

Damn, that had been hot last night. He'd been out of control. He didn't know if that was a good thing or a bad thing, and he couldn't remember the last time he'd felt that way. He'd probably been eighteen. It was a little embarrassing to be coming at Paige like an adolescent boy, but something about her wild spirit incited it. He had to admit, it felt great.

But he hadn't thought through where it was going—was he going to take her right there, in a dusty hangar, against a piece-of-shit worktable? What the hell was wrong with him? Had his hormones gone awry? He'd had no condom. His wranglers were wandering the property. The dude group was about five hundred feet away. And he had a teenage daughter now, about to come home after dinner with his elderly friends. He must have lost his mind.

And what was going to happen afterward? Were he and Paige going to become friends who screwed every now and then? Not that he'd ever turned those down—the no-strings-attached relationships had always been ideal in his world, despite, or maybe because of, their lack of emotion—but Paige Grant? Helen's *granddaughter*? The daughter of the woman who changed the course of his young life by having him put in jail? The girl who nearly became his stepsister one summer? The girl who the townspeople thought may have started the fires? And the woman he was now trying to wrestle property with? He'd truly taken leave of his senses.

He needed a new plan.

Of course, he'd like to finish the old plan first.

Maybe he'd see it through to its logical conclusion. He wanted her. She seemed to want him. They were both healthy, single adults. Her flushed skin and constant glances while they were watching the movie looked more than inviting.

So he'd take his cues from her. If she so much as leaned in and touched him in a provocative way, he'd go for it.

But then they were done. He'd let her know they couldn't move it past that, and he was sure she'd be right on board. She had to see the stickiness of this situation, too.

"I saw your lady's golf cart at your place again this morning," MacGregor said, riding up behind him. "Did you work something out with her?"

Adam pulled back on Darcy's reins. "What are you talking about?"

"You were going to talk her into selling to me."

"I didn't say that. I said she wasn't interested."

"Aw, you must have some influence, boy. You can talk her into it. I want both properties."

"Mine's not enough? You've got fifty acres here."

"I have big plans. I don't want neighbors." MacGregor's smile was probably meant to be reassuring, but it made Adam's gut tighten. But he couldn't worry about what was going to happen to the property. He wasn't in a position to worry. He just had to sell as quickly as possible—preferably with the least amount of paperwork and the most amount of cash—and get the hell out of Dodge.

"I know you can talk her into it," MacGregor added with a wink.

Adam was, under no circumstances, going to talk to Paige about MacGregor and the land exchange, except to warn her.

He turned as much as he could in the saddle to face MacGregor down. "I have no intention of talking Paige into anything, MacGregor. She does what she wants, and she has her mind made up already. I have nothing to do with her business deals."

"How involved is the mother?"

Adam laughed. "Ginger? Well, she's hell to negotiate with. But you can try."

"Ah, the hellion female—my favorite kind. Well, that means I have two intriguing women to think about now. I'll have to pay one or both a visit." He gave a smarmy smile and took off at a gallop.

Adam adjusted his hat and wondered if he'd just gotten himself into another shit-storm.

But he definitely planned to protect Paige from that guy.

CHAPTER 18

"Mom? How are you?" Paige put the phone on speaker and laid it down on the table so she could talk to her mother while she mended the curtains. They'd come out pretty after the wash and air-dry—they looked almost exactly like the ones from the movie—and all they'd need was a little touch-up here and there to the hems.

"Darling," her mom said, "I'm fine. How is everything going there?"

"What did your doctor say about the EKG?"

"Oh, that's fine, dear. Nothing to worry about. Tell me how things are going there."

Paige let a breath of relief escape at the sound of her mother's voice. At least she sounded well. She slid the curtains farther across the table and reached for her needle and thread.

"Are you resting?" Paige asked. "Are you taking time to lie down?"

"Paige, please—no more worrying. I can't bear it. How is everything going? Did the gazebo arrive?"

"Yes, I have some builders lined up here to help me put it together."

"Where did you find the builders?"

"They're Adam's ranch hands."

"Ah. And how is young Mr. Mason?"

Paige dropped the thread. "Mom, why do you call him that?"

"It keeps a nice distance. I highly recommend it. So how is he?"

"Do we need to talk about him right now?"

"I'm wondering what he's up to."

Paige picked the thread up and tried to get it through the eye again. She needed to stay in control of this conversation. "Why not ask me more about Gram's house, or the cabinets I'm refinishing, or the curtains I'm mending to look like the movie?"

"Because those things don't concern me, darling. I know you've got that down pat. Adam concerns me."

Paige gave a deep sigh.

"Has he tried to get you into bed?" her mom asked.

Paige bolted upright.

"I'm certain he's doing that, and probably snaking his way into your heart," her mom continued.

Paige cleared her throat. *Yes? He has?* Suddenly her conversation was taking on the tone of a confession, which wasn't at all how she'd planned it to go. "Mom, I need to talk to you about a few other things, some new financial considerations that might—"

"Paige, he's going to try to get you into bed. I've been talking to some people."

"*People?* What people?"

"It makes no difference who. I'm just warning you that he'll have no compunction whatsoever about—"

"What people are you talking to here?'

"Paige, darling, you're missing the point. I'm saying that more than one silly woman has fallen for him—did you know the men up there call their conquests 'summer women'? Adam won't have any trouble fooling you into thinking he wants you. He'll probably start by doing you a favor or two, just like his father, then telling you how beautiful you are, and it'll go from there. Has he told you that yet? Or called you *magnificent*? Has he used that one on you?"

Paige's head whirled. She tried to figure out where, precisely, this conversation had gotten off track and then batted aside the idea that, yes, Adam had done her a favor with the gazebo, but that's not what that was about . . . was it? And, no, Adam hadn't told her she was beautiful or magnificent, but if he did, she'd want to believe he meant those things. Wouldn't he?

"Has he told you how special you are? How he's never met anyone like you?"

"Mother, stop."

"Has he said you're different than the other women he's known in his life? That you have that special something that's been so elusive in his past?"

"I'm hanging up."

"Paige, I'm just worried. Truly, are you okay? Is he being okay?"

Paige closed her eyes. God, how did this go so wrong? This was why she could not be the woman she wanted to be: she was a coward. Especially with her mom, who seemed to know her better than she knew herself. And now she was starting to see what her mom was talking about because she was letting little doubts enter her head about that gazebo.

"Everything's going to be fine," Paige said emphatically. "Adam is a nice guy. And he's not being manipulative. And he's not bothering me. However, he has his own real estate deal going on with MacGregor, and—"

"Oh, Paige. We can't lose the land to MacGregor. You know he wants to raze the whole place and start over, and the area will look nothing like Dorothy wants it to. Does Adam know that MacGregor wants to do that?"

"*I* didn't even know MacGregor wanted to do that. MacGregor is here now. He's meeting with Adam this week, doing a dude ranch."

"That's a joke. He has no intention of keeping that dude ranch. Or the airport. Or even the orchard. I heard he wants to wreck everything and start over. Something high-tech. A bigger, flashier airport and some stores. A Starbucks was involved."

"Wait, Mom. Where did you hear this?"

"I have my ways."

"Seriously. How legitimate is this? Are these rumors or what?"

"Well, they're rumors. But they're from a reputable source."

"Mom, we can't start spreading rumors around."

"Of course not. But we can take proactive steps upon what we see as reality. Trust me on this, Paige. Convince Adam to skirt that deal with MacGregor."

"I'll try."

Her mom sighed. "I'm so proud of you, darling."

Tears sprang to Paige's eyes. She tried to focus on her needle and cleared her throat again to try to say something, but words would not come. *Proud of you, darling.* They were words Paige craved. "Thanks, Mom," she managed to whisper.

"Call me tomorrow, okay?" her mom said quietly.

"Okay." Paige hit the "Off" button quickly and turned toward the window, gazing at the beautiful meadow. Her hands were shaking.

Proud of you, darling.

She put her head in her hands. Her mom and her sisters were the most important people in her life. They were the only ones who ever came close to loving her unconditionally. And yet she always fell short. She would never be the prettiest sister or the skinniest or the most cosmopolitan. All her life she'd been the comical, fun *I Love Lucy* sister, but all she wanted was for someone to feel proud of her.

She stood and began pacing the room. And could her mom be right about Adam? He wouldn't give her the gazebo to get into bed with her, would he? And, conversely, he wouldn't seduce her just to make a different land deal for MacGregor, right? Maybe after her admission about crushing on him all those years, he'd decided to make his move and bend things his way. Had she been too impulsive? Had she been blinded by a beautiful man because of a sixteen-year crush? Did he only want to negotiate with her, and saw sleeping with her as an easy way to do so?

And what was this news about MacGregor wanting to modernize everything? Could Paige tell Adam that? It was only a rumor, and Adam said he hated rumors—as did she—but her mom was almost always right. Although Adam wouldn't trust Ginger. If Paige was going to convince him, she'd have to convince him it was her own knowledge.

She got back to work on the curtains, mending what was in her control for now.

Later she'd talk to Adam.

For now she had a house to fix.

At three o'clock the doorbell rang. It sounded like a cow mooing.

Paige pushed herself out from under the bathroom cabinet, where she was investigating a possible leak, and decided she'd have to get a new doorbell immediately. Her next thought, about who could possibly be ringing her doorbell, set her pulse skittering.

She smoothed her hair back and raced down the stairs.

When she drew the door open, it was Amanda.

"Do you think you could still bring me to the harbor today?" Amanda asked.

"Where's your dad?"

"I don't know. He's out doing ranch things. I think he went out to get the bison. He told me to tell you he was sending someone to take a look at things out here for you today at four."

"He's not coming himself?"

"I guess not." Amanda looked a little sad. Maybe she felt as abandoned by him as Paige felt right now.

"Well, I guess I can take you. This might be the last day, though," Paige said.

Amanda nodded and headed toward Paige's golf cart.

As they angled down the hill, Paige working the brake in her expert way, she lifted the huge sun hat she had in the back and plopped it on her head. She'd put her hair in a bun and had worn her huge Jackie-O sunglasses—with the floppy-brimmed hat being the final touch.

"Why are you hiding every time you take me to the harbor?" Amanda asked.

Paige sighed. She hadn't wanted to tell Amanda this part, hoping the girl would simply think she liked cowboy hats and shades. "If you must know, I'm hiding from my sisters."

"Your sisters live here?"

"Yes."

"How many?"

"Two. And their families."

"Why are you hiding from them?"

"It's kind of a long story."

Amanda stared out at the horizon for a minute. "I thought you didn't want to be seen with me."

"What? Amanda, what are you talking about? Why wouldn't I want to be seen with you?"

"I know my mom caused a lot of trouble here on the island. I thought no one liked her."

"What?" Paige pulled the cart over to the side of the road, suddenly not caring she might be spotted.

"Amanda, what's giving you that impression?" She put her hand over Amanda's, although the girl pulled away.

"My mom always told me she hated it here. And now that I'm here, I hear talk. I asked around down here by the harbor about Adam and my mom, and everyone has stories to tell. They talk about the fires and how much of a troublemaker Adam was then and how much trouble my mom was. I didn't tell anyone who I was." She suddenly lifted her hand. "I promise. I know Adam doesn't want anyone to know."

"What? Why wouldn't Adam want anyone to know?"

"He hides me up there. I think he doesn't want me down here. He doesn't want anyone to know. He's embarrassed about me, and my mom, and the whole thing."

"*Amanda.*" Paige turned more toward her in the cart. "First of all, some of the people of this island can be terrible gossips. That's a given when you're in a small town. Some people have a couple of details, and others have absolutely no idea what they're talking about—they just repeat what they've misheard before, or they make stuff up to make themselves look better. You can't take any of that seriously. Secondly, Adam is *not* hiding you up on the hill. And he is *not* embarrassed about you. He's a loner—he was that way long before you arrived. Trust me. And he's not a troublemaker anymore. He's been running that ranch with his brother—your uncle—and his dad—your grandfather—since he was a kid, and he's been working his butt off. And if he's not commenting on silly rumors down here, it's only because he doesn't care about them. He is *not* embarrassed about you. He sincerely wants you to be happy. He's scrambling to figure out how to make you happy, in fact."

Amanda gave her a skeptical glance before returning her gaze to the Queen Anne's lace growing on the side of the road. "I guess."

Paige turned and started the cart again. "I know of what I speak." Paige was surprised to hear her mom's old expression leap from her lips.

As the Queen Anne's lace flew by their cart the rest of the way to the sea-lion center, Amanda let out a long sigh. "If I had sisters, I think I'd never hide from them. I think I'd want to be with them all the time."

Paige glanced at her. Amanda's mind really jumped from one thing to another. "Having sisters is not all that it's cracked up to be. Sometimes they're a pain."

"Easy for you to say, having them. I think they'd be like having built-in best friends. Someone you could always trust. I'm glad you're not wearing a disguise because you're embarrassed of me, but I wish you weren't hiding from your sisters."

Paige put her eyes back on the road. A ripple of shame wove through her. Amanda was right—she had two wonderful sisters she should appreciate. Not everyone was as lucky as she was. Maybe instead of cutting them out, she should trust them and welcome them into her plans?

They arrived at the top of the hill above the center. Amanda hopped out of the cart.

"Call me if you need a ride back," Paige said.

Amanda nodded, then started running down the hill.

Young and old at the same time—sometimes Amanda had the wisdom of an elder and sometimes the naïveté of a child. Paige supposed she'd been the same way at fifteen.

And she also had a sneaking suspicion she'd be back at five.

At five o'clock sharp, Paige was puttering back up the hillside, Amanda in her passenger seat, with a nervous feeling in her stomach about seeing Adam again. As soon as they safely passed the wooden sign for Nowhere Ranch, Paige pulled the sun hat off her head and handed it to Amanda.

"You'll come over and watch another movie tonight?" Amanda asked.

"Oh no." Paige waved her hand in false nonchalance. "I've got so much to do around Gram's house. I have to keep up a schedule."

"Didn't you have fun last night?"

Paige's mind went from zero to sixty about how much fun she'd had—especially the part where Adam was running his hand up the inside of her thigh—but she refrained from saying that and tried to concentrate on the parts Amanda was talking about.

The movie.

Yes.

"I did have fun. But I have a lot of work to do. We can't just have fun all the time, you know, I . . ." She was about to go into a litany of protests, but she sounded so much like her mother right now she couldn't see straight. She might as well add "young lady" to her lecture and call life a wrap. "I just mean—"

"C'mon, Paige. I know you want to." Amanda gave her a sly smile that could have had numerous meanings to it.

Paige wasn't sure how much she wanted to investigate, or how much Amanda might know about her and Adam, so she simply concentrated on making the next few turns.

"And I thought about what you said earlier," Amanda said. "I see now that Adam's trying. And I want us all to spend some time together. I'll watch the movies with him if you come."

Ah, guilt.

That's what Paige needed to top things off this week.

"I'll see," she said to buy herself some time. But how could she deny that request? She knew she was being manipulated—being a wily fifteen-year-old girl herself under Ginger's thumb had trained her well—but she would still feel guilty if she didn't go.

When they got to the house's driveway, Amanda's cell phone buzzed. After reading the message, she pointed around the back. "Can you take me by the hangar?"

"Why do you want to go to the hangar?"

"I want to see if I can find that movie you were talking about—*Last Road to Nowhere*. I really want to see it."

"I don't know if your dad wants you looking around those precariously stacked boxes. The whole thing looks dangerous." Paige wondered when she was going to stop sounding like her mother. She sighed and tried again. "Let's just wait until he finds the movie."

"He's there already."

"What?"

Amanda held up her phone. There was a text there from Adam, which Paige squinted at, but couldn't make out the details.

"You guys are texting each other?"

"We just started. He asked me to come help him."

Paige nodded and puttered across the meadow. That was sweet that Adam was texting with Amanda. But now Paige would have to ignore the butterflies in her stomach about seeing him again. She was glad she'd changed clothes before heading out to get Amanda. She tugged her ponytail back in place and tried to ignore the girl staring at her.

When they pulled up to the hangar, Paige waited for her to jump out.

Amanda turned and waited for her.

"Aren't you coming?" Amanda asked.

"I don't know, Amanda, I—" Her words stalled when she saw Adam step out into the hangar entrance. A cloud of dust came up around his boots as he stopped abruptly. He looked surprised to see her, lifting his hat in a nervous gesture, wiping his brow, then placing it back on his head. But then he hung his hands on his hips in his customary show of exasperation and threw a long look at Amanda.

"I brought a helper," Amanda said cheerfully.

Apparently that detail hadn't been part of the text.

But something like a magnet drew Paige in. Or maybe it was the pull Adam had had on her for sixteen years. Or maybe it was the sight of those strong hands that had been in her hair last night, or those forearms that she knew could lift her against a wall until he did whatever he wanted to her, or . . .

Get a grip, girl.

She took a deep breath that had a bit of a shudder to it, and found herself getting out of the cart, smoothing her hand over her shorts, and stepping toward him.

"Wait," Amanda said, staring at her phone. "I just got another text. It's from Bob and Gert. Can I go over there?"

Adam frowned. "Bob and Gert know how to text?"

"They got a new phone the other night, and I've been showing them how to use it. They said they'd make me dinner again if I go over there and give them their last lesson. Can I take your cart?" She turned to Paige.

Caught unaware, Paige glanced at Adam, who shrugged. "She's been learning to drive mine. She's pretty good."

Well, this hadn't gone according to plan. Paige didn't mean to be stuck out here with all these pheromones floating around and an uncertain feeling about where they'd left off. But Adam looked less annoyed, almost encouraging. She wished he'd smile or something to give her a clue about what he wished she'd do.

"Sure," she finally said.

They watched Amanda putter away at twenty miles an hour, and Paige had the strange thought that she was letting the getaway car get away.

When she turned back toward Adam, he was still standing there with his hands on his hips, staring at her.

"C'mere, Paige," he said thickly.

CHAPTER 19

His mouth came down hard on hers. Paige thought at first he might be angry—perhaps for succumbing to this, to the inevitable, which was how she felt, too—but he pulled her into the hangar, into the doorway, out of sight of Amanda's rearview mirror, and drew her closer to his body by her waist, even though he couldn't possibly get any closer. He wrapped his biceps around her, drawing her toward him at the small of her back, almost lifting her off the ground.

He suddenly broke the kiss.

Breathing heavily, he leaned back for one second, then scooped her over his shoulder and carried her like a sack of potatoes deep into the hangar.

"Adam!" Paige squealed. She laughed as he carried her across the sawdust-strewn floor to the worktable along the wall. "This is crazy."

"Crazy doesn't even begin to describe what this is."

He plopped her on the table and moved between her legs, drawing her mouth down to his, kissing her hard, paying extra attention to her bottom lip until her toes curled. He reached around to the back of her body and ran his hands down, where his hand span covered her entire bottom, and he squeezed while he attended to her mouth.

"I haven't been able to stop thinking about you," he mumbled, moving his kisses down her neck and between her breasts.

Chills ran down her arms. She gripped his hair and tried to move him closer. She wanted more of him—more kisses, more words, more affirmation, more attention—but she wondered if they should talk first. "Adam," she whispered.

He pulled away for a second—looking as if it took every effort he had. His eyes were hooded, stormy blue. His gaze dropped to her lips.

"Don't stop," she whispered.

"You just stopped me."

"I didn't mean to."

"Are you sure?"

"Absolutely."

"Because you have a very small window here where I'll be able to."

"I'm sure."

His lips were on hers again, and his hands traced the shape of her bottom and hips and waist as if he were memorizing every curve. She tugged at her blouse to give him better access, then reached for the hem and swept the entire thing over her head.

"Should we talk first?" she whispered.

"I don't feel like talking right now," he murmured against her cleavage. "Do you?"

His mouth moved down and nipped at her breast through her bra. She gasped. "No."

She clutched his head and brought his lips closer. They were warm and smooth, and his tongue was expert at teasing, sweeping beneath her bra to hint at what was to come. His fingers came up to undo the clasp, and she held her breath. She was ready to be open for him, naked for him, but she felt bad that they hadn't talked yet.

"I should warn you," she whispered.

He backed away again.

"Warn me of what?" He seemed distracted—not really listening—as his eyes drank in her body, her bra, her cleavage, then grew hooded with reverence.

"I've been known to have calamities with this, too."

"With sex?"

"Yes." She kissed him again so he wouldn't stare at her, but he backed away again.

"What kind of calamities?"

"Broken beds, broken tables, falling off couches, that kind of thing."

He glanced up at her and slowly smiled as his fingers unsnapped her bra. "I think I can handle that."

His hands went to work exploring again while the warmth of his tongue was turning her bones to liquid.

"You are beautiful," he murmured into her left breast.

She chose not to think about the fact that this was the first line her mom had predicted. She chose, instead, to lean back on the heels of her hands and lift her body toward him. She chose to simply enjoy the fact that this gorgeous man, whom she'd loved since the day she first saw him, was calling her beautiful and kissing her cleavage and not caring at all that she was Calamity June. Whether out of joy or defiance—it really didn't matter anymore—she arched her back into him.

His hands traced the shape of her waist and hips again, moving down slowly to her bottom and thighs, moving his mouth across her stomach. Her breath caught as his tongue got to her low waistband. He undid her shorts, and she gasped as he slipped her shorts to the floor with no problem. She sat up, now in only her panties, and pulled his face toward hers, this time taking *his* lower lip between her teeth. His kisses grew more feverish as his hands slid down again, his thumbs hooking the waistband of her panties, pulling them down.

"This is going to be uncomfortable, baby," he said huskily.

Her pulse raced at the sexual promise of that: What was going to be uncomfortable? This table? His hands? What he was going to do to her once they were both undressed? Her breath caught, and she gripped his shoulders while he moved her awkwardly to get her panties off and kicked them aside with his boot. But then she wondered if he meant something altogether different—uncomfortable emotionally, between them, because of their histories and their parents and their land predicaments. But then she felt his hands again coming up her thighs and lost all train of thought. She truly didn't care right now.

The table was rough under her bottom—it was covered in peeling paint—and Adam reached under her and let her sit in the palms of his hands.

"Rock forward," he demanded, kissing her shoulder and encouraging her to the edge of the table. He lifted her just enough to get her to the edge, his shoulder keeping her balanced, and the effect was intoxicating: the cool air swirling up off the cement floor between her legs, the rough table against skin so rarely exposed, the tingling between her thighs, waiting for his touch, feeling his jeans brush up against her.

She leaned forward with excruciating need, but his fingers were now at his zipper, frenzied, pulling. Having Adam this out of control was beyond thrilling: listening to his strained breaths, watching that war rage in his head and his muscles, watching that play between strength of mind and strength of body. She knew he was trying not to think too far ahead, same as she was. She knew he was still warring with whether this was a good idea or not. But right now they both didn't care. It was exhilarating.

He brought a foil packet to his mouth and tore it with his teeth. She loved his frenzy, loved his fumbling, loved that he was shaking as he moved to get the condom on with one hand while he used the other to keep her positioned. His mouth came down to her shoulder in a kiss that was half bite, half possession, then moved to her neck, sending a row of goose bumps along her arms and chest.

"Open for me, Paige," he murmured.

She cried out the first time he thrust, and he moved one hand under her bottom, as if to protect her from the table; then he lifted her off the table completely, onto him, and her legs went around his waist. He grabbed the table behind them to steady them both, holding on to her with his other arm—his biceps pressed against her breast. He used the force of the table and the pressure of his hand to bring her all the way onto him. Energy reverberated. Paige hugged his neck. His arms now encircled her. He pumped again, hard.

Her body bumped against the table, and he cursed an apology and moved them away, but Paige felt very little except the sensation of straining against his body, to get him to reach that spot, *there*. She kept crying out as he got it, again and again, until she thought she was going to come apart, straining for that tease of pleasure. It was like a point of sky she was trying to reach, and he helped her get it *again*, right *there— oh holy, glory, sweet opening sky*—and she called out his name and arched her back while the sky filled her fingertips. It raced down her arms and into her bloodstream and burned her to her toes.

God . . .

She fell, limp, against him, and Adam paused to let her enjoy the aftershock, then pulled her once more, tight, and braced himself against the table. She felt him stiffen and shudder and say a few things that sounded like they might be blasphemous . . . then he buried his face into her shoulder.

Damn.

Adam finally managed to resume breathing. His triceps shook. He gripped the edge of the table. He was going to collapse in about twenty seconds, so he gently rested Paige on the table and tucked her head under his chin.

What was that?

He knew he'd left teeth marks along her collarbone, and had probably allowed her bottom to be scratched up from this table. He attempted to cushion her thighs from the peeling paint, then continued to stroke her hair.

Damn, but damn.

He'd gone from zero to 180 in about twenty seconds, and he couldn't even control his own release on that one. Thank God Paige came over the edge as fast as he did. That probably took a total of four minutes. If he'd had to renew his license on that, the way he had to renew his pilot's medical one, he'd be in some serious shit right now. *How is your vision, son? Just fine. Maybe too fine. Any trouble taking off? Not at all. Any trouble releasing? Well, uh . . . Any trouble controlling your aircraft? Uh . . .* He'd have his license ripped from under him in a flash.

He pulled back and tried to look at her. Her hair was in a sexy disarray around her face, and she hid behind it as she turned to look for her shorts. He could see red marks along her cheek where his facial hair had chafed her. He kept vacillating between exhilaration at finally having this beautiful woman and embarrassment that he'd behaved like a teenager in doing so.

He took care of the condom and fixed his jeans. Normally at this point he didn't care what happened next. Or what his partner thought. They were usually done, satiated, having both their needs met. But this felt different. He wanted Paige to have enjoyed herself. He wanted her to be happy. He wanted her to *like* him.

But he didn't know how to express that. He didn't even know how to process the emotions swirling through him. He hadn't ever wanted to scoop up a woman right after sex and hold her in his arms and stroke her face and make sure her skin wasn't chafed.

He also had never been so nervous that his partner wasn't meeting his eyes.

Confused, he simply stepped back and ran his hand through his hair and handed her the shorts she was trying to reach.

"I'll let you get dressed," he said, charging back out of the hangar, where the sun assaulted his eyes.

He bent to pick his sunglasses out of the gravel and started polishing them with his shirt. With his back to the hangar entrance, he squinted at the sun, waited for Paige to get dressed, calculated when he should bring up MacGregor, and wondered how out of his depth he really was.

Paige dressed slowly, carefully. When she was reassembled, she leaned back against the worktable and hugged her torso. She glanced out the door at Adam's silhouette and rubbed her elbows to wait out the thrumming. She willed her breaths to come slower, to normalize her heartbeat.

God, that man was overwhelming.

He was hot. He was passionate. That intensity that lay in his eyes ran heatedly through his muscles, too. And, apparently, though his veins.

She knew this was lust. And she was glad it was over with. It was powerful, and it was exactly what she needed. What she wanted to avoid was letting it breach into territory that felt like too much emotion, where, like her mom said, she would be in serious trouble. She already loved his voice, his work ethic, his arms, his protectiveness, his hands, his generosity, his sense of responsibility, his muscles, and the power that pulsed through his veins. If she met his eyes, and he said one more sweet thing, she was going to fall straight over the precipice of love. She needed to protect her heart.

She glanced at him standing silhouetted in the hangar opening, his eyes on the horizon. He looked dismissive. That might help. Maybe he was done now. Maybe he turned into a jerk at this point to drive his partners away. Maybe she could walk away now.

It was better than falling in love with him.

It was better than feeling guilty she hadn't told him the whole truth about her involvement in his teenage troubles.

It was better than wondering if this have-sex-in-an-airplane-hangar kind of passion was normal for him and she was just one of a string of summer women this year. *Has he done this before? Is this his usual gig? Does he meet women who visit in the summer and have brief flings and then throw them away?*

She looked around for her belt. *Does he ever fall in love with them, even a little? Has he ever found someone special? Was Samantha one of many? Will he think I'm different?*

She pressed her fingertips to her forehead. *Oh holy moly, no.* Absolutely no. This was not something she could let her mind drift toward. It made no difference whether she was exactly the same as any other woman he might have pulled to his chest, or as different as Venus. Because *she was not going to fall in love with him.* And he was not going to fall in love with her. She was here only briefly; he was leaving. She hadn't even told him the truth about their pasts; they were both going to have to get back to figuring out their properties. This was just sex. And it was more than she'd ever hoped for.

She leaned down, still looking for her belt. The force of their wild sexcapade had shoved the table back a couple of inches, and the belt was wedged beneath one of the legs. She tugged at it while her mind drifted again to the other women who probably came through here, and she wondered if she was too wild for his normal taste. Maybe he liked more sophisticated Ingrid Bergman or Rita Hayworth types. Not screaming banshees like her who would have sex in a hangar and warn him of possible future calamities. Then she chastised herself again and wondered why she was torturing herself. This didn't matter.

The belt was truly stuck. She yanked on it again with greater force, but the table was too heavy to lift alone. She bent to try to pry it out, but when she did, she noted, with curiosity, a large box shoved far underneath the bottom shelf. Its edges were puckered up around the wood from being forced there so wrongly. She walked along the other side and saw the words scrolled in black marker there, almost covered with dust: "Private."

"Adam?" She finished buttoning the waistband of her shorts. "I think I found something."

"Shove!" Adam croaked.

He held the table as high as he could so Paige could push the box from the other side. He got the belt out first and threw it to her so she could keep her shorts up.

Once she was pulled back together, she bent again to help. He raised the table into another forceful lift. "Again!" he said through clenched teeth. Paige shoved the box hard with both hands.

The table felt as if it weighed several tons and resented being moved. He took a few deep breaths before each boost. Finally, Paige gave the cardboard a desperate shove from underneath. Adam had the table hovering, and the cardboard monstrosity scuttled across the sawdust about two feet.

Adam let the table's legs thunder to the floor. "Christ!" He scowled at the cardboard box and caught his breath. The damned thing looked as though it had been wedged there for a decade. He sat down and leaned against the bottom panel of the table.

Paige slid down next to him.

For a long time, the only sounds were their ragged breaths reverberating along the tinny walls of the hangar. Adam stared at the particles of dust that were swirling in the rays of the sunset.

"I didn't mean to do that earlier—come on to you quite like that," he said.

"What do you mean you didn't mean to do that? You had a condom with you."

He laughed. "Well, hope does spring eternal. I guess what I mean to say is that I'd planned to wait—to take cues from you. But I didn't even wait that long."

"Don't be sorry for that." She threw her chin out in a cute, haughty way. "Maybe I was the one who wanted you."

A smile escaped his lips in spite of himself. He didn't know why he didn't give her more credit. There was such a strange contrast between her vulnerability and strength—it kept confusing him.

"And I didn't mean for it to happen like that," he added.

"Like what?"

"Completely out of control."

"Damn, don't be sorry for that. It was hot."

He smiled and rolled his head toward her. "It didn't bother you that I barely got your panties off?"

"No. That was hot, too."

"How about that I took you against a dirty table? In a dusty old airplane hangar? And I acted like some kind of fumbling teenager? None of that disturbs you in the least?"

"You were out of control. And that's okay. You looked like you were having fun. I was having fun. And that's okay, too. You're allowed to have fun, Adam."

He looked away. He wanted to believe that. He supposed it was true if he thought about it cerebrally. It was what Bob had been telling him in recent years, too—that he'd aged too fast. But throughout his adolescence, "fun" had had consequences in his dad's home. Ever since he'd been eighteen, his dad's "fun" meant more gambling debts, more excessive drinking, then more responsibility being placed on Adam. And when Adam had tried to have "fun" himself, with Samantha, for instance, it resulted in banishment from his dad's house and, ultimately, a daughter he didn't know about until sixteen years later. Fun had always been trouble.

Of course, Paige was fun. Maybe that's what her magnetic draw was. She was exactly what he denied himself. And he had to admit, he was like a man in a drought: he kept wanting to drink her up.

"You *did* have fun, didn't you?" she asked.

He grinned at the concrete. "Damn, yes."

"That's not usual for you?"

Adam let out a bark of a laugh. Losing all control and taking a woman against a worktable in an old storage hangar because he couldn't wait another second? *Uh, no.* But he bit back that thought.

"Not at all," he said.

"I'm hungry," she said.

He chuckled again.

The sun highlighted the dust particles like beams, and he watched the light play across her legs. Then he had the sudden, pressing thought that he wanted her again. Now. Right now.

But this should probably end. He needed to talk to her about MacGregor. And if he started talking about land right after sex, he'd be coming way too close to George behavior—so much so he'd have to throw himself off a cliff somewhere. So he nodded and held out his hand.

Paige took it and unfolded her legs in a graceful yoga move, rising to meet him. She looked up into his eyes, and he had the strangest sense of falling—into another type of responsibility, perhaps, but this one didn't have any of the negative consequences he was used to. This one felt like something he would welcome. He couldn't fully define it, though, so he just stared into her beautiful eyes with the long eyelashes for a few seconds too long.

"I'm making quesadillas and salsa," he finally said.

"A new addition to your repertoire?"

"Well, the salsa was already part of it, but the quesadillas are new. You can be my first victim."

He balanced the box up on his shoulder as they traipsed across the meadow. The meadow grasses were long where the bison hadn't come through yet, and the sharp blades whipped around their ankles. About halfway through, the large shipments of ready-to-assemble lumber for the gazebo became visible, sitting on the line between their properties.

Paige turned toward it and stared. He stared, too. And they walked the rest of the way in silence.

CHAPTER 20

The pungent smell of cilantro filled the kitchen while Adam stood at the counter and chopped a cornucopia of vegetables for his salsa.

"Are you sure you don't want me to look through this for you?" Paige asked from the kitchen table. She poked at the "Private" box with her foot.

He glanced over his shoulder. "No."

She stared at the box while she listened to the chopping sounds of his knife punctuating the silence. She couldn't believe he wasn't at least a little curious. George Mason had left a weird cardboard box, shoved roughly under a bench for years, marked "Private," named in his will, and Adam didn't want to know what was in it?

"I could report what's in it, and then you could decide if you want to look yourself," she suggested.

"No, Paige." His voice made it clear this line of questioning was over.

She looked around the kitchen. She felt sort of useless right now. And adrift. She didn't know if she should suggest a "talk" and question what this was between them. She didn't want to make it seem more than it was or scare him off. "Are you sure you don't want me to help you chop or something?"

"Relax. Let me make this for you."

She took that as her cue. *Relax.* She tried to settle back in her chair. "It smells great. How long has salsa been part of your repertoire?"

"Since I've known Mrs. Teresa Mendez, *cocinera* extraordinaire and Antonio's beautiful mother."

As if she hadn't already fallen for everything about him, the way he said that Spanish word was very sexy.

"Does *cocinera* mean 'cook'?" she asked.

"Yes. Teresa Mendez—everyone around here calls her Mama— makes the meanest salsa and the best chili enchiladas on this mountain. I'm lucky to know her. And you're lucky," he said, turning and waving the knife at her, "to *benefit* from the fact I know her."

She smiled. "Where is Teresa Mendez now?"

"She's taking care of family in Mexico, so I've been on my own for a month."

"How are you handling being without her?"

"Well, now that I know Amanda can cook, I might start handling it pretty well."

"But you're leaving."

His knife stilled. Then, eventually, it started chopping again. "Is it strange that I keep forgetting that?"

"No. This has always been your life. It'll probably take some adjusting. What will you miss most?"

"To my surprise, the list is getting longer."

"What's in the top three?"

"Maybe Bob and Gert, my horses, Rosa's Cantina. I could go on."

"Feel free," she said.

"The ranch hands, Kelly, riding, the meadow, the pond, and even the . . . uh . . . hangar is starting to become a special place."

"Glad I could contribute," she said.

He chuckled. "I'm realizing I liked a lot more about this place than I thought."

Paige wanted again to talk about what was next for them. Had they both scratched an insistent itch and now were done? It had been her original plan, too, of course, but now that she was watching him across the kitchen, enjoying this relaxed, good-mood Adam—not to mention thinking back to how incredibly hot that hangar encounter was—she wouldn't mind keeping things going for a while. She'd work hard to keep it casual. She'd work hard to keep her heart out of the way.

But she wasn't sure how to bring it up with him right now.

Plus, she'd *absolutely* have to tell him about that summer and her hand in talking to George.

And she was wondering if now would be a good time to tell him what her mom had said about MacGregor's commercial plans for the land. Maybe they should get this land talk out of the way.

She fiddled with the stack of napkins.

"Has, um . . . ," she started. "Has MacGregor told you anything about what he plans to do with this land once he buys it?"

"I figure that isn't any of my business," he said. Chop, chop, chop.

"But don't you care what he's going to do with the dude ranch and the orchard and the airport, and everything you and your family have worked so hard for?"

"I don't have the luxury of caring, Paige. I'm in a situation where I have to sell. Quickly."

"I've already told you Dorothy Silver is willing to buy. And pay more."

"I can't count on that. That offer is only thoughts and words right now. And she's not paying cash. MacGregor is here, right now, and he's ready to buy. Which, by the way, I've been meaning to talk to you about."

"But MacGregor wants to raze everything."

Adam stalled and turned toward her. "How do you know that?"

"I have it on good authority."

"What authority?"

"Ginger."

He went back to cutting. "Well, Ginger might have other motives for making me ignore MacGregor's offer."

"We can trust her."

He turned again to glance at her, and suddenly the word *we* had a lot of meaning.

He walked over with a cutting board filled with chopped onions and chopped hot peppers and dumped three huge mounds into a big bowl on the table. A smile played along his lips. "So we're back to talking about business now?"

"I guess. What kind of peppers are those?"

"Serrano."

"What are those other green things?"

"Tomatillos. So if we're going to make the dangerous slide into talking about business right after having sex, I meant to talk to you in more detail about MacGregor."

She investigated the bowl and took a good long whiff of the spicy-scented concoction. She wanted to keep her mind off the way Adam said "having sex" in that slightly cold way. But she had to remember that coldness, too. They weren't falling in love here.

She took another whiff as he walked back to the counter. "What about him?"

"He wants to put pressure on you to sell to him. Or he wants me to."

Adam saying anything about putting pressure on her had the zing of sexual overtone. Maybe it was his deep voice. Or the way his forearms grew muscled when he chopped with the knife. Or the memory of his hands roaming over her skin a few minutes ago . . .

Maybe she wasn't going to be good at keeping things separate, after all. Now she just wanted to flirt with him.

"He wants you to put pressure on me?" she asked. "And how are you planning on doing that?"

"I'm not planning on doing that."

"Right." She smiled. "You're *not* going to put pressure on me by seducing me in an airplane hangar and giving me some of the most intense sex of my life?"

"*Paige.*" He gave her a warning look over his shoulder, but he caught her smile and grinned back. "Don't do that. You know that's not what that was."

She didn't answer. She wanted to believe that, of course, but she didn't know that was not what that was. That *was* what her mother had predicted—that he'd use sex as a bargaining tool. That he'd get her into bed but without caring about her. Not that they needed a bed.

The sound of the knife on the cutting board filled the kitchen.

"My dad was an asshole," Adam continued. "He always mixed business with pleasure, and he never thought through the aftereffects."

"He did that with my mom," she said.

"I was under the impression Ginger was the user in their scenario."

"I think they used each other. Ginger lent your dad a lot of money—did you know that?"

The knife made slow, rhythmic taps until Adam filled another small bowl with cilantro. "I think I figured it out," he eventually said. "The other night I studied the books back about fourteen years, and I made some guesses about that time frame."

"He paid her back by giving her pieces of land," Paige said. "Then he left her."

"Or she left him."

"I think because of you," she said.

"He told me it was because of you."

Paige reeled a little at that, but it sounded as though it could be right. Ginger probably blamed Adam, and George probably blamed Paige. She remembered there being a lot of fights outside the door of Gram's house right after Adam was sent away. The whole situation definitely broke up Ginger and George.

Adam walked back over to the bowl with the mound of cilantro and threw it in. "I'm not fond of Ginger, but I know my dad wasn't exactly a saint in everything they had going on, either. I'm pretty sure they both screwed things up. Let's just make sure neither of us is like them."

"I'm with you."

"I don't want to get sex mixed up with money and land and negotiations."

Paige's throat was suddenly filled with cotton. Was that Adam's way of dismissing her? They had sex once, and that was enough for him? She focused on the vegetables so her hurt feelings didn't betray her.

"Of course"—Adam leaned down toward her ear—"I'm not sure I can give you up just yet."

Her heart skipped a beat over his husky delivery and sexy sentiment as she watched him walk back to the counter. *Damn.* She didn't want him to have such control over her emotions, but she didn't know how to stop it.

She nodded slowly until she could get her heart rate down. "We could come up with ground rules," she squeaked out.

His knife went back to its rhythmic sounds. "I'm good with that. You name them."

Her fingers found the napkins. "We agree this is only temporary." That was obvious. They would both be gone by the end of the summer.

"Perfect."

"We don't trade info about land or money or trade any other kind of favor for sex." That's the one that had gotten her mom in trouble. Ginger thought she was helping for love; George thought she was helping for sex. They both ended up angry and disappointed.

"That's good."

"We never talk about land or deals with our clothes off."

Adam walked back to the table with a board full of onions and smiled. "That's actually a nice visual. But you're right—I'm good with that."

"And we stay FRED."

"Fred?"

"It's sort of like friends with benefits, only it's got an end date—Friends Ready to End in Divorce."

He scraped the onions into the bowl and thought that over. "All right. FRED."

"See? We're already light-years ahead of George and Ginger." One of the napkins was in shreds, so she moved on to another. "They didn't talk, and they weren't honest with each other."

"You're nothing like Ginger," he said.

She took a deep breath. She hoped not, but she wasn't sure. She didn't want to harden her heart the way her mother had, especially toward men. She knew she'd been leaning that way, especially with her mother's warnings through the years, but she wanted to trust. She wanted to trust people. She wanted to trust men. She wanted to trust herself and her own decisions. And, especially, she wanted to trust this particular man.

"Thanks," she breathed out. "You're nothing like George."

His mouth quirked up. "I appreciate that more than you know. And, more important now, I don't want to be like him with Amanda, either." He headed back to the counter.

"What do you mean?"

"Cold. Yelling. Terrorizing. Arbitrary rules."

Paige shook her head. How could Adam think he was like George? It broke her heart to think he was so hard on himself. "You're not like that at all, Adam. Although . . ."

He looked back sharply. "What?"

"Amanda and I were driving today, and she did say one thing that I know will upset you. But it's good you know her thoughts. I know you have only her best interests at heart, and you can work this out with her."

"What?"

"She thinks you're hiding her up on this hill because you're embarrassed of her."

"*Embarrassed* of her?"

"That you see her as a mistake from your past and don't want the townspeople to know about her."

His jaw muscle danced. "That's not even *remotely*—"

"I know—I know. *I* know it's not remotely true. And *you* know that. I'm just telling you to give you a chance to make sure *she* knows that. Sometimes the way teenagers' brains work can be mystifying."

He stared at her, his scowl murderous. But, finally, he seemed to think it over and then nodded. The knife came back up to the counter, and the chopping continued.

About a minute later, he walked back to the table with a huge mound of tomatoes on the cutting board. "Thanks, Paige," he said softly.

He pushed the tomatoes into the bowl and tossed the concoction with his knife. "And wait. Can we back up a minute? I thought I heard you say something earlier."

She reached for a diced tomato and popped it in her mouth. "What?"

"Did you say a couple minutes ago that that was the most intense sex of your life?"

"*Some* of the most." She gave him a saucy grin. "In the top four." She pretended to inspect the chilies.

His eyebrow raised as he slowly finished scraping the last of the seeds off his cutting board. Eventually his mouth quirked at the corner. "I'll have to investigate this." He gave her one last glance before returning to the counter.

She ignored the heat that rose up around her cheeks and snuck a few extra glances at him.

Being FRED with Adam was going to be a heady ride.

The door banged open, and Amanda stepped through. Paige reached up to cool her cheeks.

"Hey, Amanda," she said.

Amanda smiled, threw her backpack into the corner, and went into the kitchen to watch Adam finish chopping.

She waited for Amanda to leave so they could continue their talk, but Amanda stayed in the kitchen with them until dinner. A half hour later, the three of them were enjoying salsa and quesadillas at the dining table, talking about what foreign language they'd each learned in high school, and telling funny stories about the worst teachers each of them ever had. After dinner they went into the family room so Amanda could select another movie to watch.

They sat together on the sheet-covered couch, but this time Adam positioned himself so he could rest his hand under a blanket on Paige's thigh.

Goose bumps ran up her arm through the entire movie.

When the credits finally rolled, he leaned toward Paige's ear. "Stay tonight?"

"I need to get home," she said, tossing the blanket aside and looking for her shoes.

"Are you sure?" He glanced at Amanda, who'd turned toward them to listen. Adam cleared his throat. "You can stay in the guest room."

"No." Paige found one shoe under Denny. The other was providing a small pillow for Click. It was tempting to stay. Even just to stay in the guest room or on the couch. They could talk. They could go over their ground rules once more. But Paige sensed this would be a mistake. She needed to sleep on the whole thing. The more time she spent with him, the more she could see getting attached, and that's not what FRED was about. She'd spent too many years trying to forget this guy who'd barely known she existed—and she was just now getting to a comfortable, confident, I-can-be-casual-with-you kind of place, complete with mutually agreed-on, laid-out rules—to backpedal now. She needed to think this through, then make a decision by morning that would allow her to best keep herself together.

"Let me walk you home, at least," he said.

Amanda looked up worriedly.

"I'll be back in fifteen, Amanda."

He gave a whistle, and Denny leaped up onto the couch where Adam pointed. Amanda snuggled close to the warm dog. Click, feeling momentarily abandoned by her new friend Denny, climbed up on the couch, too, and nestled between Denny's paws.

"You don't have to walk me if Amanda's worried," Paige said. "I know the way."

"Thanks, Paige," Amanda said with a relieved smile.

Adam walked her to the door and helped her with her sweater. "Are you sure?" he whispered. "She'll really be okay."

"So will I."

Paige stepped out onto the porch, and Adam followed, closing the door behind them.

"I want to make sure everything's okay between us," he said. "You're still good with FRED?"

"Of course."

"I'm not sure how to act in front of Amanda."

"I think we can focus on the 'friends' part. We can be better role models that way."

"Role models? Man." The moonlight caught his smile. "Never thought I'd be that."

"You're doing fine."

He gazed at her for a moment, then gently cupped her face, drawing her to him and kissing her tenderly. No craziness. No insanity. No frustrated desperation. No leading to another step or hinting at something next. No touching her body or pushing to another level. It was just a gentle, giving, yielding kiss—velvety lips saying good night, or he was sorry, or good-bye, or things wouldn't ever be different for them—she couldn't quite tell. When he finished, he simply met her stare.

"Thank you, Paige," he said, low.

As she walked back across the meadow, Paige brought her fingertips to her lips.

And realized she should have made one more rule about kisses. Maybe only during sex.

Because that good-bye kiss didn't feel very FRED at all.

Over the next several days, they fell into a routine: Paige would work on her house all day, Adam would show MacGregor around, Paige would take Amanda down to the harbor and pick her up, they would come back, and the three of them would have dinner together and watch another VHS tape from the movie box.

The box marked "Private" stayed in the corner, untouched, much to Paige's surprise.

She and Adam didn't have a lot of time to be alone, between the workers at Paige's house, the ranch hands helping to assemble the gazebo, the dude group at Adam's, and Amanda. But Adam let Paige know he'd like to be: his hand under the blanket each evening worked itself higher up her thigh until she gasped in inappropriate places during the movies.

"What's the matter?" Amanda would ask, turning back toward Paige.

Paige would press her lips together. "Nothing. I thought he was going to pull out a knife or something."

Amanda would look at her as if she were dense. "Why would he pull out a knife?"

"I don't know. I must not be paying very much attention."

Amanda would shake her head and go back to the movie while Adam would work the smile off his face.

Sometimes Adam would catch Paige by the waist in the kitchen, and he'd lay a quick, hot kiss on her lips, filled with promise and longing.

Once, when the dude group was off in the distance, Adam tugged Paige into the grove of trees by the pond and ran his hands along her body in one long, sweltering kiss behind the tallest oak tree—just long enough to remind her of what he could bring her to and hint at what might come next if they could find a couple hours alone.

Another time, he snuck her into the horse stables before the other wranglers came back and managed to make her come against a haystack with just his hand and a few clever kisses.

One afternoon, as she was starting to paint the baseboard in the downstairs powder room, her cow doorbell mooed, and she opened it to find Adam leaning in the doorway.

"I have an hour off. I came to say hello."

"Ah. Great. Well, hello. Is that the only reason you came?" She smiled.

"And to see how you're doing with the work, of course." He looked over her shoulder at the interior.

"Of course." She stepped back to invite him in. "Let me give you the tour."

There were workers moving about upstairs and outside, and Paige managed to show Adam two whole rooms before he had her behind a closed door and pressed her against it, kissing her neck and running a hand up her leg.

"Adam! The workers are still here!"

"I don't care," he murmured. "They'll get the picture."

"The locks don't work!"

"We'll take our chances."

"Adam!" She pushed at his chest.

He gave her a long-suffering look and then stepped out into the hallway. "Antonio!" he bellowed.

"Yeah, man?"

"Don't let anyone come up here."

"Got it, chief."

Adam came back into the room, a wolfish grin on his face, and closed the door. "How quiet can you be?"

They were like two teenagers, sneaking around the premises, and Paige loved every minute of it. The serious, scowling Adam she'd initially encountered the day she got stuck in her grandmother's window had turned into another man. He was now a winking, dimpled Adam, always looking for the next adventure. As much as she'd been crushing before, she had doubled down now.

But she still had to talk to him.

She still had to come clean.

If she could just get up the nerve . . .

CHAPTER 21

The dude group left on a Sunday.

Adam couldn't help but breathe a sigh of relief.

It was great to know he was sliding toward a sale, but nerve-racking having MacGregor hanging around inspecting everything. When MacGregor had seen the gazebo going up in the meadow, he'd barked to Adam, "What the hell is that?"

"A gazebo."

"I hate it," he'd said.

"I don't care."

"I'm not buying this property with that monstrosity on it."

"It's on Paige's property."

"It looks like it's crossing a line."

Adam turned and ran his hand over his jaw as if he were inspecting it. "Mr. MacGregor, you have fifty acres of land to play with here. If you don't like the twenty square feet that the gazebo might be taking up, you can probably talk Paige into razing it anytime after August 7. How's that?"

"You're talking me out of buying your property, son."

"I'm doing no such thing. I'm trying to help you be neighborly."

MacGregor had just growled. He was already pissed that Paige was waiting on Dorothy Silver's offer rather than taking him up on his, and doubly pissed that Adam couldn't sway it.

But Adam had kept him away from Paige. He hated the way the man stared at Paige's property or, worse, Paige herself. He'd wanted to take him out on at least twenty occasions.

And now he was gone—he'd flown back to Tennessee and said he'd be in touch. The ranch had quieted down, the bison were back in the wild after their week of vaccines and injections, and things felt normal for the first time in ages.

In fact, things felt good.

Adam didn't quite want to admit that to himself. The feeling was foreign. Even if he let himself acknowledge how good he felt, he'd have to follow up with the knowledge that Paige was part of the reason, and he couldn't completely wrap his head around that, or the fact he'd be leaving her soon.

Besides, maybe it wasn't Paige.

Maybe it was about being free.

And his plans were in motion.

As things should be.

And there was no stopping everything now.

He caught sight of Paige's golf cart coming around the side of the resort—her hair lifted on the wind as she threw her head back and laughed with Amanda. As they bounced down the road toward town, they looked over at him and waved.

An incredible warmth filled his chest. And something that felt like joy. He didn't even really know what it was, but *joy* was the word that kept coming to his mind.

Paige and Amanda both trusted him. And relied on him. And liked him. And he liked them. They'd let him take them horseback riding a few times when he could break away from the dude group, and he'd never remembered having such great days. He'd laughed and felt entirely relaxed—Amanda had proven to be a fast learner, and Paige could hold her own. Amanda seemed fascinated by the trails her mom had taken. And Adam had simply felt "at peace," if that was a real thing.

These two women were changing his life in ways he couldn't even comprehend.

He took a deep breath and looked away.

He didn't want to think about what he was giving up.

Paige went the usual way up the back road to the Friends of the Sea Lion center.

"I think he's just not into me," Amanda said.

"Maybe he just doesn't know how you feel about him."

"Or he's just not into me." Amanda gave a wan smile.

They'd been discussing Garrett on their drives, Paige trying to encourage Amanda to be herself and not worry about Garrett too much. If it was meant to be between them, Garrett would come around.

"Sometimes boys can be a little slow," Paige said. "You have to stay true to who you are. And if he likes you, he'll eventually show interest."

"Is that what happened with you and Adam?"

Paige blinked back. "What?"

"It's not like I don't know. Jeez. I see you two looking at each other. I'm not dumb."

Paige didn't know how Amanda was going to feel about that, given her mother and all, so she fumbled for the right words. "I had a crush on him when I was a teenager—about your age," she admitted into the sage-filled air.

"Was it when he was dating my mom?"

Dang. Teens were perceptive. "Um. Yeah."

"I was starting to figure that out."

"How do you feel about that?"

"I guess it's okay." She shrugged.

Paige couldn't bring herself to tell Amanda the whole story—that she'd been instrumental in breaking the couple up—and didn't know if she'd ever be able to admit that. She could barely admit it to herself, definitely couldn't admit it to Adam, and now certainly couldn't admit it to Amanda, either.

"Did your mom ever talk to you about Adam?" Paige asked.

"She never told me his name. She just said that she and my father were teenage sweethearts, and that her parents and his parents broke them up, but he never fought it. So my mom took that as a cue and left him for good. She said he never really cared about her. And that he lived in a terrible place that she never could have gone back to anyway. And he had a terrible father. And a terrible stepmom. That's all I knew."

Paige reeled a little from that. Ginger was probably whom Samantha perceived as stepmom. And those things she'd said—many were lies or exaggerations. But Paige couldn't tell Amanda any of that without calling her mom a liar. So she bit her tongue.

"But I don't get the sense that Adam was ever that bad," Amanda said wistfully, staring out at the canyon trees as they rolled by. "Maybe my mom just said some of that because she didn't want me to feel like he left both of us."

Paige couldn't believe it. "You're a very smart girl, Amanda."

The following week, while they waited to hear if MacGregor was going to make an offer, Paige was invited to dinner again. Adam asked Amanda at dinner if she wanted to have a party for her birthday.

"A party?" Amanda asked, dinner fork halted.

She glanced at Paige. Paige shrugged.

"A small thing," Adam said nervously. "You know, a few friends. Me and Paige. Bob and Gert. Maybe some of the ranch hands, Antonio and Tanya, Kelly and Joanne and Mendelson. But you can invite a couple of friends from the harbor. We can go to Rosa's Cantina, and they'll close off the bar so it's just family and friends, and maybe play pool and listen to the jukebox?"

Amanda stared at him.

Paige suppressed a smile. He didn't want Amanda to feel as if he were hiding her up here, and he was determined to find a way to make sure she understood that.

He glanced at Paige. "Is that uncool now?" His uncertainty about teenagers was endearing.

"No, it's cool," Amanda said.

Relief crossed his face.

"They have a band that comes in at eight thirty," he went on. "They might be country, though. Do you hate country?"

"I can deal with country."

More relief. He was trying so hard. Paige wanted to melt.

"Do you want me to set it up, then?" he asked, stabbing his dinner now. "You invite your friends from the harbor, and I'll do the rest."

Amanda looked at Paige. "Is this for real?"

"I think it is." Paige smiled.

The night of the party, everyone assembled at Rosa's Cantina.

Paige greeted the same group from last time: Antonio and Tanya, Joe, Little, Tony, Jen, Sherryl, and Kelly. Joanne and Mendelson were there. Bob and Gert came, of course. Gordon and Gabe came by with three of the new wranglers, whom Amanda seemed to know. Amanda had invited Garrett from down the hill.

"Is that Garrett?" Adam asked, leaning into Paige's ear as the country band started up. "He was the only one she ended up inviting from the harbor."

"Yeah. He's the brother of Gordon and Gabe."

"How exactly does Amanda know him?"

Paige stiffened. She wanted to tell him about Amanda's crush, but she didn't know if she could give up Amanda's confidence in favor of Adam's, especially since Amanda had so few confidantes.

"You should ask her about it," she said. "Hey, don't you still owe me a dance?" She whirled so she was in Adam's arms.

"Do I? You have a long memory, Paige Grant."

"And you have a short one, Adam Mason."

He chuckled and wrapped his arms around her. "Could that be my excuse for why I can't dance? I can't remember the steps."

"I think you can learn. We'll start with something slow. But for now, I'm leaving you here because I want to line-dance." A number was starting behind them, and Paige glanced over her shoulder.

Adam lifted his eyes to the crowd. "Thank you for not making me do that."

"No problem."

Paige headed out to the dance floor, surprised that even Amanda was out there, laughing with the others and participating in country line dancing with her goth chained boots, Grateful Dead T-shirt, lighter makeup, and growing-out dyed hair. Paige was proud of her for trying a little of everything. She was finding her own way.

Rosa brought out a cake around nine, and Amanda seemed shocked. Everyone sang to her, and she wiped a tear away before she opened presents. She loved Adam's flatiron—he even got a public hug out of that—plus, he gave her an envelope that had something in it that made her tear up again before she quickly brushed at her cheeks. Paige knew that Adam had been staying up the last few nights writing out that card.

Bob and Gert gave Amanda some baking trays and kitchen gadgets, Kelly gave her eight free riding lessons, Tanya and Antonio gave her a vinyl of the Grateful Dead, and others gave her books, movies, and iTunes cards.

Garrett looked stricken when she started opening gifts and turned to say something to his brother. When he made his way around the room toward Paige, he leaned toward her. "I didn't know it was her *birthday*."

"It's okay. She's not the type to care. If she didn't tell you, that means she didn't want you to get her anything."

"I feel bad."

"She won't mind. I promise."

He didn't look appeased.

"You could offer her a dance, though," Paige added.

He lifted his eyebrow.

"You're the only one she invited up here from the harbor, you know."

He looked around at the crowd as if that hadn't occurred to him. "Really?"

"A dance would be special."

He seemed to put the pieces together at once and started nodding his head. "Okay."

Paige smiled. Boys could be so dense sometimes.

She looked at her own teenage crush and realized she was getting to do that all over again.

After cake and presents, the dancing started up again, and Paige waited for a slow song. Once one started, she found Adam, who was sitting with Bob and Gert, and drew him out of his chair.

"He still owes me," she told Bob, who laughed.

As soon as Paige led him to the dance floor, he pulled her close. "Is Amanda going to notice that we can't keep our hands off each other? At least I can't while we're dancing."

"Is that a pathetic ploy to get out of this dance again?"

"It might be."

"It won't work. Besides, speak for yourself. I can keep my hands in appropriate places plenty."

"I challenge you to do so for the next hour."

She slid her hands toward his shoulders and stepped back a few inches.

"Never mind," Adam said, pulling her back. "That's a dumb bet."

He wrapped his arms around her, and they swayed to the mournful country song.

"This is nice," he said.

"I'm glad you like it. And, by the way, to your first point, she's figured us out already."

"Amanda has?"

"She cornered me in the golf cart one afternoon."

"And she's okay with us . . . you know . . . being FRED, or whatever?"

"Well, I didn't explain it like that, but she seemed to be okay with our being together."

"So what in hell are we sneaking around for? Come spend the night with me."

"We're still trying to be good role models, Adam."

"Ah. Foiled again."

The night Paige's new king-size bed arrived, she invited Adam over to test it out. They had a long, languid evening romping in the new bed, since Amanda was down at the harbor with Garrett and some of his friends.

It was fun to be with Adam in what felt like her own home. Alone. Relaxed. Comfortable. Maybe too comfortable. It felt as if they were playing house.

She watched the moonlight shadows play along the ceiling after her second orgasm of the evening and ran her fingers through his hair.

"How is the gazebo coming along?" he asked sleepily.

It was coming along beautifully. Paige couldn't stop staring at it every time she walked by. But having Adam in her own bed, dreamily watching shadows, and hearing his relaxed voice talk about home repairs made the feeling of playing house come on even stronger—making her feel sad this was going to end. She tried to conjure up her promises to be FRED.

"I thought we weren't supposed to talk about land when we were naked?" she said, her fingers still playing with his hair.

"I thought it was make promises," he mumbled.

"Wasn't it any discussion of deals?"

"I don't remember. But if you don't want to talk about wood and paint and gazebos, trust me, I'm okay with that. Instead, I can ask you about the other three."

"Other three what?"

He got up on an elbow. "You said I didn't give you the best sex you ever had. That I was among the top four. So I want to know who the other three are."

"I said the *most intense*."

"I stand corrected." He grinned. "So who are these other three?"

"We're not really going to do this, are we?"

"I sort of want to."

"Why?"

"I want to know what they did so I can top it."

Paige had been kidding when she'd said that. But if the man wanted to improve his already talented skills, far be it from her to get in his way. She took on her sauciest tone and called up her best Mae West.

"Let's just say you're almost number one." She smiled.

"What do I have to do to be number one?"

"Well, one man made me see stars once when I came."

"Is that right?" Adam crawled up her body and put his biceps on either side of her head. "What was he doing to you that you saw stars when you came?"

"That's where you have to use your imagination."

Adam grinned. "Challenge accepted, Paige Grant. Meet me at midnight in the hayloft."

After a few more chores, dinner, a shower, then a long evening of shopping for old ranch-house furniture online, Paige closed her laptop.

It was almost time to meet Adam.

Her fingers tingled with excitement as she brushed her hair and changed. As the clock ticked toward twelve, she threw her hairbrush down and skipped out into the meadow, pulling a wrap around her shoulders against the night air. The moonlight bounced off the long blades of grass that tickled her ankles, and she inhaled the scent of night-blooming jasmine. She imagined Adam in the hayloft, waiting for her, and her heart thrummed.

She couldn't believe this was happening. She knew she should stay focused on FRED, keep her heart safe, stay distant from Adam, and all that, but she could feel herself falling. She'd been crushing on him for so long—and had built up an imaginary love for a man she'd never known—but now that she'd met him, and gotten to know him, the imaginary love was starting to become real. And now that the physical intimacy was matching every one of her fantasies, he was becoming almost mythical in her mind. If she truly wanted to protect her heart, she needed to stop seeing him. Otherwise she was going to keep falling and falling until she tumbled down. But she would focus on that tomorrow. Tonight she couldn't wait to feel what he was going to do to her.

Through the dark, she could see a soft glow inside the hayloft and raced toward it, tugging the wrap around her. Once there, she pressed the heavy wooden door open. Adam was already inside, sitting in the center on a large haystack, fully dressed. He had three thick blankets thrown over a cluster of haystacks near him, and two lanterns on the ground that cast shadows on the wood. He smiled and held out his arm as she stepped inside.

She sauntered toward him, then straddled his lap, positioning herself over the bulge in his pants while he made a sound deep in his throat. He looked up at her with eyes that were liquid, adoring, begging, and thankful, until she started to move—then his eyes were suddenly anguished.

"Paige." His voice was thin, like paper in the wind.

She undid his shirt buttons, moving just enough to torment him. She wanted his shirt off—wanted to see the muscles she adored, wanted to touch them again, wanted to feel the strength in his arms, wanted his skin against hers.

"*Paige.*" He suddenly reached up and stopped her hand. "Let me do you. Undress for me."

She smiled and threw off the wrap, then unbuttoned her blouse slowly, loving the look in his eyes. They were ravaging her, devouring her, and she watched them the whole time—his pupils dark, wide, wild—while she took her time getting rid of the blouse and then starting on her skirt.

Adam sat quietly, trying to look controlled, but Paige could see the delirium there. When she got the skirt to the ground, she bent at the waist to pick it up, tossed it to the side, then stood before him in her pink bra and thong, letting him look her up and down.

"Turn around," he rasped.

She did.

Although he was trying to look restrained, his eyes told a story of a man on the brink.

"You are magnificent." He yanked her back onto his lap, against his pants, kissing the cleavage formed by her favorite push-up bra, hinting at promises of things his tongue might do, and she felt her skin prickle.

Paige chose not to think about the fact that that was the second line her mom had predicted. She chose, instead, to lean back and let him kiss her, and to run her hands through his hair while he undid her bra and adored each breast and drew each of her nipples between his lips until her toes curled.

"Lean back farther," he murmured, gently lowering her onto another hay bale behind her, her hips still in his hands. Her shoulders settled into the blanket on the bale, and she wriggled into position. The thrill of it was almost more than she could stand. Her bottom and pelvis were still in his lap, face up, and he played with her as if she were a toy. He ran his touch lightly along her stomach and brought his fingertips to the band of her panties, tugging at them, torturing her. She writhed in his hands.

"Adam, I can't wait."

"Of course you can."

His fingers were light and teasing, outlining the tiny triangle of her panties, tantalizing her until she was arching her back and letting tiny moans escape her lips.

"I can't," she whispered. The pleasure was too great, almost to the point of pain—the erotic position of her hips so high, the inability to fully see what he was doing, the teasing feel of his too-light touch, making her ache for more pressure.

"Adam, *please.*"

"Baby, we haven't even gotten started yet." He pulled lightly at the front of her panties. The combination of his expert touch and the wind whispering through the door and flickering across such intimate places of her body caused her to arch her back and go out of her mind for a second.

"Adam."

"Relax." He scooted her down, shifting himself back, and she knew what was coming next. The wind sent another meadow gust through the open door and puckered her breasts. Adam's hands splayed along her back. She writhed against him, and his other hand pulled at her panty front, and a long, slow ache settled between her legs. She waited and felt the wind and closed her eyes. Then she felt his tongue, warm and insistent.

"Oh," she cried out, not quite ready for the thrill that shot through her, and then—*again.* "Oh God, Adam."

His tongue grazed her, swiping underneath her panties, adding to the aching sensation, as he gently pulled them to one side, and let his tongue touch her, and let her cry out, and then pulled the other side, teased her again, let his tongue touch, let her cry out.

He licked and tormented until she couldn't stand it anymore—she was on a plateau in the wind, standing naked on a mountaintop, her arms open wide—and *Oh God, Adam*—she spiraled, and spun, and his tongue was flicking in and out and—*Oh please*—he entered her, wet and warm, and she pushed to meet him, and ached for him to touch her there, right there—*Oh there, oh yes*—and she arched her back and kept spinning, and splitting, and pushed to meet him again for—*Oh there, yes, Adam, there*—and then—

"Oooooooh God," she cried out as he finally touched the ache, and then the ground wasn't there.

She was weightless and floating, and the wind was carrying her down.

When she opened her eyes and was able to focus fully, she looked straight up through the hayloft, where a skylight had been opened that she hadn't noticed before.

There she could truly see stars.

While the wind made a hollow whistling sound, and Paige lay still, a pressure started between her eyes, and a couple of quiet tears trickled down each side of her face.

They weren't tears that belonged to a particular feeling—they weren't from sadness or relief or fear—they were simply tears from too much emotion in general, too much emotion felt for this one man, who was still holding her with his enormous hand splayed beneath her back, where he'd bent her backward. The tears felt like a relieving of pressure, the pressure of too much of everything, as if her body could handle only so much feeling, and the rest needed to be squeezed out in a couple of salty drops.

As the feeling of the uncomfortable hay against her shoulders came into her reality, and the wanting ache between her legs was replaced with a feeling of satiation, and she could hear the wind outside again, she knew she was back to the existing moment.

Adam adjusted her panties, straightening them in a sweetly clumsy gesture, then reached forward and pulled her up.

He wrapped his arms around her waist and pulled her toward him, keeping his eyes on her.

"No good?" he said, smiling.

She laughed.

He tucked her head under his chin and held her there like a child. They simply sat like that and listened to the wind coming across the meadow, rocking together on the hay bale.

CHAPTER 22

Adam worked all the next day on the long front drive into the ranch, which needed new gravel along the side of the rosebushes. Antonio and Gordon came to help, and the three men donned their work gloves and parked their gravel-filled wheelbarrows under the sun along the quarter-mile stretch.

He appreciated the help, and he liked having someone to talk to. He especially liked having someone who could take his mind off Paige. Mostly he needed to know it was possible. Because he'd been thinking about her almost incessantly for the last fifty-six hours and needed to know he hadn't lost all his senses.

Last night had been incredible. And damned intense. He hadn't meant for it to be—intense, that was. He'd meant for it to be hot. He'd meant for her to anticipate. He'd meant for her to come. He'd meant for her to see stars.

But he hadn't meant for the intensity of the end of the night, when he'd pulled her into his lap and held her quivering body and felt her tears on his neck. He hadn't meant to have his own heart feel so full and want to hold her forever and feel that kind of power in a unity he hadn't known existed. He hadn't meant to pull the blanket up around them and settle them into the softer hay and fall asleep with her under the stars. He hadn't meant to wake up with her in his arms, and stare at her sleeping face as the morning light came through. He hadn't meant to spend the daybreak wondering how he was possibly going to say good-bye soon . . .

His phone buzzed in his pocket, and he scrambled to get his gloves off. He stood in the beating sun, wiped his forehead, and leaned on his shovel near a rosebush.

"Yeah?" he said when he saw it was Bob.

"Adam, I have great news."

"Let's hear it."

"MacGregor just made an official offer, so we can start escrow."

The wind left Adam's lungs in a whoosh. He'd been waiting to hear this news for nearly six months. He'd been doing everything for MacGregor's approval—fixing roads, fixing the house, selling off animals, making promises, making plans, going over numbers, making calls, mending fences, dealing in bison, and not sleeping at night. And now he was getting the news he'd been waiting for the whole time.

"So we have thirty days?"

"Yep. Thirty, exactly."

He took a deep breath and wondered why he wasn't more elated. "That's great."

"I thought you'd be a little more excited. What's wrong?"

"Nothing. This is great. Good work. I'm impressed you carried this off. I'm just . . ."

He couldn't even think of how to fill in the rest.

He was glad to have his plans fulfilled, but he was sad to be . . . what? Leaving his family home for real? Leaving the people he knew and loved? Starting over?

He knew it was all those things.

But there was something else now. Something that felt as if it was a beginning that he wasn't letting bloom. Something he hadn't known he needed, but now he wondered how he'd live without. Something that had kept him warm all night and made him smile first thing this morning when he realized it was still in his arms.

Adam suddenly had the terrible awareness that he'd let happen what he'd never intended to—he'd fallen for Paige Grant.

But she had not fallen for him. She'd told him too many times. They were staying FRED. And he'd never be accepted in her family anyway. Especially by Ginger. And how would they be a couple? Either he'd have to move to LA, which he couldn't do because of Amanda, or Paige would have to follow him to Alabama. And Paige probably didn't want to move to Alabama or start life with a teenage daughter. He could ask, but he'd probably freak her out. He'd be like Ted or Todd or whoever with the red frame.

He might just have to ride this one out. Enjoy her during the time they had left but not expect more than she could give.

Then he'd pack up his new little family of two, including Denny, and head out to start a new life alone.

He'd get Paige out of his mind.

He owed this to Amanda.

Paige stood in the yard, admiring the pansies she'd planted around the freshly painted gazebo, when her phone began jangling "It's My Party."

"Hi, Mom."

"How is everything going, dear?"

"Fine. How are you?"

"Great. I'm getting all kinds of encouragement from my doctor."

"That's great! Like what?"

"Like how strong I am, how well I'm doing. And I got the go-ahead to travel. So guess where I'm visiting?"

Silence filled the line while Paige willed her mom to say something other than Lavender Island. *Anything else. Anyplace else. Anywhere else.* She clutched the chair in front of her.

"Lavender Island!" Ginger squealed.

"No, Mom."

"Yes!"

"No. You can't."

"Of course I can! I can't wait!"

"No. It's not a good idea."

"Whatever are you talking about? I'm already packing."

"You don't need to come."

"'Need' isn't part of this. I want to come, Paigey. I can't wait to get out of town. And I can't wait to see you. And you must be so lonely there without your sisters. Aren't you lonely?"

Paige thought about the last several nights she'd spent in Adam's arms and thought, *Nooooooo*. But she couldn't think of how to tell her mom she'd been lying all this time about Adam. And now she'd have to reveal the truth of Amanda, also. Plus—

"And guess who else is coming?" Her mom's voice sounded as if it was quivering with glee.

"I can't imagine."

"Dorothy Silver!"

"*What?*"

"She wants to come and see the progress of the place so far."

"But, Mom, I'm nowhere near done! There are lots of fixes to do, and I hardly have any furniture, and the gazebo floor still needs to be stained, and—"

"You don't have any beds yet?"

"Well . . . one." Paige squirmed, thinking of how much fun she'd had there.

"Chairs? Couches? Anyplace we can sit and have some coffee together?"

"Just a dining table and three chairs, one of which is broken. I'm shopping for new furniture online, but I haven't found the right pieces yet. I've only ordered two side tables so far."

"Well, then, maybe we can stay in town. Dorothy was planning on that anyway—she's bringing her entourage. But I'll stay in town, too, if it's easier."

Paige was surprised her mom would do anything for her that was "easier." But before she could start hyperventilating any further about Dorothy's probable first impressions, she imagined the circus the famous actress would bring. As much as Paige fantasized about sitting across a dining table from the screen legend, and hopefully getting the part in her new movie, this whole early visit might be a nightmare.

"If she's in town with an entourage, and coming up here to check things out during the day, this wedding won't be a secret from the public for long—or Olivia and Natalie, for that matter," Paige pointed out. "This is going to be all over the papers. And if it's not all over the papers, it will be all over town anyway with gossips like Kilner."

"No, she wants to keep a low profile."

"On this island? Good luck."

"We'll be careful. You're doing well hiding. Natalie and Olivia still don't know you're there."

"Only because I don't have to go to town every day. I think it's a mistake, Mom. Dorothy might lose faith in us. I know—and you know—we can have the wedding done and looking gorgeous, but Dorothy might see how it looks now and get worried."

"You just have to manage expectations, darling. That's my forte."

Paige sighed deeply and knew she'd lost this round. Her mom was a woman on a mission. Always.

"When are you coming?" Paige asked, admitting defeat.

Maybe she could get furniture in another few weeks and have the gazebo nearly done and at least have the place looking more presentable if—

"Next week."

"Next week?" Paige gasped. "Okay. I'll see you soon, Mom."

She hung up before her nervous fingers dropped the phone. *Next week?* How was she going to have everything looking good by then? And how was she going to keep Adam and her a secret? And what about Amanda? Her mom would be filled with criticism as soon as she learned that Adam and Samantha's temporary relationship had resulted in a teen pregnancy. This was going to be a disaster.

Paige scrambled to her feet and raced to her notes on the kitchen counter, reprioritizing a few lines of her spreadsheet, when her phone jangled to "My Heroes Have Always Been Cowboys."

"Adam. How are you?"

"I have some good news." His despondent note didn't match the words.

"I have news, too. But you first."

"MacGregor made an offer."

Paige felt the blood drain from her head. She eased herself into a dining chair and splayed her shaking hand across the table. She knew this time would come, of course. It had always been so. But hearing it now, as reality, had an effect she hadn't foreseen. She'd been having so much fun with him, falling into their comfortable and sexy new rhythm of life—the horseback rides, the movie watching, the dinners with Amanda, the sneaky kisses, the incredible sex—that she'd been able to ignore that this life had an expiration date. It felt like a time always set in the future, and she would be the one calling the shots. But now the expiration date was finite, and it was Adam's call—probably thirty to forty-five days.

"Congratulations." She tried to muster enthusiasm in her voice.

This was what he wanted. It was what Amanda wanted. She needed to be happy for them. She *was* happy for them. *Right?* She lifted her fist in a silent victory salute to convince herself she was *so happy*. This was great! Things worked out for the people she'd come to care for!

But her heart kept falling, and her mouth was going dry.

She took a deep breath and tried to inject her voice with an upswing. "That's terrific, Adam." *There.* That sounded kind of convincing. "Did it go according to plan? Is it exactly what you wanted?"

"Yeah." Adam's response was strangely short.

"So what does this mean, now, time-wise?"

"Thirty days, but I can leave anytime now. Bob can handle the details."

She sighed.

"Bob will go to probate court and see if anyone else shows up to bid," he added. "If not, MacGregor will take the property."

"Great," Paige said in her fake falsetto. "I'm glad everything worked out for you."

Adam paused for another long time, then she heard him blow out a breath. "I can stay a couple more weeks, though. I hope we can spend as much time together as possible before then."

Tears sprang to Paige's eyes, and she immediately berated herself. Her sadness was selfish. She needed to be happy for them. She shouldn't have gotten attached. They were supposed to be FRED.

"Maybe," she said with another forced lift, "except my news kind of ruins that."

"What's your news?" he asked quietly.

"Ginger's coming. Along with Dorothy Silver."

"When?"

"Next week. They'll definitely ruin our final weeks together."

A long silence followed.

"I can handle Ginger, Paige," he said, low.

"I can't."

Paige sighed. They'd always avoided this discussion. It had been obvious that he was openly seeing her in front of his family and friends although she was hiding him from hers. She just hadn't wanted to bring it up. But now it was there in the spotlight.

"I take it you haven't told her we've been . . . spending time together?"

"No," she admitted.

"I don't blame you," he said. "But don't worry about her. When she's here, I'll stay out of your way if that's what you want."

"That's not what I want."

"It'll be all right. I'll take my cues from you."

Paige hung up and tried to decide how she'd handle this. She just needed to be honest with her mom. She'd tell her that she'd started out with a business arrangement with Adam, but then their relationship grew. Or their attraction, rather. Or their FRED friendship. Whatever. And maybe it made her less effective in convincing him to sell to Dorothy, and maybe she'd lost the sale a long time ago, but that's just the way it was. They'd at least compromised on the meadow, even though Dorothy would probably lose access to the orchard. Dorothy would be disappointed. Her mom would be disappointed. And Dorothy might not want to buy the property, ultimately. But Paige had tried. Ginger would think Paige lost the deal because she'd gotten "soft," that she'd let her heart get in the way of business. Paige could already hear the words.

But Paige couldn't turn her heart on and off like that. Maybe she wasn't a businesswoman and never would be. And maybe she didn't want to be. Were finances really more important than love? Well, okay, it wasn't exactly love when it was one-way. But were finances more important than connection? She'd connected with Amanda, connected with Adam, even connected with the townspeople, and this had been one of the most fun summers of her life. Her soul had never felt so settled. She didn't know if she'd simply been righting wrongs—the wrong of her thirteen-year-old summer, where she'd pined for a boy who never noticed her—or if it was something different that her almost-thirty-year-old soul needed. But either way, this summer had been worth it.

If they lost the Dorothy Silver deal because the ranch didn't look identical to the movie, that would be terrible. But they'd spring back. And her mom would eventually forgive. And Paige would always have this time to remember. Her memories of this place were now good ones instead of awful ones. And she'd helped Amanda. And she'd helped Adam. She felt wonderful.

She stood and looked out the window at the enormous gazebo, which she was proud of.

When her mom came, she'd just have to be strong. She'd have to be strong about her convictions, and about her feelings toward these people and how feelings were okay. She didn't want to go back in hiding—hiding her true self, her true feelings, her true personality—just because her mom thought it was bad business sense. And she didn't want to hide her feelings about Adam and Amanda. Just because her mom had had bad experiences with one Mason man and had never trusted his son didn't mean Paige had to carry forth the tradition. Just like Amanda didn't have to follow in her mother's footsteps, and Adam didn't have to follow in his father's, Paige, too, didn't have to follow in Ginger's Louboutins.

She'd simply come clean with her mom about her fling with Adam, and enjoy her last couple weeks of FRED openly.

Let the chips fall where they may.

CHAPTER 23

The next day was their newly traditional Sunday horseback-trio ride to the ocean, but when Paige arrived at the stables, Amanda wasn't there.

"She took the news of the sale pretty quietly," Adam said as they saddled Tempest and Ophelia. "She said she had a stomachache. I'm not sure what to make of that. I thought she'd be happy."

"Maybe she has to process it as another change," Paige suggested, lifting her own saddle the way Adam had taught her.

Darcy and Lizzie were going to Kelly later that afternoon, and Adam looked at them longingly.

"It's a lot for her to take in," Paige added. "She's been through so much."

Adam swung onto his horse. "I'm sure you're right. I just need to settle her somewhere she feels permanent. Let's go. I want to show you something today."

They rode past the pasture, along the pond, and then down a ravine toward a woodland entrance that Paige had never seen before. They brought the horses to a slow trot as they wove their way through the thick forestry, which smelled of pine needles warmed on the earth, and then down another trail that switchbacked twice before it opened to a clearing with an incredible view of the ocean about fifty feet down. They rode to what looked like the end of the earth, with the ocean stretching out forever in front of them. Adam hopped off and looped Tempest's reins around a tree.

"We'll let them graze. Follow me."

"Where are we going?" She watched him head down an embankment that led to a steep rock formation down to the water, then scrambled off her horse and followed.

"Remember you said the hangar was like a museum?" he called over his shoulder as he navigated the climb. The ocean roared in front of them, while the earthy, clean scent of wet land drifted up around them.

Paige climbed over a sharp embankment to keep up. "Right," she called ahead. "All those aviation records dating back to the 1940s."

"Wait until you get a load of this place."

She balanced over the next ledge and jumped down behind him. This is where her Calamity June tendencies sometimes came into play— in situations that were already dangerous, and she managed to make them worse.

"Adam, are you sure you want me down here with you?"

"Of course. What's wrong?"

"Well, remember I told you about the curse? I really can be Calamity June in places like this."

She followed him down a few more ledges that looked like black lava stones, the sea spray bouncing upward, getting thicker along her arms and in the wisps of her hair.

Adam waited for her to get to the same rock he was on, then pulled her up beside him. "Paige." He cupped her face. "When I first met you, you threw your chin in the air and told me you didn't want to be called Calamity June. So here's the thing. You need to stop calling yourself that, too. You are not dangerous. You are not cursed. You are wild and free and exciting, and that's what everyone loves about you."

The ocean crashed in front of them as Paige steadied herself on the rock. Did Adam just say "love"? He wasn't exactly claiming the feeling himself—he didn't say *he* loved that about her, simply "everyone"—but it still took her breath away. It was only a few sentiments removed, and she wanted to take it. She was working on mustering the courage to ask him to repeat it, or clarify, or something—touching his forearms—when he suddenly reached for her hand.

"We're almost there." He tugged her forward.

After two more jumps down, their heels landed into the soft sand right behind a tiny beach, maybe ten feet across. Just beyond another rocky ledge were the ruins of a structure Paige couldn't quite identify: cement walls, red-tile roofs, steps, and maybe a tower. Seeing the evidence of human life so far out here on this secret cove—but now buried in Neptune's graveyard—took her breath away.

"What is it?" she whispered.

"A seaplane port." Adam wandered out onto the beach. "Can you see where the ramp is, slightly underwater? And there, where those red roof tiles are, that was a bell tower on the ticket building. That wall over there was the start of the seaplane hangar, and those arches formed the station and waiting area. This was a gorgeous piece of architecture in the 1930s."

"Did your family run this, too?"

"My mom's grandfather did. Charlie Chaplin's half brother, Syd, was setting up seaplane service to various California islands for Charlie's Hollywood friends, so service here was added then, in about 1919. My mom's grandfather bought the ramp in 1934 and built it into this whole port. Ultimately there were three planes here. That ramp was unique—it was a turntable, so they could land in the ocean, then put the wheels down and roll up onto the turntable and turn it toward the hangar. It was something else. It was shut down when the island was taken over as a training ground in World War II. After the war was over, though, the roads started to get washed out by storms, and they never reopened it. I wanted to bring it back to life, but I never got a chance. The roads up that way were taken over by the Conservancy, and I petitioned to refurbish this area and make it into a museum."

"Why didn't they go for it?"

"It's expensive. And it's on the wrong side of the island. The main road that originally drove out of here was washed out in 1953. See? It's over there."

Paige peered around the rocks.

"It would be hard for people to even get here to see it unless the entire road was rebuilt. The only way down is the way we came."

"It's amazing, Adam," she said breathlessly. "What a piece of history."

"I agree. It's the only piece of land I still own."

"You *own* this?"

"My dad, for some reason, made me a partner on the title to this property. It's not very valuable because you can't build anything on this tiny stretch of sand—and the rocks there prevent any building up that way—so those old seaplane ruins are all there's room for. But this is the last thing I have of my mom's. I can't part with it."

"It's beautiful, Adam."

He nodded, staring out at the crashing waves. Then he sat down in the sand and patted a place for her to join him. "So what's your seaplane property?"

"What?" she asked.

"That secret you keep that you don't quite want to tell anyone." He skipped a rock over the water.

"How do you know I have a 'seaplane property'?"

"Everyone does."

She helped him find another skipping stone while she thought that over. Could she tell him hers? She'd been keeping her yoga-studio idea secret for years now—quietly attending classes, getting her credentials, saving money, and scouting sites—but she'd never told a soul, fearing people would laugh. She couldn't bear to have someone crush her dream like that. It was all she had. It was the one place she never felt like Calamity June.

"I've, um, I've always wanted to open a yoga studio," she finally said.

He turned to look at her.

She waited for him to laugh, or at least smirk, or ask her why he never saw her doing yoga, or take a quick skim of her fuller body out of disbelief, but he didn't do any of those things. He just nodded his head and watched the ocean. "Where would you like to open it?"

Tears of relief sprang to her eyes. She launched into her whole plan, describing how she envisioned it with teak walls and floor-to-ceiling windows looking out at a grove of trees, maybe near one of the riverbeds in LA or by one of the valley parks.

"And I want to specialize in yoga for people with chronic conditions, who might think they can't do the positions. There's an asana for everyone."

She demonstrated a few of the routines she'd designed, and he even tried to do a few of the moves as she posed him. He listened to her for nearly an hour, and asked a million questions that helped her give shape to her dream.

"So why are you keeping this a secret?" he asked.

"I'm worried people will laugh at me."

"Why would anyone laugh?"

"I don't look like a yoga instructor, and my mom wants me to be an accountant or take over her event-planning business or something."

"Paige, don't let anyone talk you out of this. If you see this for yourself, make it happen. You don't need permission from anyone."

He was right. The more she talked about it, the more realistic it seemed.

"And you have *your* dream right here, along with your own private beach?" she asked.

"That it is." He surveyed it, then gave her a wolfish grin over his shoulder. "Want to get naked on it?"

"Please tell me you didn't have girls here all the time."

"Absolutely not. You are definitely the first. And only."

"All right, then." She reached for his shirt, eager to see what his muscled chest would look like against the sand on this private beach. "Get over here."

Later that afternoon, after they'd both made it back to Paige's house, had a late lunch, checked on Amanda, showered, and then had another romp in Paige's new bed, Paige headed downstairs to get them both a tall glass of lemonade.

Her heart was light with joy—she'd had a beautiful afternoon with Adam and was newly inspired about her yoga studio—and all she could do was postpone thinking about the end of the road for them. He would've been a beautiful man to spend a lifetime with. But he had his own agenda with his own teenage daughter, and Paige wasn't being invited into their lives across the country. And she had never imagined that kind of life for herself anyway—she had never even pictured getting married, let alone having a teenager. Or living with a rancher. On a ranch. Or a pilot. In Alabama. Or wherever he ended up. And she definitely never imagined getting married to her teenage crush.

He had said that word—*love*—but he didn't mean it the way she craved to hear it. He'd said her spirit was what "everyone" loved about her, and he might be included, but he wasn't exactly saying that. Her shoulders sank. She'd always run away from the word *love*—Todd and the other boyfriends of her life had always wanted to invoke it too early for her jittery taste—but somehow it wouldn't have seemed too early for Adam. Maybe because she'd loved him most of her life, or maybe because he was the man she needed to hear it from—she didn't know. But now she craved the word from him again.

But that was futile thinking.

They'd agreed to FRED. And she couldn't change the rules on him now. If she tried, he might go running the other way. And she wanted to enjoy what little time was left.

As she shut the refrigerator door, she thought she heard something outside. She whirled, pitcher in hand, and almost let the lemonade shatter at her bare feet. Coming in through the kitchen door, complete with pinched face and sunglasses, was her mother.

Six days early.

CHAPTER 24

Paige stood with her mouth agape as Ginger bustled into the kitchen, chattered a few hellos, and set her Hermès scarf and purse on the island. As soon as her sunglasses were off, Ginger twirled slowly and took everything in.

"Well, I thought it would be further along, but . . . ," she said, offering up what seemed like a begrudging nod and smile.

Her smile stopped midway when Adam landed at the base of the stairs. He was fully dressed after his and Paige's last tussle in the sheets—his blue work shirt now buttoned, his jeans now buckled, his hat in his hand—but as he smoothed his hair back, Paige knew her mother was reading the situation correctly.

As Ginger's eyes widened, Adam ambled forward. "Ginger. It's been a while."

Ginger's fingertips touched the wood grain as if she were hanging on. Her gaze swept slowly from Adam's descent from the bedroom to Paige's disheveled hair and misbuttoned blouse.

"I see I'm just in time," she said icily.

"Mom, I was going to—"

"How are you?" Adam held out his hand.

Her mom took it, but only for a second and only at his fingertips, then busied herself with her purse in a gesture that Paige recognized as nervous. "You look just like him." Her voice first sounded accusing, but then Paige noticed it held a note of awe.

"Mom, what are you doing here so early?"

"I came to see how things were going. I got an interesting phone call. Perhaps my timing was off. I can see now why things weren't getting done around here." She tied the scarf back around her neck and lifted her purse.

"Look," Paige tried again. "This isn't—"

"I'll be outside," Ginger said in Paige's direction. "I wanted to see the property and see the views again. Come see me when you two are done."

She bristled out the door.

"Sorry." Adam touched Paige's elbow. "I didn't realize who it was until I got down the stairs. Let me go with you to talk to her."

"No. I need to go alone."

"I want to . . . talk to her. Or defend you. Or something."

"Defend me?"

"I want to tell her what a great job you're doing. You've knocked yourself out around here, and I want to let her know that our spending time together had nothing to do with anything. This place looks worlds better from when you arrived. I know she's going to be less than thrilled with the idea that we're sleeping together, but—"

"I told you she doesn't know."

"I thought you were going to tell her."

"I thought about it. But I didn't have time. I mostly told her we weren't," she whispered back.

"Weren't what?"

"Sleeping together."

"We weren't?"

"Well, we were, but I told her we weren't. Or I didn't admit we were. Or . . . whatever. I just didn't tell her anything."

"Paige." He pivoted her toward him. "You're a grown woman. You can do what you want. You can open a yoga studio, or live wherever you want, or date whoever you want. Don't let her bully you."

"She's not bullying me, exactly. She just wishes I was stronger."

"You *are* strong." He cupped her face. "And you're beautiful. And you're perfect. And you don't need to keep proving yourself to her."

"Just like you don't need to prove yourself to your dad?"

He cocked his head and let go of her face. His eyes went into storm mode.

"Adam, I know you have that box sitting in your kitchen because you're afraid of what's in it. Or maybe what *isn't* in it, more likely. You always wanted his approval, just like I always wanted my mom's. So don't give me that 'you're a grown-up so it doesn't matter what they think' crap. It *always* matters. To some of us. Those of us who never got that approval growing up will keep fighting for it for the rest of our lives. And I feel bad that you didn't get to finish your fight. But your dad would be proud of everything you've done here. And so would your mom. And maybe your dad couldn't show you or tell you while he was here, but maybe all he had to give was whatever is in that box. Maybe some of your answers are there. Maybe your fight is over."

Adam stared at her for a long time, his blue eyes going from stormy to calm.

"That's all he had to give?" he asked. The bitterness in his voice didn't call for an answer.

Paige watched as his scowl returned, his eyebrows furrowing, first looking thoughtful, then frustrated, then pained; then the pain was released altogether. Finally, he reached up and took her face in his hands again.

"Thank you, Paige," he said, almost in a whisper. "Are you sure you don't want me to go with you?"

"I'm sure."

Once Adam left, Paige took a deep breath and glanced at her mom way out across the property, about a hundred feet, standing at the edge of the cliff, staring at the ocean view.

She sighed. She'd have to get this over with.

As Paige approached, she watched her mother's shoulders, weakened from chemo—they seemed shorter and narrower—but yet still in possession of such power.

"Are you sleeping with him?" her mother asked, her back still turned.

Paige's heartbeat picked up. Immediately on the defensive, as usual, she took a deep breath and pressed her hands into her pockets. "Yes."

"How long has this been going on?"

"I tried to tell you a few times, but before I could—"

"I thought we went over this, Paige. I told you about him, and about his father, and—"

"Mom!"

Ginger took a sudden step backward and blinked back surprise at Paige's abruptness.

"You do *not* let me finish a sentence," Paige said. "Will you let me speak?"

Ginger's eyes went wide. She nodded.

"Thank you." Paige let out a slow exhale. Her heart was still skittering over a few beats. She paced a few times in front of the view. Once her heartbeat felt as though it was settling down, she fixed her voice into something that sounded steady. "I didn't mean to lie by omission. I meant to tell you a few times. But you jump in immediately with your commentary and opinions and direction and judgment, so I wasn't able to complete a thought without getting wrapped around the axle. You bully me into saying what you want me to say, and you pressure me into buckling under your opinion."

"I don't bully you!"

Paige knew that would hit a nerve. She took another deep breath. "You do. You put your opinions onto me and expect me to take them up for you."

"Like what?"

Paige looked at the grass. She didn't want to upset her mother. But suddenly she realized how desperately this needed to be said. "Like I don't want to act anymore. And I don't want to go into the event-planning business. I want to open a yoga studio."

Her mother stared at her as if she'd just said she'd like to ride to Saturn. "A *yoga* studio?" she sputtered. "What on earth would you do with a *yoga* studio?"

"Didn't you say you enjoy the moves I've been teaching you and your friends?" Paige asked.

"Well, yes, but—"

"*That.* That's what I want to do with a yoga studio."

Empowered from her planning with Adam earlier, she went on. "I'd like to teach specifically for women dealing with chemo or pain or chronic conditions, and show them which moves they can do safely that might help with pain management."

Her mom simply blinked.

But Paige felt relieved, strong, and ready to fight. "And secondly, you've imposed your opinions regarding how terrible Adam was."

Ginger shook her head. "Don't try to make him my fault, Paige. He was a troublemaker. He was just like his father."

"No, he wasn't, Mom. You might have said that to him, or said it to George, but that didn't make it true. *George* was the troublemaker. He was the one who took your money. And he tried to give it back in land, but that was never good enough for you."

"This rocky land is useless."

"My point is that he tried, and you rejected him, and you broke each other's hearts. But transferring that onto Adam or me wasn't fair."

"Adam was just like him, Paige—can't you see? With all that gallivanting around, and he started those fires, honey."

"That was never proven. And I can't imagine he did."

"Then who did?"

"I have no idea."

"You and Adam were in both places. So if it wasn't you . . ."

This was the old argument. And the old story. The entire town seemed to have something to say about it and an opinion to weigh in with. But when the first accusations came down on "Calamity June," Paige had been the one to tell her mother that Adam was in both places, too. She felt ashamed now that her tattle-telling had gotten him in so much trouble, but her mom had taken it too far.

"I didn't want you to get blamed," Ginger said. "I was protecting you."

Paige nodded. She appreciated that. And she knew the fact that George hadn't given Adam the same benefit of the doubt was what had ruined their father-son relationship forever.

"But Adam was traipsing around with that girl all the time—do you know I caught them in George's bed with their clothes off? He had trouble written all over him, Paige. Who knows how many girls he'd been with?"

"That girl, by the way, was named Samantha, and they had a baby together."

Ginger's eyes widened.

"The 'baby' is here now. She's sixteen. Her name is Amanda. Samantha raised her in Alabama and didn't tell Adam about her, but then Samantha died six months ago and sent Amanda here, and now he's taking care of her. And he wants to do the best thing for her. And he's knocking himself out. And, in addition to his daughter, he takes care of animals—horses and cats and dogs—and people. He helps Kelly with her career and takes care of his brother and employs all the people up here and takes care of Gert and Bob, and—"

"Bob *Hastings*?"

"Yes. Do you remember Bob?"

"Of course." Ginger shook her head. "Go on."

Paige tried to get her bearings again. "Adam's a wonderful man is all I'm saying. He's kind and generous, and everyone on this ranch loves him. I had sex with him because I wanted to."

Ginger turned away quickly.

"He didn't pressure me or ask me for anything," Paige continued. "He *liked* me, Mom. And I like him. But we both know this is a strange, temporary situation, and we don't plan to continue anything. We're adults, and we wanted this, and that's just the way it is."

"Paige, put yourself in my shoes. You just sent your daughter up a mountain to take care of a business issue that you wish you were strong enough to handle. She goes up the mountain and gets seduced by a stepson you never trusted and who spent time in jail. Don't you see how I must feel about this? Don't you see how guilty I feel? Like I've sent you into a wolves' den? I just don't want you to get hurt."

"He wasn't your stepson."

"It felt that way."

"And he was released from jail."

"He had a warrant even before that—remember?"

"It was for jaywalking, Mom. They said that to keep him for questioning."

"Still."

"And he spent time in jail because you threatened to call the sheriff's department if George didn't."

"It was for his own good."

"I don't think he would see it that way. He didn't start that fire. And you broke up a family."

"That was probably for his own good, too. Can you imagine if he'd married her and gone to Alabama? He'd be a different person. And he wouldn't have any of this."

"That wasn't your call."

"You seem to be forgetting that you're the one who initiated that call."

Paige tried to swallow. That was the part she could barely admit to herself.

"Does he know that?" Ginger asked.

Paige shook her head.

"Then you're both being dishonest." She turned to gaze out at the sunset. "I don't want you to get hurt."

"I'm not going to get hurt."

Her mother glanced up but didn't respond. Paige felt frustrated that they were at a standstill, but she'd show her mom. Ginger was frighteningly right about so many things—about MacGregor, about George, even about Paige. But she couldn't be right about Adam, too, could she?

"I got a phone call from Dave MacGregor," Ginger suddenly said. "He's the one who told me you and Adam were seeing each other."

"Dave MacGregor called you?"

Ginger nodded.

"If you knew about me and Adam, why did you ask?"

"I didn't believe him."

Paige sighed.

"But the other thing Dave MacGregor said was that he'd been trying to negotiate for our property and that Adam had said to go to the source and to call me directly. Did you know that?"

Paige reeled. She knew she wasn't a very good businesswoman, but she didn't know Adam had so little faith in her, also. She had actually thought he might be one of the only ones who did have faith in her. What was all that talk about her not being Calamity June and being strong and perfect? What was that whole pep talk about following her dreams? Did he not believe any of that? Was her mother right? Was he feeding her lines?

She shook her head.

"You can't do business with men you're sleeping with, Paige. I don't know how much clearer I need to be. You couldn't convince Adam of anything because he already saw you as soft. And now he'll keep telling you what he knows you want to hear so you'll keep sleeping with him."

Tears threatened in the back of Paige's throat. Had she botched this as terribly as her mother was laying it out? Had she been blind? Selfish?

If so, she would straighten it out.

She took a deep breath.

"I'll fix everything."

Adam headed out to the barn to meet a grain-feeder inspector he'd lined up.

He hated to leave Paige alone to deal with Ginger as a one-man army, but she'd said she could handle it. Plus, she was certainly used to dealing with Ginger—he knew she could do it. But he still would have liked to have helped.

He'd take his cues from her, though—it was her family, her life. He could only get involved as much as she'd let him.

And what was all that she'd said about his dad? Could she be right? Could he be structuring his life to impress a man who was no longer able to be impressed? Could he be chasing after some kind of acknowledgment he was never going to get? Was the rest of his life destined to be this futile grasp for something, unless he changed it now?

The inspector was there, peering at the grain feeders with his clipboard. Adam walked him through each one to show the faulty tubes. Just as he got to the last one, his cell phone rang. He glanced at the number. *Bob.* It was weird having Bob use a cell phone all of a sudden. He'd have to thank Amanda for her tutoring.

"Excuse me," he told the inspector, turning to walk back through the barn door. "Yeah, Bob."

"I have bad news about MacGregor." Bob was never one to mince words.

"What is it?"

"He's pulling out."

"Pulling *out*? What do you mean? He already submitted the offer."

"He's allowed to do that."

Adam let a string of swear words float though the phone.

"I know," Bob said. "But it's legal and true."

"Did he give a reason?"

"It doesn't matter."

"I want to know."

Bob sighed. "He said he was pulling out because you weren't able to get him the Grant property, too."

"That son of a—"

"Adam."

"He's an asshole. I don't usually let feelings get in the way of business, but I'm sort of glad our property isn't going to that prick. Were you not going to tell me that part?"

"It does leave you an option, but I wasn't going to share it with you. I knew you wouldn't take it. I knew you'd do the right thing."

All Adam could think of was Amanda and what she was going to say, how disappointed she'd be. And especially how disappointed she'd be in him. He hated to let her down. He may have let his dad down, and maybe even his mom. But he wasn't going to screw this up, too. He'd let Amanda down for sixteen years—being a deadbeat dad without even knowing it. And now he wanted to fix it. He pressed the bridge of his nose to keep his head from pounding.

Then he thought of Paige. And a tiny part of him was glad he'd have a couple of extra weeks with her. She was still leaving, of course, right after the Silver wedding, but at least he'd be around to say good-bye. And he could enjoy every second of her until she left. He pushed the selfish thought away as soon as he had it, though—it felt like a betrayal to Amanda—but he couldn't ignore the way his heart pounded faster.

"So what are our options, then?" he asked Bob, trying to get back to business.

"You'd have to convince Paige to sell to MacGregor. Or you'd have to admit defeat."

Bob was right. He couldn't convince Paige to sell to MacGregor. There was no way. She had her own thing going on, and even though he worried he'd look bad to Amanda, his pride didn't matter. He'd find another way.

"I admit defeat," he said quietly.

"I knew you would."

It felt as if a rope tightened in Adam's chest and made him stand taller at Bob's words.

"Of course, it'll delay your inheritance even further," Bob said.

"I know."

"You'll have to start over."

"I understand."

"We'll have to get your dad's debts paid off."

"I get it, Bob."

"You could consider Silver's proposition."

"That's not until late August. Paige said Silver is going on a three-week honeymoon and will negotiate when she gets back. I need to get Amanda in school before then."

"You might have to consider selling your other property, then, and fast."

Adam ran his hand through his hair. That's what he'd been trying to avoid. He'd wanted to hang on to the seaplane property no matter what. It was his mother's. He felt as though it was the last thing he could do for her, and now it felt as if he was failing her, too.

But his mother was gone. And Amanda was right here in his life, needing him. And he had to take care of her now. He hoped his mother would have been proud of him for taking care of her grand-daughter first.

Also, he'd suddenly had the thought that if he could give Paige some of the sale money to start her yoga studio, he would. He hated to see such a beautiful, talented woman give up on her dreams because she was too busy helping everyone else. Paige deserved to be happy, and she deserved to get the best out of life. He wanted to do this for her.

"Go ahead." Adam could barely get the words out.

He hung up and realized, for the first time, that sometimes he did let feelings get in the way of business. When they were the right thing to do, of course.

And when they were for a beautiful blonde named Paige.

Dorothy Silver came with an entourage of about fifty people: personal assistants, private yacht captains, doctors, acting coaches, friends, at least one old lover, four cameramen, two videographers who were film-ing the whole thing for a documentary, and someone who might have been a personal sommelier. Together, they wandered through the ranch house about four people thick. Dorothy kept touching the tendrils of hair that spiraled from her 1960s-style turban, and looked at the entire house as if in a dream.

"It's just like I remembered," she whispered about fifteen hundred times.

Clutching Paige's arm as they walked behind the entourage, Ginger glanced over every now and then and raised her eyebrows when Dorothy would gush over something. They were both holding their breath over everything she said. And they were nervous about her asking about the orchard. They knew Dorothy loved that part of the ranch—it was a crucial scene in the movie, when Dorothy's and Richard's characters chased each other around the trees and realized by the end of the scene that they were in love, after an apple conked her on the head. It was kind of a corny scene, but Dorothy wanted to re-create it. She wanted it for the documentary and for the wedding itself.

The entourage slowly flowed outside, where Dorothy put her gigantic round sunglasses back on and gripped the arm of one of the personal assistants. Together, they wandered to the gazebo.

Ginger squeezed Paige's arm. "She's going to love it," she said. "You did a beautiful job."

There, the entire group stopped and stared. The gazebo had been finished late one midnight—the bright-white paint finally covering the whole edifice, which stood like an enormous wedding cake in the middle of the meadow. Wooden scroll details looked like frosting, and Mr. Clark had sent forty-five flats of pansies to rim the base and create a frothy burst of color. A heart-shaped weather vane, straight out of the movie, which Paige had found on Craigslist in a miracle of fate, topped the gazebo now after Antonio had performed feats of strength to get it up there at two a.m. while she navigated from below. The weather vane now spun prettily in the wind, a cupid's arrow racing after a heart.

The entire entourage seemed to let out a collective sigh.

Beneath her sunglasses, Dorothy let a tear escape.

Then she turned toward Paige. "It's perfect, darling."

Ginger squeezed Paige's arm. Dorothy reached back to her, and Paige took her delicate hand. Being invited into Dorothy's embrace was more than she'd ever hoped for.

"Did we talk about your debut in my movie? You have your SAG card, right?" she whispered into Paige's ear.

Paige thought she might die from joy. But she held off answering until Dorothy had the whole story.

Dorothy gripped Paige's arm and asked about the gazebo, the rocks, the view, and then came the question Paige had been dreading. "Will we have access to the orchard? Can we go there now?"

Paige glanced at Ginger and took a deep breath. She'd been rehearsing how she was going to say this, and she'd tried to come up with a solution for how they might reconstruct that scene without the actual orchard being part of the wedding. But before she could get the words out, she heard a *yes* behind her.

She whirled to see Adam jogging through the meadow.

He came up and put his arm around her. "Yes, you can have access to anything you need."

"What?" Paige whispered.

He leaned toward her ear. "I'll explain later. Just say yes."

They wandered around with Dorothy, and she asked a million more questions: Could Adam take her to the orchard? Could she hold his arm? Wasn't he handsome? Didn't he remind everyone of Richard? Could her staff stay on the property? Could her crew stay there? Could *she* stay there? Could she stay with Adam?

"Paige might get jealous," he whispered.

Dorothy giggled, and he patted her hand.

She turned and looked at Paige with a grin and another level of admiration.

They made plans for some of the staff to stay in Gram's house, some to stay at Adam's resort, three to even stay inside Adam's house, and guests to stay down the hill and at the Castle.

At the end of the day, even Ginger was looking at Adam with a modicum of approval.

That evening, Adam hauled himself to the kitchen and dropped his backpack on the table. He was so glad to have been able to help Paige.

But there was someone else he needed to talk to.

"Amanda?" he called.

She didn't come out of her room. Maybe she wasn't back yet from the stables or the pond. Or maybe she was spending time with Rosa, who was teaching her how to make tortillas.

He wandered around the house for a minute, his eyes riveted for some reason on the damned box that still sat in the corner.

He stopped in front of it, staring the thing down.

All his dad wanted to give . . .

Adam nudged the side with his boot and stared at the writing as if it were going to change. He looked at the ceiling and ran a hand through his hair. Maybe Paige was right. This might be all his dad wanted to give. And that might have to be enough. Adam couldn't keep chasing after some kind of acknowledgment he would never get for the rest of his life. That would make him truly a miserable, angry bastard.

He tried to get to a place of forgiveness, but suddenly the idea that he now had to sell the seaplane property and let down his mother's legacy made anger lash up inside him again, slashing at a place behind his heart, making his chest constrict.

He took a few steps around the box.

He'd bury it. That's what he'd do. He'd stab the damned thing with a kitchen knife, then drop-kick it into a ditch behind the house and bury it. He tore off his jacket and went back into the kitchen for a knife. He shuffled from one drawer to the next, flinging open one after another. Denny made crazy-eights around his legs.

He found the right knife on the side of the sink and lunged for it, then swiftly moved to the dining area, lifting the heavy box to his shoulder with a sharp exhale. He marched toward the back patio, one hand gripping the knife at his side. Denny nervously pattered at his feet.

"Go back into the house, Den," he grumbled.

He didn't need his damned dog to see him acting like a madman. But Denny just looked up at him, trotting along, not ready to abandon anyone.

On the patio, Adam threw the box onto the wooden planks. His fingers clenched into fists, giving him a grip on the knife handle that felt like expertise. He could already feel the knife thudding through cardboard. He could predict the spent feeling of anger it would unleash.

But he glanced again at Denny, who was looking at him with sad brown eyes, and suddenly, inexplicably, Adam stopped.

He dropped the knife. Landed on his knees. He pressed his hands into his thighs and let out a throaty sound that started as one of his favorite cusswords and then ended in some kind of anguished moan.

"You bastard. You're not winning this one." A pressure surprised him as it came from behind his eyebrows, and his eyes suddenly filled with tears.

His gaze landed again on the knife, and he picked it up gingerly this time. He used the flashing edge to lift the corner of the box. He was not letting his dad win anymore. He was going to accept this lame gift from his father, then stop feeling anything toward him at all. He was going to stop going after an acceptance that would never be his. Then he was going to be his own man. Dad: fifteen thousand. Adam: one.

The packing paper came out in fistfuls, which Adam tossed on the patio. Beneath the paper was a huge stack of letters, wrapped in red ribbon. *Ribbon? Good Lord.* Why would his dad tie letters in a ribbon? As he pulled the stack out, turning it over, witnessing the carefully tied bow, his hand became increasingly unsteady. His breathing shallowed. He leaned heavily into his thighs, afraid to take another item out.

This wasn't his dad's box.

It was his mother's.

He took a few more breaths, glancing out at the meadow to make the tears retreat, then looked deeper inside. He missed her so much. He could suddenly remember her scent, her soft hands, her voice. His hand shook as he pushed aside more packing paper and saw his mother's whittling tools, one of the flutes she liked to make out of birch branches. He gently moved them aside and saw a box of medals her father had earned in the war, and a framed photograph of his grandfather shaking hands with FDR in front of the little airport in 1935. The glass was cracked across their faces.

Adam had to look up again, until the tears went back. He couldn't see a goddamned thing. He shoved the balls of his hands angrily against his eyes and then reached in until his fingers wrapped around a plastic bag. It was filled with yellowed photographs. There were about seventy, shuffled like an old deck of cards, the corners turning up. One by one, Adam drew them out, barely breathing, laying each one on the porch next to Denny, who sniffed at them.

"Son of a—" he whispered to Denny.

His eyes stilled on a shot of himself as a young boy—posing in his pajamas, beaming from the kitchen table. Another was him sitting on the porch eating popcorn, grinning from atop a brand-new bicycle. There were some of Adam and his father, his dad making him laugh, lifting him in the air. There were a couple of Noel as an infant, and several of both boys with their mother, which Adam suddenly remembered his dad taking. There were some with the old horse they used to have, Tilly, and some of Adam as a five-year-old, fishing in the pond, his dad right behind him, showing him how to hold the rod.

He put the stack down shakily. His breaths were coming short and fast, rasping through his chest. He hadn't remembered those better times, but there they were, in Kodak, corners curling. The bad times had always come to his mind easily, shoving everything else from view, but there were good times, too, with his father. Now he remembered. He remembered the way his father had taught him to fish, even after his mother died. How he'd showed him how to throw popcorn in the air and catch it in his teeth when he was a teenager and they'd been cracking up on the back porch. How his dad had gone with him to the May carnival because he'd won an award in high school. How his dad would lift him in the air when he was a kindergartner and say, "Pretend you're a pilot, Adam. You're going to be a flyer. Just like your mom." How his dad had laughed with them. How his dad had taught him to ride that bike in the photo.

He looked at another handful of pictures of him and his dad and Noel. Farther down were stacks of little cards, written out in his mother's handwriting. His chest gave a painful tug as soon as he saw her familiar scroll, but he read on. They were recipes. For his mother's pies. The ones she used to make at the harvest.

His dad was giving him this box, his mother's box—willing it to him, singling it out—because he knew he'd take care of it.

Adam swiped another tear away, then tunneled to the bottom of the box, where he found twenty or thirty other items of memorabilia from his grandfather's airport. There was an old logbook, an old leather helmet, a real set of pilot goggles. He sat back on his haunches. "Son of a—" he whispered to Denny again. He could definitely set up a museum with this.

Over the next half hour, he turned each item over in his hands, then carefully packed them back into the box, along with the key that would open the metal container at the bottom. They were bonds, probably purchased for him as a child, and his mother had kept them there. It wasn't a fortune, but it would be enough for him and Amanda to start over.

He packed the key on top and closed the flaps on the box. Then he stood up and stared down at it, realizing he'd almost buried the damned thing.

Now he looked at the box with a new feeling.

It was the feeling of freedom.

And his first feeling of gratitude toward his father.

When Amanda came home, Adam was sitting at the dining table.

"Hi," she said. "Look at these tortillas I made. I'm going to roast some meat tonight for soft tacos just like Rosa's." She smiled and headed straight past him to the kitchen to turn on the oven.

"Amanda, I need to talk to you."

She glanced back at him with a concerned frown, then plopped down across from him.

He didn't know how to lead into this, so he took a breath and blurted it out. "The ranch sale fell through."

He waited for the disappointment to sprawl across her face, but instead she looked blank. He worried that he may not have been clear.

"We can't leave," he clarified. "Not yet. We'll have to stay awhile. But I'll come up with another plan. I found some lost money that was mine, and I think I can make it work for us—it's enough to at least move us to an apartment in Alabama and get you enrolled in your art school."

He waited for her disappointment again, but none came. She simply looked blank.

"Are you okay?" he asked.

"I'm starting to like it here."

He lifted an eyebrow.

"I like volunteering at the center, and I like some of the people here, and no one is bothering me about my mom, and . . . you . . . you seem to like me now."

His chest had been rising with hope, but her last line sent a dagger through it. Is that all she thought he could muster for her? A begrudging "like" after all these months? He realized this was where he needed to set himself apart from his father. He shook his head. "I *love* you, Amanda."

He reached across the table for her hand. Much to his surprise, she didn't pull away. He let out a sigh of relief and realized how scared he'd been to do that. Had his father been similarly scared? Had his father thought his children would have rejected him? Would they have? Had they? It was entirely possible the lack of affection had gone both ways.

But he was done with this cycle now. He needed to be brave about this and let his pride go. He needed to show this girl how much she was loved.

"I know we got off to a rocky start," he began, "but I think we just scared each other. I didn't know you existed, and you didn't know I did. I think we're both the types who need time to adjust to a new reality."

The way she slowly nodded her head reminded him a little of himself, or maybe even Noel. And definitely his mom.

"Once I adjusted to the idea of you, though, I couldn't have been happier," he added.

She looked up with doubt.

"I couldn't have been happier it was *you*. And all I wanted to do then was make things up to you. I'm sorry I wasn't there for the first part of your life, but I promise I'll be there for the rest. I just want to take care of you. I want to provide for you, and raise you where you're happy, and be the kind of dad mine was not."

"You didn't have a good dad?"

Adam sighed and looked at their hands. "He tried. At least I think he did. I was reminded an hour ago of how hard he might have tried. But my mom died when I was young, just like yours did. I know how hard that is. My dad never made the adjustment to her death, and never seemed to know how to take over or treat us with love. He treated us like ranch hands. I think he just didn't know what he was doing. He didn't have a lot of love himself growing up. But I . . . I don't want to be like that. I don't know what I'm doing, either, Amanda, but I'll try. I promise."

"You're not like that."

He looked up.

"I can tell you've been trying really hard," she said. "And you're very fair. And you're nice. I'm glad you're my dad."

Tears clogged the back of his throat. He cleared it and had to glance away.

"It's been especially nice since Paige has been around," she added. "You've been different since then."

He was finally able to meet her eyes. "Is that right?"

"She seems to show you how to love."

He was surprised a sixteen-year-old could be so insightful. The tears kept threatening in the back of his throat.

"Yes, Paige is very special."

"Is she very special to *you*?"

Adam nodded.

"Maybe you should get married."

He smiled. Her wisdom and her naïveté were still entwined. "It's not that easy. Paige has her own life. She has things she wants to do, and following around after me isn't one of them."

"What about staying here?"

He blinked back at her. All his old reasons for leaving were gone now. He didn't hate this place anymore; he could probably pay back his dad's debts if he sold the seaplane property; the Conservancy seemed desperate that they wouldn't have a bison wrangler anymore; and the town—Kelly, Antonio, Joseph, and the rest—would be guaranteed to keep their jobs. The only thing left, really, was Amanda herself.

"What about your art school?"

"I might be able to find some classes out here for my senior year, maybe. If not, maybe I'll work with Rosa at her cantina after school and then apply to a culinary college next year."

"*Culinary* college?"

"Yes. Culinary art. I was accepted to the Culinary Conservancy at the art school."

His mind whirled back to their conversations. *Damn. Of course.*

He studied her carefully as a peaceful look came over her face.

"You'd truly want to stay here?" he asked.

"Yeah. And that way, you can ask Paige to marry you."

He laughed again. "Still not that easy. She has things she wants to do. And she has to be in love with me first."

"Aren't you in love with her?"

His gaze snapped back up. *Was* he in love with Paige? He knew he loved her spirit. He knew he loved her spontaneity and her silliness and her fun and her laughter and even her crazy calamities. But even with all that, she also had an iron-hard determination to make things work, even when pieces were falling around her, and he loved that, too. He loved how she loved her family. And how she'd earned Amanda's trust—it took a special person to do that. But mostly he loved how he was when he was with her: he was a better man. Paige made him better. And he trusted her.

"Maybe I am," he said quietly.

"Then you should work on that," Amanda said. "Now I'm going to get this dinner started. You go take a shower and then invite Paige over. Wear your blue shirt she likes."

Adam was still blinking back his sudden awareness. But finally Amanda's specific recommendation sunk in. "She likes my blue shirt?"

"Definitely."

"How do you know?"

"Girls know these things. And invite her for a walk after dinner. And don't wear your hat when you go outside—it covers your eyes. Plus, she likes your hair."

"She likes my hair?"

"Absolutely. Now go get ready. I'll make you guys a dessert."

An hour later, Adam paced the dining room, inhaling the amazing scents of whatever Amanda had in the oven.

"Stop!" Amanda said, laughing. "Relax."

The doorbell rang, and he lunged for the door.

When he caught sight of Paige, his heart heaved into an unrecognizable rhythm.

What the hell was the matter with him? He hadn't been this nervous since he flew a plane for the first time. He needed to relax. He wasn't going to ask her to marry him, for God's sake. He just needed to find out how she felt. And be honest about how he felt.

He'd never told a woman he'd loved her. In fact, he'd never told anyone that. Except Amanda just now. And maybe his mom, he hoped. But he'd never even told Noel, never told his dad. He'd never told Bob or Gert, even though he loved them both like parents. Those were not words he knew how to say.

And he wasn't even sure that's what he felt with Paige. Was it? Given the way he was sweating and nervous right now, when nothing had changed except his awareness that he might have stronger feelings for her than he knew, he figured something might be up.

"Apparently Gram had a wine cellar!" Paige said, lifting a bottle. She giggled in that cute way of hers and barreled through to the kitchen. "We'll celebrate."

"What are we celebrating?" he asked, shutting the door behind her whirlwind personality.

"Dorothy Silver, of course. It's perfect! I can't thank you enough, Adam. You'll have to tell me what happened to change your mind about the orchard. Wow, it smells amazing in here, Amanda."

Amanda smiled and looked up from the bowl where she was stirring rice.

"So what happened with MacGregor?" Paige asked with a little squeal. "And, man, I have to tell you the nice things Dorothy said. I can't believe . . ."

Her next phrase stalled as she looked back at the dining table, which Amanda had set with nice china and silverware. A few candles were in the center, already lit. It looked desperately romantic. Adam was instantly embarrassed he'd let Amanda do this.

"Wow. This is so nice." Paige looked up at him with a brow raised. "Did Amanda do this, too?"

Adam nodded.

Amanda moved toward the table with the bowl of rice. "Who's ready to eat?"

"Amanda, this is beautiful," Paige said. "And the dinner smells delicious. Thank you."

"No problem," Amanda said. "Special occasion."

"Special occasion? What's the special occasion?"

"I'll let Adam tell you."

Adam rolled his eyes. *Thanks, Amanda.*

"What's the special occasion?" Paige asked him.

"Let's eat, and you tell me all about Dorothy, and I'll tell you about MacGregor, and then we'll go for a walk and we can talk about special occasions." He pulled her chair out for her.

Seeming appeased, she sat and let him and Amanda serve while he shot warning glances at his daughter from across the kitchen.

Paige's excitement bubbled over as she chattered on about Dorothy's perusal of the property, described every member of her entourage, and how Dorothy had been convinced Paige should have the movie role. Paige practically panted the words out. Then she stared at both of them and let out a squeal. Adam felt his salmon going dry in his mouth. She was definitely leaving.

"What about the yoga studio?" he asked.

Paige blinked at him. As he watched her, he could almost see the confusion, joy, then a return to confusion play across her face.

"I need the money," she whispered. "This will get me there. Stepping-stones. So what happened with MacGregor?"

"The offer fell through."

Paige's eyes went wide, and she put her fork down. "Adam, no! I'm sorry! What happened?"

He couldn't tell her that it was because Paige and her mom wouldn't give up their land to him, too, so he just shrugged. "Didn't work out."

"What are you going to do?"

"Sell the seaplane property."

"No! You love the seaplane property!"

"It'll be fine." He didn't want to worry Amanda, so he gave her a reassuring smile across the table. "Let's talk about something else."

They talked more about Dorothy and moviemaking, and Paige regaled Amanda with tales of what the Hollywood Film Library was like, and the famous people who came in for research.

When dinner was over, Amanda shoved them toward the door for their walk, saying she'd have dessert baked for them by the time they got back. She all but winked as she closed the door.

"Wow, she really wanted us to go on this walk, didn't she?" Paige asked. "Where are we going?"

"Amanda wanted us to go to the Top of the World, but we don't have to go that far."

"Oooh, are we going to make out there?" Paige shot him a cute glance.

Adam chuckled. "I'm always up for that."

"With Dorothy so happy, and my mom pleasantly surprised, I think my mom isn't even going to mind so much that we're spending time together." She reached for his hand.

Adam let her take it and marveled at how sweet it felt. He couldn't even remember the last time he'd held hands with a woman—probably high school. His more recent encounters were good for getting laid, but nothing that ever led to the sweet, pure gesture of holding the hand of someone you knew and trusted. He stared at their entwined fingers for a second and realized this was what was missing in his life—a friend, a companion, a lover, a confidante. Someone you wanted to share everything with. Someone you told your seaplane-property secrets to and who trusted you with hers. Someone you wanted to help with her dreams. Someone who believed in you. Someone you loved. He was missing a Paige.

"So what's the special occasion?" she asked.

"Amanda and I made a big decision today."

Her face lit up, and she turned toward him, walking backward. "What?"

"We're going to stay."

Paige stopped abruptly, and he almost tripped into her. *"What?"*

"We're staying."

He could almost see the wheels whirling through her head. But her smile was fading fast, and he didn't imagine the wheels were turning his way.

"How are you going to make that work?"

"It won't be easy. I'll need a lot of Bob's help to get things revved back up. The seaplane property should pay off the debts, and then everything else will go to me and Noel. As long as I can figure out how to make things profitable again, I'll be okay. The Conservancy offered me more money if I stayed—seems they don't have a lot of bison wranglers lined up. And I figure it'll be a five-year struggle—it'll be like starting my own business again—but then I'll be back on my feet."

"What about Amanda?"

"She wanted to stay." He shrugged.

"What about art school?"

"I guess it was culinary arts, and she thought she could find some classes here or work with Rosa and then apply to a culinary college. She said she was starting to like it here. Bob and Gert are already becoming like grandparents to her, and the townspeople are making her feel welcome. I think she's finding a sense of community here she never had in Alabama."

Paige nodded. "That's great, Adam. I mean it . . . that's really great. Maybe I can visit you."

He stalled. "Visit" was not what he wanted. He'd love for her to live with them. He'd love to have her in his bed every night and every morning, and kiss her forehead awake, and ride with her every week, and skinny-dip with her until they got caught, and sit out on the porch with her and Denny as the sun set behind them. But he couldn't bring himself to say any of that. It sounded selfish. Paige needed to get on with her own life and pursue her own dreams. She hadn't gone into FRED thinking things were going to suddenly change on her at the end.

"I'd love that," he said.

She glanced up, looked as if she was going to say something else, then stopped.

"Hey, we don't have to go to Top of the World," he said. "Amanda's probably got our dessert already baked. Let's go back and see what she has."

Paige paused, as though she didn't want to give up the walk just yet, but she finally nodded and followed him back.

He wanted to get out of there. He wanted to get out of the cozy night that was reminding him of what he might have had if he'd been bold enough, and smart enough, to see what he had right before him. If he'd forgiven Ginger a long time ago. If he'd forgiven his dad. If he'd looked past his own problems and had seen the gift he'd been given.

Now it was just too late.

CHAPTER 25

Three days before the wedding—Paige couldn't believe it had crept up so quickly—everything was in place. She'd been running around like a possessed person for the last week to make sure of it. Her mother was down in Carmelita in one of the swanky hotels. Dorothy and Richard and their dual entourages would be flying in the next day. The workers would arrive in two days. The coordinators would show up in three.

She'd even arranged for a private charter to take her back to LA right after the two p.m. wedding. She needed to be there by eight p.m. for a specially arranged dinner with Dirk and the director to discuss the movie part. She was pretty sure she already had it, based on Dorothy's winks and encouragement, but she needed to be there anyway. Dirk was overjoyed.

Most of the other pieces for the wedding had come together smoothly. She and her mom truly were a good team.

The gazebo was the pièce de résistance, but Paige had spent a lot of time cleaning up the orchard, too. They'd established plans for where the white satin bows would go and where they would do a cute scene for the documentary, re-creating the moment Dorothy and Richard fell in love. The film crew had set up their lights, cables, and dollies and had strung miles of electrical wires.

As Paige ran back and forth every day among the workers, the wedding coordinators, the film crews, her mother, and various Dorothy Silver entourage members, she'd glanced around for Adam, but he'd vanished. He'd seemed to be avoiding her. She knew he was busy, too: various town members were coming up to visit him and help him fix the back end of his property where it led to the rocky cliff toward the seaplane ramp—a lot of tree trimming and brush clearing needed to get done for him to get it on the market. If he could clear it enough to show where a road might go, he would get top dollar. He'd seemed surprised that so many Carmelita residents would drive up to help, but they were all relieved he hadn't sold to MacGregor. They knew he'd keep the Mason property—and the orchard and the bison ranch and the air-strip—just as it should be. They even set up a fund for him to try to pay off George's debts themselves so he could keep the seaplane property, too, and maybe make it into a museum. He'd seemed humbled and shocked by their generosity.

But that was the last day Paige had seen him. Otherwise, he'd been like a ghost.

At first she thought it was a matter of circumstances, but then she started to wonder if he was avoiding her on purpose. Maybe he was done with FRED. Maybe he was done with her. She tried not to be hurt by that, because that would make her mother right. And she tried to remember that she'd always known this was short-term, and that she'd had fun with him while it lasted, and she was the one leaving—she'd laid out the rules. He hadn't broken any promises or any trust, and she needed to accept that and move on.

At least that's what she told herself.

Her heart, however, was apparently not listening. Late one after-noon, while tying her three-hundredth bow around a tiny pot of wed-ding almonds—a 1950s Dorothy-Richard first-wedding throwback, to be sure—four huge teardrops escaped her eyes and wet the wooden dining table. *What the heck?*

Paige swiped at her cheeks with her fingertips and quickly moved the rest of the almonds aside so she didn't have a pastel-candy mess on her hands in a moment. *Dang.* She didn't want to be this way. She didn't want to feel hurt. She wanted to be in control of her emotions. She wasn't supposed to let her heart get in the way.

And yet the tears kept coming.

She wiped at her cheeks a few more times just as she heard the back door open.

"Yoo-hoo," her mother said.

Paige snagged an empty netting circle and patted her eyes. "Hey, Mom."

The netting was completely ineffective. Paige went for her sleeve instead.

Her mom circled her for a moment, then set the bags she'd brought on the kitchen counter next to Paige's VHS copy of *Last Road to Nowhere.*

"What's this?" Ginger asked.

"Oh, I ordered that for Amanda. She wanted to see it."

Ginger nodded and glanced back at Paige. "What's wrong?"

"Nothing. I . . ." Paige didn't know how to finish the sentence. She dabbed one more time at her cheeks with her sleeve and turned away. She didn't want to get into this with her mom.

"Where's your knight in shining armor?" Ginger asked from the kitchen. She started unloading wedding-morning marmalades, made fresh on Lavender Island, lining them across the counter.

"What?"

"Adam. You haven't been around him much lately."

Paige stood and began a trajectory toward the coffeemaker. "I think our summer fling is over."

Ginger watched Paige fumble with the old machine, then fluttered her away. "I'll do it."

Paige returned to the dining table and plopped down.

"So is this one of those moments where you want my opinion or don't want it?" Ginger carefully measured the coffee and arranged two cups.

"I guess I want your opinion if it's positive."

Ginger laughed. "That sounds about right. Well, if you want mine on this, I think you might be letting a good thing slip away."

Paige was sick at the flurry of emotions skittering through her—chief among them were sadness, doubt, and fear. And now, after her mother's admission, shock. "I can't believe you just said that."

"I can admit when I'm wrong."

"Since when?"

Ginger smiled and waited for the coffee.

Paige stared at the blue delft vase and sighed. "I don't know, Mom. There are a lot of things I still need to tell him."

"He came to talk to me."

"What?"

Ginger poked at the coffeemaker as if to make it work faster, or maybe to avoid Paige's eyes. "Yes, he came to apologize. He introduced me to Amanda."

Paige's jaw felt as though it had dropped to the table. "*What? When? Tell me what happened.*"

Ginger made her wait through a little more fussing with the appliance, which Paige recognized as one of her mother's delay tactics. Finally, Ginger turned and leaned against the counter.

"Yesterday. He came to apologize to me—for blaming me all those years about his severed relationship with his father when it wasn't me."

Paige held her breath. "Did he know it was me?" she whispered.

"No. He said it was him. He said he and his father both had trouble expressing their feelings and their trust in people, and that if either of them had been able to bridge that gap back then, things might have been different."

Paige let out another breath. That sounded like her and Adam, too. Apparently, they were both having trouble trusting and, therefore, expressing their feelings. But she didn't want things to be too late for them, too.

"What else did he say?"

"He introduced me to Amanda and said what a wonderful girl she was and that he wanted me to meet her. She is a cute girl. And he said he knew he'd made some bad impressions on me back then but wanted me to know he'd changed and wasn't the clueless boy he'd been. He wanted me to know what a fabulous job you did here and how hard you worked, and he hoped I'd give you all the credit. Paige, I admit I was wrong about him. He looks just like his father and has all the charm and appeal, but he's a different kind of man. He really does care about you, honey. And if you care about him as much as I think you always have, I think you should tell him so. You made a good choice in him, even when you were thirteen years old."

"You knew I had a crush on him then?"

"Everyone did, dear." She turned to pour the coffee for both of them.

Paige laughed. "Adam didn't."

"Well, boys can be dense. But he's grown-up now. And he can see exactly what's in front of him. You are a wonderful find."

Paige fiddled with the napkins. "Maybe I'm not."

Her mother brought the coffees to the table. "What are you talking about, dear? You're lovely. You are one of a kind, and any man would be lucky to have you."

Paige smiled. "I appreciate your blind faith in me, Mom, but I haven't been all that with Adam. I haven't even been completely honest. I never told him I was the one to tell on him to you and George."

Her mother quietly sipped her coffee at that, then stared into her mug and let out a lengthy sigh. "I'm sorry for all those years I made you distrust men, Paige. It was wrong of me to impose my own opinions and experiences on you. I was just choosing the wrong ones. But dishonesty begets dishonesty. The more you distrust men, the more you'll withhold. And then you'll completely withhold your honest self. Pretty soon you're holding everyone at such an arm's length, and being so quiet about who you truly are, or what you want, that you'll never let anyone get close to you."

"I didn't want to tell him because I didn't want him to hate me."

"You didn't want him to see the real you."

Paige stared at her untouched coffee and realized that was the truth.

"I'd say trust him," her mom said.

Paige lifted an eyebrow. "All these years you've been telling me not to trust men, and now *this* is your advice? A complete one-eighty?"

"A woman has the right to change her mind." Her mom took a sip of coffee. "But, yes. That's my advice. Trust him to make the right decision about a relationship with you, but you have to give him the true *you* first."

Paige nodded again. Her mom was right—she had to give Adam the true her. She needed to tell him that she'd been the one to tell George and Ginger. He might hate her, and might never forgive her, but she had to give him that option. If he chose to forgive her, they could perhaps move on and have something truly meaningful between them. But if she never told him, they absolutely *never* could. She'd always distrusted others in relationships, but now she realized it was a two-way street. *Be completely honest to expect complete honesty in return.*

She also wasn't Katharine Hepburn or Lauren Bacall or any of the other sophisticated femme fatales she was trying to put on for him—she was just goofy, sometimes silly, find-an-adventure Paige Grant. And that would have to do. If he couldn't love that about her, she'd simply have to accept that fact. But she couldn't get him to fall in love with someone she was not. It was time to take her armor off. It was time to be her real self. It was time to be proud of who she was.

Paige scooted her chair back and grabbed the VHS tape off the counter. "I'll have my coffee later, Mom. I have to go find someone."

Paige ran across the meadow, the grasses no longer whipping at her ankles but now becoming dried and matted.

When she got to Adam's back porch, she pushed the hair out of her eyes and stared at his back door for a long moment before taking a deep breath and knocking.

"Hey." He opened the door in his bare feet and low-hanging blue jeans. Paige swallowed a sigh. But he had the look of a stranger now. He didn't reach for her, didn't grab her around the waist for another hot kiss, didn't even smile at her in his naughty, intimate way. He just opened the door wider and ushered her in.

"I've missed you," she said.

"I've missed you, too, Paige."

His words were uttered with politeness. Seeing his downcast eyes as she walked into the house like some distant visitor brought another threat of tears. How had she let them get to this place? Had her fear of opening up brought them to this awkward, terrible end?

Her heart thrummed at all she had to say, and what it would take to say it, and she took another deep breath. "Adam, I need to talk to you."

Adam welcomed Paige into the kitchen, as he'd done so many times, but now his heart was encased. He wasn't going to lay it raw anymore. He loved Paige. He knew that. But he would never hold her back. Paige was young and vibrant and free, and she needed to follow her dream, which started by taking this role in Hollywood. He tried to be happy for her. He'd been convincing himself all week.

"So did you call my guy to ferry you out right after the wedding?" he asked, heading into the kitchen to get her a drink. Adam had offered to fly her, but she'd admitted she was afraid to fly.

"Yes, everything's set. Thank you so much."

Maybe he could get her to visit. Maybe she'd come after she got the part, or after she played it. They were only twenty-six miles across the sea, after all. And she had her sisters here. She'd be back sometime.

"I've missed you," she repeated, stepping toward him.

He nodded. Amanda was in the next room, watching *From Here to Eternity*, but he wanted to wrap his arms around Paige right now and take her to his bedroom. Or the hangar. Or the hayloft. Or maybe to the pond or the woods or her bed or the gazebo. He wanted to say good-bye properly and leave things on the warm, comfortable note they'd hit earlier in the summer. But he also needed to keep his heart hard. This was difficult enough as it was. It would be easier for everyone if they kept things simple from here.

"I ordered this from the Hollywood Film Library," she said, thrusting a tape of *Last Road to Nowhere* at him. "I made sure to get it on a 'vintage' VHS for Amanda's amusement."

Adam smiled. "She'll love it. We'll watch it together."

His heart felt as if it were sinking like a rock. Seeing her again—her beautiful smile, her doe eyes, her soft hair that fell around her face—and knowing he might never see her again was crushing him. He tried to get up the courage to say some of the things he needed to say, but he didn't want to come off like a needy, pathetic jerk. Instead, he hardened his heart further and turned away.

"You might need to go now, right?" he asked.

Ass.

Paige looked up at him with those eyes that killed him. "Do you have a minute to talk? It might be our last night of peace and quiet before the wedding workers start descending tomorrow."

"I thought you might have things you needed to do for the wedding."

"I do, but I . . . I have some things I want to say."

Unless she was saying she wanted to stay, he didn't know if he wanted to hear it. A few weeks ago, he would have wanted to hear anything—how much fun she'd had, how much she enjoyed the great sex. He'd have eagerly listened to how much she'd loved the laughs, his salsa, their horseback rides, the ranch. But now he didn't want to hear that. Because now it would only drive home the point that, while he wanted so much more of her, she'd had enough of him.

"Adam, I—"

He held up his hand. "I don't know if we need to do this. Do we?"

She looked up at him as if he'd just slapped her. Her eyes teared. She took a step back. Bit her lip.

His chest crushed again. He was such an ass. He couldn't do this to her. As much as he wanted to harden his heart so it wouldn't hurt so much, he couldn't. He'd have to let her say whatever she wanted to say. If it drove a knife through him, so be it.

"Can we go for a walk?" she asked quietly.

That would just drag this out. But he would do it, for her. "Sure."

She nodded and headed back out the door.

He set *Last Road to Nowhere* down on the table and followed behind her.

Time to fall on the sword.

Paige bit her lip as they wandered across the yard, and she tried to figure out how to start. Dusk was starting to fall, changing the sky to a deep purple over the dried grass. The evening was mild, but she wrapped her arms around her torso as they kept up a brisk pace.

Unable to formulate anything that might cushion the blow, she simply blurted it out. "I haven't been completely honest with you."

Adam slowed and turned slightly toward her. His eyebrows formed a deep frown as he stared down at her; then he looked back at the horizon they were marching toward. "Go on."

"When we were kids—that summer of the fires—my mom wasn't the one who told George on you and had you sent away." The words were coming in a rush now.

His scowl grew deeper. "She wasn't?"

"I was," Paige said. "I told on you. I went to your kitchen, and she came with me, to tell George. It wasn't Ginger. It was me."

Adam stopped and turned toward her completely. He stared at her for a long time, his face alternating between fury and disbelief. "You thought I started the fires, and yet you've been *sleeping* with me?" he asked.

"No! I never thought you started them. I never said that to George. I just told him about you and Samantha—that you were there, too. I didn't think it was you. My point was that it could have been anyone. I didn't think he'd have you thrown in jail, Adam. But, I must admit, I did want them to break up you and Samantha." Tears sprang to her eyes. What she had done, and saying it out loud, hit her full force in the chest. She wanted to reach up toward him—touch him, stroke his face, hug him—but his expression looked murderous. She didn't dare. "I'm so sorry," she whispered into the space between them.

He glanced between her and the road. "Paige . . ." He couldn't seem to even find the words. His face was a mask of incredulousness and anger.

His phone rang in his pocket, but he ignored it and turned to face the sunset. "That drove a wedge between me and my dad that lasted forever."

"I know," she whispered. Tears flowed down her face now. She couldn't help it any longer—she needed to touch him, just a gentle touch, to let him know how sorry she was—and she reached up for his shirt, but he stepped away.

"And Samantha . . . ," he said. "When her parents took her off the island, she left without looking back. I don't think she ever believed me. Those years I lost with Amanda . . . that was why."

"I know," Paige said, choking on a sob. "I'm so very, very sorry, Adam. If I could do it all over, I would."

His phone rang again, but he simply turned away. The anger on his face was morphing into pain, and Paige didn't know which was worse.

"And you let me hate Ginger all these years, even though it wasn't her," he said.

Paige nodded weakly as his phone rang again. She glanced at it, a minor panic starting in her chest. Multiple phone calls were never good. "Are you going to get that?" she asked.

He yanked his phone out and glanced at the screen. "It's Bob."

"Go ahead. It sounds urgent."

"What do you need?" he barked into the phone.

Adam didn't take his eyes off her. He looked as if he was looking at her for the first time—and not liking what he saw. Something Bob said made his brows furrow even deeper. "Calm down. What are you talking about?"

He listened for a second, then shook his head. "I'm on my way toward the Top of the World, I—"

Suddenly he looked behind him. And a slew of whispered curses followed.

Paige followed his gaze and saw a huge plume of smoke lifting out from behind the trees.

The meadow was on fire.

CHAPTER 26

Paige ran behind Adam into the front yard, where they both stopped short when they saw the blaze roaring across the dry grass toward the gazebo.

Amanda raced out of the house right then, looking toward the meadow herself, her mouth dropping open at the sight of the violent flames.

Adam moved toward the resort, but Mendelson was already running out along the deck.

"Is anyone else in there?" Adam shouted.

Mendelson shook his head.

Adam then turned toward the stables.

"I've got to get the animals," he yelled to Paige. "Go back to the road. Take Amanda. Start heading down the mountain."

"But my mom!"

"Your mom is back there?"

"She's in the kitchen."

A few more whispered oaths flew out of his mouth as he stared across the meadow, but—within seconds—he was running in that direction.

"Adam!" Paige screamed.

He turned. "Go *back toward the road*," he repeated. "Take Amanda."

Paige didn't need to question where he was going. There wasn't a clear way out for her mother. There were some back trails that led away from the house on the other side—the trail the intruder took weeks ago—but her mother wouldn't know where to find them. Fear clogged her throat as Paige watched Adam disappear into the smoke. But she had to get Amanda out of here.

She ushered Amanda back toward the house on a jog. Denny was barking frantically. Paige scoured the house for Click. She was starting to have flashbacks to the fires before. But even those hadn't been so close to homes. To her home. To animals and memories and life and the people she loved.

Once they found Click, they grabbed the struggling kitten and dashed across the pasture toward the stables. Paige's pulse raced erratically as she watched a pickup truck come the other way, then another and another, lining up along the ridge to help. But then she coughed. The sky was filling with dark smoke and ash.

"Amanda, put your shirt over your mouth." She showed her how to pull the collar up and breathe through the fabric as they ran toward the trucks. Paige found it easier to wrap Click in the hem of her shirt, also.

They arrived at the stables near the main road just as the wranglers were pulling the horses out of the stalls and directing them toward one of the three trailers they'd brought. Amanda rushed forward to help, and keep the horses calm. When they were loaded up, the wranglers jumped back into their trucks, waving Amanda and Paige toward them. Smoke was everywhere.

"Amanda, go with Gabe!"

"I want you to come, too." Amanda looked at her with panic. "And I want to wait for Adam."

"Adam went back for my mom. He'll probably try to evacuate her the other way. He'll come out of the woods trail down by the harbor, and he'll be okay. We have to get you to safety." She guided Amanda toward Gabe's truck.

"I saw you guys fighting."

Paige blinked through the smoke at yet another of Amanda's non sequiturs. "What?"

"I saw you fighting. Out the window. You're not breaking up, are you?"

"Amanda, we can talk about this later. I need you to go. Take Denny. Go with Gabe."

"I want to help."

"You can help by leaving so we don't have to worry about you."

Paige ran up to Gabe's truck and opened the passenger door for Amanda, urging her in along with Denny and Click. She looked at Gabe. "You two, hurry!"

"There's room for you!" Amanda scooted over.

Paige looked up at the long line of trucks pulling up. "There's a bucket brigade coming. I want to help."

Paige saw the entire community spilling out of pickup trucks—Rosa, Little, Joseph, Sherryl, Antonio, John from town, Billy Joe from down the block, Mendelson, and Mendelson's son, David, and about fifty others—all with buckets or hoses. This community was wonderful. They'd never let anything happen to one another. As much as Paige disparaged the small-town mentality of Lavender Island, in times like these, she realized its value. That mentality might include rumors and gossip and everyone knowing everyone else's business, but it also meant that when someone was in trouble, everyone was there to help. Her eyes welled up again as she saw them move quickly toward the pond. Just then the island's two fire trucks pulled up the dirt road.

"I promise I'll be safe," she told Amanda. "I'll see you in an hour or so." She tapped the side of the truck for Gabe to leave and then turned and ran toward the brigade.

At three in the morning, word went out that the fire was contained.

Adam dragged himself to Rosa's, where everyone had gathered. He'd raced toward Helen's house, found Ginger, and literally carried her down the side trail toward town. She seemed to only weigh about eighty pounds, weak with her chemo treatments, perhaps, and his adrenaline made short work of getting her down the hill. About a fourth of the way, he'd met four men from the Carmelita Hotel—old Mr. Perry and his three burly sons—who'd come up to see what the smoke was. He'd handed Ginger off to them.

"Take her to the hotel," he'd panted. "I have to get the Grumman."

They'd nodded and started back down with Ginger as Adam flew back up the hill and across the meadow, choking on the smoke, to get to his Grumman S-2T. They'd used the plane to put out many fires in the past, but he never thought he'd have to use it for his own property. Sweat had dripped from his forehead as he maneuvered the plane back and forth, first dropping the twelve hundred gallons of retardant across four acres, then returning to the ocean for additional bucket drops. Between the plane and the fire trucks, and the bucket brigade saving the outlaying properties, the fire was contained in about an hour.

Rosa had supplied everyone with free food and drinks in her cantina to keep them going through the night. The moon was still on the horizon, hovering, not quite ready to give up her reign. Adam headed through the bar, shouldering his way through the crowd, looking for Amanda and Paige.

Everyone clapped him on the back and told him what a great job he'd done. But he didn't feel he had. He knew they'd lost the gazebo and most of the meadow. The trees on the perimeter of Paige's house were blackened to scraggly spokes of branches. And his job was in no way complete until he laid eyes on both Amanda and Paige.

He suddenly caught sight of Paige coming out of the women's restroom in a flurry, her eyes looking ravaged and panicked.

"Paige!" he shouted across the room.

She didn't hear him and seemed to be moving toward the front door.

"Paige!" he tried again.

He pushed his way through the crowd, trying to get to her. He had to tell her so many things—he wanted to tell her he loved her. He wanted to tell her he was furious with her. He wanted to tell her he could forgive her for what she'd done in the past, but he had to work through the fact that she hadn't trusted him enough in the last couple of weeks to tell him the truth about it. He wanted to tell her she was beautiful. He wanted to tell her she infuriated him. He wanted to tell her she made him feel a thousand emotions he'd been shut off to for far too long. And mostly he wanted to tell her he was glad she was alive.

When he finally caught her elbow and turned her around, she still had the panicked look on her face.

"What's wrong?"

Her eyes looked wild; her mascara had blackened the rims of her eyes, and one streak stained her cheek.

"Adam, we need to go!"

"What? Why?"

"No one can find Amanda," she said.

CHAPTER 27

No one knew where to look first. Everyone was in Rosa's Cantina or around it, having all participated in the fire containment, but it was hard to find anyone in particular. Gabe was missing, too. It didn't make sense that they'd have gone anywhere but Rosa's. Paige scrambled to think if she had his phone number. She'd already texted Amanda about eight times, but the teen wasn't replying. And Adam didn't have his phone any longer—he confessed he may have dropped it when he ran across the meadow to get her mom.

"I'm going to find Bob," Adam said.

Paige nodded. That was smart. And she would search for Gabe.

She pushed through the crowd and asked if anyone had Gabe's number. When no one said yes, she wondered if Amanda might have asked Gabe to take her down to Garrett.

Adam found her again. "Bob went back home to keep an eye on Gert. I'm going over there," he said.

He looked exhausted, spent, with rivulets of soot coming out of his hair. She felt terrible for him, but she also felt awful about what had happened between them. She was desperate to apologize, but now was not the time.

"Will you wait here for her?" His eyes were tired, pleading.

"Of course," she said. "I wanted to stay here and try to find Gabe. I also wonder if she might be with Garrett."

"Why would she be with him right now?"

Paige stalled. She probably should have told Adam about this, too.

"Paige?" he asked again. "What do you know about Garrett?"

"Did you ask her about him like I told you to?"

"No. What do you know?"

"She had a crush on him," Paige admitted in a whoosh. "That's who she was seeing when she was going down to the sea-lion center."

He looked stunned. "Why didn't you tell me that?"

"I just . . . I didn't want to betray her confidence."

"So you betrayed mine?"

"It wasn't . . . it wasn't that easy, Adam. I wanted her to tell you herself."

He looked as if someone had just stabbed him in the back. He actually winced and moved away from her.

"Adam—"

"I need to go." He backed toward the door. "We need to find Amanda right now. I'm going to Bob's."

Adam raced to his truck, willing his brain to stay in the present and focus on the task at hand: he had to find Amanda. He tried not to think about how betrayed he felt by Paige, and her not telling him about being the one to seal his fate when he was eighteen. That moment had changed everything in his life—she must have known that. And the fact that she didn't say anything until now—while they'd been growing closer and closer—felt like a huge chasm he couldn't quite bridge in his mind. Here, he'd thought for a brief crazy second that he might have a relationship, maybe even something leaning toward *marriage*—did that word seriously enter his head? But he'd lost his mind when he'd thought that. That was insane. He clearly didn't know her. And she clearly didn't trust him. This latest, smaller secret about Garrett just made him wonder what other kinds of secrets she was keeping from him. He'd thought that maybe he'd been different, special to her somehow, someone she could trust with anything, but now he realized he wasn't.

"Adam, wait!"

He turned to see Paige running toward him.

"Let me come with you!"

She didn't wait for an answer but instead piled into his passenger seat.

He was glad she didn't wait. Because right now, he couldn't decide whether he wanted to be near her or as far from her as possible.

He climbed in the truck himself and roared down the street—Bob's house wasn't far, but Adam wanted his truck so he could tear down the mountain if necessary to turn up every rock and stone to find Amanda.

Once he screeched into the driveway, both he and Paige ran to the door.

When Bob opened it, he looked similarly alarmed. No, he hadn't seen her. No, he hadn't heard from her. He tried to remember if he'd seen Gabe.

Gert came into the living room in her robe and slippers, her hair piled on her head. She tapped her fingernails against her cheek in a nervous gesture while she listened to everyone trying to put together clues. She finally shouted, "Wait!"

They all turned toward her. "What about that thing Amanda did on our phone, Bobby? The GSS?"

"GPS?" Adam asked.

"Oh! Yes!" Bob got out his phone and started tapping buttons. "That's right! Gert, do you remember how she did that?"

"Let me get my notes." Gert came bustling back with a stenographer's notepad filled with her scrolling handwriting and flipped the pages around. "Wait. Here. Okay, Bobby, go to 'Contacts.'" She looked over Bob's shoulder. "Then 'Details.'" He did as she said. "Then hit 'Location.'"

"Got it!" Bob said joyfully. "It says she's down at the harbor! By the ferry. Or wait. No. It says she was there forty minutes ago."

"Oh dear," Gert said, flipping her notes another page forward. "Remember, that means her phone might have died then, and that's the last location it has for her?"

"It's a good place to start." Bob looked up at Adam.

"Thanks, Bob. And I'm friggin' impressed with both of you." Adam tore back out of the house with Paige right behind him. They flung themselves back into the cab.

As they barreled down the mountain, Adam leaning forward with worry, Paige glanced at him and thought about how similar they probably looked to George and Ginger coming down the mountain for *them* during the fires sixteen years ago. Suddenly she could understand the worry and frustration their parents had gone through—and all the protection involved afterward.

"She'll be okay," Paige said.

Adam nodded and didn't look at her.

Although cars weren't allowed in the town, emergency vehicles were, and Adam drove as though his truck was one right now—running red lights, flying through empty intersections, and screeching into the harbor.

Hardly anyone was out moving around yet, and they still had a half hour until the first ferry left at dawn. As they squealed into the passenger disembarking area and skidded across empty pavement, they could see Amanda's lone figure sitting on a low harbor pylon in the distance. Adam let out a relieved breath and slowed the car. He cut the headlights and jumped out.

"Amanda! What the hell are you doing?" he yelled.

She twisted toward them, her face streaked with tears that glistened under the streetlight.

Adam stopped in his tracks. "What's wrong? What happened?"

"Are you mad at me?"

"Of course I'm mad at you! You had us worried to death!"

"No, I mean . . ." She looked over Adam's shoulder and saw Paige. "Paige? What are you doing here?"

"I was worried, too."

"But didn't you guys break up?"

"Break up?" Adam looked as if he were going to tear his hair out. "What are you talking about?"

"I thought I was breaking you guys up. I saw you out the window. I thought you'd be mad at me."

"How would you be breaking us up? And what are you doing down here? And where's Gabe, or Garrett, or whoever was driving you?"

"Gabe and Garrett have nothing to do with this. I walked down the hill. I was going to leave the island. On the first ferry. I"—a sob racked her—"I thought you'd hate me once you found out."

"Once I found out *what*?"

"About the fires."

Adam froze. Even under a lone streetlight still aglow in the rising dawn, Paige could see the color drain from his face. "What are you talking about, Amanda?"

"The ones from a long time ago. I thought I heard you talking about them when you left the yard, and I thought you'd both break up, and then you'd"—another sob shook her shoulders—"you'd hate me, and especially when you figured out that . . ." She pressed her hands into her face.

"Figured out *what*?"

"That my mom started them," she said from under her palms. "It wasn't Paige. It wasn't you. It was my mom."

Adam recoiled in the rising daylight. Paige's mouth dropped open.

They both stood in silence, Paige's mind whirling back to the events of that summer so long ago. Her memory waded through the first fire, on the hill, by the boathouse, and the second one, and then . . . she glanced up and could see Adam staring into the pavement, too, his own memories probably flooding back.

"But . . ." Paige tried to remember the details. *It couldn't have been possible, could it?* "Samantha was with *you* during the first fire," Paige said to Adam, her voice nearly a whisper. "In the boathouse."

"No," Adam said, turning back toward her. "She wasn't. She'd lit some candles. She said she had to check on something, and she went out, back down the hill, and told me she'd be back. Once I smelled smoke, I busted out the door and tried to find her. She was running up toward me when I came out, and I grabbed her hand and got her out of there."

Paige's eyes widened. *Could it be?*

"But she wasn't near the stables during the second fire," he said. "You were, right? She said she'd been in town."

"No. She was there," Paige whispered. "I saw her. I thought she was waiting for you. You were there, weren't you? Your horse was saddled."

"No. I was on a ride that day. I'd saddled Bartlett for her."

They both looked back at Amanda as the realization dawned slowly on both of them that this was probably the truth. The stories had been passed down to the next generation as half-truths and half-understandings, as rumors always were. And Adam and Paige had each had only half the story.

As Adam stared harder at Amanda, her face crumpled again.

"Amanda," he said.

She sobbed harder.

"Amanda, it's not your fault," he said.

Her shoulders shook as the tears came in earnest, and she wiped at her face.

"Amanda? Look at me."

She finally did.

"It's not your fault."

"I"—the crying racked her shoulders—"I thought you knew. I thought everyone in town knew. And I thought you, and they, would hate me when I got here. But then I realized you *didn't* know. And they didn't. And Paige didn't. She was wearing disguises for another reason. And I felt like maybe you accepted me because you didn't know. But when I heard you and Paige arguing about it, I thought you'd break up over it, and then *that* would be my fault, too, and then you'd know, and you'd hate me anyway, and—"

"Amanda, no." Adam reached out for her and drew her toward him. "No. I will never hate you. And none of this is your fault. You are not breaking me and Paige up. We might need to talk, and we might have some arguments, but that's between her and me. You never have to worry about that. And your mother's mistakes are certainly not your fault. Got that? Just like my father's mistakes are not my fault, and Paige's mother's mistakes are not her fault." He glanced up at Paige over the top of Amanda's head. "Okay?" He seemed to be asking Amanda, but he was looking right at Paige.

Paige nodded back to him.

"Okay, then. Now that we all understand this, I think we need to get a few hours of sleep and start making plans. Because we've all got a lot of work ahead of us." Another glance up at Paige. "And a lot of ashes to clean up. And a huge wedding to throw in two days, which is going to take a miracle. But we can do it. Right?"

Amanda nodded in his embrace.

"Let's go." He leaned down and kissed Amanda's forehead. "I love you."

Paige's chest constricted when she heard him say those words, although she knew they weren't meant for her. They sounded amazing. And she wished he would say them to her. But he never would. Her worst fears were realized—she'd lost him by telling him the truth. But she'd had no choice. It was the right thing to do.

His "I love you," though, seemed to go straight to the heart of the girl who might need it even more right now.

"Thank you, Dad," Amanda whispered into his shirt.

And Adam's eyes teared up.

CHAPTER 28

When they got back to Nowhere Ranch, dawn was breaking over the tips of the pine trees. Adam parked the truck and encouraged Amanda to go in the house and get into bed. Paige slid out of the truck door and moved, slowly, toward the meadow cast now in gold, with an orange haze hanging in the air.

It was charred.

The gazebo was gone.

The woods along the perimeter were blackened and smoking, and the orchard was half-gone, smoke rising off the ground. The house, luckily, was still standing but covered in gray ashes that extended throughout the acreage, clinging to the ground, casting the entire property in a ghostly, deathly pall. The edge of the meadow was lined with police cars, their lights still flickering into the orange-tinged morning.

Paige's eyes watered, and she brought her hand her mouth. What was she going to do?

"It might not be so bad." Adam's deep voice came from behind her.

She couldn't even turn around. Of course it was. Everything was ruined. Especially everything between her and Adam. Their relationship was now as damaged as this charred meadow before her.

"Adam, I'm so sorry," she said.

"We can talk later." His voice was a monotone. It didn't sound like forgiveness.

"But I'd like to talk now. I've ruined everything. I'm so sorry."

"The meadow will be okay. You'll bounce back from this. Just like you always do."

She didn't mean she was sorry for the meadow. But as she started to open her mouth to say so, he stopped her.

"Here's what I'm talking about"—he looked up and pointed behind her—"that."

She followed his gaze. Across the meadow, coming down from the road, were scores of townspeople piling out of cars. They held hammers and toolboxes, wood panels and lumber pieces, paint cans and ladders, sawhorses and tarps. They brought weeders and mowers and whackers and hoses. Mr. Clark's staff walked down with wagons of flowers and flatbeds of soil. Mr. Fieldstone wheeled down four grocery carts full of water and snacks. Doris and Marie were there, holding skeins of white fabric and taffeta. And Natalie and Olivia followed, with Elliott and Jon behind them, each carrying brooms and tubs of soap.

"Where do you want us?" Natalie asked.

Paige began laughing and crying at the same time, her hand over her mouth.

As the army came around her, Olivia dropped her broom and threw her arms around Paige. Nat followed suit.

"You didn't think we'd abandon you, did you?" Olivia asked into Paige's hair.

"I can't believe you guys came. I'm so sorry I didn't tell you I was here."

"Mom told us everything," Natalie said. "I can't believe you didn't call us for help."

"I thought you guys would be mad that Mom and I weren't listening to you."

"Paige, you and Mom *never* listen to us," Olivia said. "Why should this be any different?"

"But I ruined everything." Paige looked around. "I lost the wedding. Mom's business is going to be devastated by this." *And I lost the love of my life.*

"Not when we're all done helping you," Natalie said. "Now tell everyone where you want us. We've got to get going if we're going to have this looking right in two days."

Paige turned to scan her new army with tears in her eyes, then looked for Adam, but he'd wandered away, disappearing behind the crowd.

Then she got everyone to work.

For the next two days, Lavender Island hardly slept. It felt as if the entire town was at Nowhere Ranch. Mr. Clark and his shop provided the lumber, paint, manpower, and tools to resurrect the gazebo. Gordon, Gabe, Garrett, Luke, Olivia's Jon, and John-O from town all managed to reconstruct the entire thing by working for forty-eight hours straight.

Adam coordinated the orchard after the fire investigators left. They'd determined the fire had started by accident through an electrical short in the film crew's wires that had led out to the orchard. After the investigation, Adam and Pedro cleaned up the charred remains; then Antonio and the ranch hands joined Joseph, Little, Gil, Keith, and others to cut down the burned trees and nurse the remaining ones, babying the soil with fertilizer and water and neatening up the rows.

A forestry crew came in to chop down the dead pine trees on the edge of the forest, which made the land look as if it had been opened up another few acres and ended up being a blessing in disguise by opening the ocean view.

Olivia, Natalie, Doris, Marie, Bob, Gert, Kelly, Amanda, and a host of others from town worked on the yard around the house, sweeping the ash off the roof and out of the lawn and bushes, and reworking the lawn and acreage to revitalize the soil and ground. They sprayed with a green fertilizer designed to rejuvenate growth and, in the meantime, made the property look almost verdant. Mr. Clark's crew kept a constant supply of fresh soil and fertilizer and flowers coming from town, and Kelly and Amanda worked together to organize the new plantings around the house and the new forty-eight-hour gazebo.

By the time the catering and decorating crews started to arrive with the wedding chairs, tables, runways, flowers, taffeta, and bows, the yard looked almost as good as new.

And the gazebo was once again a centerpiece.

Paige ran into Adam again and again during the shuffle, and she wanted to stop and talk—at least further apologize—but there was so much to do in so little time that they both kept moving.

The next thing she knew, she was peeking through the crack in her curtains on the big wedding day—the sun was shining, crisp and clear. It was a perfect day to have a wedding. It was a perfect way to start a life.

But her life felt as if it were ending today. Whatever life she thought she might forge forward with Adam—realizing, now, that's what she longed for—was done. There would be no life for the two of them.

She wondered at the feeling of loneliness that had hollowed her bones. Despite being surrounded by so much love the last few hours, so much help, and so much goodwill from her sisters and the town and Nowhere Ranch, she had the feeling of being an empty shell. Every time she saw Amanda or Adam working on the new meadow, all she could think of was loss. Their glorious summer together already felt light-years away as Adam avoided her eyes and Amanda gave her sad smiles. At the end of the nights, watching Adam walk back to his house with his arm around Amanda, all Paige could feel was despair. She'd made a terrible mistake by not being forthright and open with him.

The dress she'd reserved for the wedding slithered over her hips. She'd have to say good-bye today. She'd say good-bye to Adam. She'd say good-bye to Amanda. She'd say good-bye to the townspeople.

She didn't know if she had it in her, though. Maybe if she just slipped away and got on that private ferry quietly, they'd forget about her. Maybe she'd forget about them. Maybe all of this would seem like a dream in a few months. Maybe Adam would forget about this summer, too.

Outside her bedroom window, activity was bustling. She stood and watched for a few minutes as the florists put the last touches on the gazebo, which was strewn with ribbons and bows. Rows of white chairs were aligned to await the guests, with Doris and Marie securing pink and yellow flowers at the ends. Kelly followed behind them and added long white ribbons. The three of them giggled and went to talk to the instrumental trio that had been gathering to one side of the gazebo—a harpist, a flautist, and a violinist—all women. They chatted and seemed to make friends in no time.

Paige dropped her gaze and left the window. She was going to miss Lavender Island. And all its residents. Especially certain ones. But she couldn't think about love right now.

Instead, she went downstairs to make some coffee.

"So what's the story with Adam Mason?" Olivia said from the coffeemaker.

Paige froze in the kitchen doorway. She hadn't even realized her sister had arrived.

And . . . her *other* sister?

"Good morning, Paige," Natalie said from the dining table, where she was sitting in workout clothes and reading the *Lavender Island Gazette*.

Paige wandered in beside them and took a seat at the table. "What are you two doing here so early? How's Mom?"

"Mom's fine. She's resting up at the Castle in her fit-for-a-queen room. She'll be here at ten. But we came to learn about Adam," Natalie said, turning a page. "We sensed some weirdness."

"Weirdness?" Paige asked.

"Weirdness," Natalie verified. "Furtive glances. Avoiding eyes. Mumblings as you passed each other in the meadow. Longing double takes. You know—weirdness."

Paige sighed. She'd have to tell her sisters about her summer with Adam sometime. And, frankly, it was sort of a relief to have them here to tell. She didn't realize how much she'd missed them.

"Would you like some marmalade and toast, Paige?" Olivia was snapping open marmalade jars. It had been their tradition to share toast and coffee together with their mother whenever they helped her with event mornings. Husbands always stayed home, and it was just girls.

"Sure."

"So this weirdness . . ." Natalie put the paper down and pushed her own plate aside. "It appears to us like falling-in-love weirdness."

"Does it now?"

"It does. Yet we both have a hard time believing you fell in love with Adam Mason, who you have oh-so-affectionately been calling the 'Weird Hermit on the Hill' for about as long as we can remember. So spill it, Paige. We want to know everything."

Paige took a deep breath and dove in. She told them everything: the butt in the window, the intruder, the hot tub, Amanda, staying at Adam's house, seeing Olivia and Lily at the hardware store, *everything*.

She even told them about the hayloft sex. And the hangar sex. And the seaplane-property sex. And the new-bed sex. And . . .

"I just can't believe this is the same Adam Mason you've been making fun of for years," Natalie said, smiling. "Although I don't know what was wrong with you—he *is* gorgeous."

"I told you a long time ago he might surprise you," Olivia told Paige, finishing her last bite of toast and pushing her plate aside. "I used to see him at the market from time to time, and I always thought he was hot."

"Olivia!" Natalie said.

"What?"

"First of all, I don't think I've ever heard you use the word *hot*. And second, didn't we say that commenting on the sexiness of future brothers-in-law was off-limits? Though Paige was always the biggest culprit."

"Oh jeez, he's not going to be your brother-in-law!" Paige rolled her eyes.

"What went wrong, sweetie?" Natalie turned to Paige.

"Once I told him the truth, I lost him." Paige could feel a hot cry burning her nose right as she said it. "I'm still glad I told him. But he won't be able to forgive me. We're over."

"It sort of sounds to me like you didn't tell him the *whole* truth," Natalie said.

"Of course I told him the whole truth! What more was there to say?"

"It sounds like you left out a key element."

"*What are you talking about?* I told him everything. I laid myself raw."

"No, you didn't."

Paige resisted the urge to yank on Natalie's long hair like she had when they were kids and she was mad. Instead, she fumed into her coffee.

"I told him *everything*," she mumbled.

"Did you tell him you loved him?" Natalie shot back.

Paige frowned. "No. I mean about the past. The part I was withholding."

"Aren't you withholding the fact that you're in love with him? And always were?"

"That has nothing to do with—"

"But it does, Paige." Olivia reached across the table and cupped Paige's hand. "Like Nat said, it's a key element. You need to tell him that part, too. It's part of you. It's part of the truth. And he deserves to know. At the very least, it'll change the way he feels about you. But at the most, it'll change the way he feels about himself. And that's a wonderful gift to give. Even if your relationship has ended."

Paige stared into her coffee and thought that over. Not that it would change his level of forgiveness, but Paige could at least let him know he was always loved. That she did everything out of love. And a little infatuation, too, but definitely love. She'd truly always loved him. She was definitely not one to admit such a thing to a man—especially a man who was angry at her—but she should be. As her mom had said, she had to be brave enough to start being, and showing, her true self. Always.

"Okay," she said into the quiet kitchen.

"Okay?" Natalie sat up straighter in her chair. "You'll do it? Ooooh, this is so exciting!"

"It's not exciting," Paige said. "Nothing's going to change. But you're right. I need to have the balls to do this."

"Is that a lovely Lauren Bacall quote?" Natalie grinned over her coffee cup.

"I'm not trying to be Lauren Bacall anymore," Paige said. "Just me. I'm just me."

"And that's perfect," Olivia said. "Go get him, girl."

Outside, guests were arriving, hoping to get a great seat for the lavish affair. Two enormous tents had been set up—her mom always did the tents at the last possible second for celebrity events because it was an obvious marker for paparazzi—but now they were in place, and guests were starting to stream in. Dorothy had said the entire island was invited—anyone with a Lavender Island ID—because she was so grateful to everyone for their help in getting her dream setting in place. It was going to be exciting to see all the Lavender Island residents rubbing shoulders with Old Hollywood this afternoon.

Paige wove her way through the first tent, around the decorating staff, around the chairs and flowers, and tried to peer over everyone's head for Adam. He'd said he'd be an usher today, and the ushers were supposed to be there by ten.

Not finding him in the first tent, she headed for the second, which was farther back toward the orchard where the reception was going to take place. As she trekked across the field, which had been decorated in almost a mazelike fashion with potted hydrangea shrubs, a crowd began migrating across the meadow and pointing toward the sky. She followed their gaze and saw the sun glinting off a bright-blue plane.

Noel.

Paige knew he was flying in this morning. And Adam would probably go out to meet him. She'd love to catch Adam before Noel did, though. Once the crowds started coming in—including the Colonel, George, Sugar, Doris, and Marie, some of her favorite senior citizens from Natalie's job at Casas del Sur—and Adam got busy with his brother and other Lavender Island residents, it would get harder and harder to talk to him. And her ferry left at three p.m., right after the ceremony.

She stepped around a giant elderberry bush and rushed into the second tent. The lavish setting was draped in white tablecloths and sparkling crystal, awaiting the bride and groom, their first dance, and the fun postwedding hoopla. She scanned several tuxedo-clad men, who were either decorators or waiters setting out more china, and almost took out a whole table with her fluster, but she couldn't spot anyone who looked like Adam. Quickly she rushed back out. Maybe he was still at his house?

She tried to make her way hurriedly across the meadow past the crowd waiting for Noel, but she got caught up in his entourage. She glanced toward the airstrip, trying to step around a group of suit-clad Nowhere Ranch wranglers who were waving him down, and somehow caught his eye.

He had the classic look of a younger brother—no responsibilities, easygoing, happy. The Nowhere Ranch people buzzed around him, clapping his back and hugging him. He had blond hair like Adam's, only purer. While Adam's was thick, Noel's was soft and curled and pale. His face was round and almost cherubic—his smile spreading across his face, lighting up his eyes. He looked as if he would fit as comfortably in a bar, running with a band of boys, as sitting in a parlor to placate a grandaunt.

Paige tried to hustle faster, but, much to her horror, Noel steered his followers in her direction.

"And who are you?" He took several long strides toward her and held out his hand.

She reluctantly turned toward him. "Don't you remember me, Noel? It's Paige." She offered everything quickly: her handshake, her greeting, her glance into his eyes.

He didn't let go of her fingertips. "You're going to have to give me more than that."

"Paige Grant."

"She's here with Adam," came Kelly's voice from over her right shoulder.

Noel looked at Kelly as if she'd materialized right there on the lawn. "Squeaky!" he said, dropping Paige's hand and stepping around her to scoop Kelly in his arms. He gave her a loud smack on her cheek.

Kelly laughed and shook her head, keeping a hand possessively on Noel's chest, but the energy between them was clearly one of old friends.

"I do remember you now!" Noel turned back to Paige. "Helen's granddaughter. So you're here with Adam now?"

"I'm not *with* Adam, exactly," Paige said crisply. "I'm looking for him now, though. I'm a little desperate—"

"All right." He threw a smile Kelly's way. "I can see some symmetry to that. And desperate for my brother sounds good."

Paige didn't know what that meant, but she didn't have time to ask. "I'll see you," she said instead and rushed toward the house.

When Adam stepped back into the path of the flowering bougainvillea vines, Paige was gone. He cursed under his breath and looked across the gathering crowd. He could have sworn he'd just seen her there.

This was going to get crazy here today. But he needed to talk to her. He wanted to at least say a proper good-bye. And give her a proper hug. And, truth be told, he'd love to give her one more thorough kiss. Because even though things hadn't worked out for them—clearly she didn't have enough trust in him to fall in love—he at least wanted to let her know he forgave her.

He'd taken a few long walks over the past few evenings—many to the Top of the World—and had thought everything over. He'd realized that she hadn't known the series of events she'd been sparking when she talked to Ginger and George about him. Her actions were age appropriate, really—a young teen trying to get out of her own trouble, not blaming someone else, just trying to wriggle out of her own problems. He knew she'd meant no malice toward him personally, then or now.

But it was harder to wrap his mind around her choice to not say anything in the last few weeks. How could she have been sleeping with him—presumably growing closer—and not have told him? Did she think he'd explode with the kind of fury his dad would have unleashed? Could she not trust that he wouldn't? Or did she simply have no plans to get closer and wanted to only stay FRED? Had she thought their sleeping arrangement would end if she said anything? Either way, all paths seemed to lead to the same place: She didn't trust him. And if she didn't trust him, she couldn't love him.

But he wanted to see her today and tell her that he'd loved each day he'd spent with her. He'd loved being with her this summer.

And he might not tell her this part, but he'd loved her.

As he strained to see over everyone's head, though, and find Paige again, he saw his brother traipsing through the meadow.

It was great to see his little brother again. He'd heard his plane and immediately looked forward to reuniting. Plus, he needed to wrestle him away from everyone at some point to tell him everything about Amanda and losing the seaplane property before he heard details from someone else. Adam had almost done it on the phone earlier, but it felt like information he should share in person, especially the being-a-new-uncle part.

But first Adam had to find Paige. He was starting to feel the clock ticking down on their time here. And he had some things he really needed to say.

The music started up with an instrumental trio, indicating the wedding was just a half hour away. And Paige was leaving right after the ceremony. Adam wandered through the crowd, starting to feel desperate. Finally, a heavy hand landed on his shoulder.

Noel greeted him with his trademark grin. "Hey, bro. I met your lady friend. Our old neighbor, huh? She grew up pretty."

"Where'd you see her?"

"Meadow. I wanted to touch her hair."

"Hands off," Adam said, frowning.

A slow grin spread across Noel's face. "That sounded serious. Is there something I need to know?"

Adam looked away. He didn't want to talk to Noel about Paige. It felt too private, too surreal. Talking about summer girls at the boat dock, or summer women they'd seen at the jazz festival was one thing. But talking about Paige was different. Things between them seemed as though they needed to stay between them—their own private circle of two. He'd miss her more than he could imagine, but their summer would always be a private memory for him.

"I need to talk to you about something else, but now is not the time," Adam said.

"So how did you two rekindle?"

"Noel, seriously."

"Just tell me."

"Drop it."

Noel shrugged good-naturedly as if he had no intention of dropping this whatsoever, then smiled. "Good to see you, man." He clapped Adam on the shoulder.

Adam smiled back. It was good to see Noel, too. And he owed him this explanation. Maybe he could rush it quickly and then get back to finding Paige. He took a deep breath as he listened to the instrumental trio playing off to the side and tried to figure out how he was going to say this.

"So what's your news?" Noel said over the lively violin.

Adam looked at the fake-green spray in the charred meadow grasses. He ran his fingers through his hair. He'd just have to blurt it out. He had things he needed to run to.

"I have a daughter."

Noel's jaw went slack.

Adam took a perverse satisfaction that he was finally able to stun an expression off his brother's face. After twenty-nine years.

"A *daughter?*" Noel's words came out more as expulsions of air than actual words.

"A daughter, yes. She's sixteen."

If Noel could have possibly looked any more shocked, Adam didn't know how to produce it. His brother's mind seemed to be whirling a million miles an hour. He might have been doing the math.

"Samantha?" he finally asked.

Adam nodded. "She died. And left Amanda to me. Amanda's here now. I'll have to introduce you. She's great. She looks almost exactly like Mom."

"Wow." Noel stared at his hands, then swiveled his gaze out toward the trees. "Before you said her age, I almost thought you were going to say it was your new lady. But this is crazier."

"And she's not my new lady. Stop saying that. And I have to sell the seaplane property. I'm sorry for letting everyone down about that, but it had to be done." *There.* It felt good to blurt everything out. Adam let out his breath.

When Noel didn't respond, Adam looked up. Noel was giving him one of his don't-bullshit-me looks.

"First, if I hear you say those words again, I'm going to beat the hell out of you," Noel said.

"What words?"

"Anything about letting everyone down. You're not. And you never have. You've been the rock of this family for a long time. Hell, since you were fifteen, I think. And you never let us down. You always saved us, in fact. Did you know Mama Mendez calls you 'The Rock'? She says it in Spanish, of course—*La Piedra*—but she says that when she calls me."

"She calls you?"

"Sometimes."

"Why?"

"To tell me how you're doing. I figure she'll give me the real low-down." Noel grinned. "Anyway, no more of that. And don't worry about the seaplane property. I've only been here for twenty minutes and I've already heard three rumors about the townspeople starting a Seaproperty Fund for you, so that explains that. I trust you. What's meant to be will be."

"You trust me? Just like that?"

"Adam, you're the most trustworthy person on this island. Everyone knows that. Now on to more important things, like why you said that gorgeous friend of yours is not your new lady. And why she's desperate to find you."

"She's desperate to find me?"

"I think she said desperate. Or maybe she said 'despondent.' Not sure." Noel grinned.

"When did she say that?" Adam's blood began racing through his veins as he looked over his shoulder.

"About fifteen minutes ago. She went that way. But since we've been talking, I saw her walk back over there." Noel nodded toward the orchard.

"What the hell, Noel? Why didn't you say anything?"

"I just did. I was waiting for her to be alone. I think she is now. You've got fifteen minutes before the ceremony, man. Go." He slapped Adam on the shoulder just as Adam spun away.

Fifteen minutes wasn't quite enough for the good-bye he'd envisioned.

But it would have to do.

It was long enough for a guy's heart to break anyway.

CHAPTER 29

"Adam!" Paige let out a breath of relief when she spotted him jogging in her direction, looking around—she hoped, for her.

He looked amazing. He had on a black tuxedo with a crisp white shirt, the collar held around his neck by a soft-blue tie that was the same color as his eyes. The crispness of the shirt came around his neck in an oddly containing way—not how she was normally used to seeing him. But rather than look uncomfortable with the containment, he simply looked gorgeous.

As he turned near the boxwood maze, Paige stepped back to try to wave to him, but she lost her footing in the planter and toppled into a hydrangea bush.

"Oof," she squealed. She landed sideways in the shrubbery.

She pushed against the leaves, her hands poking through the spindly branches and giving her no leverage, then tried to shift to one side to maybe roll out. But finally she managed to get her feet underneath her and back out, her bottom jutting in the air.

"These things always thwart my getaways, too." Adam's voice was suddenly right behind her.

She glanced over her shoulder. He stood, with his hands in his pockets, and watched, amused, as she backed her bottom out.

She finally straightened. "Thanks for the help."

"I guess I was too busy enjoying the view."

Her cheeks heated as she dusted herself off.

He was looking her up and down. "You look stunning."

His eyes had already told her that. She had to glance away.

"It needed a little greenery," she said, picking a few leaves out of the fluttery sleeve of the dress.

A silence filled the space between them while he shoved his hands in his pockets and seemed to calculate what he wanted to say next. "Paige," he finally ventured, "I need to say a few things."

She shook her head. Her heart was pounding. "I have a lot to say, too, Adam. And I think I should go first."

The music trio led into a livelier tune—designed to encourage people to find their seats now—and they both turned toward it nervously.

"Can we go somewhere else?" she asked. "Quieter, maybe?"

"I'm not sure we can find a quiet corner on this ranch today."

"Maybe back here?" She grabbed his arm and pulled him back with her about ten feet; then she thought twice about that spot and moved him another ten feet toward the orchard. It was getting quieter and quieter, so she kept tugging at his tuxedo sleeve. Pretty soon they were in the center of the orchard, in the middle of the cameras and camerapeople and wires that had been reconstructed for the documentary. The music slowly rolled into the traditional "Wedding March." Paige let the familiar notes shatter her a little, wishing she could have had the gift of Adam falling in love with her.

As the "Wedding March" hit its louder notes, the camerapeople looked up at once. "Are they *starting*?" someone gasped.

Bodies went into frantic motion—cameras were wheeled back, lights were killed, grips jumped up from the ground. Paige and Adam pressed themselves back within the whirlwind, steeling themselves against one of the still-standing apple trees to let everyone by.

When the frenzy dissipated, Paige looked up into Adam's eyes.

"I don't want you to miss the wedding," he said.

"This is more important." Paige swallowed around the sudden feel of cotton in her mouth. She stared at the spared rows of orchard grass for a few more seconds and inhaled the sweet scent of apples as she gathered up her nerve. "Adam, I wasn't entirely truthful with you earlier."

He lifted his eyebrow and stared down at her. "There's more?"

"Yes. I left another part out."

He nodded slowly and stared at the ground. "Go on."

"The part I left out is"—she took another deep breath—"I love you."

The words came out in a whoosh of air and fear and honesty. They hung there, between them, as Paige watched Adam's face change from surprise to relief to something that looked more like disbelief.

"You *love* me?" he asked.

She nodded slowly. She could hardly stand up.

"But how . . . how could you *love* me?"

Paige frowned. "What do you mean, how could I love you? I could love you because you're a wonderful person. You take care of everyone on the ranch, even people and animals you're not responsible for. You are kind and giving and generous. You try to fix everyone's problems. And for the problems you can't fix, you find someone who can. You're sweet. And funny. And you love old movies. And you ride a horse like a Western hero. And you make a mean salsa. And you make me see stars when I come."

The corner of his mouth quirked up. "I heard that was an important requirement."

"You make me laugh. You make me happy. You love Amanda and Denny and Bob and Gert. You're smart and handsome, and you make me stare at your body every minute I'm with you . . ." She looked up into his eyes. "How am I doing?"

"You're doing okay." He smiled, but then his eyes took on a solemn hue. "But I don't hear the word *trust* in there, Paige."

"*Trust?* Of course I trust you."

"If you trusted me, I don't understand how you could have kept your secret from me all this time."

She gulped. Her eyes filled with tears again. He would never be able to forgive her—her worst fears realized. "Adam, I'm *so sorry*. I feel sick about what I did. I just—"

He held up his hand. "No. I forgive you for that, Paige. I really do. I forgive the young Paige for trying to point out the injustice of what she saw as unfair finger-pointing. I get that. But what I can't get around is that *now*—in this time we've spent together—you didn't trust me enough to finally tell me. What did you think I'd do?"

She shook her head. "I don't know."

"Did you think I'd rail? Like my dad? At *you?* You know I'd never—"

"No! Adam, no. I don't think you're like your dad at all."

His shoulders visibly relaxed. "Okay. That's a start. What, then?"

"I thought you'd hate me, and that you'd end everything we had together. And even though, at first, all we had was FRED, I didn't want that to end. But then, as we grew closer, I was more and more afraid of what I would lose. I was afraid of losing you. But I finally realized that if I couldn't be honest, I'd lost you anyway."

"Afraid of *losing* me? Paige, you weren't in danger of losing me. I was falling. Hard." He stepped closer. "Fast."

Falling? Adam was *falling* for her? She couldn't quite reconcile what he was saying with what she'd always dreamed, and then what she'd feared losing.

"But," Adam said as he stepped even closer, "if we want to have anything, we have to be able to trust. You have to trust me. It kills me to think you can't."

"I do," she breathed out. "I trust you. But I realize I have to open myself up, also. I had to tell you the truth about being in love with you, too. I was learning to be honest with the details and actions of the past, but still not quite able to open up about how I *felt*. But now I am. I love you, Adam. And even if you can never forgive me, I want you to know that everything I did was out of love. And fear that you wouldn't love me back."

He stared at her for the longest time, as if trying to assemble the pieces in his head, then smiled. "I guess this isn't like Ted?"

"Who?"

"Ted. The guy with the frame."

"Todd."

"Todd. Whatever."

"No . . . not like Todd." She tried to inhale.

But maybe it was. Only she was the one rushing to the declaration. But now she could understand where it came from. It came from a raw opening of your heart, a total throwing of caution to the wind. Total trust. A moment of being completely honest, and putting yourself out there to maybe get hurt, but knowing you needed to say it anyway. It came from feeling the love intensely and wanting to give it back. It felt wonderful. And free. And honest.

She looked up at him and tried to catch her breath again.

"I love you, too, Paige," he said quietly.

She stared at him and blinked. *Did he just say . . . ?*

No. He couldn't have.

"What?"

"I love you." He quirked a grin and wrapped his arms around her. "Too. Paige."

She shook her head to force everything to make sense. "But you can't."

"I can't?"

"We were being FRED," she said.

"We were. And I didn't want to change the rules on you. But things changed for me."

Her heart continued its erratic pace as she tried to make sense of what he was saying. "When?" she asked.

"Maybe when I saw your backside stuck in that window."

She smiled. "But that's when you first met me."

"Exactly. I can be slow."

"But you have . . . *summer* women. Who you meet all the time."

Adam frowned. "Where did you hear that?"

"My mom. She's a pretty reliable source."

"Paige, you are so far in another league from anyone I've met before, I can't even begin to tell you."

"When . . . when did you start to feel this way?" Her voice was coming out breathy. She could hardly believe what she was hearing. Adam *loved* her?

"Things started to feel different the night I got home from the dude overnighter."

She managed a weak smile. "Right before we got caught by Amanda wrestling with the paint cans in the hangar?"

"Yes, but you're ruining my Hallmark moment here. When I got home from the dude overnighter, I came across the meadow that night and scratched Denny behind the ears, and I saw the lights on and knew you and Amanda were inside. And it scared the hell out me, Paige, what I was feeling right then. Because it felt like I was coming *home*. To you. It felt right that it was you."

She brought her hand to the front of her neck as if to loosen the words that suddenly seemed lodged there. "Why haven't you . . . why haven't you *said* anything? Why did you agree to FRED?"

"Maybe the same reason you did."

She gave a weak smile. "Fear?"

"Yep. Or maybe because I'm an idiot," he added. "And then, later, when I realized you wanted to leave, I didn't want to hold you back. I wanted to ask you to stay with me and Amanda, but I can't ask that of—"

"*Yes!*" she said.

"What?"

"*Yes*, I'll stay!"

"But what about the island? You don't like the island."

"I'm finding a lot of things I love about it—the hangar is becoming a special place."

He smiled. "I hear ya there. But what about the small-town nature and the rumors and all that island stuff you hate?"

"I'm realizing that, despite the gossiping, when push comes to shove, these islanders are here for one another. I forgot about that sweetness, but I saw it again when the meadow was in trouble—when *we* were in trouble. They came to help."

"It took me by surprise, too." He nodded. "It's good to be reminded. What about the scorpions and raccoons and snakes?"

"All right, I'm still not used to those. But if you take the girl out of LA, maybe you can teach her. So did you really mean that? You want me to stay?"

"Absolutely. But the most important consideration is that I didn't want to get in the way of your dreams. You need to pursue what's important to you."

"What's important to me is you."

His face softened. His arms grew tighter around her. "What about the Dorothy Silver role?"

"I'll find another way to make my dreams happen. But my first dream, always, was you. I've dreamed about you since I was thirteen and saw you kiss Samantha, and wondered if I might turn into a sophisticated girl like that—someone with Veronica Lake hair and a mysterious Ingrid Bergman smile. I wanted to be that kind of woman from then on. I wanted *you*, Adam. I have since I was thirteen."

He stared at her for a long minute, then reached up into her hair and cupped her cheek. Staring into her eyes, he gave her a serious look. "For the record, I'm not an Ingrid Bergman fan." She smiled. His kiss was warm and gentle, full of love and adoration and trust and care and protection and, most of all, longevity. It was the most romantic kiss she'd ever experienced. Until something hard hit her head.

"Crap! What was that?" She brought her hand to her head and saw an apple roll into the dirt.

Adam smiled and brought his finger to his lip, glancing at the blood on his fingertip. "I think you bit me."

"Sorry. An apple just fell on my head." She twisted to look for the culprit.

"Paige Grant, I look forward to a long, exciting life with you."

She kicked the apple into the grass with her high heel and touched his lip where she'd bit him. "Are you sure you want to take your chances with me?"

"Absolutely."

"You've been forewarned—there will be crazy calamities."

"I look forward to that." He smiled and leaned down to give her a long, toe-curling, albeit slightly bloody, kiss. "Now, we have a wedding to rush to."

He grabbed her hand and pulled her through the apple orchard.

Paige stepped into the wedding tent, still holding hands with Adam, which attracted more than one stunned glance.

Noel lifted an eyebrow and grinned at his brother. Amanda smiled smugly and nodded to Paige. Bob and Gert stared and then hugged each other. Ginger brought her hand to her mouth and smiled. And Natalie and Olivia did hyper quiet-claps under their chins.

It seemed the whole town was staring at them as they snuck down a side aisle and slipped into two vacant seats.

The wedding was elegant and very Hollywood, and everyone cried when Dorothy and Richard repeated their lines from twenty years prior. They admitted they'd known from the start that they were each other's first and true love, and that time never changed a thing except made it stronger.

After the ceremony, the guests moved toward the reception tent, but Dorothy wanted to toss her bouquet. As she turned her back and flung her bouquet of yellow-and-white daffodils over her shoulder, Paige saw a pair of rough hands reach up and snatch the flowers out of the sky. She dropped her hands out of defeat, then came face-to-face with Adam, who stepped through the crowd—as Rosa, Kelly, and Doris shoved him good-naturedly—and he dropped the bouquet into Paige's hands.

"That's cheating," she whispered.

"However it needs to happen," he whispered back into her ear.

The guests moved again toward the tent, and Adam smiled and pulled her through the maze of hydrangeas, past the rows of wooden chairs, alongside the gazebo, and straight through the meadow.

"Adam," Paige said, laughing, while he undid his tie, "everyone's going to wonder where we went."

"I think they know where we went," he said, tugging her up his back steps, past the kitchen, and into his bedroom. His shirt was coming out of his waistband faster than she could get her breath.

"But don't we need to talk to everyone—tell Amanda and my mom and Noel and my sisters that we're changing our plans?"

"We'll tell them later," he said, kicking the bedroom door closed.

"But, Adam, don't you think—"

"*Paige,*" he said, exasperated. He reached up to push his hands into her hair. "Trust me."

She let him undo the fabric tie and button at the side of her silky dress; let him hold her, naked, in the middle of the floor while he kissed her so deeply her knees began to tremble; and, finally, let him pull her carefully into the cocoon of the bed.

And, for the first time of many to follow, she completely did.

EPILOGUE

The day had finally come.

The Mason Apple Fest had a brightly colored banner hanging over the new ranch entrance, decorated with hand-drawn apples and vibrant fall leaves—and a prediction of hundreds of excited Lavender Island guests over the two-day event.

Paige stood with her hands on her hips, the crisp November breeze swirling her hair around her shoulders, and surveyed their work: Kelly and Joseph were donating horse rides for the kids at the corral; Rosa's Cantina was donating enchiladas, tacos, and *cervezas*; Antonio and Tanya were running the game aisle for the kids; Little was manning the karaoke booth; Gabe, Gordon, and Garrett were handling the bobbing-for-apples booth; and Gert and Amanda had been baking pies all week for the famous pie booth.

The booths were set up throughout the meadow, which had been covered with straw for the event and had colorful pots of mums and hay bales sitting throughout. The gazebo still stood sentinel, now with autumn-orange, magenta, and yellow mums around the base, with large haystacks topped with pumpkins at the step-up entrance. The heart-shaped weather vane still spun on top, reminding the residents of the recent wedding that had been such a wonderful, coming-together moment for Lavender Island.

Dorothy Silver had, indeed, purchased Helen Grant's property, despite the fire. Or maybe because of it—her film crew took full responsibility for the electrical short in the orchard and paid top dollar to nurture what remained back to health, as well as paying the asking price for the house. Dorothy planned to use the property as a quarterly escape from her regular home in Beverly Hills, but she didn't mind at all if her new neighbors, Adam and Paige, used the meadow or the gazebo whenever they wanted, and she was adamant about using whatever they needed for the Mason Apple Fest.

Dorothy had been disappointed that Paige didn't want to try out for the movie part, but she finally pulled Paige aside and whispered that she understood.

"Acting is a hard life," she'd said, looping her arm through Paige's as they'd strolled across the meadow one afternoon. "It doesn't bode well for love. If you find love first, take that. And I see that you have." She'd nodded toward Adam out across the pasture, who'd been riding toward the corral with the bison. Dorothy followed up her smile with a wink.

Paige still couldn't believe her sexy bison wrangler was in her life every day. She'd moved into his house after much begging on his part. As soon as she'd acquiesced, he'd asked if there was anything she wanted to change—that it was her home now, too. He'd said she could change *anything*—he really had no love lost for any of it. The only thing he wanted to keep was the direct entry to the resort lobby and one lamp that reminded him of his mother.

So Paige and Amanda got to work. Paige also enlisted Natalie's help, and Amanda enjoyed getting to know Nat, too. Natalie was still doing event planning for the senior apartments in Carmelita, but she was expanding into interior design, as well, and Paige thought her design skill was second to none. The three women drew up plans and ideas over the course of several weekends. Amanda designed her own room. Paige got rid of the weird old kitchen cabinetry. And they divested the family room of the scary white sheets in favor of a fresh, cozy modern design that looked like a page right out of a Pottery Barn catalog. Paige framed a bunch of pictures for Adam that he'd found in the box his dad left him, and they added new canvas prints along one whole wall of Adam with Amanda and Noel, as well as Adam and Paige. Adam's eyes grew misty when he saw them.

Now, as Paige watched the first of the Apple Fest guests arrive in their golf carts, she straightened the pie-booth banner and winked at Amanda and Rosa. Amanda had spent every day for the past month trying to perfect her grandmother Ellen's recipes off the recipe cards found in Adam's box, and she was certain she'd mastered it.

"Hey, hands out of there," Amanda said, pushing Adam out of the way and readjusting her new Apple Fest apron.

"Don't I get a free piece?" he asked. "I was your taste-tester for a whole month. And I ran the risk of weighing four hundred pounds by now."

Amanda smiled and handed him a plate and a fork. "Fine. But you were the one who kept insisting on eating the entire pie, Dad," she said. "I was only asking you to *taste*."

Adam chuckled and dug into another piece. "Just trying to be fair."

"Thanks, Amanda." Paige looped her arm through Adam's fork-holding one and began strolling with him toward the next booth. "Should we check on the others?"

"Do we have a kissing booth somewhere? We could check that one out."

Paige smiled. "We have bobbing for apples. Will that do?"

"I definitely want to see you try that one."

Paige giggled. "It should be popular. Gabe, Gordon, and Garrett are running it."

"Ah, that means my daughter will be spending time there."

Paige gave his arm a squeeze. "Garrett's fine. You have to get used to her dating sometime, and this is a nice boy to start with. He treats her well."

Adam took another bite of pie and thought that over. "That's all that matters, I guess."

"And besides—having the Stone boys there will bring in a huge crowd, and the bobbing-for-apples booth is donating *all* its proceeds to our Fighters Week." She gave his forearm another squeeze.

Adam and Paige were both excited about their new dude-ranch setup, in which one week out of every month was going to "Fighters Week" for cancer-recovery patients. They'd designed the weeks as strength builders—some physical activities, such as archery and horse-back-riding and rope courses, plus Paige's new hatha-yoga courses, and then some emotional strength building with speakers who they would bring over from the mainland. Amanda was going to help prepare healthy meals, which they would enjoy around campfires or outside around the spa under romantic twinkle lights, and Kelly offered to help out with horse and animal therapy, which the guests would love. They had their first group planned in two weeks—Ginger would be one of the first guests, along with some of her friends from her oncology offices in LA. Ginger hadn't been able to stop marveling and praising the whole idea among her LA friends, and now Adam and Paige were booked through the summer. They couldn't wait to keep expanding the program.

"Hey, do we have time to sit for a minute?" Adam asked, nodding toward the gazebo.

"For a few minutes. The band should be here to set up in about a half hour."

They climbed the gazebo steps and sat in the far right side of the octagon, where they relaxed almost every evening. Denny was lying on the floor right where their feet always rested, as if waiting for them. Click hopped around Denny, looking as if she wanted to play, and

Denny gave her his usual I'm-tolerating-you-because-you're-so-cute look. If dogs could roll their eyes, Denny would have. But the two had become unlikely friends. Click finally gave up when the old dog simply laid his head down and let Click snuggle up between his paws.

"Everything came together," Adam said, laying his empty pie plate on the gazebo bench.

"It did," Paige said, snuggling against his flannel shirt.

"Except the mums—did you notice?"

Paige sprang upright. "Mums? What happened? Which mums?"

"The ones out here." Adam waved his hand over the gazebo rail.

Paige jumped to her feet and peered over the side. Sure enough, the fall-colored mums only reached about three-quarters of the way around the gazebo. The whole back quarter was bare. "What *happened*? Didn't Mr. Clark have enough? It looks ridiculous. Maybe we can call and have him quickly fill in with some daisies, or—"

"Paige."

She looked back at Adam, who was sitting languidly on the bench. "It's okay. Come over here."

She reluctantly left her inspection of the unfinished flowers and plopped down beside him. His shirt smelled like woodland and apples, and she cozied up to him once again, stringing her fingers through his and looking out at the festival booths, which she could be proud of, even if the dumb flowers were unfinished.

"I did it on purpose," he said.

She twisted her neck to see him. "What?"

"The flowers—I had Mr. Clark only finish them partway."

She sat up and stared at him. "Why would you do that?"

"You said the other day that Elliott—I really like him, by the way, we went out for beers the other night. Anyway, you said he bought flowers for Natalie every month and had almost filled the entire perimeter of his house, and that she'd agreed to marry him when that was done."

Paige nodded. "I'd say two more months, tops." She smiled at the image. "But what does that—" Before she could form the question, Adam was grinning.

"I know you're a little skittish about how fast I've been moving things along," he said, "but I can't wait to spend the rest of my life with you, Paige. I can't wait to ask you to be my wife. But I want to respect your comfort level. I wondered if you'd be up for the same plan as Elliott and Natalie? But I can't wait long enough to fill the perimeter of our whole house—I was thinking our gazebo."

"But . . . wait, what?" Paige glanced over the rail at the almost-filled octagon.

She had been a little nervous at Adam's speed, but he'd continually told her that marriage was his plan. And, frankly, she couldn't remember any longer what she was waiting for. She loved this man. He clearly loved her. She loved his daughter and his dreams and this life they were building together.

"I think," she began, "yes."

Adam snapped out of his languid pose. *"Yes?"*

"Yes."

"You mean, when I get this planter filled, I can ask you to marry me?"

"I'm thinking yes."

The smile that spread across his face was everything Paige needed.

The band suddenly appeared in the meadow, hauling their gear toward the gazebo, and Adam and Paige cleared out of the way with Click and Denny, heading toward the ranch entrance where they'd start greeting guests. Adam kept getting out his phone, in between a few last-minute orders to the ranch hands who were helping out at the barbecue. Finally, they arrived at the entrance to their property.

There, right beneath the freshly painted sign that proudly proclaimed the new name, Hope Ranch, Paige saw Olivia puttering up the hillside in her golf cart with Lily in the passenger seat. Behind her were carts Paige recognized as Doris's and Marie's. Marie shared her cart with her ninety-five-year-old beau, the Colonel, from Casas Del Sur, and Doris was riding with a woman named Sugar. Behind them, it looked as though Mr. Fieldstone was coming, along with Mr. Clark and then Elliott and Natalie. Bob and Gert came from the other direction, right on cue.

As each of the arrivals parked in the makeshift gravel parking lot, they piled out. All seemed to have their arms loaded up.

With mums.

Paige turned toward Adam quizzically.

He gave her a sheepish grin. "Just neighbors helping neighbors out."

Paige blinked at the long rows of people holding the potted plants. "They *know* already?"

"I told them it was my plan, but we didn't know if you'd agree yet. Once you did, I put the word out. I think they're on my side."

They all came forward, smiling and handing their potted mums to Adam and Paige, clapping Adam on the shoulder, and offering congratulations to Paige.

"I'll bet this isn't quite what you had in mind when you saw my butt in that window?" Paige asked, leaning up on her tiptoes and giving Adam a kiss.

"No, I must say my thoughts may not have been that noble in that exact moment." His arms reached around her, and he smiled. "But I'm glad I did, Calamity June."

And Paige stretched up farther to kiss him again and tighten her arms around his neck. She planned to never let go.

ACKNOWLEDGMENTS

Love on Lavender Island has had a long life. In its original form, it was the manuscript (then called "Earning Wings") that won me a finalist spot in RWA's Golden Heart awards for unpublished authors. But it wasn't quite right. It needed finessing. I loved the hero and the setting, but everything else needed to be readdressed. So when it came time to write Paige's story, I thought, *What if I gave* her *Adam Mason?* and my wheels started spinning. I got rid of the old heroine, threw Paige into the story, kept finessing it, added Amanda, added Ginger, added the Grant sisters, and finally came up with this newer version, which I love. I hope you all love it, too!

As always, there were a lot of people who helped me shape the story, both the original version and the new.

My biggest round of thanks goes to historical-romance writer Tricia Lynne, who has been my most amazing critique partner for a crazy-long *nine* years now. She questions me in all the right places, pulls things out of me to improve the story, and always challenges me to be my best. She knows exactly where to add more emotion, more description, more action—and I follow her advice to the letter. I can't thank you enough, Tricia!

I also want to thank my earliest beta readers who gave me so much great feedback to make me a better writer and catch the high scores that got me the finalist spot in 2012: Nancy Freund, Michelle Bailat-Jones, Debi Skubic, Kristi Davis, Crystal Posey, and Michelle Proud.

For the later version:

Thanks go to my mom, Arlene Hayden, for always being willing to talk about plot points on the phone and help me out of plotting jams.

Big thanks to my brainstorming Firebirds for always-fun and funny ideas. Especially, for this book, Sheri Humphreys, Lorenda Christensen, Tamra Baumann, Pintip Dunn, Jean Willett, Priscilla Kissinger, Pamela Kopfler, Wendy LaCapra, and Lexi Greene, who offered calamity ideas that made me giggle.

And extra thanks to friend Tamra Baumann for keeping me on deadline for this book—we were "sprint sisters" for this one, and she really knows how to lift up and motivate.

Thanks to beta readers of the new version: Arlene Hayden, Debi Skubic, Mary Ann Perdue, and Barbara Young.

Big thanks to readers and Facebook page fans Debi Skubic and Tracy Dodd Wickman for suggesting on my Facebook page the fun names for my town stores. Debi named the bookstore (Book, Line, and Sinker) and Tracy named the toy store (Once Upon a Toy). I love having devoted and clever readers!

I also want to thank my amazing agent, Jill Marsal, who goes above and beyond in every single way. I'm so lucky to have her.

And thanks to my editor, Maria Gomez, at Montlake, with an additional shout-out to my developmental editor, Charlotte Herscher—thank you for bringing out the best writing in me. And the copyeditors and cover designers at Montlake are fabulous—thank you all.

As I was finishing this book—about six weeks from the final deadline—I was diagnosed with breast cancer. A whole team of people rallied behind me to help me deal with the fear and panic, and then take the steps I needed to start on the road to treatment. *And I wanted to finish the book!* When you're *six weeks away* from completing your dream, it's hard to stop. Everyone's support—even if it wasn't directly about the book—really allowed me get it done. All my fellow writers, coworkers, publishing team, and readers—thank you for getting me to the finish line on my fourth book, which is a dream I still can't believe I'm living.

And, during my cancer fight, a huge, huge, heartfelt thanks to my family and friends. Cancer can take away a lot of things—your hair, your confidence, your security in the future. But one of the things it can never take away is the amazing knowledge that family and friends are there no matter what. I knew that theoretically, but when I needed them in reality, they came through so fast and lovingly I didn't even know how to respond. (Mostly I cried!) (Like every day!) My husband was my cancer hero, and he cared for me every single day—he's always been my Superman. My family and friends (and that includes reader friends!) sent so many encouraging texts, phone calls, cards, letters, prayers, chemo scarves, chemo caps, dinners, pep visits, cozy gifts—I felt so loved, supported, and encouraged. It really helped me through.

I thank you all *so very* much, and this book is dedicated to you.